00066 52246

D0599902

 **libraries**

Possilpark Library
127 Allander Street
Glasgow G22 5JJ
Phone: 0141 276 0928

This book is due for return on or before the last date shown below. It may be renewed by telephone, personal application, fax or post, quoting this date, author, title and the book number.

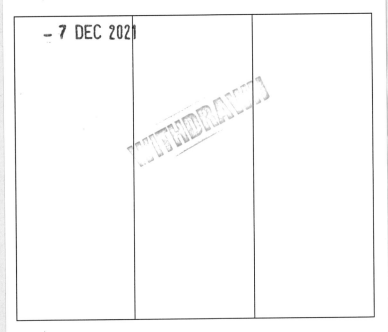

- 7 DEC 2021

WITHDRAWN

Glasgow Life and its service brands, including Glasgow Libraries, (found at www.glasgowlife.org.uk) are operating names for Culture and Sport Glasgow.

Glasgow
CITY COUNCIL

Daily Mail

'Compelling'
Heidi Swain

'Emotional and affecting, this is an absorbing read'
Sun

'A magical mix of wit, warmth and poignancy'
Trisha Ashley

'Alliott is always an absolute joy to read'
Veronica Henry

'Emotional and engaging, I was completely absorbed'
Sarah Morgan

'Another blissful read from Catherine Alliott'
Hello!

'Evokes the perfect summer romance'
Cornwall Life

'A wry look at life in the wealthy environs of the
Oxfordshire countryside . . . page-turning'
Oxford Mail

Behind Closed Doors

CATHERINE ALLIOTT

PENGUIN BOOKS

PENGUIN BOOKS

UK | USA | Canada | Ireland | Australia
India | New Zealand | South Africa

Penguin Books is part of the Penguin Random House group of companies
whose addresses can be found at global.penguinrandomhouse.com

First published by Michael Joseph, 2021
This edition published by Penguin Books 2021

001

Copyright © Catherine Alliott, 2021

The moral right of the author has been asserted

Typeset by Jouve (UK), Milton Keynes
Printed and bound in Great Britain by Clays Ltd, Elcograf S.p.A.

The authorized representative in the EEA is Penguin Random House Ireland,
Morrison Chambers, 32 Nassau Street, Dublin D02 YH68

A CIP catalogue record for this book is available from the British Library

ISBN: 978–1–405–94074–0

www.greenpenguin.co.uk

Penguin Random House is committed to a
sustainable future for our business, our readers
and our planet. This book is made from Forest
Stewardship Council® certified paper.

For Ali

I

I arrived at my parents' house to find that, as usual, my sister had beaten me to it. As I crunched up the gravel drive to the crumbling red-brick farmhouse, I spotted Helena's shiny blue BMW already parked squarely outside the gabled porch. The front door to the house was wide open. As I drew up beside her, Hector, my parents' aged spaniel, came out to greet me, wagging his tail sheepishly. He turned to look apologetically at the rumpus coming from within. Voices were raised in anger. I could hear my mother's shrill tones complaining that she could hardly be to blame for smashing a bowl she didn't even know my father had won for school cricket seventy odd years ago if he insisted on cutting his toenails on her copy of the *Daily Mail* she hadn't even read yet.

'Always on the letters page,' I heard her cry as I got out and patted Hector. He cringed and took up position behind me, very much staying outside for this one. 'Which he knows is my favourite page. And then he trims his nasal hair on the arts reviews – and we all know the reason for that!'

'If you're implying I shed my personal detritus over Lucy's husband's column for unattractive reasons, I call that poor form,' my father's voice rejoined mildly. I stiffened at my name.

'Why can't you use your own paper? That's what I want to know.'

'I find a tabloid a more convenient size. And anyway, you don't read it.'

I sighed and made my way towards the fray. Ducking under the low beam of the front door, I saw the parquet floor of the hall was strewn with umbrellas and walking sticks which had clearly been thrown in anger from the wooden hat stand, upended on its side. In the sitting room beyond, my parents were squaring up to one another either side of the inglenook fireplace. The Persian carpet was covered with bits of broken china. Helena, looking pompous, was positioned between them, arms outstretched, palms up, like an Italian traffic cop. All she needed was white gloves and a whistle. Hovering to one side, eyes shining delightedly, was Mrs Cummings, the neighbour who'd summoned us.

'Thank you, Mrs Cummings, it was very kind of you to ring us, but I think we can handle this now,' Helena was saying, glancing at but not greeting me. I didn't greet them either, there didn't seem much point. It was business as usual at Pope's Farm, and to express upset or astonishment at the scene would be ridiculous. My parents had had another fight. My mother was worse the wear for drink and my father not far behind, but managing to seize the moral high ground on account of being far more of a functioning alcoholic than my mother. He had an air of practised bewilderment as he faced my mother, which naturally only served to stir the pot. Mum, slight and elegant in heels, her face red, fists clenched and quivering with rage, suddenly lunged at him. He ducked and she tottered and fell sideways – into a gleeful Mrs Cummings, who shrieked hysterically and sidestepped out of the way, rather unhelpfully, clutching her heart.

'You see?' seethed Helena, lowering Mum on to the sofa. 'This *cannot* be ignored any longer, Lucy.'

'Thank you, Mrs Cummings,' I repeated more firmly, glaring at my sister in a must-we-do-this-in-front-of-the-neighbours way. 'We've got this covered now, but thank you for your call.'

'Well, I was only trying to help,' she said rather huffily as I escorted her to the front door. 'I wouldn't want anyone to get hurt. And of course I *did* think of ringing social services when I heard the breaking glass, but you've always said—'

'That we'll deal with it, and so we will. And I think you'll find it was a china bowl rather than a cupboard full of glass, but thank you.'

She glanced regretfully over her shoulder as she went down the drive, back to the barn conversion next door, where once we'd kept hay for the horses. Pity we still didn't, I thought, as I shut the door on her.

'Busybody,' I muttered, going back into the sitting room. 'She must have been listening in the garden, for crying out loud.'

'We couldn't do without her,' Helena reminded me tersely, as if my parents weren't there, or were senile, which they weren't.

'Oh, I disagree, I think we should do quite well,' objected my father. 'When a long-married couple can't have the most basic of conjugal rights, namely a flaming row, in the privacy of their own home, things have come to a pretty pass, as that wretched nosy parker would say.'

He began picking up pieces of his bowl, not looking at either of us, and although defiant, I could see he was embarrassed.

I went to the kitchen for a dustpan and brush with Helena on my heels. 'They're both so *pissed,*' she whispered in urgent tones as I opened the broom cupboard. 'It has to stop.'

It didn't occur to me to wonder how Helena would go about achieving this, because I already knew. She wanted care: twenty-four-hour care, preferably, with my parents under close watch. All booze locked away, obviously, and presumably with some sort of armed guard. Sheltered Housing were words she used a lot, before getting out brochures for an over-seventies estate in Amersham, where residents had access to a pool, a spa, restaurants – and a range of bars, I'd pointed out last time she'd shown it to me.

'Yes, but with like-minded people who would shame them into behaving, don't you see? Peer pressure and all that. And there'd be a warden.'

'Like being back at school. Which they'd both hate,' I'd told her. 'And which they'd resist with every fibre of their being.'

'Well, they might hate it to begin with, but they'd pretty soon get used to it.'

Again, like boarding school: the first couple of terms utter misery, but thereafter, not too bad actually. And

4

the final years decidedly jolly as one gained seniority, which, in my parents' case, really would be the final term. The final curtain. As I gathered the dustpan and brush from the cupboard, I wondered if she was right. My parents rattled around in this erstwhile farmhouse in leafy Buckinghamshire where Helena and I had grown up, and drank themselves to a standstill most nights. It could often end in tears, admittedly, but no bloodshed or genuine fisticuffs had occurred yet, and but for the noise of smashing china, was it really anyone's business what they did with their own property if no one got hurt in the process?

And nor were they alone. Mum and Dad still entertained on a regular basis, and many of their friends were in the same state. Nancy De Courcy, Mum's BF and a fearsome pony club mother in my youth, had passed out in her soup the other day, apparently, whereupon everyone had chortled and agreed it was lucky it was gazpacho. So what? She'd been cleaned up, laid out on a sofa like a stiff, according to my father, while the rest of the guests pushed on through. She even came round to enjoy a glass of Château d'Yquem with pudding, before being driven home together with husband Archie by a *very* nice chap who'd come to collect them. As I pointed out to Helena, if that was our children, we'd think they'd behaved terribly responsibly.

'Yes, but they're not children,' she'd objected. Helena wanted them to act their age: to play canasta and watch *My Fair Lady* with other 'moved on' folk, and, a tiny bit of my brain wondered, let her get her hands on the house.

I went back to the sitting room and found my father settling Mum in her favourite armchair, propping her feet on a footstool, adjusting her cushions. She was reaching out for his hand in thanks, her pale blue eyes watery as she squeezed it. Daddy brushed aside her apologies for breaking his cricketing bowl, and as I swept the small pieces he'd missed, he bustled off to the drinks cupboard, muttering about getting her a little pick-me-up, and one for him too. For the nerves. I knew it was hopeless to suggest this was not the most sensible option, and even Helena only got as far as opening her mouth – and shutting it again. We sat on the sofa opposite, watching dejectedly as my old dad, tall, rake-thin, still elegant and suave at eighty-six in his whipcord trousers and starched shirt, handed my mother, equally thin, and beautifully dressed in ancient Chloé (a few stains on the skirt perhaps), with her lipstick askew and too much eye shadow, what looked like a bucket of neat gin.

'We had a marvellous time at the races the other day with the Montagues,' he told us, settling into his own armchair, as if absolutely nothing had happened and Helena and I had just popped down for a social. 'Didn't we, darling?'

'Oh, it was splendid,' my mother agreed. 'Quite the highlight of my week.'

'Your mother's got a new suitor,' he told us confidentially, winking roguishly. 'A retired endocrinologist, a professor, who's moved to the village. He took us in his Bristol. Widowed, obviously, and of a rather earnest bent, but your mother worked her magic as usual.'

Helena and I forced tight smiles as Mum chortled, cheering up enormously. She patted her hair. 'I can't think what your father means.'

Helena and I could. Part of the fabric of my parents' marriage involved spectacular flirtation on my mother's part which always went absolutely nowhere but amused my father no end.

'And then, blow me down,' she'd say around the lunch table in our youth, about some poor besotted admirer, 'he made a terribly improper suggestion, after I'd simply agreed to help him choose some cushion covers in Beaconsfield!' Whereupon Dad would roar with laughter. Somehow it didn't feel quite so funny, these days. Dad, too, would still regale us with his conquests, but they were tamer in nature: the girl in the chemist who, in her quest for the right knee bandage, had asked him to roll up his trouser leg, to which he'd retorted, 'Only if you will!'

This charm offensive to anyone deserving enlivened their days, and no doubt reminded them of younger ones. And let's face it, there's precious little charm about these days. It's hardly crime of the century. But it was about all there was left, now. Because the awful truth was that Mum's eyesight was deteriorating to such an extent that she was practically disabled – although, God help us, she still drove – and any help came in the form of my father, who shielded and protected her, but who faced his own disabilities, with what he dismissively referred to as his gammy legs. How long could this situation go on?

'Have you eaten?' I asked helplessly.

They looked at each other rather vaguely as if trying to remember. I got to my feet and went to the kitchen with Helena on my heels, hers much higher and sharper than mine. It occurred to me that she'd clearly just abandoned her desk in the City and headed straight down, believing I couldn't be trusted to take control.

'This time we have to at least insist on AA for Mum,' she told me as I opened the fridge, more through hope than expectation. Sure enough, a lemon for the gin and a packet of curly ham greeted me. I retrieved the ham and, realizing the fridge was filthy, quickly shut the door.

I sighed as I turned and regarded my very professional sister, the one who'd made such a success of her life: an equity partner in a major accountancy firm – although, as my son Ned said when I mentioned Helena's triumphs in envious tones, when had making a success of one's life on those terms ever got anyone into the kingdom of heaven? If my daughter Imo was present she'd roll her eyes and disappear, but Ned's simple faith, which exasperated me on many occasions, was a comfort to me where Helena was concerned. Not that I necessarily felt I had a free pass into the holy stratosphere, but some half-remembered parable about camels and eyes of needles helped.

'You know as well as I do, AA's a shock tactic,' I told Helena, as the music accompanying the *Countdown* clock suddenly blared through. 'Dad knows it too.'

In fact they'd regarded us in abject astonishment, eyes

wide like children, when Helena had broached it some time ago.

'But we're simply social drinkers!' Mum had exclaimed, lifting her glass to her lips and getting most of it down her chin.

My father, who was more astute, hadn't responded, but his frown and small headshake to his eldest child quashed even Helena, who tucked her pamphlet away. My father's authority was still paramount and absolute. His years on the local bench as a magistrate after four decades in the City at a stockbroking firm and, before that, active military service as a young man, bringing with it a collection of medals, were not to be ignored. And he and his dear lady wife, erstwhile mannequin for Norman Hartnell and appearing in no less than three issues of *Vogue* in the fifties, were not to be treated as senile dribbling fools, whatever the circumstances.

'Hels, there's nothing more we can do,' I told her gently as I cut the dry bits off the ham. I knew this was anathema to her. Helena thrived on control. 'We've got Irene coming in once a week, and Dad isn't totally incompetent. We can do no more.'

'Except hotfoot it down here every time the alarm goes off.'

'The false alarm, actually. From busybody Cummings. No, I suggest we don't. I'll speak to her later and ask her not to overreact again.'

'Unless, of course, she sees a corpse in the garden.'

'As long as it is a corpse, and not just Mum and Nance

coming round from mild comas on sun loungers like it was before.'

Her mouth twitched. 'Well, quite.'

She buttered the toast I handed her, the bread being too stale to eat fresh, and then popped in some ham and mustard. We added two glasses of lemon barley water and went back to the sitting room to find them merrily competing over the quiz show.

'Sensibility!' roared Dad, who could still do the *Telegraph* crossword before breakfast. 'Any fool can see that!'

They took their sandwiches, Mum oohing and aahing about them being cut into triangles, and then ate them with relish, whilst Helena and I discussed who would do a major shop. She would, she decided, since she was here, there being no point going back to the office now. When we'd rustled them up a little fruit salad from a past-its-sell-by assortment in the fruit bowl, we prepared to go. As we got to our feet, Mum declared it a *'very* happy luncheon', reaching up from her chair to take our hands in girlish delight. Her wide, happy smile glowed, as if we'd just sprung a surprise party on her.

'*Do* let's do it again soon. We don't see nearly enough of you girls. And bring the children next time, don't you think, Henry?'

'Oh yes, let's make a party of Mrs Cummings' summonses. So much jollier,' he chuckled.

'Oh no, we don't want her,' frowned my mother. 'Dismal old witch. If I didn't dislike her so much I'd give her a voucher for Elizabeth Arden. If only she knew how a little rouge would improve her.' She attempted to get to her feet.

'Don't get up, Mum,' Helena told her gently. 'Dad will see us to the door.'

She demurred and sank back into her armchair, and my father did just that. Once we were outside in the drive, well out of earshot, he assured us quietly that all was well. And sweet though it was of us to worry, there was really no cause for alarm. And no, they absolutely didn't need any more help. None at all. He wouldn't meet my eye, though, when he kissed me goodbye, and he didn't see us off as he usually would, smiling and waving in the drive. Instead, he hastened back inside, to Mum. Except it was more of a shuffle than a hasten.

Helena sighed as the door closed softly behind him. She opened her mouth to opine, then shut it again, defeated.

'How's everything with you, anyway?' I asked quickly, before she could get second wind.

'Oh, fine,' she said in surprise, wrong-footed. 'Non-stop as ever. I've got an associate director starring in a white-collar fraud trial on Monday and he hasn't quite decided if he's pleading guilty or not, which is a minor wrinkle. But other than that, yes, fine. Up to my eyes and single-handedly keeping the wheels on a highly expensive domestic bus. Business as usual.'

'Ant's ill?' I asked sympathetically, managing not to add, 'again'.

Helena's husband, a delightfully shambolic, charming actor who of course didn't get paid when not working, suffered a bit from hypochondria, which sometimes meant even longer stretches of inactivity. It drove Helena insane.

'He's currently got a lump on his leg which naturally he thinks is bone cancer, even though every clinician tells him otherwise. He's supposed to be auditioning for *Richard III* at the National, so I told him to bloody well get on with it and do it with a limp as well as a hunchback. No director's going to mind that. But, of course, he won't. Needs a fourth opinion. And how's Michael?'

'Oh yes.' I made myself smile but delved quickly in my bag for my car keys. 'He's on good form.'

'So I hear,' she said lightly, but it was the lightness of steel. 'The word is you'll soon be cosying up to some Swedish woman called Ingrid in your own jaw-dropping, inimitable style.' She eyed me beadily, but then saw something in my face: naked sorrow perhaps; fear even. She instantly regretted her jibe and, instead, reached out and put her arms around me. We held on tight.

'Don't do it this time, Luce,' she whispered into my hair. 'Do something else. Something brave. Leave him, hm?'

I shut my eyes and tried hard not to cry. I nodded as I stepped back. She still had her hands on my shoulders as I retrieved my keys. I couldn't look at her.

'I'll help,' she promised earnestly. 'I didn't mean that about the expensive bus, we've got pots of money. I'll help, OK?'

I managed a laugh as I got in the car, still avoiding her worried eyes. 'No need,' I told her, shoving on my sunglasses, which were conveniently on the dashboard. I shut the door and buzzed the window down between us which gave me a moment. 'No need. I promise. All's well. But thank you,' I told her, meaning it. I stretched out my hand and squeezed hers. Still not looking at her, and knowing I was on the cusp of dissolving, I started the car. Then I performed an immaculate three-point turn in my parents' drive, gave her a cheery backward wave, and drove away.

2

As I drove home, I gave a long, shaky sigh into the privacy of my steering wheel. It was more one of exhaustion than anything else. More to do with the effort of keeping up appearances, the constant need to be on high alert. Helena had caught me unawares. And she was right, of course she was right. This time I really should be brave. Leave Michael. Ned and Imo said the same and they knew how much courage it would take. Up to a point. But then again, old habits died hard. Particularly when I'd had such success with my methods in the past. This sounds like an eminently foolish thing to say, but my husband's particular brand of philandering was something I knew exactly how to deal with. I prided myself on it, because it was one of the few things, concerning Michael, that I did well. His more awful proclivities I had no control over. But just as some wives dealt with depression, anxiety – hypochondria, like Helena – my particular strand of man management took the form of subtly diverting my husband's feet from straying to the sunny side of the street, where, as an attractive man, temptation beckoned, and back to the more prosaic side, where his family lived. Which might sound counterproductive – many adulterous husbands are easier to live with, apparently, but sadly, mine didn't fit that mould. Fortunately, I knew exactly what to do.

The first time it had happened, I'd cried myself to sleep – in retrospect, more through shock than grief – but I'd had small children at the time. Also, things weren't so bad. It was early days. I'd thought about it, at length, and decided I didn't want a divorce, so no, I hadn't confronted him. Instead, I'd confronted *her*. In a manner of speaking. When Michael was away, I'd contacted the lady in question and asked her if she'd like to play tennis. I knew her vaguely – I usually did, indeed once it had been a friend of mine – and I knew she played. I'd done my research. I remember her surprise, but she'd come. We'd had a game at my club, and then I'd bought her lunch afterwards. She was rather nice, actually. They usually were nice. Over lunch, I learned that she loved modern art, and so I later bought tickets to the Hockney exhibition at the Royal Academy. I invited her. Michael was still in America, seeing shows on Broadway. By the time he came back, it was all over. His embryonic affair, I mean. Sally was too pleasant and too well meaning to countenance an affair with a man whose wife she liked, and contrary to public opinion, not all divorced, middle-aged women are predatory bitches.

So that's what I gambled on: conscience. Only once, it nearly hadn't worked. Had threatened to backfire. A rather sharp, married woman called Tara Harding – an actress in a play Michael had given a rare good review, I wonder why? – had refused to play ball. On arriving at our house for supper at my invitation, she'd flirted outrageously with Michael all night, right in my face, as if to say – bad luck. Fortunately this had infuriated her small, balding, screenwriter husband who, the following week, decamped the entire family to the South of France for the summer, where Michael was too lazy to follow. That was the other element I relied on: Michael's laziness. Unless it was easy, and on a plate in front of him, he couldn't be bothered.

And the latest one had indeed been easy, and the plate had been at a supper party at the Taylors', who, it occurred to me now, as I drove home, were not only friends of mine, but of Helena's, too. Michael's attraction to Ingrid, a Swedish interior designer, had been so blatant that Millie Taylor, our hostess, had even tried to intervene. When Michael and Ingrid had stayed at the table long after everyone had retired for coffee, she'd hastened back to join them, pink-faced with embarrassment. Later, I'd texted Millie for Ingrid's number, on some pretext about wanting to re-do our kitchen in a Scandinavian style. I knew she knew, but frankly, at this stage, I didn't care. That's how low I'd sunk. It had no doubt gone straight back to Helena.

Actually, that's not true. Of course I cared, it was totally demeaning; but it was necessary if I wasn't to be further humiliated. I sighed as I joined the heavy M40 traffic back to London. And I'd hate you to think this was a constant surveillance mission, a never-ending stealth operation. It wasn't. Michael and I had been married for twenty-eight years. We had two grown-up children, and I could count on one hand – well, all right,

two, but only just – the times I'd had to step in and . . .
you know. Operate. And neither was I alone in this.
Melissa, my best friend, did it too. Turned a blind
eye. Or at least she had done, until she'd failed to observe
the cardinal rule, if you want to remain married, which,
trust me, many women, for a variety of reasons, do. She'd
hurled his laptop – on which she'd found the evidence –
out of the bedroom window and deposited his clothes
in a bin bag on the steps of his girlfriend's house in Chiswick. Except they weren't in the bag, they were scattered
all over the steps, cut into tiny pieces. Melissa lives near
me now, across the road in Fulham. In a tiny rented flat
she can barely afford. Dominic, her husband, moved into
the large Chiswick house belonging to his girlfriend.

And therein lay the rub for many wives, I thought, as
I cruised along in the middle lane where I didn't have to
think. Money. Not that it bothered me much. Not at all,
actually. But I'm ashamed to say I used it as my foil. If I
divorced Michael, as Helena, and even Ned and Imo,
who knew the pitfalls more intimately, said I should
(Imogen reasoning down the phone from New York
about it being time now, and Ned from his tiny modern
rectory above the chip shop in Ealing, persuading me
they no longer needed protecting), I told them it worried
me. Or I pretended it worried me. The financial implications. Instead of the all-consuming fear I couldn't voice.
Where would I live, I asked them? Where would Dad
live? And then I'd rattle on about the house being re-
mortgaged to the rafters and the debts eye-watering,
and the position, frankly, impossible. They'd go quiet. A

mixture, perhaps, of knowing what I couldn't say, and not wanting to hurt me by voicing it. So much subterfuge. So much deceit. Was it necessary? Of course it was. If it protected people's hearts. People's lives. Pitfalls? Ruddy great man traps.

As if in defiance, in a sudden show of uncharacteristic boldness, I pulled out into the fast lane. I overtook a lorry, but ducked back in fright as a Mercedes roared up behind me. I sank back to a more restful seventy in the middle lane. And it wasn't as if life was awful all the time, I reasoned. It wasn't as if I hated him every minute of the day. Although recently, as I'd lain in bed and looked at him, admiring his profile in the mirror in the en suite bathroom – still square-jawed and handsome, steely-grey hair swept back from a high forehead, eyes clear and blue – something much worse than hatred had consumed me. Something closer to homicidal rage had made me turn over, so that I couldn't see him.

We'd just had sex, on that particular morning. I didn't want to, I hadn't for a long time, but somehow I knew it was in the rules. Always in the mornings, and usually once a week, on a Saturday. To set him up for the weekend. And to celebrate a week pretending to work, but actually lunching and drinking with his cronies in a pub in Soho, all of whom, except one old soak who propped up the bar in fingerless gloves, were male. Michael preferred male company. He wasn't really interested in women. He didn't understand them. But even Michael couldn't in all conscience slope off to the pub on a Saturday, so sex in the morning put him in a good mood for the weekend. Thereafter he played the diligent father and husband, welcoming the children when they came home, which wasn't so much these days, carving the roast, and hinting jovially at potential grandchildren. Neither of my children was married, so it wasn't that jovial. Our children, I should say. Except they felt more like mine because they were my proudest possession, and Michael's was his ego.

Michael was a theatre critic, and I nearly prefaced that with 'respected', which he had been in the old days, but now I think he was just feared. His column in the *Sunday Times* had been shifted to Mondays, then cancelled, and now he only featured occasionally in my mother's *Daily Mail*. Latterly, he'd written regularly for a glossy magazine, but after he'd single-handedly closed one too many shows, he'd been asked to leave. The gentle young editor, blinking with embarrassment, had asked him to come in, which was brave. In his office, he'd asked him to step down, because, on the whole, he said, they only reviewed plays they liked, as who wanted to wade through a poisonous review to be told they shouldn't see it? They were a smart, country magazine but eager to promote all things cultural. To get the county folk up to town, or to support their local provincial theatre. Michael's famous temper, spoken of in hushed tones in newspaper circles, had surfaced. He'd turned the editor's desk over, leaving the poor man lunging for his glasses on the floor as he stormed out to meet his boorish colleagues in Soho.

And along with his quiet threats, which made me go

cold, that was the thing I feared, I thought, as I parked the car an hour or so later. His temper. He'd never raised a hand to me, ever, but his fury could be so vile; his words so wounding; the things he called me, which I won't repeat, so crushing, that occasionally I wished he would hit me. Sometimes it took me so long to recover, that not even Melissa or Helena could reach me. I shrank into my quiet, dark shell. And wrote. For days on end. And of course I never complained to the children. I kept the picture as rosy as possible for them, as I always had done when they were younger, trying to shield them from the worst of his rages. They knew, though. They'd seen it. And been on the receiving end of the quiet threats too. I sometimes worried it was why Imo had chosen a university in America and stayed there ever since, and why Ned had remained very close, down the road in Ealing, but turned to God.

And actually, I thought, as I climbed my steps and put my key in the front door, and as classical music filtered through to me in the hall, the sun pouring through the French windows at the back of the house, rosy was what we most certainly pretended we were, a lot of the time. We rubbed along quite genially, until the next storm clouds gathered. And naturally, the more you pretend, the more you convince yourself it's the truth. Some days were even good. As Michael's voice, strong and musical (not unlike that of Simon Callow, an actor he greatly admired and knew a bit) boomed through, I knew this was a good one. I shut the door behind me with relief.

'Darling!' he called, getting up from his desk in the corner of the kitchen. He removed his reading glasses and came to greet me. He was very tall and broad, what you might call a commanding presence. He set his hands on my shoulders and looked down at me, concerned. 'What a day you've had, what a mission! Are you completely knackered?'

'Utterly,' I agreed, relieved. Perhaps he'd had a pay cheque. Or lunch with Patrick; that always put him in a good mood.

'I got one of those M&S fish pies for supper. I popped it in at about seven, so we can eat soon. Drink?'

'Please,' I agreed as I followed him into the kitchen. I didn't drink much, as a rule (it featuring too strongly in my family's repertoire) but I'd had a long drive. I perched on a stool at the island and watched as he poured me a glass of something cold and white. The kitchen, I noticed, was tidy. Rather sparkling.

'You've had a clear-up,' I observed, glancing around, surprised.

'Well, I decided you were right. If I'm determined to work here, rather than in the study, I've got to get a grip. It is, after all, the engine room.'

Michael and I had, historically, both worked either side of a large table in the study, me writing my novels, and Michael his critiques. In the old days it had been pleasant. But as tensions rose, and as his career hit the skids, a mutual tacit agreement had forced him in here. It had certainly helped both work and general relations, but it caused chaos domestically. I smiled and sipped my wine, noting the desk in the corner which he'd tidied into neat piles.

'Sometimes I think it would be better if I was the one in here,' I commented. 'After all, I spend so much time here, or in the garden. And you always loved the study.'

'No, no, your need is greater.'

It was true, but magnanimous of him. A rare admission. I needed a proper desk. My books might not sell many copies, or bring in much money, but I was prolific. Relentless, some might say, still writing a book a year. As a result, my publisher in Bloomsbury was able to give me a small regular advance each time. In the early days, I'd had a reasonably successful run, but the murder mystery market had been swamped recently by sophisticated psycho-noir thrillers. My gentle *Midsomer Murders* style, with my feisty detective, Susie Sharpe, at the helm, had rather fallen out of favour. Still, Frankie, my lovely editor who'd become a true friend, nevertheless did everything she could to usher Susie forwards; and sometimes, to our mutual delight, she appeared not just in a back room at WHSmith, but in the supermarkets too, where my more mature readership found her convenient to pick up with their Ovaltine. Recently, I wondered if my heroine's level of forensic ability had begun to reflect the cosiness of the demographic I attracted. The other day, I'd heard her say airily: 'Oh, I think the body can keep. Pop it in the freezer overnight and I'll get the pathologist to look in the morning.' That would never have happened in the old days. Susie Sharpe – who in real terms was probably about a hundred and four – was in danger of becoming Susie Blunt. Nevertheless, she forged on, hopefully brightening the days of retired gentlefolk, who were often kind enough to write and tell me as much. And what little my books continued to bring in still eclipsed Michael's meagre salary. It was nice of him to acknowledge this.

'How were the aged Ps?' he asked sympathetically, reaching into the freezer for a bag of frozen peas.

'Oh, predictably in denial. Lots of assurances they were fine and everything was going swimmingly. But it really is the seven ages of man down there.'

'Sans eyes, sans teeth, sans everything,' he quoted.

'Well, not quite everything, but certainly sans any modicum of restraint. Dad's more on it, of course, but only marginally. They sent their love.'

They hadn't, but Michael smiled and nodded in gracious acceptance, knowing they hadn't either.

The games people play, I thought, getting up to lay the table as he poured peas into boiling water and checked the pie. But if they don't, I thought later, after a convivial supper at the kitchen table, the television on low in the corner, the necessary third wheel to turn to in times of trouble, if they don't play games, what then? Surely there was no escape from reality, which was often so ugly and stifling? I climbed the stairs to bed, leaving Michael to watch *Newsnight*. He'd doze in front of it, before coming up later, when I was asleep. Always a blessing. Crossing the bedroom to draw the curtains, I gazed down a moment into the lamplit street below. It was damp with rain. I turned and went through to the bathroom. Surely daily life was more bearable if one acted a part, if one pretended one was someone else? I switched on the bathroom light, catching my eyes in the mirror as I did. They were strained. Because yes, such theatrics were a strain. That was the trouble. I averted my gaze and busied myself with cleaning my face with a cotton-wool pad, something I could do without looking, determined not to prolong the scrutiny. And let's face it, lots of people's lives were strained, I thought, tossing the pad in the bin. Lots of people just buggered on. Because what was the alternative? Being myself? Where had being myself ever got me in the past?

3

I met Ingrid Schroeder, my husband's potential lover, at the Arts Club, where I was a member. I couldn't afford it these days but I kept up the subscription – albeit with eyes slightly averted when the email came through – because, in my mind, it was central to my operations. Call it subliminal, but I felt being on home territory played in my favour, gave me a tiny advantage, which put my guest on the back foot – historically, likewise, the tennis club, now prohibitively expensive. In any event, it was the rendezvous of choice and a good one. Nevertheless, when I came up the steps from Green Park tube, it wasn't without some trepidation: a little flutter of nerves. I was ten minutes early so as to be in situ when she arrived. To my surprise, however, when I'd pushed through the old oak doors, greeted the doorman and walked into the members' room, Ingrid was already there. She was perched on a stool at the bar, a glass of white wine in hand. Given that you had to be a member to buy a drink, I was taken aback. She was talking to a tall, portly-looking chap with attractive, smiling eyes who was leaning on the bar beside her, listening attentively.

'Lucy,' she said coolly, looking round as I approached. She didn't get up to greet me, which meant I had to bend down to kiss her cheeks. 'I was early and made the awful faux pas of swanning in and ordering a drink, not knowing that wasn't the form. This gallant gent saved me and put it on his sheet – wasn't that kind?'

'Very,' I agreed, shaking hands with the gallant gent, who introduced himself as Tim Farrow, a publisher I'd heard of slightly, but who certainly wouldn't know me. He politely pretended he did, though, and we exchanged a bit of publishing small talk and then he excused himself and said he was off to lunch at the members' table. He disappeared into the dining room, but not without giving Ingrid a last wistful glance. She was well out of his league.

Ingrid was one of those ice-cool Scandinavian blondes who would have been ravishing in her youth and was still quite something. She had a slightly transatlantic lilt to her Nordic accent, having been brought up in various different countries by a rich industrialist father, but had married a fellow Swede, Lars Schroeder, who was in property, and they'd settled over here. But the marriage was shaky. Open, even. All this I'd gleaned from her manicurist, after Millie Taylor let slip she and Ingrid had a regular Tuesday slot at a nail bar in Parsons Green. See what I mean about research?

Obviously, there were quite a few nail bars in Parsons Green, but it didn't take long to breeze into some of them, claim Millie had recommended the joint, and then, after three had shaken their heads, locate the right one. Fourth time lucky. I've never been to a manicurist in my life, but according to Fatima, who filed, buffed and polished me, it was high time I did. She also told me how lovely Millie was, and how she admired Ingrid's style. But the crucial nugget came when she told me Ingrid was writing a book, about interior design. This was a gift from God, as far as I was concerned. All prospective authors were wide-eyed at the prospect of an introduction to an agent or a publisher, which, of course, was exactly what I suggested when I rang her. I'd opened with the Scandinavian kitchen makeover, and she'd said she'd come round and give me a quote. She'd asked where I lived and, when I'd told her, she'd sounded surprised: said she was literally round the corner. Obviously I didn't want her popping round, so I said I'd love to see her work first, and she'd blithely directed me to her shop, and her manager, Helmut, as I thought she might. I'd agreed to go – and later, of course, decide, with regret, it was too expensive – but wondered if there was anything I could look at? A website, or even a brochure? The rest was easy. She'd bitten.

I settled myself beside her now at the bar and we chatted a bit about the club: how cosy it was, albeit a bit run-down. And then Ingrid glanced around, blue eyes searching.

'Is she here?' she asked, referring to my agent, Sonia, who was in fact in Hampshire seeing her newborn grandchild for the first time. 'Or did you say she's meeting us later?'

'Later,' I agreed. 'If she can make it. But she did actually send a text saying she was slightly held up with an author. She said she'd do her best, though. Ingrid, you look amazing, have you been away?'

'Portugal,' she said shortly. 'Just a long weekend in Lisbon.' She frowned. 'So . . . maybe we should make it another day? Rearrange? I could easily do some shopping today.' She began to gather her suede bag with its slinky gilt chain from the bar.

'Oh, you never know, she may yet show. Just a tonic water, please,' I said to the barman, who was raising his eyes enquiringly at me. 'And could we see the menu, please? I'm starving, aren't you?' This with a beaming smile at Ingrid, who was looking a little disgruntled.

'Well, I suppose we may as well eat now we're here,' she said petulantly. Lord, she was bad-mannered. What did Michael see in her? She was gorgeous, of course; sleek and shiny and with long silky hair, too long, possibly, for late forties, and she'd had some work, I decided, looking at her very smooth brow. Not that a man would probably notice. It was subtly done, and she'd sensibly avoided her lips. We ordered a salad apiece. Then we moved to a little table in the corner, and as we chatted about how nice the Taylors were, she became a bit more genial. After the salads arrived, I glanced surreptitiously at my phone, which wasn't actually allowed in here.

'Oh.' I pocketed it quickly. 'Sonia's definitely not going to make lunch,' I explained, 'but she's going to try to join us for a coffee later. Now. Tell me all about it. The book! It sounds amazing. Do you have any pictures?'

She brightened and pulled out a tablet, then hid it quickly under the table as the barman frowned. I swivelled around to take a closer look. Shot after shot of typical Scandi room sets whirred past, all blond wood and bleached floors but with a twist, she told me, in case I hadn't spotted it, in that the walls were flocked velvet, suede sometimes, and the upholstery too, making the juxtaposition all the more vivid. And all the more alarming, I thought privately, as I oohed and aahed, gushing extravagantly, thinking – only rich industrialists, surely? But Ingrid was encouraged by my laying it on thick and began to thaw a little. She even managed to smile when, on learning she'd taken the pictures herself, I declared she could be a photographer, too.

'D'you think? Well, you're very kind. You must come and see it, if you really like it. My shop, I mean. It's in Chelsea Green.' Of course it was.

'I'd *love* to,' I enthused. 'I'm hopeless at interior design. I could really do with some good ideas. Did you study it for years?'

Clever Lucy, clever. She hadn't, of course; she was self-taught, and had been set up in a jiffy either by Daddy or her husband, but loved that I thought she was a professional and not just a rich housewife filling her days. So off we went again on her 'instinctive eye' and 'unfailing feel for colour', so that before long I knew exactly what she and Michael had in common: themselves. And actually, I was disappointed. Usually they were nicer than this. I began to have a slight sinking feeling. Conscience, my trump card, was not feeling so strong.

'Will you open another shop?' I asked eagerly, as if I simply couldn't wait and hoped it was next door. 'You know, expand?'

'I might,' she said, pale eyes widening, and I could tell

it hadn't occurred to her, but she was encouraged I might think she could make an empire out of her plaything. Perhaps an upmarket IKEA? She was beginning to thoroughly warm up and even gave a tinkly little laugh as she knocked back her wine. I admired her hair and she ran a hand through it. Normally at this point in the proceedings – indeed, long before – the other party might politely ask *me* a question, albeit, in the case of Tara, the actress, in a bored, offhand fashion, but not our Ingrid. As I moved on to the rocks on her fingers, gazing rapt and appreciative at the glittering spectrum, she ran me through each heirloom. Only when we'd exhausted this did I ask about her children, which usually *had* to lead to mine, together with a chummy, self-deprecating eye roll about our adored but impossible offspring. A sharing of photos and tips. But Ingrid didn't conform.

'One, a girl, Sophia. Rather spoiled and princessy at the moment.' I waited, but she didn't expand. Neither did she reciprocate.

'I've got two,' I volunteered, rather desperately. She nodded. Sipped her wine. 'And . . . how old is Sophia?' I ploughed on.

'Seventeen. She lives mostly with her father in New York.'

I felt my heart pound. 'You're divorced?'

'Oh no, that would not be financially viable, but we lead separate lives. It's much easier.'

She smiled thinly and I was about to agree warmly that this was, of course, the ideal scenario, when I realized this was the only thing I should absolutely not agree with her on. I was slightly floundering now, to be honest, when luckily, a friend of mine, a smiley Irish author called Maggie Healy, chose that moment to interrupt. She swept across from the bar and materialized before us in a long floral dress. She kissed me warmly on both cheeks, bending down to squeeze my shoulders.

'Lucy! It's grand to see you. I was wondering where you'd been hiding yourself! Sorry to interrupt,' she shot a wide, apologetic smile at Ingrid, 'but I couldn't resist beating you to it. Look what Sonia's just sent me!' She had her phone hidden in her bag and glanced back to check on the barman, who was luckily distracted. 'Lucy and I share an agent,' she explained to Ingrid. 'Take a look at that, now. Isn't that the sweetest babe you've ever seen?'

I looked. At a very lovely, smiling photo, which became a video, of a beaming Sonia. She had a newborn wrapped in a shawl in her arms and looked every inch the proud grandmother. I felt my throat tighten. 'Isn't she the most gorgeous bundle of joy? Augusta Sarah, born last night, on the stroke of midnight.' Maggie turned her phone inclusively, so Ingrid could see.

'So . . . that's your agent?' asked Ingrid, peering, confused. 'With the baby?'

'Taken two minutes ago. She hotfooted it down there this morning when she heard the news. But you knew that, didn't you, Luce? You're in the WhatsApp group?'

It seemed I had neither breath nor words to draw on.

An awful lot of blood seemed to be leaving my face. My mouth opened mutely.

Ingrid fixed me with her cool blue eyes. 'I don't believe we were ever meeting your agent here,' she said quietly. 'I think you got me here to divert me, in some insidious way, from something else.'

Maggie looked horrified. Also baffled. She dropped the phone back in her bag. Then, making wide, apologetic eyes at me, she muttered her excuses and melted away.

'I'm not interested in your husband, Lucy,' Ingrid went on, never taking her eyes off mine. 'He took me to lunch yesterday, and we had a nice time, but I shan't be going again. And not because I've been warned off by you, or because in some weird way you tried to befriend me, but because he's not my type. Believe me, though, if he had been my type, I wouldn't let a little ruse like this stop me.'

She shot me a defiant look. Then she gathered up her suede bag and got to her feet. She adjusted the gold chain over her shoulder and turned on her heel. I watched as she threaded her way through the room. Despite the great legs, her skirt was a bit short and tight, although none of the men in the bar would have agreed with me. Their eyes all strayed from whosoever they were talking to, to follow her out. A female editor I knew smiled and rolled her eyes despairingly at me. But I couldn't move my face at all. I just sat there, in the corner, frozen.

Maggie, sweet Maggie, beetled back. She took Ingrid's

seat beside me, and then my hand, distressed. She asked me quietly, 'What on earth . . . ?' I licked my lips and told her, in halting, whispery tones, what I'd done. Or had tried to do. She didn't speak. Didn't judge. She just squeezed my hand. As my eyes welled up, she led me out of the bar to the Ladies. There I had a bloody good cry in her arms. Later, sniffing and balling bits of tissue from the loo roll she handed me, I assured her I was fine. She saw me downstairs and got me an Uber. And she wouldn't say a word, not to anyone. She promised. I knew she wouldn't. I trusted her. An old friend, who actually wouldn't be a bit surprised. Not really. She watched me go, sadly, into the London traffic.

Michael was waiting for me when I got back and he'd been drinking. As I closed the front door behind me, I knew at once this was a very different atmosphere to the one I'd encountered yesterday. I walked down the hall to the kitchen and he came towards me from where he'd been waiting. A muscle was going in his cheek and the familiar anger vein was throbbing in his forehead. He'd called the club, he said. I'd been so long, he was worried. Asked the doorman who I was lunching with, who'd signed in as my guest. He said he knew my nasty little ways of old. Knew exactly what I was up to. He began to shake with fury, his face florid. He said he was mortified, thoroughly ashamed of me, that I was a complete embarrassment. And then it started. How nobody liked me, nobody. I had no friends; people only accepted me for my association, by marriage, with him. His friends all pitied him, wondered why he stayed with me, this timid soul who churned out drivel. Terrible disposable book after disposable book. I was a laughing stock. He said pity was the only reason he stayed with me. That he knew I'd be destitute if he left me. The house, in a covenant organized by trustees of his parents, belonged solely to him. He knew I'd be on the streets. He said he despised me. All this, as he prowled around me, whisky on his breath, hissing in my face, leaning in now and then for my ear. Michael was always careful now, not to make too much noise.

I groped for a stool. My legs were wobbly and I always physically shrank under the verbal abuse, often with my head bowed, my eyes shut. Still he prowled, and hissed: about what a pathetic creature I was. Overweight, fat, ugly. An insult to my sex. And all this, actually, I could take. As long as I took cover, thus, in silence. I knew, from his sister, that when they were younger she'd suffered similar insults when he'd been thwarted in some way. She'd repeated some of the things he'd just said to me word for word, so although it left me breathless, I could take it. I waited, mute and trembling, on the kitchen stool, for him to finish. In the past, of course, when I was younger, I'd retaliated: shouted, screamed even, but that would only kick-start something extra – something he'd yet to say, about the children – so I didn't. Finally he bent right down to put his face close to mine, that vein pumping in his forehead, to deliver his last insult.

'And don't you ever think of leaving, you sad little bitch. Because you know what I'll do. You know I'll find you. Or someone else.'

34

I froze, waiting for him to elaborate. To tell me about the accidents that happen daily. A girl who fell from a high-rise window only a block from Imo's in Manhattan. How, in Ned's church, a huge lump of plaster had dropped from the ceiling, wounding a parishioner. He didn't. Just a lot of heavy breathing, the whisky fumes revolting. Still I waited, though, and when I knew he wouldn't go away until I glanced up, I did. He spat in my face. I didn't brush it away, I knew the rules.

Finally I sensed him moving off. There was a rustling behind me as he collected his door keys from his desk in the corner. Then he blundered heavily past me through the kitchen. Down the passageway he went, and then the front door slammed behind him, rattling in the frame.

I raised my head and wiped my face. My hand was trembling. He'd be off to Soho to meet his buddies: a few alcoholics, out-of-work actors, none of whom had families any more, all of whom had been deserted. Boozing, ageing luvvies, who would have been there all day. And there he'd stay, until they were finally chucked out, in the early hours. Michael would pour himself into a black cab and trundle, expensively, home. He wouldn't come up to the bedroom, I knew – thank God. He'd prostrate himself on the sofa in the study, and there I'd find him in the morning.

And then, the nightmare would continue: for days, weeks sometimes. A different sort of treatment: silent, deadly, brittle and tense. No words would be exchanged, and during that time, I'd determine to leave him, once and for all. Go to the police. Tell them about his threats. No bruises, of course, he was too clever for that, and I could almost hear the police sighing in my head. Telling me many people threaten to do things when they're angry. Still, this time I'd do it. And just as I'd be building up to it, with Helena there too, for moral support, he'd come home beaming, almost as if he knew. The sun would come out and he'd have flowers in his arms and tickets in his pockets for Venice, just the two of us. And I can hardly bear to tell you this, but something inside me would crumble. My resolve. All the tension of the last few weeks would dissipate, and I'd feel such ridiculous relief flood through me. And I'd try not to picture Helena's face, contorting in disgust and incredulity, as I found myself on an EasyJet flight a few days later. I'd text her, assuring her all was well, and that I was having really rather an amazing time. She wouldn't reply.

But not this time, I thought, as I sat there chilled and still, for what, I realized, when I glanced outside, must have been ages. It was getting dark. This time it would be different. I'd actually report him. And then disappear. Go abroad, maybe. To America, to Imo. Aware I'd resolved this countless times before, I climbed the stairs to my bedroom. Neither hungry nor thirsty, I drew the curtains and got undressed. But I couldn't face brushing my teeth. That mirror in the bathroom, so shaming. I just crawled into bed.

Some time later, I heard him return: his key in the door; it slamming shut. Then a shuffle down the hall towards the kitchen, and thence the study. A light appeared around my door frame for a few minutes, then darkness again. I shut my eyes, exhausted but sleepless. And then, an hour or so later, when I was still wide awake, I heard a crash. Breaking glass. I lay still, shocked. Then I heard a voice, Michael's voice, a shout. And then a cry and a thud. I sat bolt upright in bed. What the fuck? Had he woken for a pee and crashed, pissed, into that glass coffee table? Knocked a lamp over? Silence, now. I leaped out of bed and flew to the door in my nightie. Terrified at what I might find, I froze, my hand on the knob; but then, resolute, I opened it and crept down.

The house was in darkness. I passed the children's old rooms on the next landing, then their bathroom on another, and stole on down the stairs to the hall. The kitchen was very dark, but I felt my way through and pushed open the door to the study. A bright stream of light, a torch, suddenly swung round and was in my face, blinding me. The light was dazzling in its intensity and stopped me in my tracks. There was heavy breathing too. I was terrified. I stood, frozen. Then came to my senses.

'Hey!' I shouted, instinctively covering my eyes with my arm.

All of a sudden, it was gone. Snapped off. Darkness fell, and as my eyes acclimatized, the intruder, who I instantly realized I'd disturbed, was off. Out the way he'd come, flying through the open French door, a pane broken where the latch hung. I fleetingly saw him leg it down the garden. Just as the moonlight had briefly illuminated him, it was also enough to reveal Michael. He lay motionless, face up on the floor, between the sofa and the coffee table. Beside him was a bucket, which already had vomit in it. His face was deathly pale and there was a small pool of blood beside his head. I stared. Didn't immediately move. Don't ask me why. But the room still had the air of someone fast-moving and violent passing through it. And that dazzling white light. The breathing. So close. I felt violated.

Then I crouched in my nightie. I felt his pulse. Very faint. And blood was seeping still, from his head. Beside him was a heavy marble lamp stand, a wedding present. The shade was off, away in a corner. We didn't have a landline, and when I reached in Michael's jacket pocket, on the sofa arm, for his phone, it was out of charge. I'd have to find mine. I realized my movements were slow, though, and my breathing was very laboured. Very . . . considered, almost. Where was it? My phone? Upstairs? No, of course not, it was still in my bag, in the kitchen on the island. Somewhere in the distance a light went out. I darted out and found it.

When I returned, I sat down on the sofa, looking at Michael on the floor. I felt numb. Weirdly disconnected from my body. Michael seemed miles away. Yet he was right at my feet. Vast and motionless. All at once, he looked very close. Such a big man. His mouth was open as if in shock, eyes shut. Two buttons on his shirt were undone and there was a yellow curry stain down the front. It took me a while to avert my gaze. I'd never seen him so defenceless. I looked at the phone in my hand. I'd been out all day, so maybe it was out of charge? It wasn't. There was twenty per cent left. I raised my head. The French door was hanging on one hinge. We had good locks, so the frame had been forced too. The garden, long and thin, was illuminated by the moon. He must have legged it over the wall and vaulted into the next garden, I decided. It was high, the wall, but not insurmountable. I looked at the phone, limp in my hand. I must be in shock, I told myself, although I sort of knew I wasn't. And I have to tell you, I was neither trembling, nor terribly scared, as I picked up Michael's wrist again. This time the pulse was barely there. I sat on the sofa and waited. I felt extraordinary. Other-worldly. As if it wasn't me sitting there at all.

At length, I tapped a number into my phone. Raised it to my ear. When the ambulance arrived, minutes later, from Charing Cross, the young team of paramedics checked Michael quickly on the floor, before placing a blanket calmly around my shoulders. The elder one sat beside me. She told me quietly and very gently that my husband was dead. I wasn't really surprised. In fact, I wasn't surprised at all.

4

Michael's wasn't the first life I'd had a hand in ending, actually. During the course of my writing career I've obviously seen off quite a few individuals; it's something of an occupational hazard. But fiction aside, in real life, I'd killed someone else. It was an accident, of course, and years ago, but still, to this day, harrowing.

Helena and I had been going to a party and I'd just passed my test. I was seventeen to her nineteen. In the country you learn to drive at a young age, unless you want to be dependent on your parents, or dreadful public transport, so Mum and Dad were not unduly concerned when, one night, they saw us both off. Helena was in the passenger seat, having promised not to drink and to drive us both home. The party wasn't her age group, so it was less of a big deal for her. I was at the wheel, dressed up and excited. We'd literally barely left our lane, we were scarcely a mile from home. And it was his fault, luckily for me, the motorcyclist's. I don't mean luckily – there was nothing lucky about that terrible night – but he flew across the T-junction when it was my right of way, and I was travelling quite slowly. And then he didn't really stand a chance. In my darkest moments I still see him, somersaulting fast through the air in black leather, and then plastered against the windscreen, his face, through his helmet visor, towards us. I still hear Helena's piercing screams, her hands over her face, as I sat shocked and silent beside her.

After that, it's a bit of a blur. Police cars arrived, sirens blared, blue lights flashed. My parents arrived, white-faced, in the fading summer dusk. I remember a police station in the local town and a kind female detective, my parents beside me. Helena sobbing quietly. Then nothing, really. It was the end of the summer holidays and I went back to school for my final year to take my A-levels. My friends were kind, sympathetic, but I found I couldn't talk about it. Didn't want to. And I couldn't for some time. Not when I went to university the following year, where I thought it would be a relief for people not to know, where I could turn to a new chapter in my life, to be someone else; but in a way, it felt almost worse somehow. I felt as if I was hiding something. Deceiving everyone around me.

He was a local boy, not much older than me. Nineteen. He'd lived two villages away in Barrington. I'd written to his parents, the hardest letter I've ever had to write, saying how deeply sorry I was, but I hadn't got a response. He'd been on a technical training course, learning to be a bricklayer, and eventually, a builder like his father. He was their only son, although I believe there was a daughter. I say I believe, I know. For a while I became obsessed with the family, wanting to know everything I could about them. But later I found I couldn't maintain what had become a self-imposed determination not to forget him. A penance. It brought me too low. I became dangerously introverted and quiet. I recognized it myself, without going to a therapist or anything, so I took action. Went the other way. I threw myself into university life, parties, and made new friends, good friends actually, and at more of a remove than my school friends, so it was easier.

Boyfriends I found difficult, though. I dated one or two people, but when it came to the more intimate, confiding nature of the relationship, I came unstuck. When one boy told me, slightly teary-eyed in bed one night, that he'd never got on with his father ever since he discovered he'd had a long affair, that it compromised all his childhood memories, I knew that was my moment. Knew I should reciprocate with a confidence of my own. An admission. But even though it hadn't been my fault, I still found the magnitude of ending someone's life, of taking someone's child, leaving such a hole in a family of four (like mine) of such breathtaking enormity, that if I struggled to comprehend it, how could I expect anyone else to? Also, I knew it would define me. Change me into the girl who'd killed someone, with that aura of pity and fascination around her. And so I broke it off, the relationship. An avoidance technique I would use repeatedly.

I was reading Modern History at York, and whilst most of my girlfriends on the course majored on feminist subjects, like patriarchy and female oppression, the suffragette movement, the rise of political empowerment for women, I concentrated on the survivors of the battle of the Somme. On why they never spoke of the horrors of war. I wrote about PTSD, and why men were subjugated and marginalized in that they were ordered to take lives, whereas women weren't. I championed for men's rights, in a way, and for their voices never heard. I got a first.

When I left, I went home for a while and wrote quite a lot of poetry. I also did a fair amount of cooking and gardening, but as my parents pointed out, I needed a proper job. I wasn't sure about proper, wasn't sure I deserved a career, but I knew I had to do something. And so I went to London and cooked directors' lunches for a large firm of City accountants. I think Dad got the job for me, through contacts. I had no formal training, but I knew enough from Mum to put a boeuf bourguignon for twelve on the table and follow it with summer pudding. One of the young directors there took a bit of a shine to me and asked me to a party. I was trying to get over myself more, and so, even though he was a bit clean-cut for me – Paul, he was called, very ex-army and Winchester – I went anyway. And it was there, at a house party in Clapham, that I met Michael.

Michael was holding court in the kitchen, clearly a colourful character. He was telling amusing anecdotes, and generally playing to a very appreciative audience. All the people there were much older than me and when Michael's eye fell on me as Paul and I went across to get a drink, I could tell it was in an 'ah, fresh meat' sort of way. An older man distracted for a moment from his familiar coterie of writers, journalists and actors, of

43

which this gathering, Paul had told me, was comprised. Paul was an accountant for some of them, and I think rather flattered to be invited.

'The white's filthy,' Michael told me, as I picked up the bottle. His eyes were hooded and pale blue: slightly bloodshot perhaps, but sexy. They forced me to meet them. 'Here, have some of this.' He reached behind him for a bottle of red. I didn't drink red as a rule, but accepted the glass he offered me. I smiled a thank you, and instantly let Paul lead me away, although I knew Michael's eyes were on my back.

It wasn't an unpleasant feeling, actually, knowing, as the party wore on, that this jovial, very tall and good-looking man, for no reason other than my youth, I suspect, and my novelty value, had his eyes trained on me for the rest of the evening. It was a hot summer's night and we all danced in the garden on the terrace: Michael with a stunning but rather sulky-looking red-head in tight leopard-skin who shot me savage glances occasionally; and me with Paul, who was sweet but incredibly earnest, asking me every five minutes if I wanted to move on, or go out for supper.

Suddenly they were right beside us, Michael and the redhead. Michael was facing me. He had a good sense of rhythm, unlike Paul, who, to compensate, was gyrating rather too energetically. Michael was smiling mischievously, right into my eyes. It was too much for the redhead, who stormed off, which meant the three of us were dancing together, which suddenly struck me as terribly funny. It was his sheer force of personality that did it, his chutzpah. It should have been annoying, but I got terrible giggles. Paul was obviously miffed and, apologizing profusely, I followed him off the dance floor to somewhere quieter in the garden. He was alive to the situation, though, and when some friends of his came across for a chat, and then suddenly Michael was beside us again, siphoning me off, he didn't object. He carried on chatting to his friends. That left the two of us smiling at one another under a pear tree.

'Go on then, what is it?' I asked, three glasses of red wine in and emboldened.

'What's what?'

'Your well-honed, well-versed opening gambit. Your chat-up line that hasn't failed you yet and which you're about to unleash to devastating effect.'

His eyes brightened delightedly. 'Who says I'm even interested?'

'You do. With your body language and your special effects – which include ignoring the girl you probably arrived with. Charming.'

'Unlike you, you mean?' he said, glancing at Paul in his group of friends.

'I met Paul last week. I don't suppose he'll be too distressed.'

'Whereas I've known Celine for years, and our on-off relationship is decidedly off at the moment.'

'Right.'

We seemed to have discovered a great deal about each other remarkably quickly and I for one would have liked to slow things down. Aware, however, that it was me

45

who'd got the ball rolling so fast in the first place, I decided I couldn't really cry foul.

'Still, I agree, it seems indelicate to share the same space with them. To parade our mutual attraction quite so blatantly. Come. Let me lead you up the garden path.' He waggled his eyebrows and nodded further down the garden.

'There's nothing mutual,' I said, my mouth twitching. 'I've literally just met you.' Nonetheless, I found myself following him down the garden, which was long and grassy and lit with fairy lights in the trees. It was like a garden friends of my parents might own. Indeed, the whole thing was incredibly grown-up and beguiling, and despite my protestations, I felt ridiculously excited.

And excited was something I hadn't felt since the accident. Ever since I was a little girl, I'd had a profound crush on someone. The family dog; Brad Pitt; Pierce Brosnan; the boy in the village shop with floppy hair and a devastating smile; Mr Simons the music master, who closed his eyes when he played the violin; and then a real boy, called Chris, who'd taken me to the pub a few times, a friend of Helena's. And then, after that – nothing. For years. Just an empty space and a glaring white light thereafter. It was as if that side of my head had died, with Liam Stephens, in the crash. Chris I didn't see again, despite his entreaties, his phone calls, and at university, as we know, the white light and the empty space persisted. However much I tried, I never felt a thing. And previously, even with Brad and Pierce, it was not just a crush, but true love. These people would consume me. I'd make up stories about them, about how I'd save them, perhaps, from an accident – ironic, obviously – or become best friends with their sisters. So that even when I was alone, I never felt I was. Even if I was sewing, or walking the dog, I always had my love. I never felt lonely. But now, when I was on my own, I did.

Something about Michael, though, made my heart peek out a little from the shadows: made me curious, despite myself, to look. Call it animal magnetism, which sounds rather brutish, or sexual attraction, which isn't much better, but whatever it was, within moments we were walking right through the garden and out of the gate.

'Hang on.' I came to. 'Where are we going?'

'Just to the shop. I need some cigarettes. Walk with me? Tell me, what are you doing with that boring young man?'

'Paul's not boring, he's sweet. He just doesn't wear his charisma on his sleeve like some people. He'd probably feel it was attention-seeking.'

His eyes lit up in delight and he suppressed a smile. 'For someone you met five minutes ago, you seem to know an awful lot about him.'

'I try to be perceptive, particularly when I'm asked out to a party. I find it helps.'

'He looks like a bank clerk to me. One of Eliot's thousands pouring over London Bridge.'

'Nice to see you wear your learning so lightly, too. Are you one of those people who litters their conversation with literary allusions to put others at a disadvantage? Or are you just showing off?'

This time he threw back his head and laughed outright. 'Definitely showing off.'

The shop was shut, predictably, and so we went to the pub and got cigarettes there. Obviously we had a drink, too, so that by the time we got back to the party, Paul had gone. Celine too. Michael scratched his head with theatrical bewilderment and regarded the thinning crowd.

'Good Lord. It seems I have no other choice but to escort you home.'

He did, in a taxi, and, to my surprise, he didn't ambush me. He just dropped me back at my flat and said goodnight. But not before he'd got my number and then clearly asked the driver to wait. The taxi didn't trundle off until I'd found my key, opened the front door, and shut it behind me.

I found myself thinking about Michael the whole of the following day as I cooked. When I delivered my coq au vin to the assembled directors in the dining room – Paul thankfully not amongst them – it was with a cheery smile, so that a couple of the elder statesmen smiled back, not averse to having their lunch delivered by a pretty young girl. But they looked surprised, too, so that it occurred to me that perhaps I hadn't smiled much, historically.

He didn't ring that evening, nor the next, but the following night the phone went and I found myself pouncing on it before Helena could. She looked at me in surprise. I dragged it out to the hall and sat on the stairs as we chatted. We agreed to meet on Saturday. I went back in. Helena raised her eyebrows and looked at me in amusement.

'You look like you've just had sex.'

'What d'you mean?'

'Your eyes are huge and your face is flushed and your hair's all over the place.'

'Crap,' I scoffed, but I smoothed my hair down quickly where I'd obviously been flipping it back and forth as we'd chatted.

'No, I'm thrilled. Haven't seen you look like that for years. Who is he?'

I told her. She nodded slowly. Was silent.

'You know him?'

'Only by repute. Ant does, I think. You might be a bit careful, hon.'

'What d'you mean?' I bridled defensively.

'No, nothing terrible. Just . . . well, he's older, and therefore a bit more – you know.'

'Experienced?'

'Exactly.'

'Well, he's bound to be, surely?'

'Oh quite,' she said quickly, not wanting to rain on my parade. 'It's just, I've heard he gets what he wants.'

I shrugged. 'I may not want him.'

She smiled. 'That's the spirit.'

I did, of course. And my excitement grew as, on our first few dates, he was terribly chivalrous, much as he'd been at the party, I was able to tell Helena triumphantly.

He didn't try a thing. Just took me out for the most delicious supper at L'artiste Assoiffé, which had parrots and sofas and golden retrievers and a menu that made my eyes water it was so expensive, and then dancing, and then home. Once back, he simply kissed me, albeit rather thoroughly, on the steps of my flat in Gloucester Terrace, and then he hailed a taxi, so that actually, as I watched him go, I was the one wanting more.

Helena had smiled thinly at this, but said nothing. I assumed it was because she was rather agreeably surprised, and irritated she'd been wrong. It didn't occur to me she might recognize a practised technique. In bed, I played the evening back to myself, line by line, word by amusing word.

For Michael was very funny. Once, a friend asked me what he was covering with the constant jokes, and I couldn't think what she meant. And when we did sleep together, a month or so later, he was kind and lovely, but not intense or declamatory, as boys of my age had been. He didn't seem to want anything from me, which made him all the more attractive. In fact, it was me, as we lay in his bed overlooking Onslow Gardens, the French windows open to the night, who asked him questions about his past, his life. His parents, I knew, had both died, hence the rather plush pad in South Ken, his sister in a similar one down the road, but I didn't ask him about that: I asked him how he came to write. He admitted it was a form of therapy after losing his parents, something he'd taken solace in, so that when he asked me in turn about my poetry, which I'd once vaguely admitted to, I found that, remarkably, and no doubt in recognition of something similar, I was able to open up.

'I killed a boy once,' I found myself saying. 'In an accident. I was driving. I hit his bike. I found writing helped.'

I didn't have to say any more. He understood immediately. He nodded at the ceiling. Remained silent. After a while, he spoke.

'Does it still help?'

'Yes.' I hesitated. 'But these past few weeks . . . well. I've needed it less, I've found.'

He smiled, accepting the allusion to his presence in my life.

'You've filled a dark hole,' I went on, emboldened.

He swallowed, and I could tell he was moved. 'D'you want to talk about it? The accident?'

I did. And I also told him that it was the first time I'd ever shared and explained my past. I told him at quite some length. How it had happened. The images I remembered from that night. An old woman, running in her apron from a cottage in the lane, her hand over her mouth: stopping dead, then turning back to phone the police. The way Liam had slid, eventually, off the car bonnet on to the road. How I'd once walked past his mother in town: how we'd both stiffened with recognition. I'd seen a photo of her in the local paper, at the funeral, and of course, she'd made it her business to know who I was, even though she'd never met me. My parents had insisted on going alone to the coroner's court. I told him how a boy in a leather jacket had deliberately knocked into me in a local pub. Spilled the drinks I'd been carrying. A friend of Liam's, I later learned. How moments like those had set me back, sent me reeling. There were many terrible moments, a lifetime of them, which is different, naturally, to a terrible lifetime. I told him how I'd been incapable of talking about my feelings, even though my family had tried, principally because I felt there was no script for a tragedy like this. How I knew my life had changed immeasurably. How I used to think of Liam every single day, and had imagined that would persist forever. And how, to my shame, it had begun to stop. Was more intermittent. When I'd finished, Michael was silent.

I'd been lying on my back, but I rolled over and lay in the crook of his arm. We were silent for a while, and I could tell he was thoughtful. I asked him about his parents, then. He turned and looked at the bedside clock. It was two in the morning.

'Another time, little Luce,' he said, giving me a squeeze. 'I'll tell you about it another time.'

He didn't, though. And in a small part of my head, I realized I'd given him something very precious. Something very intimate. A part of myself, if you like. And he hadn't reciprocated. And he never did.

5

The first time Michael surprised me was on a plane going out to Majorca. He wasn't on the plane, but a stewardess came down the aisle bearing a bunch of flowers. She stopped beside me. Then she checked my seat number and handed them to me. They were from Michael. I flushed with delight.

'Oh my *God*!' My girlfriends got up out of their seats and crowded around. 'You've got flowers! How did he *do* that? Oh my God, he is *so* gorgeous. Luce, you are *so* so lucky!'

I was. I really was and I knew it. Flushed with pleasure, I handed the small posy of white roses back to the stewardess who promised to put them in water. Then, when we got to Majorca, I transferred them to a vase in the room I shared with Sara for the week. I felt a thrill of pleasure every time I saw them on my girls' sunbathing holiday. How had he managed that? Talked the stewardess into it? Well of course, Michael would find a way.

When we got back to a heaving Stansted, at some godforsaken hour in the morning, girding our loins for the Tube to London, he surprised me again. Because there he was, smiling at the barrier, ready to whisk me away to his flat in his convertible MG. No room for anyone else, sadly, by the time my luggage was in, so my girlfriends – who, if they had boyfriends, had boys their own age who barely even had cars – were left gaping in astonishment. I was indeed a very lucky girl.

We were an established couple by now, and did pretty much everything together, although Helena encouraged me to have my own life. She said it was healthier, and I got the point of that, to keep up with friends my age, even though I was totally immersed in his glamorous, clever Cambridge set. They were mostly in the arts, either actors or writers, and had met in the Footlights, which Michael hadn't quite got into. He'd wanted to act, he told me, but hadn't cut the mustard. Michael had lots of friends, and was very much the life and soul, but strangely, after a party, he was always quiet on the way home. I knew not to break into his thoughts. If I did, he'd snap at me for wittering, but then instantly recover and apologize profusely: say he'd forgotten himself, which was a good way of putting it. He genuinely had.

My own friends he indulged now and then, but he wasn't overly keen on mixing too much, and I could see why. He'd moved on from chat about internships and the cost of London rentals forcing them out to places like Crouch End, which he'd never even heard of. He was polite, but I could tell it bored him.

So following Helena's advice – and trust me, my sister's quite bossy – I went on my own to supper parties, one of which was indeed in Crouch End. When I emerged at about midnight, there he was, in his blue

MG, waiting for me. I stopped in surprise on the pavement. The passenger door swung open and I leaned in and stared at him in astonishment.

'What are you doing here?'

'Back end of bloody beyond,' he grumbled. 'How are you supposed to get home from here? No cabs are ever going to take you.'

'Tube,' I told him as I climbed in, 'like the rest of the world. I cannot believe you've driven over here! That is so sweet!'

I did, indeed, think it unbelievably sweet, and it happened a couple more times. Closer to home in Clapham, and then, down the road, in Fulham. Helena's eyes widened when I told her.

'He sat outside Sara's supper party waiting for you?'

'Isn't that divine?'

'Or slightly creepy?'

I frowned. 'What d'you mean?'

'Well, hasn't he got a life of his own? Why does he have to keep such firm tabs on yours?'

This was so like Helena, who'd been dumped a couple of months ago, and, as always, when she was unhappy, lashed out at the nearest person – her flatmate and sister. The situation was often tense in the flat. In her unhappiness at losing Ant – who was completely gorgeous, incidentally, a kind, unassuming boy, unable to take the heat of high-maintenance Helena – she increasingly took it out on me. With this in mind, when Michael suggested I move in with him, I thought it a good idea. I'd get to be with my boyfriend, and Helena would be better off sharing with a friend, who she'd have to be more considerate of. Plus I knew Millie, her best mate, was looking.

My family, however, were not so thrilled.

'I thought you liked him,' I said in surprise to Mummy when, having been encouraged to come on my own, I went down for the weekend. I was chopping a salad with her in the kitchen.

'I do,' she said carefully. 'But Luce, you're only twenty-two. And he's thirty-one. And much as I can understand he's ready to settle down, I'm not sure you are. I'd say you've got a lot more living to do. And he's only your first serious boyfriend since . . . you know.'

'The accident,' I said shortly. 'Liam.' It still hurt to say it, that name, but not as much, I realized. Now that I shared the guilt and sadness. Now that someone was carrying some of the load with me. And that that some-one should be anything other than loved and thanked by those around me, for bringing me back into the real world, from out of my dark place, seemed to me an abomination. A travesty of justice.

'It's Helena, isn't it?' I seethed. 'You've only met him once and you and Daddy both said how much you liked him. Helena's poisoned you against him.'

'Now that's much too strong,' said my mother mildly, doing something creative with radishes and simul-taneously taking a sip of her Martini. 'Helena's just concerned. And you're right, we have only met him once, which isn't much, considering you're moving in. It's Ant who's concerned, actually.'

'Ant? Really? You know he's finished with her, by the way.'

'Yes, but that's another story, and one that I agree doesn't cover your sister in glory. Trying to make him buy a flat when he's got no money and leaving copies of *Brides* magazine lying around. But the point is, Ant would never speak badly of anyone.'

There was no disputing this. Ant had been going out with Helena for years, he was a local boy and was very much part of the family. But the only contact Ant had with Michael was professional, which was bound to be fraught, as I pointed out to Mum now.

'Actors hate critics. They're scared of them, it's well known.'

'Not all of them, he says. He says Michael can be spiteful.'

This was unusual for Mum, who, equally, rarely had a bad word for anyone, and I looked at her in surprise. 'In his writing, yes. Sardonic, satirical humour. Acerbic, sometimes. But also very funny. That's his *job*, and also his trademark. Surely Ant can see that?'

'Of course he can,' said Dad, coming in and reaching for a bottle of red from the wine rack for lunch. He put it between his knees and pulled the cork, then did the same with another. 'And personally, I think children have got to make their own decisions. So if we could have an end to all this girly chitter-chatter, I'd be grateful. The De Courcys are even now making their way up the drive in their new Jag, Nancy no doubt POA – pissed on arrival – and in need of a sharpener to stop her sobering up and becoming belligerent. Cecily, what's that fillet doing sitting on the side? It surely needs a canter round the oven, no?' He reached across and popped the beef in the Aga. 'Rare is one thing. Heart still beating is another.'

Dad's word, as ever, was final and we shut up. I was still slightly seething and Mum was clearly flustered, having uncharacteristically spoken out as coached by Helena. Through we went, however, both a bit pink, to greet Nance and Martin. The former was indeed POA and we settled down to enjoy a noisy, convivial luncheon. No more was said that weekend on the matter, my mother, not the bravest, clearly feeling she'd done her bit. I'm not sure Helena would have agreed.

I'd made an excuse to Michael about going home on my own. Usually we were together at the weekends. I'd said it was to do with talking about inheritance tax or something. My family never talked about things like that. They wouldn't know what it was if it slapped them in the face, which it probably would one day. But I knew Michael would fall for it, seeing as it was a subject he knew a great deal about.

He and his sister Amanda had inherited quite a lot when his parents died. I didn't know how much, just that they were reasonably wealthy, and that when they'd gone to live with their grandparents, it had all been kept in trust. Which was why, it transpired, Michael was able to live so well and be a theatre critic, not, as his lifestyle might suggest, an investment banker or something. Even if he wasn't a raging success, it certainly looked as if he was, as he himself would admit. 'Important to look the part, even if it is only a part,' he'd quip, which I liked. Although, as a pissed friend of his pointed out one night, Michael was always quick to tell a joke about himself before someone else did.

Anyway, I did move in, or flounce out. Helena and I had had another blazing row. This time it was about Michael's sister, whom Helena had met at a party. Having realized the connection, she'd then had a frank-and-fearless with her about the death of her parents, as only Helena could. Amanda had told her how, in a hotel bedroom in Greece, they'd both died in their sleep of carbon monoxide poisoning. And how this tragedy had left Amanda not only bereft, but traumatized. How, as a result, she'd never been able to make any real connection in a relationship. How, as soon as it got serious, she broke it off. For fear of getting hurt. For fear of abandonment later.

Helena, probing and inappropriate as usual, had asked if she thought the tragedy had had the opposite effect on Michael? That through his own fear of abandonment, he'd make the connection too tight? Be too controlling? Amanda's eyes, already no doubt swimming with booze, had widened in the light of this amateur psychologist's claptrap. Yeah, she'd said. Yeah, you could well be right. In fact, it had happened before, to an ex of his called Rachael. She genuinely felt Michael followed her sometimes. She'd look behind her, and there he'd be. So Rachael had broken off the relationship. And sozzled old Amanda had said that of course she *adored* darling

Michael and didn't want to judge, but it was only natural they'd *both* suffered, as a result of such a brutal separation. She said it was why she found it so hard to stick at a job, to keep friends, and all manner of psycho-babble people blame their shit lives on, as I'd screamed at Helena, gripping the handles of my cases in the hall. I knew from Michael that Amanda blamed a lot of her loafing around, her trust-fund existence, her bust-ups with friends, on the death of her parents. But Michael wasn't like that. He never even *talked* about it, for God's sake. I'd had no idea how they'd even *died* until Helena told me – which obviously irritated the hell out of me – why couldn't she just mind her own fucking business? Why couldn't she just 'STAY OUT OF MY LIFE!' I'd screamed at full volume at her. And then I'd slammed out and clattered down the stairs.

Helena and I didn't speak for a while after that. When we did, Michael and I were already planning our wedding, having recently discovered I was pregnant. Well I know, it wasn't ideal. And the thing was, I'd become so brilliant at the rhythm method, which Michael had told me about. I'd stopped taking the Pill because he'd sweetly said he didn't want all those rubbish hormones and toxins in my lovely young body, and it had been working perfectly well for months, until blow me down, I missed a period. I did a test and there it was: the famous blue line. We went home and told my parents. They were brilliant, in fact. I'd actually already rung ahead and told Mummy, and I'd quite wanted to go and speak to them on my own, but Michael insisted it looked bad if he didn't come, particularly since we were getting married. And yes, I was thrilled we were. I mean, obviously I'd moved in, so in some unformed, hazy way, my intention must have been to marry. But it was just all so sudden.

Mummy and Daddy *were* brilliant, but they were also quite serious and quiet. They listened, and thanked us for coming to tell them of our intentions, but the whole day was rather subdued. And Daddy didn't get the champagne out as I thought he would. My family can turn anything into a celebration, which this surely was.

On the way home, Michael leaned across and patted my hand. 'All right, little Luce?'

'Yes.' I turned back from gazing out of the window. 'Fine.'

'Your parents were so good about it, weren't they? I mean, given the circumstances?'

'Yes. They really were.'

I knew, though, that had it been Helena and Ant, an unplanned pregnancy, a mistake, a wedding, there would have been whoops of delight. My mother would have clasped her hands in joy. Daddy would have rushed to the drinks cupboard. Ant would have stammered a sheepish apology, whilst Daddy pooh-poohed it, saying, 'Nonsense, dear boy!' Whereas Michael had slightly stolen the show. Done all the talking about how things were going to be, and how he was going to look after me. Patting my hand, like he was now.

Two days later, I received a letter from my father, and I can't tell you how unusual that was.

Dearest Puss,

Forgive some interference from a crumbling old fool, but something in your demeanour yesterday inclined me to put pen to paper. The thing is, my love, I'm slightly concerned. Are you happy? Is this genuinely what you want? Because Mummy and I can't be sure. I can see it's what Michael wants, and I'm sure he really loves you, but darling, do you feel the same? Because if not, please, please examine your options.

In the first place, you don't have to have the baby, this isn't the 1950s. If that idea is morally abhorrent to you, as Michael said it was, then of course, we understand. But please know that we would also one hundred per cent support you as a single mother. You could come and live with us and we would welcome you with open arms. Or, why don't the two of you live together, but wait a year or two to get married? It is far from unusual to have a toddler at a wedding, these days. What I'm trying to say, my love, and no doubt in a clumsy fashion, is that you do have alternatives. You don't have to get married now.

I'm in London on Friday seeing Mike Dubarry about some terrible new scheme he's got for flogging wine to the French — aka ice to Eskimos — but could meet for lunch? How about Wheelers, one o'clock?

Anyway, have a think.

Best love,
Daddy

I stared in wonder. Stood up from the stairs where I'd been sitting reading it. Michael's voice behind me made me jump.

'All right, little Luce?'

I swung around. He was at the top of the stairs.

'Yes, fine.'

'Who's the letter from?'

I stared at him. 'Helena. Haranguing me again. Apparently I've got some of her clothes.'

'As if she hasn't got an entire shop-full!'

'Well, quite.'

I pocketed the letter. And then later, something made me burn it. I rang Dad and said all was well, but thank you. And we were both quite brisk on the phone. Quite . . . polite. I knew it was as far as he'd go.

We got married in Twickenham, in the same church where Michael's parents had married, and where they were buried in the churchyard. Obviously I showed a bit in my dress, but everyone said I looked lovely. I would have preferred a registry office, under the circumstances, but Michael insisted, and the vicar didn't seem to mind. There was quite a lot from the vicar – a family friend – in the address about Michael's parents. And quite a lot in Michael's speech, too. About how he wished they could be here. He had to stop as he got emotional: whipped his hanky out. Amanda was sobbing quietly and had to be led away. It wasn't really the most joyful of occasions. And if I'm honest, in a funny sort of way, I felt a bit miffed. He never spoke about his parents to me, and yet here he was, talking openly to lots of people. But the moment passed. And it was good later on, when my family and friends hit the champagne at the reception and danced like mad.

Michael said later that they hadn't shown enough respect: that my father should have mentioned his parents in his speech, which was too much about me. I was flabbergasted. We had a furious row, on our wedding night. I wasn't to know it was to be the first of many.

Imogen was born in September, and then, rather swiftly, Ned followed. After that, I said, no more. And made sure of it, quietly. Michael wasn't always very nice to them. He shouted at them. Not when they were babies, but certainly as small children, a lot. And at me, a lot. We grew to fear him. Imogen once told me she hated him. She was about fourteen at the time. She burst into noisy floods of tears and said her most fervent wish was never to see him again in her life. The jokes were all reserved for his friends now and his temper had become terrifying. Much worse than the clipped irritation I'd previously witnessed, which had no doubt masked the real thing. In those early days of our marriage, it was loud and voluble. The hissing came later, after a concerned neighbour knocked on the door. A couple of times, actually. Asked if everything was OK.

And to be fair, his rages were often sparked by not knowing where we were. It panicked him. He needed to know at all times where we were going, and who we were seeing. Once or twice, he tried to drive a few friends away, but he never succeeded. Indeed, it was *his* friends that seemed to dwindle, rather than ours, although we never mentioned it. Never said – what's happened to so-and-so? He was extremely sensitive and we'd prick his pride at our peril. And naturally, we found our way through all this, as families do. Melissa, living across the road by now, was very helpful. She worked for a big IT firm, and she helped us set up private email accounts to the friends he wasn't mad about, something I had no idea was even possible, and the children stood their ground on social media and their own phones. I knew he looked at mine, but I had an old pay-as-you-go one, too, locked in a jewellery box in the cellar. Luckily I wasn't interested in social media and I resisted any suggestion of setting up an account for my books.

By then I'd written a novel, while Michael was in the pub. When he learned of its existence, he'd derided it, but then it was published and he was astonished. He would never sanction me going back to work – we'd had a furious row when I'd said I wanted to cook again, maybe even try and start a catering business – but this was different. This kept me at home, and brought in money, too. We were very short by now. The trust fund, which had seemed so substantial years ago, was now barely enough for two people, let alone four. So although he scoffed at my oeuvre, in a way it played into his hands.

I'd managed to get an agent, Tom, through a friend who wrote, and Michael insisted on coming with me to our meetings. Then Tom left the agency, and Sonia took his place. After that, I was allowed to go alone, although if Ron, the CEO, was present, Michael came too. My publishers were wide-eyed at this and initially, Frankie, my editor, poked fun. But then, when one or two of my plot lines necessitated Miss Sharpe investigating problems of a patriarchal nature, she didn't joke about it any more. Sonia tried to broach the subject with me once over lunch, but when I clammed up, she stopped. By now Michael had stopped reading my books, dismissing them as nonsense, so I was safe. But whenever I drew a character just a bit too close to my husband, I'd wake up in the night, drenched in sweat. And I'd be at my desk early the next morning, re-jigging it.

Money went into a joint account, which he controlled, in that he monitored every transaction I made. But he wasn't particularly mean. Plus, there are other ways. Melissa, again. On her suggestion, I opened a separate account for my foreign rights, and thus siphoned off some money for the children when they were at university. He was less generous with them. And if you're wondering why I was brave enough to do these things, but too scared to leave, it was because I knew he'd find us. And it would be worse. He'd told me it would be. And showed me how. Once, when he was in New York and I said I'd take the children to my parents' for half-term, he forbade it. We went, nevertheless. When we got home, a day after him, he was all smiles and hugs; he'd even made us a cake. That night the three of us were very sick. I'd thought it was the fish pie Mum had given us the night before, but when I rang her from the kitchen to see how she and Dad were, Michael took the cake from the side and, never taking his eyes off me, scraped it slowly into the bin. I stuttered a goodbye to Mum, chilled to my bones.

So no, I never left. But I encouraged the children to go, and Imo did. She went to Princeton University in

New Jersey, which she adored. I'd urge her to stay with her friends in Connecticut too, when she was invited in the holidays. She was a popular girl. And even though she worried she was away too much, from me and Ned, she did, she stayed away.

But Ned dealt better with Michael. He didn't shout and scream as Imo did; he blanked him. Ignored him. I think he was clever enough to find a place in his mind to retreat to, when necessary. I'm not even sure he listened: just mentally tuned him out. He certainly never answered back, which of course infuriated his father. And as I say, Ned didn't go far. Away from home at eighteen, yes, but only to Oxford, where he read Geography. Then to Clapham, sharing with friends, while he worked in the City. Which just left me. And Michael. And increasingly, his women.

But no more. I watched, now, in the study, all these years later, still in my nightie, but with a coat over the top, as the ambulance crew picked up the stretcher. A blanket covered his face. The police and forensic teams had gone. They'd taken a while. All the blood samples and prints had been taken, the crime scene thoroughly trawled. It was getting light outside. The two women in high-vis jackets who'd been the first to get here walked the stretcher down the hall and through the front door to the road. I followed as far as the door. Saw them slide him into the back of the ambulance and shut the door firmly behind him. I watched as they drove off down the street. Disappeared around the corner. Yes, he was gone. Michael no more.

6

It was one of the things Melissa asked me, after the funeral. Why, when she knew I'd grown to hate him, did I mind about the women? Surely it had been better when he was with someone, his attitude more relaxed, slightly less angry. And a break from him, too. Why didn't I just turn a blind eye, as she had with her husband? Until she'd cracked, of course, and told the whole street. Helena was with us at the time. We were in the pub, down the road from the church in Twickenham where we'd just buried Michael with his parents. When I'd paused, she didn't butt in to answer for me as she normally would, because she knew the answer. Helena knew everything about me, irritatingly.

'I think,' I said, choosing my words carefully because I didn't want them to impinge on my friend, 'the crucial difference was you loved Dominic. Hoped it would all go away. Which is understandable. A lot of women do it. But I was very unhappy with Michael. So yes, you'd naturally assume I wouldn't care.' I felt my fists clench on the table. 'But that felt like I was surrendering my entire life to him. All dignity. All semblance of a marriage. It would be like wearing a label saying – I don't mind who he shags, because our marriage is over. And I had too much pride for that. I wasn't going to sacrifice everything for him. Not when I'd given up so much else.'

Melissa looked thoughtful. 'Yes, I get that,' she said slowly.

'Plus,' I went on quietly, 'I felt responsible for the mess I'd made. I felt I'd brought Michael into my family, that it was my fault. I felt shame, I suppose, that I'd let everyone down. So I did the one thing I could do. I got rid of his women. To make the whole thing less shabby.'

'Shame is the last thing you should have felt,' observed Melissa, squeezing my hand.

Helena made a how-many-times-have-I-told her face to my friend as we sank into our gin and tonics at our corner table. We were all dressed in black, but no one felt under any compunction not to speak ill of the dead – that would feel like blatant hypocrisy. A monumental sham. Although we would, of course, change our tune when the children approached, which they were doing now. The door to the pub garden had flown open, and on a blast of fresh air, Helena's daughters tumbled through in their school uniforms, followed by my own, more elegant, daughter in black silk. We sat up straight and adjusted our faces into bright smiles.

'Isn't she gorgeous?' breathed Tess as Imo peeled off to the Ladies. She hastened to perch on the arm of my chair, glancing back at my daughter over her shoulder. Maudie, her identical twin, settled on my other chair arm, auburn curls windswept, eyes shining.

'We've had a whole twenty minutes with her outside,'

Maudie told us confidentially. 'Look at her dress when she comes out – even at a funeral she's glam.'

'Marc Jacobs,' Tess informed her and I realized they both smelled of cigarettes and Polos. 'And the shoes are Jimmy Choo. She bought them in Paris with Ben, before she dumped him.'

'Oh – you two! There you are!' Ant appeared through the same garden door, looking pink and flustered. 'You were supposed to be going to the car. I've been looking everywhere for you.'

'Darlings, do go with Daddy,' urged their mother. 'I thought you'd gone ages ago. Ant, what are you *doing*? They should be back by now.'

'Gave me the slip!' he said, exasperated.

'Don't you think our parents are misguided, Lucy?' asked Maudie quietly, picking up her mother's drink and taking a sip. 'There's more education in a day like this than any old maths lesson. It's surely a lesson in life. Why can't they see that?'

'Did you know that in Catholic countries the dead are laid out for days before the funeral?' Tess informed us. 'Annabel Rossi's grandmother was on the kitchen table for five days. She told us in hockey.'

'How unhygienic,' observed her father. 'Come on, in the car.'

'In a coffin, obviously,' Maudie said, giving him a withering look.

'Go on, you two,' Helena said absently. 'If you go now you'll still be back in time for afternoon lessons.'

'Double physics for me,' Tess complained bitterly,

ignoring her mother and helping herself to some peanuts. 'Only very pushy parents would make their children go back for that. By the way, I hope you don't mind, Lucy, but I've told Ned there's never been a better time to pull in a dog collar. *Fleabag*, obviously.'

'Don't mind at all,' I smiled.

'In our day it was Richard Chamberlain,' their mother observed, unwittingly succumbing to her daughters' distraction techniques. 'There's nothing new about that.'

'Oh yes, *The Thorn Birds*,' Melissa said, remembering. 'Wasn't he gorgeous? And then there was that priest in *Jamaica Inn* before that.'

'Really?' Maudie contrived to look completely fascinated. 'Any more you can think of? Are those your cigarettes, Melissa? I didn't know you smoked.'

'Only occasionally.'

'Helena smokes occasionally, but she doesn't think we know.'

Helena looked at Ant, exasperated. 'Take them away!'

'I'm trying!' He wrung his hands hopelessly.

The twins got up with weary sighs. 'We'll go. For your sake, Lucy. We don't want Ant and Helena's woeful lack of parenting skills to add to what has already been a very difficult day for you. It's embarrassing enough for *us* to witness it, let alone you and Melissa. How long is Imo staying for, do you know?'

'Not long, I'm afraid.'

'Shall we quickly go and ask her?'

'No!' squealed their parents in despair.

More eye-rolling from my nieces but out they trudged,

with much mock staggering and weakness at the knees, blowing us kisses as they went. As Ant hustled them off to the car, telling them that of course they didn't need to say goodbye to everyone again, they'd done that twenty minutes ago, Helena suddenly got up and darted after them, fussing over Tess's trailing skirt hem.

Melissa and I exchanged amused smiles. Helena's lack of parental control was a joy for the rest of us to behold. So strident, so successful in every other sphere of her life, yet so utterly subjugated by her frisky, mercurial, fourteen-year-old daughters. Ant was always going to be a pushover as a parent, no surprise there, but the fact that Helena was too had been a glorious revelation. Had the twins been anything other than sweet-natured and joyous, it could have been a disaster, but they weren't, so it wasn't. They'd inherited Ant's easy-going temperament, together with Helena's high spirits.

They were replaced by my own children, who came across to join us. 'All right, Mum?' asked Ned, putting a hand on my shoulder.

'Yes thanks, darling.' I patted his hand. Looked up into his kind blue eyes. 'All the better for a stiff gin, though.' Then I made a face. 'Well, it's a single actually, what your grandfather would call a dirty glass. I'm driving.'

'I think Granny and Grandpa are wondering if it's OK to go?' asked Imo, perching on the chair arm Tess had vacated. I looked at her slim, delicate face, her pale blue eyes, so like her brother's, etched with worry. She hadn't seen her grandparents for a while and had been shocked at the change in them.

72

'Of course, they've had such a long day. Are you sure you're happy to drive them, darling?'

'Yes, I'd like to. It's just Amanda . . .'

We glanced across to where my parents, exhausted and spent, slumped on a leather sofa by the fire, were being monopolized by Michael's sister. Some long, drunken monologue had been unfolding, I learned later, about the idyllic childhood she and her brother had enjoyed, and what a golden boy he'd been. Such a talented writer and a wonderful husband and father. A marvellous brother too, always there for her, and she was going to miss him so much. All of which was bollocks, of course, because Michael and Amanda rarely saw one another, and when they did, fought ferociously. My father, seeing us look, rolled mildly despairing eyes. My mother's were shut.

'Rescue them, darling, and I'll go down later in the week. I'll cope with Amanda.'

'Well, she certainly can't drive,' muttered Helena.

'Oh, she hasn't done that for years. I think she got a lift here . . .' I glanced around the pub, but everyone had gone apart from us, not that terribly many people had come to the funeral and still fewer to the pub. 'Didn't she come with some of his Soho buddies? I can't see them . . .'

'They've all sugared off,' said Melissa. 'Stayed for the free drinks but then went. Don't worry, I'll take her.'

'Oh Melissa, that's above and beyond.' It was. Half an hour of Amanda's views on the universe was half an hour too long.

'She'll be asleep in moments and I'll put the radio on. Somewhere in Chelsea?'

'Tregunter Road, off Redcliffe Gardens. Thanks, hon.'

She got up, slim and elegant, her dark hair in a neat chignon, my greatest friend and ally, who sadly, I saw too little of these days. Her work mostly took her away to Silicon Valley, where they were desperate for her skills, and where she spent most of her life in hotels. She'd sworn she hadn't flown across specially, but I couldn't be sure. She drained her drink and I watched her cross the room and neatly extricate Amanda, bidding my parents, who brightened immediately, goodbye. They were very fond of her. Dad managed to haul himself up from the deep sofa, reaching for his stick and thanking her with his eyes. He received a huge wink from Melissa. She frogmarched her mildly protesting charge across the room to us for the swiftest of goodbyes.

'But I thought maybe I'd stay a bit . . .' Amanda was mumbling. Her streaky blonde hair was all over her face, which, once very attractive, was now rather puffy. Her heavy make-up was smeared. She was wearing a smart black suit but it was very creased. She frowned petulantly. 'Lucy, surely you could take me—'

'No, no, Lucy's very tired,' Melissa told her. She turned her charge around smartly, barely allowing her to say goodbye, and then with one hand under her elbow, marched her through the garden door and outside. Melissa had once been in the Territorials.

My father staggered theatrically across when they'd

gone. 'Refreshing to meet someone who lives life even more precariously than we do,' he said weakly.

Imo giggled. 'Made you feel saintly, Grandpa?'

'For five minutes, but your grandmother was up to the competition and wasn't going down without a fight. Give us a hand, Ned, dear boy, and we'll heave-ho her upright. Pour her into the motor vehicle. Oh, and don't forget her teeth, I think she's sitting on them.'

'She took them out?' asked Imo, horrified. She hurried to help her brother retrieve them.

'She's got an ulcer. They were giving her gyp.'

'Ah.'

I watched as Imo and Ned, with as much dignity as possible, gently helped my mother to her feet. She seemed to have a beer mat stuck to her cardigan and her skirt was all rucked up at the back, but Imo sorted her out with humour and kindness, whereas Helena and I might have been more exasperated. Ned retrieved her glasses from the floor and polished them before he gave them back to her. Helena and I watched grimly. How dare they get so old?

'You know her latest thing,' Helena muttered in my ear. 'She's decided to give Wednesdays a miss.'

'What?'

'Apparently her great-aunt did the same thing, the legendary Fanny. Took to her bed on a Wednesday. Declared there were too many days in a week, and that no one needed more than six.'

'Helena, I've made a decision,' I said, as we watched Ned and Imo begin the search for coats and handbags.

'I'm going to go down and look after them. Live with them.'

Helena's head swivelled round sharply. She stared at me, astonished. But then, as the answer to all her prayers suddenly became more than a distant light shining on the horizon, she wasn't able to disguise her relief, even though she tried to.

'Oh no, Luce. You don't want to do that. I mean—'

'I do, actually,' I interrupted. 'I've thought about it.' I hadn't really. The epiphany had just come to me now. 'I can't possibly stay in the house any more. Not after . . .'

'No,' she agreed quickly, although I could tell she was surprised. I could see the cogs whirring. 'Maybe a rug?' she said tentatively.

I managed to suppress a smile. 'No, it's not just that,' I said, although it jolly well played a part. 'It's the fact that I don't *have* to live there any more. There are so many bad memories.' This much, at least, was true. 'I just don't want to stay.'

'Right. No. I do see that. Of course. A new chapter. So you'll sell?'

I made a face. 'Terrible time, don't you think?'

'Yes, ghastly. Nothing's moving. So, maybe let it?'

'That's what I thought,' I said anxiously. 'What d'you think?'

'Definitely let it. Till the market improves. I'll tell you when. But Luce, to live with Mum and Dad . . . talk about falling on your sword.'

'Well it won't be forever, will it? Let's be realistic.' We watched as Imo helped our mother towards the door.

Mum glanced across at us and Helena and I nipped to our feet. We kissed them all goodbye, promising to see them very soon. Then, with Imo's assurances that she'd manage, and with Ned slowly walking with my father, chatting and smiling the while and watching carefully as he shuffled down the step to the garden in his orthopaedic shoes, we resumed our seats.

'You mean,' Helena went on in a hushed tone, 'you'd stay until . . . ?'

'I don't know,' I said quickly, not knowing the answer to this myself. I shrugged. 'God – who knows what will happen? Which one will go first? Whether they'll need care?' I hesitated. 'What I don't want, though, is to be tied to any decision I make now.'

'Oh God, absolutely,' she said vehemently. 'You know I'd never do that.'

'No, I know you wouldn't. And I didn't mean you, really. I meant myself, actually. Don't want to feel any guilt, should I change my plans. I don't want *any* firm plans about the future. I just want to see how it goes.'

Helena nodded slowly. 'Well, I won't pretend it's not a huge relief, Luce. But you know as well as I do, the longer you stay, the harder it'll be to leave. Talk about the martyr's crown.' I swallowed and averted my eyes. She wasn't to know I rather needed one. 'And if there's one person who actually deserves a break, who deserves to live a little, it's you.'

'Yes, but that was never going to happen immediately, was it?'

'Why not? Let's not pretend you've just lost a beloved

husband. You've had your emotional life on hold for years. You don't need some ostensible period of recovery.'

'No, but I need a period of readjustment. Just to be me. To be on my own, without anyone. Surely you can see that?'

'Well, you won't be on your own, will you? You'll be with them.' She was quiet for a moment as she mulled it all over. As ever, a plan began to form. Helena loved a plan. I saw it taking shape in her head. She picked up her drink and sipped it: pretended to sound casual.

'Daniel De Courcy has always rather held a candle for you, you know.'

'Helena!'

'You know who I mean, don't you? Nancy's son from—'

'Yes, I *do* know who you mean. But I do not want to discuss any potential rural hook-ups at my husband's funeral, thank you very much!'

'Just saying,' she said, with faux indignation.

'Just replying!' I glared at her.

She made a face. 'OK, have it your way. However, I think you should know – and I know this from all my divorced girlfriends – that attractive single men of our age get snapped up mighty fast. It's frightfully unfair, but they do. Whereas single women—'

'*Helena!*'

'Right, right, fine,' she muttered, but I could tell she was pleased she'd said it. Got it out. 'I'll do the bill,' she told me, as if she was now doing me a huge favour. She picked up her handbag.

'No, *I'll* do it.' I got up.

'Well, it's hardly worth fighting about, a few rounds of sandwiches and some drinks.'

'No, but I'll take it out of his estate, eventually.'

'Oh. Right. Good plan.' She sat down smartly. 'Which I've asked one of the juniors in the legal department to sort out for you, by the way.'

'Oh, yes. Thanks so much.' I actually was very grateful for that. Grateful to have a smart, professional, well-connected sister to organize probate. But did she have to pull that card out now? Maybe she hadn't done it deliberately. Perhaps I was being uncharitable.

When I'd paid, we made our way to the car park. We passed a plate-glass chalet complex and I caught a glimpse of our reflections in the window. A couple of middle-aged women, hats in hand, in shoes that pinched, dressed in black, looking weary.

'Do they know, by the way?' Helena asked. 'Mum and Dad? Your plan? Oh, well done, Ned!' We'd turned the corner and literally bumped into my son, who'd just seen his grandparents off. He saw us exchange a guilty look.

'What plan?'

I cleared my throat. 'Darling, I've decided to go and look after Granny and Grandpa for a bit. Well, to go and live with them, actually.'

'In the cottage?'

'Well, eventually, yes. Although I might have to start off in the house.'

He looked thoughtful. Then he nodded slowly. 'Yes, I thought you might.'

'Did you?' I stared at him, astonished. 'Blimey, I've only just decided it myself. When did you think that?'

'As soon as Dad died. I thought – Mum won't go it alone. Which I think you should, incidentally. Have a go, rent a flat somewhere, spread your wings. I thought – she'll probably go and live with Granny and Grandpa. Use them as her big excuse.'

Helena's eyes lit up with delight. It was a heroic effort on her part to hold her tongue.

'Ned! You're an effing vicar! That is so uncharitable. Do you not think I've got some sort of kind, familial motivation too?'

'Of course. You love looking after people, and you're brilliant at it. Look at me and Imo – we could have been basket cases but we've turned out all right, hopefully. And all thanks to you. You've pretty much devoted your life to us, for which I'm eternally grateful, by the way. But now you're going to do it for Granny and Grandpa. When actually, it's your turn.'

I gaped at my tall, good-looking, fair-haired boy, who'd given up his own life purely in the service of God and others. But I knew, even as I was about to say it, that actually, he hadn't. Ned was doing exactly what he wanted to do. He always had done. He'd always been true to himself. I regarded my son and my sister, the latter triumphant at being backed up by her intelligent nephew, but clearly battling with a pyrrhic victory, because naturally, she also wanted the parental problem solved.

I snorted with derision. 'Anyone would think I didn't have a career! Didn't do anything for myself!'

Ned inclined his head, conceding this, but not saying, as I knew he was thinking – ah yes, the career. The convenient, solitary one. The one that always kept a weather eye on any trouble. Because there was no denying it had been mutually convenient. It might have worked for Michael, but it worked for me, too. When the children were young, arriving home from school, I'd always been there: always been on hand to deflect any unpleasantness. And I'm not sure cooking in a boardroom in the City or running a catering company elsewhere would have afforded me that. Certainly in the holidays. Which were often a diplomatic minefield, as Michael's irritation at having the children around bubbled over. Or boiled. We were silent, the two of us, as all the years of dodging and diving, of ducking and weaving, flooded back. The bad memories. The necessary compromises.

'But of course, it's a laudable decision,' said Ned quickly, seeing my face. It might have collapsed a bit. 'And G and G will be delighted, I won't deny that.'

'They will, won't they?' I said, brightening. I was looking forward to telling them.

'Undoubtedly. But I'm telling you right now,' he grinned and tossed his car keys in the air. Caught them. 'I'm not protecting you from Imo.'

'Ha! Neither am I!' agreed Helena. She kissed us and scuttled off to her car. Ned kissed me too and went to his. As I watched my sister purr past me in her BMW her smile was annoyingly smug.

7

Imogen was, as Ned had rightly predicted, incandescent with horror at the plan. When I opened the door to her the following morning in the spring sunshine, she barely said hello. In fact, she didn't.

'What's all this about you deciding to bury yourself down in Little Snoring?' she demanded, striding past me down the hall. I watched her go with eyebrows raised. Then I closed the door behind her and followed her down to the kitchen. 'On some misguided mercy mission, just so you can polish your halo? We all know G and G can easily afford a carer, and the last thing they'll want is you sacrificing yourself on the altar of Granny's alcoholism – which is what you're doing, incidentally.'

She took off her glamorous houndstooth coat, flung it on a chair and flopped down on the kitchen sofa, facing me. She pushed her silky cream sleeves up, as if for battle. Her blue eyes were bright and determined.

'A carer?' I enquired mildly, crossing to fill the kettle at the sink. 'Can you really see that happening?'

'Well, eventually it would have to, wouldn't it?' she said defiantly. 'I mean, when they really can't resist any longer?'

'Yes, but that point comes when the shit has really hit the fan. When the paramedics are resuscitating them, or

82

when the courts are involved. Or even men in white coats. They simply will not agree to it, Helena and I have tried for ages.'

Imogen stared at me, tight-lipped. Then she abruptly sat forward. She put her head in her hands and massaged her brow with delicate fingertips. Both my children were fair, fine-boned and delicate, perhaps another reason I'd always felt so protective of them. They were like beautiful, ethereal, fairy children. Looks were deceptive though. This one was used to controlling things, like her aunt, and this unwieldy situation, which had foxed us all for a few years now and was getting bigger by the day, was anathema to her.

She jerked her head up suddenly, eyes wide in despair. 'It's like dealing with children,' she said, exasperated.

'Yes,' I agreed simply. 'It is.' It helped, of course, that she'd spent some time with them yesterday. I wondered what she'd made of the house, the crumbling decrepitude. It wouldn't suit her right now to say, of course. 'That is indeed what they've become.'

She chewed her thumbnail. 'It would have made more sense if you'd gone when Dad was alive,' she said darkly. 'Then I would have been totally up for it.'

I didn't answer. Instead I put a cup of black coffee on the table in front of her and perched on a stool at the island. I watched her stir her coffee and cogitate. Suddenly she looked up.

'So odd,' she said abruptly. 'That he's not here.' She glanced around the kitchen: then through the open door to the study.

'I know.' It was the first time, I realized, she'd been back. I let her take in the lack of him, with all its complicated resonances. Sadness, perhaps, for the father-daughter relationship she'd never had. After a bit, she came back to me.

'No word from the police, I suppose?'

'No. The best they can do is assume a petty thief who bungled a burglary. Petty enough to wear gloves, though; he left no prints. Oh, and the sergeant was sharp enough to deduce that he made his entrance and getaway over the wall.' I jerked my head garden-wards. 'Note the trampled hebe bush and the footprints in my flower bed. Even I had spotted that.'

She shook her head. 'Pathetic. D'you know, I read in the paper the other day that only seven per cent of crimes are solved in London. Seven per cent!' Her eyes boggled. Then she shrugged. 'Still. What do we care.' She gulped, though, as she said it.

I saw her gaze fall on his desk in the corner, which I'd tidied and cleared. All his papers and files had gone. It had looked so empty when I'd done it, I'd put a vase of flowers on it. Then I'd taken them away. It had seemed a bit crass, somehow. Like a jibe. I'd taken his comfortable chair away, too, with its squashed velvet cushion; put it in the cellar. I went and sat beside her on the sofa. 'Imo, you know what you said yesterday? At the funeral?' I said gently, breaking into her thoughts.

'What?' She came back to me, her face perhaps paler than when she'd arrived.

'About coming back to London. Your posting, with the bank. Is that – you know – coincidence?'

'It is, actually. I was offered it a month ago. I mean, it's a promotion, for sure. Investment Associate with a really nice team. And I thought – come on, girl. You can do this. Confront your demons. Live in the same city as him.'

I nodded. 'And now?'

'Well, now I'm glad I'd made that decision while he was alive.' She turned her cool blue gaze on me. 'Glad I can say that. That I was going to be brave.'

I smiled but my eyes filled. 'Yes. Well done you.' I squeezed her arm. My heart wrenched for my gorgeous, bold, big-hearted girl, who'd done so bloody well, despite the obstacles. But there was another elephant in the room too, not in the shape of her father. Something Tess had let slip, which I'd already suspected.

'And the only reason I didn't tell you earlier, when I took the job,' she said reading my thoughts, 'was because I knew you'd worry. Knew you'd think – oh God, what's happened.'

'So, it has happened?' I asked. 'You and Ben . . . ?'

'Are no more. And my decision, Mum, so no tears.'

I gave a wry smile. 'It always is your decision.'

'I know. But he just wasn't – you know. A long-term prospect.'

I nodded. Couldn't possibly comment, obviously, because I'd never met him, but he'd sounded lovely. A lawyer she'd met through a friend. She'd sent me Whats-App pictures of them, all through the autumn and winter. Snaps of them on skating rinks, wrapped up against the cold in huge coats and scarves, his arms around her; or on the ferry going to work, her head on his shoulder, Manhattan in the background. A nice-looking young man: slim, dark hair, glasses. Geek chic, Helena had said approvingly, when I'd shown her.

'And it's not that *I* don't think he's a long-term prospect, it's that he doesn't.'

'Oh.'

'His parents divorced when he was eleven and it was messy. He doesn't believe in the institution of marriage. Says vowing fidelity to one another forever is an out-dated anachronism, particularly when we're all going to live to be a hundred. He didn't see why we couldn't just live together, go on as we were. Have babies, even. So I thought – why waste my time?'

'Quite.'

Imo did want to get married – and show me a girl who doesn't, she'd say caustically, and I'll show you a liar.

'So you broke it off?'

'I did.'

'But, you miss him?' I asked tentatively.

She narrowed her eyes thoughtfully but they didn't mist up. 'I miss the idea of him. I miss having a boyfriend, and not having to look again, if you know what I mean. And Sunday nights are shit, obviously. But other than that . . .' She looked far away, out of the French windows. Then back to me. 'I won't miss his conviction. Or his pedantry. Or the way, because he'd read Greats – he was a Rhodes scholar – he always had to make classical allusions.'

'Sounds like Boris Johnson.'

She threw back her head and let out a great guffaw. 'If you only knew how different he was.' She grinned. 'But yeah, he didn't wear his learning lightly. Which, of course, is an insecurity. Like wearing glasses when he didn't need to. I put them on one day. Clear glass. And I couldn't un-know that, d'you see?'

Oh dear.

'So actually, I'm looking forward to coming back.' Suddenly she smiled, her lovely, bright, sunshiny smile, all faint lines on her face vanishing for a moment. 'Looking forward to escaping the Big Apple and all its scrutiny.'

'Ah, like me then,' I said lightly.

She smiled wryly. 'Yes, OK, point taken. We're both running away. But I'm running to London, Mum. To the exciting, humming Square Mile with a bumper salary and a whole raft of different, interesting people. I'm not sloping off to Little Snodgrass, or whatever that bonkers village is called.'

'Sneaton, as you well know. And it's not entirely sleepy. A mobile library calls once a week and by all accounts the church bring and buy is an absolute sizzler.'

Imo rolled her eyes. 'You're a lost cause. But don't get too cocky and complacent, oh mother of mine. Don't start taking up tapestry just yet. I'm not done here. I'm going to have a word with Grandpa.'

That was an error, if I'm honest, on the part of my oh-so-intelligent, Harvard Business School graduate daughter: to warn me. Because after she'd gone, to look at a flat – not to rent, but to buy, in Notting Hill, which made me so proud – I was fully prepared for my father when he rang.

I was in the car when I saw his name flash up on my phone, off, like Imo, to see an estate agent, but on a very different mission. I quickly put him on speaker.

'I've just been talking to Imogen. It's out of the question,' were his first words. Again, no hello. What was wrong with my family?

I cleared my throat. '*Au contraire*, Papa, it is very much the question, and it has been for some time. But be that as it may, this is not about you and Mum, this is about me. I want to get out of this house, and I want to get out of London. I also want to live in the country, so why can't I come and live with you?'

'Because, as Imo says, you're burying yourself. No one lives in the sticks until they're decrepit, like us. There's nothing down here for you.'

'Oh, I don't know. I'm looking forward to some home cooking.'

'Well, you can cross that off your list for starters. It's become rather eccentric. For pudding last night we had incinerated baked apples covered in shaving foam which I'd left on the draining board and your mother had mistaken for cream.'

'My point entirely. You need help.'

'And my point is that we roared with laughter and had a choc ice instead. We are managing extremely well, thank you. Also, I have just forced a confession out of you. You *are* coming down to help, and not for your own benefit. I won't have it, Lucy.'

He only called me Lucy when he was angry, but I wasn't having it either. I was angry too.

'The incident the other day wasn't a one-off, Dad. I know you're struggling. Waitrose in Thame rang Helena and she paid them forty-three pounds. Mummy had been doing a little light pilfering again.'

He paused. 'She gets forgetful. Forgets to pay.'

'And had parked on a roundabout while she got her shopping? I thought we'd agreed she wouldn't drive any more, Dad?'

'She found the keys.' He sounded weary. 'I'd left them out, by mistake. And the police were terribly nice, Luce.'

I sighed as I stopped at some lights. 'Yes, and they were nice when she filled up with petrol three times and drove away without paying.'

'Nancy's done that once, she told us.'

'I doubt it. I expect she was being kind.' Nancy was Mum's very switched-on BF.

'I think we all know Nance has many admirable traits, but that the milk of human kindness flows like glue.'

I smiled as the lights went green and I moved off.

'My point is that you and Helena expect her to be exactly the same woman she was ten years ago, and of course she's not. But she's not barking.'

'No, I get that – hang on, I'm just parking, I'm in the car.' I'd pulled into a side road and was slotting the car into place, only a few yards from my destination. I took the phone from its holder and held it to my ear. 'Of course she's not the same woman, and we don't expect her to be. We don't expect her still to be – I don't know, chairing the NSPCC, or organizing meals on wheels like she was a few years ago. But she has deteriorated quite quickly recently, and we are building up to a crisis here, Dad. And frankly, I have just had my own crisis. And much as I was desperately unhappy with Michael, I still need to lick my wounds; in peace and quiet, sure, but also, if possible, not entirely alone. Surrounded by familiar people I love. And not in that quiet, empty house surrounded by bad memories. Let's be even-handed here. It *is* about you and Mum, but it's also about me. I *want* to come home. Would very much like to, please. If you'll have me.'

There was a silence on the end of the line. I glanced up at the estate agent's window. As I activated my parking app, I could tell he was thinking about it.

'And you'd live in the cottage?'

'Of course.'

'It's a bloody mess.'

'I know.'

To call it a cottage was a huge exaggeration. It was an ugly pebbledash bungalow, thrown up in the fifties with no doubt zero planning permission. Certainly before my parents' time: a throwback to the days when the farm-house had staff, no doubt. A gardener, perhaps. It had been derelict for years. There was a sitting room perma-nently covered in bat poo which had our ping pong table in it, two bedrooms, a bathroom and a kitchen.

'I'll have a look at it this afternoon. See what I can do.'

'Do not! I'll sort it out myself when I come. It'll give me something to do.'

There was a pause. Then: 'Your mother's delighted, of course.'

'Is she?' I smiled. 'Dear Mum!'

'She's getting the horse trailer ready. Thinks you're both off to the local gymkhana. She's keenly anticipating the bending race.'

'Right,' I said faintly. I swallowed. 'Dad, *is* it dementia? I know you say you've had all the tests, but it sounds jolly likely.'

'No, no, not that. The hospital were quite categorical. Just a few lapses in concentration; and, of course, I ham it up a bit.' Oh, did he. If my mother was naughty, my father was worse. He'd do anything for a laugh, so one never quite knew where the joke stopped and reality began. 'But I won't pretend, if you're really serious, that I won't be delighted to see you myself. Maybe to – you know. Get the place in order a bit. But we're talking a few weeks here, possibly a month or two maximum, yes? Just for the summer. And just to get *you* back on your feet again too, hm?'

'Of course,' I agreed. I got out of the car and locked it. Then I walked down the road to the estate agents. I gazed through the window at the glossy photographs and particulars spread before me, looking at long-term rental prices. Not bad. Not bad at all, especially if I went for a year. Two years even. 'Just for a few weeks,' I agreed, before bidding him goodbye and clicking my phone off. Then I pocketed it, and sailed through the door into the office.

8

Time passed. But not long actually, only a few days. Estate agents work like quicksilver in London, particularly when there's a commission in the offing. They sent some Rupert round to look over the place, he liked what he saw, and then they got going: photos were taken, particulars were printed and put on the web – it looked rather smart, actually, and for a moment I wondered why I was going. But the following day I opened the door to my first prospective tenant. I'd forgotten, of course, that Ned had said he might pop round for a coffee, so that when I discovered the two of them together on my doorstep, it wrong-footed me. Being grown men, however, they'd managed to introduce themselves and ascertain what the other was doing there. As they stepped inside, Ned introduced me to the stranger, whose name was Joshua Cohen. He was slim, dark and not terribly tall, with glasses rather like the ones I'd seen on the face of Imo's ex-boyfriend. He was possibly a bit younger than me and had the look of a young Jeremy Paxman before he got cross and arrogant. I was about to extend my hand, but then wondered if one did shake hands with viewers, and since he didn't remove his from his overcoat pockets, I didn't. We exchanged a few pleasantries and then I led them down the hall to the kitchen where I'd been brewing coffee, the aroma from which, I'd read in a colour supplement, was seductive when showing a house. When I got to my fragrant kitchen, however, I realized I only had Ned with me. Mr Cohen had peeled off. Raising my eyebrows at my son, I went back to find him in the sitting room.

'Sorry.' He turned to me abruptly. 'I was just looking at your shelves. I saw them through the window.'

'Oh yes, quite a few, I'm afraid.' They were floor to ceiling on both sides of the fireplace and crammed. 'But you don't have to fill them with books like this, I just happen to have rather a lot. You could put ornaments or whatnots on them.'

He raised his eyebrows. 'I happen to have rather a lot, too.'

'Oh. Splendid,' I murmured. He'd gone again, ahead of me, making his way to the kitchen. Which left me following him. It occurred to me that Jeremy Paxman had always been arrogant.

'What's all this, Mum?' Ned was perched on a stool at the island, looking at lemons I'd arranged attractively in a large shallow dish. He picked one up and grinned. 'Gone a bit Tuscan?'

'It was in the *Sunday Times* last week,' said Mr Cohen with a smile. 'That and the smell of coffee. This is the third house I've seen with the same vibe.'

They laughed in comradely fashion and I pretended to join in. I wanted to tell him I'd never said whatnots in my life before just now. 'It was the *Observer*, actually,' I said smoothly, crossing to my percolator.

'Oh, sorry. I get both.'

'Yes, me too.'

Ned's eyes widened at my tone. He replaced the lemon.

'Nice kitchen,' said Mr Cohen, breaking a silence I obviously should have been the one to fill.

I beamed, remembering myself. 'Thank you, I love it.' I did, actually.

It had been bought on the strength of a two-book deal which had been labour-intensive in the writing, but very satisfactory in the spending. Even Michael had agreed that the three weeks we'd spent living off micro-wave meals while it was fitted had been worth it.

'It was handmade in Somerset,' I told him proudly. 'By artisans, in an atelier.'

'Oh really? As opposed to carpenters in a joinery?' He grinned. Was he laughing at me?

'Or even chippies in a workshop,' observed Ned, rather disloyally I felt, which they found equally funny. Lovely to have so much male bonding in my kitchen, I decided with a tight smile as I went to get some mugs. I felt my visitor's eyes on my back.

'I was sorry to hear about your husband,' he said abruptly. I turned from the cupboard with my mugs, surprised. 'Obviously the estate agent told me,' he said. 'Apparently it's called the three D's.'

'Sorry?'

'Reasons for selling. Death, divorce and debt.'

'Oh, right. Except I'm not selling.'

'No. But I can see it would be hard to stay.'

94

'Well, yes. It is. In all sorts of ways.' Ned and I managed not to look at each other. 'Do you have a family, Mr Cohen?' I swept on quickly.

'Josh.'

'Josh.'

'I do, but they're staying on in Paris.'

'Oh, right. Gosh, you'll miss them, won't you?'

'The children, yes, certainly. But my wife, no. We're separating.'

'Oh. I'm sorry.'

'No, don't be. It was high time.'

His candour was refreshing, as was his matter-of-fact delivery, and I wondered if this was the way forward for me. The way to reveal that I too was well shot of my other half. On the other hand, I decided nervously, circumstances might differ. I also wondered if, had I been happily married, I might have been rather shocked. I decided that in the real world I no longer inhabited, I might have been.

Ned cleared his throat. 'Shall I make myself scarce, Mum? Come back another time?'

'No, no, it won't take a moment to show Mr Coh—Josh, around. I'll be back in a mo. You finish making the coffee, darling.' I went to the fridge to pour some milk into a jug.

'In fact, if it's all right by you, I'd rather poke around on my own, if you don't mind,' said Josh. 'These houses all have an identical layout and I've seen three already.' He smiled. 'No dark secrets, I take it?'

The jug slipped from my fingers and smashed on the floor. Milk shot everywhere.

'God!' I lunged for a dishcloth in the sink. 'So stupid,' I muttered, mopping and squeezing as Ned put the bits of broken china in the dustpan he'd got from the cupboard. 'No, no secrets. Absolutely not. Do have a good look around.' I threw the J-cloth in the bin, my face hot. Ned calmly put the milk carton on the island but as Josh disappeared, he was watching me, I could tell. I gave the simmering percolator a degree of unnecessary attention.

'How did you find Imo?' I asked, with my back to him, before he could say anything.

'Hm? Oh, fine. On good form, I thought. I mean – all things considered. She looks great.'

'Imo always looks great.' My daughter was very beautiful. 'But in herself? Sad about Ben?'

Ned sighed. 'Mum, you've got to stop worrying and treating us both as boxes to be ticked. Imo will find someone. She's just – you know . . .'

'A bad picker?' I turned to look at him properly.

'Is that what worries you? That you were, so she will be?'

'I think it's why she gives up so easily. James, Tommy, Ed – and now Ben – and there was nothing wrong with any of them! I think she panics.'

Ned sighed. He'd heard it all before. 'Whereas I won't pick at all. Poor Mum.' He got up and put an arm round my shoulders, squeezing them and giving me his naughty grin. He looked just like his grandfather.

'Darling, if you *are* gay, you know you can tell me. I've told you that a million times.'

'You have, but I'm not.'

'Or bisexual?'

'You say that so weirdly. Why all the syllables? Sex-u-al.'

'Ned . . .'

He laughed. 'No, not that, either.'

'So, hetero.'

He shrugged. 'I guess. If you must have a label.'

'I must. And you're not even a priest, like Damien. It's allowed, for God's sake, in the C of E, and—'

'Mum, breathe. Breathe.' He led me to a stool, where I slumped down, defeated. 'You'll last longer. Anyway, Damien is gay.'

'Is he?' I brightened. 'Oh good, he's finally come out. Well, lucky Marion.'

Ned grinned and poured the coffee. 'Yes, you'd like that, wouldn't you?'

'It would give me something to work with.'

'You mean scouring dating sites?'

I blinked. I hadn't considered this. Could one? For other people? 'Maybe.'

'Yes, Marion's been busy. But she still likes to double-check. When Damien goes home for the weekend she says – hello, darling, lovely to see you. Still gay?'

Ned barked an incredulous hoot up to the ceiling. I smiled wryly. 'Yes, well, you can laugh. Wait till you have children.' I sighed. Glanced up at the ceiling. 'D'you think he's all right up there?'

'He's fine. Having a good old poke around. Much the best way to see a house, as he says. Anyway, I didn't come to talk about Imo or me, I came about you. And not about moving – I'm coming round to that. At least for a bit. But I saw Sonia the other day.'

I got up and pretended to look for some biscuits. Sonia might be my agent but she was also a very good friend and she knew my children.

'I bumped into her in Waterstones. Sit down, Mum. She says you're not answering her emails. About signing a new contract.'

I breathed heavily into the cupboard where I was conducting my spurious search: wondered if I could confess to this priest son of mine that I no longer had an urge to write. No longer needed my therapy. I turned and gave it a whirl. He listened in silence. Then nodded.

'Yes, I can see that. I understand that, with Dad gone, another world is not so . . . well, I get it. But wasn't it also something for you?'

'I've just explained, it was *all* for me. No one else. But with your father gone, it's no longer necessary.'

'But you were good at it. *Are* good at it.'

I shrugged. 'I'm OK. You and I both know I can do it standing on my head. I was churning them out. And let's not pretend it's brain surgery.'

Ned and I didn't do bullshit, so he didn't protest. He tried another tack. 'But what will you do? I mean—'

'Do?' I interrupted, irritated. 'What is this obsession with doing? Why should I have to *do* anything? I've been *doing* all my life, surely it's time for a bit of bugger all?

Even a bit of fuc—oh, hello! Sorry, didn't see you there. How did you get on?'

My prospective tenant appeared in the doorway, rather fortuitously actually, in the light of my son's interrogation, and before my language got too fruity.

'Yeah, I like it.'

'Oh good! Do you?' I beamed, delighted.

'Well, there are a couple of things I wouldn't mind changing, but on the whole it works.'

'Oh? Really?' I bridled instantly. 'Like what?'

'Well, the television is antiquated and the fridge is too small. Plus there's an awful lot of clutter, which I presume you're taking with you?'

'Clutter? What clutter? This fridge is American, by the way; I just resisted one of those vast ostentatious ones. What clutter?' I'd tidied the entire house yesterday, until my fingers were numb. Taken bin bags of rubbish to the tip. My cupboards looked like Benetton displays, which was why I hadn't minded him peering around in them. He should have come last week.

'Statues in the bathroom, that kind of thing.'

'Oh, my lovely Nefertiti! Don't you love her? Well clearly not. And that marble one is Diana, goddess of the moon, but I can take her with me, if you like?'

'And all the blue and white china?'

'You don't like it? It's antique.'

'Mum, furnished really just means bare bones,' Ned interjected. 'Sofas, beds, tables, that kind of thing.'

'Of course. Yes, of course. I know that.' I straightened

up. 'Well, you can be sure I'll pare it down to the very . . . bare bones, Mr . . . Josh.' I nodded curtly. I wasn't sure I liked this man. He was ungracious and uncomplimentary. 'Would you like to see the garden?'

He shrugged non-committally. 'Sure.'

I led him through and out of the French windows to the terrace. It was a beautiful spring day and this was my sanctuary. Any love I could no longer pour into my children, I poured in here.

'Have a wander round,' I suggested.

Another shrug, but he ambled off. Would it hurt to comment on how gorgeous it was before he went, I wondered? But I held my tongue.

The small raised terrace looked on to an immaculate rectangle of well-tended grass, surrounded on three sides by suitably distressed walls at which I'd been known to throw yoghurt, to age them. All were clothed with delicate creepers, and carefully espaliered fruit trees which were now in blossom, the apple the palest pink and white. Below, the beds positively billowed over with late spring flowers. Tulips, slightly dishevelled and decadent, like beautiful courtesans after a night out, were the softest blush Dutch ones from my very exclusive catalogue: they bowed their heads over a sea of blue forget-me-nots, nearly over, but not quite. Poised to replace them, and just starting to bud, in fact, were my all-time summer favourites, frothy lime-green *Alchemilla mollis*, which would spread and scramble everywhere like eager children, replacing the bluebells I cultivated in small clumps. An ancient wisteria, of the Chinese variety, so white, climbed the back wall I shared with my neighbour and dripped its elegant, pendulous flowers like huge, milky teardrops. Whoever lived behind had trained climbing roses on their side, and in the summer, they crawled over to mine. My neighbour had taste: they were softest yellow and classy.

I'd trained a few of the less heavy wisteria branches around and over the roof of a shepherd's hut, which was perched at the bottom of the garden, so that right now it dripped with blooms. The hut, painted tasteful pale green, stood at a jaunty angle in the corner. I'd bought it thinking I might work there in the summer, but Michael had been against it, so it had become a garden shed. Unfortunately, it was the only thing I hadn't got round to sorting out yesterday and my prospective tenant was even now making his way . . . oh God. I sprang into life and hastened after him. As he opened the door – too late, a large rake sprang out, hitting him squarely on the head.

'*Ooow!*' He bent over in agony, holding his forehead.

'Oh Lord – I'm so sorry.' I rushed up, horrified. 'It is rather full. It was literally the one place – are you all right, Joshua?'

'*Josh!*' he roared, rather unnecessarily, as he straightened up. 'And I'm fine.' He glared at me. 'Do you always set traps for prospective tenants?'

'Of course not, and it was hardly a trap. How was I to know you'd go in the shed?'

'Well, call me optimistic, but I thought it might yield something more promising. I thought I might work in there, actually.'

'Oh. Right. Yes, well, so did I. That's why I bought it.'

'So why didn't you? he asked accusingly. I stared at him. His bespectacled face was quizzical, intense. But not unattractive. If you like that sort of thing. I swallowed. Impossible to tell him, of course, that Michael had wanted me right under his nose, where he could see and hear me, and not making calls or sending emails at the bottom of the garden, so I told him instead that the windows were too small.

'Ah.' He nodded. 'Not enough natural light.'

'Exactly. And cold in the winter.'

'But you've got a stove in there?'

'No, I haven't.'

'So how come you've got a chimney?'

I felt I was on *Any Questions*. And he wasn't playing *Just a Minute*, either. 'It came with it,' I said testily. 'The stove can be fitted at a later date, if required. If you must know, I liked the look of the chimney. I thought it looked quaint and rural. I saw a picture of David Cameron's. His had one.'

'Ah.' He looked pleased. As if that summed me up, which of course it didn't. Well, a bit, but not entirely. Not by a long chalk. 'So it's purely cosmetic?' *God*, he was annoying. We were making our way back to the house now.

'Until it's appropriated, converted and therefore operational, yes,' I said, as if pedantry was clearly required. As we emerged through the French windows Ned glanced up from his phone and took in our faces.

'What's up?'

'Josh wanted chapter and verse on the shepherd's hut, that's all.'

'Hardly! I just didn't expect to be ambushed by it!'

'Ambushed?' asked Ned.

'A rake fell out and caught him,' I said smoothly, aware I was behaving rather badly but unsure why. 'And I'm terribly sorry,' I added stiffly. 'It was my fault. It's too full.'

'Not at all,' came back an equally stiff rejoinder.

Ned sighed and drained his coffee, none the wiser.

'Yes, well, you might want to empty it, Mum, before you go. I'll give you a hand, if you like. And fascinating though this slice-of-life drama is, I feel I must be getting on my way. I have a funeral to conduct.'

Josh glanced at him, alert. 'You're a vicar?'

'I am.'

'How interesting. I often wonder if I should have liked that.'

Ned and I both blinked at him in surprise. Joshua Cohen was not a name to automatically suggest an Anglican vocation.

'For the other team, obviously. A rabbi. Or a doctor, perhaps. But there we are. The decisions we make early in life do rather constrict us, don't they?' He looked rueful.

Ned smiled. 'Not necessarily. I only became a vicar a few years ago. Changed horses in mid-stream.'

'Oh? What were you before?'

'A hedge fund manager. Bye, Mum.' He pecked my cheek. 'Don't see me out, I'll manage.'

'Oh no, I'll come down.' I hastened after him to the door. When I'd opened it for him and we were out of earshot on the step, I muttered: 'God. Rude, isn't he? Typical Parisian. He's clearly been there too long.'

'I rather liked him,' he said consideringly, glancing back beyond me down the hall. 'At least he says what he thinks.' He turned back to me. 'Anyway, don't forget the thrust of my little mission here today, hmm?'

'What was that?' I genuinely had forgotten.

He eyed me kindly. 'To do things for yourself. To stop worrying about other people.'

'Oh. That. Yes, of course I will,' I lied.

He gave me a funny, sad smile, and then he sauntered off down the steps to the street. I watched him go, his thin shoulders hunched in his leather jacket against the chill wind.

When I went back to the kitchen, Josh was turning up the collar on his own coat. 'I must be off. I'll be in touch. I've got one more to see in Prothero Road, but I might not bother. When do you want to move out, incidentally? I mean, if I decide to take it?'

'Oh, I'm ready to go now. I'm going home, you see.'

He frowned. 'Home?'

'I mean, to my parents. For a bit,' I added, in case that looked sad.

'Oh, OK.' He couldn't look less interested, actually. 'Well, I'll be in touch. Via the estate agent, of course.'

'Yes, quite.' No need to communicate directly was implicit.

I led him to the front door and opened it for him. I

managed a bright smile as he went out. He looked at me thoughtfully.

'Nice chap, your son,' he said. 'Interesting.'

He descended the steps into the street in his rather oversized black overcoat. Perhaps that was the Paris look this season? He certainly had the carefully knotted à la mode scarf. I watched as he went down the road in the opposite direction to Ned, but also, I noted with some relief, in the opposite direction to Prothero Road.

9

It wasn't strictly true, what Ned had said back there in the kitchen, but I knew what he meant. He hadn't changed horses: he just hadn't initially been allowed to get on the one he wanted. He'd been keen to go into the Church from an early age, ever since he was confirmed at school. The lessons he'd received in preparation for it had fascinated him, and he'd come home wanting to talk about them, discuss it. Added to which he was a chorister, so he was in chapel a lot. He said there wasn't much he heard in there that he disagreed with. At Oxford, his environment became equally ecclesiastical since he was on a choral scholarship, and I must admit, on the occasions I went to Brasenose to hear him sing, sitting in the intimate, ancient chapel, the sermons, often given by visiting preachers, were inspirational. I wasn't surprised he was impressed, although Imo, a non-believer, would mutter cynically that if you couldn't get a motivational speaker somewhere like that, where could you? After university, however, he'd been persuaded by Michael to at least look at other jobs. Ned had explained that what he planned to do wasn't exactly a job, it was a calling, and Michael had flown into a terrible rage. He said he hadn't spent all that money on a private education for his son to fritter it away in some country parish giving sermons to one man and his dog, and he could bloody well think again.

Ned had put up a fair amount of resistance, helped by me and Imo, but he was a sensitive soul, and one day, after Michael had taken him out to lunch – suit and tie job at Simpsons in Piccadilly – he'd caved in. Said he'd be happy to try banking, like Imo. He'd been very pale when he'd returned. I'd asked him to tell me what his father had said, but he wouldn't. Imo had tried too. Obviously Michael and I had a huge row about it, which had been absolutely vile, and had taken ages for me to recover from, but neither Michael nor Ned were ever going to tell me what had gone on. I knew that.

So Ned, on the strength of his CV alone, and with no strings pulled from us because we didn't know anyone, had gone for a few interviews in the City, and, against all the usual old boy network odds, had secured an internship, and then a coveted job at a hedge fund. To his credit, he said he found the job interesting, and of course, it was highly rewarding, financially.

I'd been surprised at the way he'd been able to seemingly effortlessly suppress his real desire, and I'd tentatively brought it up with him when he'd been there for a while. He'd smiled.

'Just because I'm religious, doesn't mean I'm not ambitious. I'm making a shedload of money here, Mum.'

I was even more surprised.

And then, one day, exactly five years to the day after he'd started in the City, he resigned and enrolled at St John's College in Durham, to prepare to be ordained.

He was a grown man now, with resources enough to do exactly what he wanted. I wondered if that had been his game plan all along, to accrue some money and then go his own way. Even Michael knew when he was beaten. Ned barely talked to him anyway at that stage, and Michael made no attempt to persuade him; he just har-rumphed about it being a total waste of brain power.

'How so?' asked Ned, on one of the few occasions when we'd gathered as a family. It was Christmas Day, I believe. With my parents, at Pope's Farm.

'What – hedge funder to parochial parson? You can't see that isn't a waste?' he'd spat, over the turkey. 'Who's going to listen to you, anyway? I'm surprised the Church has even accepted you. You've compromised your belief – sold your soul. You're tainted with the whiff of money.'

Since it was Michael who'd forced him to compro-mise, there was a collective intake of breath around the table. But Ned stayed calm.

'Doesn't seem to have hindered Justin Welby, does it? Eleven years in the oil business before he was ordained. And by the way, I fully intend to be an archbishop.'

This silenced even Michael, who'd gaped at him like a goldfish over the parsnips. My father's eyes had gleamed with delight, and as I followed him out to the kitchen with some empty plates, I heard him mutter 'touché!' as he tossed a sprout to Hector, who caught it in his mouth.

No one ever said anything like that in public, though: no retorts, no jokes made, no teasing. Certainly no one mentioned the fact that, unbeknownst to Michael, yet quietly celebrated by the rest of the family, Ned had already published papers on the relationship between finance, ethics and religion, which had been commented on by various bishops, and was making quite a name for himself at Holy Trinity Brompton, where he worshipped. Anything like that was kept firmly under wraps. We, including Dad, who had been in the Special Forces, were far too scared to stir the pot. I was scared that if I took Michael on, he'd take it out on the children. Dad was scared that if he squared up to him, he'd take it out on me. The children were scared on my account and – well. You get the picture. In fact, I'm almost certain that Michael had suggested something along those lines at his lunch with Ned, hence Ned's willingness to drop his dream so quickly. But I don't even want to think about it. Nor, indeed, did I have to, now. Michael was dead. And no one, amongst his immediate family, was going to pretend that was anything other than a relief. Except Amanda, of course.

Amanda was on the phone most days, sobbing and wailing, wondering how I was. And of course I had to sort of pretend I was bearing up, which was strenuous, so in the end, I'm afraid I didn't always take her calls. Maybe one in three. Because she'd be on the phone for hours. And recently, she'd been rather insulting. Calling me hard-hearted. And the odd thing was, when he was alive we hadn't really heard from her much, because it seemed to me they disliked each other so. Michael called her a dismal old bitch and on the odd occasion I had lunch with her, in some smart Chelsea restaurant of her choice, she'd complain bitterly about him, wondering how on earth I stood him, before frowning at the end of the meal, and wishing she could remember who paid last time. I'd sigh and reach for my purse. Like many rich trust-fund children, Amanda was tight. I felt sorry for her now, because after all, her only remaining blood relative had gone, but as Helena said, I really didn't need to land myself with Amanda, when I was finally free of Michael. And now she'd taken to popping round. Sure enough, just as I was gathering my strength to work out what I'd need to clear out before the lodger moved in, the doorbell rang and there she was on the doorstep.

'Just don't answer the door!' Helena said later on, when she and the girls called round for tea. They'd found me limp and exhausted on a sofa in the sitting room. Amanda had just left. My sister plonked herself down on the end of the sofa. I curled my legs up to accommodate her. 'You've got a spy hole – use it! Then if it's her, creep upstairs and lie doggo on the bed till she's gone!'

Hard to explain to Helena the feeling of physical terror Amanda inspired in me, courtesy of her connection to Michael. She'd think I was mad if I told her that recently, when the doorbell went, at increasingly odd times and with no message beforehand, that old terror would literally take over my body. I'd notice my hand trembling as I reached for the doorknob.

'Yes – or,' exclaimed Maudie, fresh from school and still in her hockey kit, muddy knees included, 'when you hear the bell, lie under the window seat like this!' She demonstrated by flinging herself to the floor and lying like a corpse, eyes shut, hands on heart.

'But what if she creeps right up to the window before she rings the bell and Luce hasn't got time?' said Tess, wide-eyed. 'Or, even worse, sees her make a dash for it?'

'Turn to stone,' commanded Maudie, leaping up from under the window and demonstrating. 'Like musical statues. There's a disease you can get, which turns you literally to stone. It's called Stone Man Syndrome.'

'Stop it.' Tess was gripped. 'Where did you hear that?'

'It's in Ant's medical bible, that big black one. Remember when he thought he had a stomach ulcer? Almost called an ambulance? It's the next one down.'

'Calm down, girls, that's enough. Lucy is wrung out enough without your hysteria,' Helena told them.

'Speaking of ambulances,' Tess turned to me avidly, 'did you hear that Ant had one on their holiday last week? Blue flashing lights, sirens, the lot! He thought his heart had stopped.'

'I did hear,' I said, trying not to smile as Helena rolled her eyes.

'Only the third time we've had an ambulance on holiday,' she muttered dryly.

'It always happens on a romantic mini break,' Tess told me quietly, perching next to me. 'I can't imagine why, can you? Too much for the old ticker, perhaps?'

'And this time, it was in Paris,' Maudie informed me. '*Quelle drama* on the Champs-Élysées.'

'And *quels* fit doctors at the hospital. If *only* we'd been there.'

'Ah monsieur,' Maudie affected an outrageous French accent, 'ees thees your *petite fille*? But she is soo beautiful!'

'*Ah, mais une autre fille! Très, très belle,* far more *belle* than the other one!'

'*All right,* girls, enough,' scolded Helena, but not ferociously.

'He couldn't feel his pulse,' Tess confided, reaching for my wrist and finding mine. 'And Helena had popped out to do some secret shopping at Chanel while he had a nap, so he panicked. And you'd think he'd be so good at it by now, wouldn't you? After all, he takes it twice a day. Ooh, Luce – yours is raging! Met someone already? Ned says you've got a hot lodger.'

'Ignore them,' Helena told me. 'Ned called by this afternoon with some books he thought the girls might like. He just said he was nice.'

'Actually, he's neither,' I told them. 'He's a rather surly Parisian. Well, English actually, but he was living in Paris until things went pear-shaped with his wife. And not bad-looking, I suppose.'

'Doesn't sound too terrible,' Helena mused. 'Not that you want anyone,' she added quickly, seeing my face.

'Ooh, that's not what you said earlier,' said Maudie. 'To Ned. You said Lucy didn't need a mourning period, given that the marriage was over long ago.'

'Girls, I do wish you wouldn't listen on the stairs to adult conversation. No good can ever come of it. Ned did say, though,' she said, turning to me, 'that you're not writing. Is that right?'

'Just for the minute,' I told her, not wanting to expand.

Not wanting to explain, as I had done to Ned, about how I no longer felt the need to control a cast of characters, in a way that I couldn't control my own life. I no longer needed that power. And it *was* a power. It was I who rounded their personalities, moulded them into shape, gave them little traits, peccadilloes, foibles; I who delved into their past, their families, discovered what made them tick. The autonomy I lacked in real life was exerted on my cast – my friends, actually. They were so real to me, and I became so close to them, that I always felt genuinely sad to say goodbye. And then needed that gap, in between books, before I could take my leave of them, and create some more. Except Susie, of course: she was my constant. She prevailed in every book. My best friend. I could rely on her, always. But I didn't need her now. And that had been such an extraordinary revelation. A bombshell, actually. Susie was as dead to me as Michael was. Helena hadn't lived here as Ned had done. She wouldn't fully understand. She'd question, pick holes. Talk about displacement mechanisms being what drove many people to creativity, but that couldn't be the *whole* picture, she'd argue: find other ways to enable me to pick up my pen. Because, of course, if I was busy, my family didn't have to worry about me. She'd settle down to flex her argumentative muscles, which I really didn't want. Luckily, the girls were nudging each other, and seemed to be building up to something.

'Go on, spit it out.' Their mother sighed, easily distracted by her offspring.

'Apparently,' Tess turned to me, perched back on the window seat beside her sister, 'Imo said that when you tidied up the house, you found some clothes of hers. She said you saved them for us. She texted us.'

'Is it true?' breathed Maudie, shutting her eyes and clasping her hands as if in prayer.

Imo was their absolute idol. They stalked her constantly on Instagram, and made no secret of their adoration. In fact, there'd been a little scene at the funeral as they'd fought to sit next to her. Luckily Imo had two sides, and Dad had changed places with Maudie with a grin.

I got up and handed them a black plastic sack from under the piano. 'Here you go. Feast on that. Bags, belts, all sorts.'

'Oh – and hats!' Maudie exclaimed, nearly disappearing inside it. 'And proper Levis! Jewels! Dresses – *boho dresses* – oh deep joy! No, Tessy, I saw that first – *no*!'

'I'll take that,' said Helena, wrestling the bag from their hands. There was an unseemly tussle. 'To be sorted out at home,' she declared, but she looked flustered and I knew she'd struggle with that.

'Maybe take it in turns to choose?' I suggested.

'Oh, good plan,' agreed Helena, casting me a grateful look. This, the woman who brokered multi-million-pound contracts for a living.

'I'll pick first,' Tess said firmly. 'I'm the eldest.'

'No – why should three and a half minutes make any—'

'Toss for it,' I interrupted, reaching for my handbag on the floor. I found a coin and threw it in the air, caught it, and asked Maudie to choose. She chose correctly. 'Right. Maudie goes first.'

For a moment, everyone was silenced. I had a feeling

such closure was unusual in this household. Helena seized a rare advantage.

'Come on, girls,' she commanded. 'We're off. Leave Lucy in peace.' They got to their feet, grudgingly. Helena kissed me goodbye. 'Bye, Luce. And give my love to Mum and Dad. Good luck with that, by the way,' she said grimly. She hesitated and seemed about to say more, but then made her way to the front door.

'Just until you're better, she means,' Maudie whispered to me, when her mother was out of earshot. 'Co-defendants often need company, Ned says.'

'No, he said co-*dependan*—'

'Girls!' their mother shrieked, exasperated, from the hall. 'Come on! You've got homework to do!' She reappeared, brandishing the bin bag, like bait.

'And good luck with Daniel,' Tess told me, as Helena disappeared again. 'We've heard about him.'

'Except we've already looked him up on Facebook, and oh Luce – no hair!'

'Or not much,' agreed Tess.

'And if he's a friend of Helena and Ant . . .' Two pairs of sparkling hazel eyes widened meaningfully at me in pert, pretty faces. 'Well,' they finished sadly.

But I wasn't really listening. I was thinking about what Maudie had said – co . . . what?

Their mother was calling them now from the car, gesturing madly. Getting quite pink. The girls kissed my cheeks.

'Give her our love,' Maudie insisted urgently. 'Imo, I mean.'

'And tell her we dream of New York – always!'

I smiled as they ran to the door. Imo had kindly hosted a half-term treat in New York last year, meeting them at JFK, taking them shopping, out to restaurants. They'd stayed at her apartment in downtown Manhattan. They'd never quite got over it. But my mind wasn't on that, either. I walked slowly back to the sitting room. What was it Maudie had said? Co-something or other? I reached for my phone to google it – or take a stab at it anyway – when I saw a message. By mistake, I opened it. It was from Amanda. I prepared to recoil from her insults, but this was different.

'I am so sorry. I am such a cow. Always bothering you, please forgive me. You're the only true friend I've got. Tell me I'm forgiven and I promise I won't bother you again.'

I tapped back. 'Of course I forgive you, Amanda.'

She was back in an instant.

'It's been such a long dark tunnel and sometimes I wonder if I'll ever come through it. But it's not fair that you've been the butt of all my sorrow.'

'It's fine, I promise.'

'Thanks hon. I really appreciate you understanding. You see, ever since he died . . .'

And then she was off. On and on she went. And on and on I answered, because, I reasoned, she wasn't being mean now, and I was just so relieved she wasn't insulting me.

Half an hour later, when I'd finally got rid of her and agreed to meet at some point – nothing definite, you understand, some undefined date in the future – I went down to the kitchen to make some pasta for supper. I felt a bit better. A lot better, actually. I didn't like any unresolved aggravation with Amanda. It left me feeling anxious. As the water boiled, and I got a jar of pesto from the fridge, I tried again to recall what Maudie had said. Then I remembered. I googled it. Stared. Oh, what nonsense. I tossed my phone on the side and busied myself draining the spaghetti in the sink: a great waft of steam rose up, clouding my vision.

IO

When I arrived at my parents' house a few days later, it was not without a degree of trepidation. My breezy assurances to the rest of my family that nothing could be simpler than moving in and looking after my aged parents, transplanting my life to theirs and adapting to country living, was beginning to echo rather hollowly in my ears. Let's just say the magnitude of what I'd done had started to dawn. As I crunched up the gravel, which boasted quite a few potholes, through the rather gloomy avenue of rhododendron bushes towards what was to be my new home, I gazed around with a critical eye, as if seeing it for the first time. The post and rails fence to the paddock beyond was broken, but then that often happened after a windy winter. The garden was overgrown, but then it had never been neat: always a rather confused and eclectic collection of low maintenance shrubs, my parents claiming to be either too busy or not terribly interested, so *plus ça change* there. I came to a halt some distance from the door and turned off the engine. I sat for a moment, thoughtful.

Saying goodbye to my old home had not been a problem. Pretty Fulham house though it was, I felt no sentimentality about it, and as I'd handed Josh two sets of keys I'd told him as much. I'd even given him a bright smile and said I hoped he'd be very happy there, even though I hadn't been. He'd frowned.

'You weren't happy here?'

This happens to me quite a lot, recently. I think things, and then they just sail out of my mouth, unfiltered. Maybe it's because I spend a lot of time alone and converse mainly with myself.

'Well, only because of personal circumstances. The house itself I adored, and my garden is a triumph. I hope you'll keep it going. Are you a gardener?' I asked, seamlessly changing the subject.

'Not at all,' he said slowly, his eyes on me, thoughtful. He came to. 'Although I suppose I could water things, if that's what you mean?'

We were in the kitchen at the time, and he looked doubtfully out through the open French windows to the riot of tasteful late spring blossoms, mostly blue and white, bursting forth from every conceivable square inch of bed amongst a backdrop of elegant foliage. I sensed this was a man who didn't stray outside at all ordinarily, unless to go to a library. His bookish countenance – books were practically all that he'd arrived with, in huge packing cases – and the fact that I'd discovered he was a lecturer at King's College, plus the look of horror that came over his face as I handed him a pair of secateurs from the kitchen drawer, did nothing to dispel this.

'Yes, watering would be great. But maybe deadhead too?' I suggested gently.

'Which is what, exactly?' He looked nervous.

'Just . . . snipping off . . . the dead heads,' I said, hopefully not too patronizingly. Golly, a professor should surely have worked that out. 'But not if it's too much trouble,' I added quickly. 'Just a bit of watering would be perfect.'

In my mind's eye I saw all my carefully tended exotics, my lovelies, my Madame Grégoires, my Albertines, my Constance Sprys, wilting and dead within weeks. But so what, I reasoned. I'd have another garden, a much bigger one, at my parents'. And there was only so much I could ask of a tenant.

'Right,' Josh had said shortly. 'I'll do my best. What do I do with the heads?'

'Well, you either gather them in an attractive distressed trug in the manner of an Edwardian lady pretending you're in rural Gloucestershire, as I do, or you let them fall in a mess on the ground.'

'The latter,' he said, looking at me with curiosity. 'Do you always live in a world of make-believe?'

'I used to,' I said, thinking this was rather a personal question, but on the other hand I hadn't half invited it. 'But not any more. Now. Dishwasher, washing machine, heating, I've told you about. I think the boiler is self-explanatory. Is there anything else?'

'Don't think so.' He stuck his hands in his overgrown coat pockets and looked around warily. It struck me he looked a bit lost, all of a sudden. I thought of his family back in France.

'Where have you been living up until now?' I asked kindly.

'Oh, with a colleague and his wife. They had a spare room so I've been there for a couple of months. It was rather nice, actually. Kensington.'

He looked at me, slightly competitively, I felt.

'Oh, right. Well, I'm sorry you're slumming it down in Sands End, but I'm sure you'll struggle on. Now, I've left you with milk and bread, and the tea and coffee jars are full. Also the sugar.'

He nodded and moved towards the study as I muttered, 'No no, my pleasure,' to myself. He opened the door. Aside from getting Molly Maids in to clean it assiduously once I'd got the go-ahead from the police, the door was always firmly shut.

'You worked in here?' he asked, peering in.

'I used to,' I said shortly. 'OK, I'm off. Good luck.'

'You too.' He shut the door and looked at me curiously. It struck me it was the first pleasant thing he'd said: a recognition of the fact that there were two of us embarking on new chapters in our lives here. But there was no way I was going to prolong the conversation and say something whimsical like that, so I just nodded and made my way out to my car.

The car itself was crammed to bursting with cases, bags, dresses, coats on hangers and bulging bin liners. Behind it was a trailer that Ant had borrowed for me, courtesy of some TV set he'd been working on. That, too, was full, the roof forced on with some effort. But an awful lot of stuff had gone to Oxfam. Not Nefertiti, or Diana, I loved them too much, but a fair amount of blue and white china, masses of clothes and books, and generally a great deal of clutter, because, as so many people told me, I didn't need it in my life any more.

Apparently I didn't need to hang around for legal reasons, either. The police had finally called, to apologize for their lack of progress, and when I'd explained I was decamping to the country they'd been understanding. They had asked for my parents' address, though, in case they needed to get in touch with me again.

So now here I was, sitting in my parents' front garden, gazing up at the brick and flint farmhouse minus the farm – that had gone long ago, before their time – in what might be described as leafy stockbroker belt, or the semi-rural, commutable Home Counties. To the left of the drive, hidden in the dark shrubbery, was the cottage. Dad had apparently got a local builder in to tart it up in readiness for me, which Helena and the children were pleased about, since it would give me some independence. I believe Helena had had no small part in initiating that, and of course I was equally pleased. No way did I want to live with Mum and Dad. I was dying to see it, but hadn't been allowed down because Dad had wanted it to be a surprise. I realized now that I could hardly see it at all. When I was young, it had been in full view of the house, an ugly pebbledash eyesore, but over the years the shrubbery had sprung up, and all I could make out now were the gables, green and wooden and in need of some paint. That was a relief. Not that my parents were remotely nosy, quite the opposite. They were far too caught up in their own lives. But it would be refreshing to have a degree of privacy.

As I got out, my father, no doubt having heard the car, flung wide the front door, wine glass in hand.

'Darling!'

I grinned. Anyone would think I was arriving for a party, not to care for my decrepit parents. Tall, slim, only slightly stooped as he rested on his stick, and still with a reasonable amount of silver hair swept back off a high forehead, my father looked every inch the genial host he always was. Despite the freshly laundered shirt, some strange grey tracksuit bottoms and, of course, the brown Velcro shoes from the back of the *Telegraph* gave him away. The shoes I was used to, the trousers I wasn't.

'Sorry about the horribly naff kecks,' he said, giving me a kiss and seeing me glance. 'It's all I can wear with the wretched legs. And my feet are webbed now, as you know. It's only a matter of time before I embrace galoshes.'

I grinned. 'You look great, Dad. How's Mum?'

'Oh, in fine fettle, generally, but in a fearful fuss today. She's burnt the lunch and the kitchen looks like a crematorium. But luckily, it's only the Frobishers coming. Jeannie's almost blind and Dickie's taste buds are so jaded he laces his cornflakes with Tabasco, so it couldn't matter less.' We went inside. 'Ah, here she is. A vision of loveliness, albeit in smoke grey.'

My mother appeared in the hall like an apparition from Hades. Dressed for Ascot, minus a hat, her face, silk dress and hair were blackened with soot.

'Would you know I've had a drama?' she asked anxiously, coming to kiss me.

'Not remotely,' I assured her, removing her glasses, which were filthy. 'But you might do better by cleaning these.' I wiped them for her. 'Mum, they're sunglasses.'

'Yes, because everything is just so bright these days, isn't it?'

'Well, not inside, surely. Come on, let's get you cleaned up. I hear the Frobishers are coming?'

'Yes, it should have been the Pattersons as well, but Reggie's got a gippy tummy so they're coming tomorrow instead, with the De Courcys. Better change this frock.'

'Right. Do you have guests every day?'

'No, no, just a bit of a flurry at the moment. We've been rather lax at entertaining. And only at lunchtime.'

'Although we go out a fair bit,' reflected my father. 'But not on a Wednesday. As you know, your mother takes to her bed.'

'I'm not surprised. I'd be on my knees. Can you cope?' I called after her as she mounted the stairs to change.

'Of course I can cope. I've coped for eighty-four years. We're not entirely past it, you know!'

And off she went. I made my way through the sitting room and beyond to the blackened kitchen: surveyed it in dismay.

'Why aren't you using the Aga?' I asked, blinking in surprise at some new, tiny electric appliance in the corner, the door hanging open.

'Your mother's taken against it. Says it's too hot in the summer. Plus, it's been on the blink a bit, recently.'

I laid my hand on it. 'Well, it's gone out, Dad. It's stone cold.'

'That's it!' he said cheerfully. 'Hence the new one.'

'Not just a case of re-lighting it?'

'Lord, no. Nothing as simple as that.'

I made a mental note to ring the Aga man in the morning and glanced in the new oven at some black blobs on a blackened baking tray. 'What are these?'

'Stuffed tomatoes.' He grinned. 'Thoroughly stuffed, actually. Drink, darling?'

'Um, in a mo.' I was peering in the fridge. 'So . . . what's the main course?'

'I believe it was a large pork pie from Waitrose with all the filling removed, re-stuffed with pigeon, tomatoes, green peppers and anchovies.'

'And where is that?' I glanced around, my mother's eclectic meal plan coming as no surprise.

'In the bin.'

'Burnt?'

'Tiny bit. We haven't quite got the hang of the cooker.'

'So what's on the menu now?'

'Oh, the usual default position,' he said brightly. 'Surf 'n' Turf.'

'Fish fingers wrapped in bacon?'

'Exactly.'

'Shall I rustle it up?'

'If you wouldn't mind.' He turned. My mother had reappeared, still quite dishevelled, but in a clean floral dress. 'Darling, you look lovely! Give us a twirl.'

Mum obliged girlishly and then dropped a shaky curtsey as Dad roared his approval. Helena and I often observed that our parents were like a couple of Italians:

either at each other's throats – well, mostly Mum at Dad's – or deeply in love and happy. It seemed I'd happened upon the latter today, which was a blessing. When it transpired they'd been to the races a few days ago, with old friends the Gordons, and that Harold and Dad had both won a packet on the last race, which they'd celebrated with lashings of champagne, I realized why. Spirits were still high.

The Frobishers arrived madly early as old people do, so there was no time to look at the cottage or even get a suitcase out of the car. Their car purred up the drive just as I was sourcing some tinned sweetcorn, there being literally nothing else. I put some plates in a low oven and went through. Jeannie, my godmother, who I adored, a dirty diamond pinned haphazardly to her vast bosom, and Dickie, her suave, still elegant husband, with a slight limp from a polo fall, were delighted, if amazed to see me.

'But darling – what will you *do* down here?' Jeannie reached to take both my hands in hers, always tactile. 'You'll go mad with boredom. It's just a short break, I take it?'

'Er, well, no. Actually, I'm sort of here to look after them.'

She blinked. Looked astonished. 'Them? Oh no, darling. They don't need that.' She laughed. 'The very idea!'

My mother, as if on cue, sailed in with the fish fingers on a platter, followed by my father with a bowl of sweetcorn. We all filtered through to the dining room, which was freezing as usual. Aside from that, however, it was a convivial meal. I noticed Jeannie had to be gently guided to her chair by Dickie and then tapped away to find her knife and fork, and that Dickie shut his eyes for five minutes after the main course. Also that my mother ate very little but commandeered a bottle of white wine which she drank steadily, whilst Dad ate and drank heartily but remained entirely compos mentis, if extremely voluble, throughout. But other than that, it was unremarkable. And to be honest, if I hadn't been looking for those things I might not have noticed them. It was only when Jeannie knocked her glass over and Dad went to the kitchen for a cloth that I noticed he had gloves on when he returned.

'What are those for?' I asked as he mopped up.

He looked surprised. 'These? Oh, at about three o'clock I get a bit chilly. Always have done, especially in the extremities. All goes a bit numb. Now, your mother and Jeannie are having a little Sauternes with their pudding, can I tempt you?'

Mum and Jeannie were beside themselves now, noses practically touching across the table, about dear old Max Harrison, who, at Towcester the other day, had offered his services to the clerk of the course to ride in the four thirty after an injured jockey retired. He'd last ridden in a point-to-point in Tripoli before weighing in was in the rule book.

'Should have taken him up on it!' roared my father, who, together with the pudding wine, had brought in a plastic tub of Wall's Neapolitan ice cream, which looked circa 1990. He began doling it out. 'He's a first-class jockey, won the four hundred guineas at Cheltenham in 'sixty-six. They missed a trick there. Dear God. There they are.' He stared. The next spoonful had brought up, like a fishing trawler, a pair of spectacles. 'Good Lord. I'd quite given up hope. Dickie! Remember I accused you of theft and grand larceny last time you were here hoovering up my victuals? Look what I've just found!'

My father had a cavernous voice and Dickie, who'd nodded off again, jerked awake. Everyone bellowed with laughter as Dad dipped the glasses in the water jug and set them aside. Pudding and wine consumed, Jeannie suddenly pushed back her chair and declared it was time. I assumed they were off, but to my surprise everyone got up with alacrity and my parents led the way back into the sitting room. They all shuffled behind the sofa, where, I'd failed to notice earlier, our old bridge table was set up. With much apologizing to me, they hustled eagerly to their seats, and then proceeded to play at least six hands of bridge.

'What, after all that wine?' Helena said dubiously when I rang her later.

'Sharp as tacks, all of them. It was like they'd suddenly come alive. Snapped into gear. Huge cards, obviously, for Jeannie and Mum, and pressed right up to noses, but all sitting ramrod straight, even Dickie. Highly competitive too, and complete silence all round, only speaking when it was their turn to bid. Extraordinary! I felt like the old granny, sitting by the fire with the colour supplement.'

Helena was silent. And, I could tell, slightly disappointed. 'But how did they get home?' she demanded. 'If they'd drunk all that wine? And Dickie's inclined to nod off and Jeannie's half-blind?'

'Camilla came for them at about five. I hadn't realized she'd dropped them off too. Remember Camilla? The daughter?'

'Yes, had a bit of a nervy breaky after the ghastly Torquil left her, but used to be rather fun. A huge party girl.'

'Well, she doesn't look so fun-loving now. In fact she looked completely wild-eyed and stressed out. As we found their coats and sticks, she was spitting to me about what a bloody nightmare the whole thing is. Jeannie and Dickie are in a converted barn in her garden, apparently. Dickie put her straight on that, though, saying it was *his* garden. Nothing wrong with his hearing, clearly.'

'Oh yes, she and her new boyfriend are in the big house now.'

'Yes, but she said that, frankly, it's a poisoned chalice. Worse than having teenagers. All they do is enjoy themselves whilst she ferries them from pillar to post and clears up after them. Sounds familiar?'

'But they can't have fun all the time, surely? They're too incapacitated for that,' Helena said, irritated.

'Well, that's the thing. Apart from the physical side of things, they're all on sparkling form in the marbles department. Honestly, Hels, even Mum gave a very spirited defence of Boris over lunch. All horribly politically incorrect, of course, about how she couldn't care how many love children he had running around as long as he was up to running the country, and how girls these days should grow up about having their bottoms pinched because she'd lost count of the times she'd been chased round tables or ducked out of a lift when she realized who she was getting in with. Imo would have had a fit. Especially when Dickie kept patting my knee and telling me sympathetically I'd be fine, soon, and that they'd find me a nice young man. They were making a fuss of *me*, Hels, hoping *I'd* be all right.'

She went quiet. 'Perhaps you hit a good day.'

'I'm not so sure. When I asked Mum later about the little Waitrose incident, she said; "But I simply forgot, Luce. I was miles away. Haven't you ever done that?" And I had to admit, I had.'

'What, stolen from Waitrose?'

'No, but got to the door and the alarm's gone off. I was at the self-service when I did it, filling my straw basket, baguette on top in a rather picturesque manner. I think in my head I may even have imagined I was in France. I must have forgotten to pay.'

There was a silence and I wondered if Helena had too.

'Never!' she snorted when I asked her. 'I was just wondering if you'd inherited some of Mum's loopy genes!'

It was my time to be quiet. Helena found Mum's charm and eccentricity intensely irritating.

'So what are you saying?' she asked brusquely. 'You don't need to be there?'

'No,' I said slowly. 'I'm not saying that. I'm just saying

that even this short amount of time with them has shown me they're not incapable.'

'Fish fingers for lunch!'

'Yes, but so what? Some people would think it's equally lunatic to slave away over Ottolenghi for hours.' Helena, I knew, after putting in a twelve-hour day in the office, regularly did just that.

'And the cottage?' she demanded.

'Ah, the cottage,' I said nervously, knowing she'd freak. 'Well, that's another story. Let's just say I'm very definitely in the spare room for the minute.'

I bid her goodbye, inventing some spurious excuse about Mum wanting me in the kitchen, and hastened away.

II

There'd been a fair amount of stalling about seeing the cottage – procrastination tactics, I realized, in retrospect. Once Camilla had carted her parents home my parents insisted on washing up first, before we went across. Obviously I did the lion's share while they plumped cushions. When we'd got things straight, though, I suggested again that we pop over. My father said it was getting dark. I said surely the place had lights? He then explained that the silver still needed polishing and that if he didn't do it now, he'd forget. He sat down firmly at the kitchen table with a duster and the Brillo, glaring at my mother. That seemed to galvanize Mum. She met the challenging look defiantly, straightened up and stiffened her back. Suddenly she was up to the task.

'Yes, let's go,' she declared. 'Danny's still working there, of course, but he won't mind.'

'Danny? What – the builder? Is he? I didn't see a van.'

'Oh, he walks, leaves all his stuff there. And don't forget,' she adopted a twinkling, merry countenance, 'you'll need a certain amount of imagination!'

With her words echoing in my ears and my father avoiding my eye as he polished away, the two of us went outside. Picking our way through the undergrowth in the dusk, I held Mum's arm. Slowly we made our way through the long grass and what remained of the gravel path to the front door of what we quaintly, and anachronistically, called the cottage. The door stuck a bit so I gave it a shove. It still wouldn't open so I gave it more heft. In I flew, into what can only be described as a building site. I stumbled to a halt. A wall had come down between the hall and the sitting room and the remains of it, together with the sledgehammer, was still in a pile of bricks on the floor. Floorboards were up, joists were exposed, and wires hung from walls. A single light bulb hung from the ceiling and a broken window let in a cool breeze. In the midst of all this dystopian chaos, Danny was indeed very much in situ. Hunched beside a pathetic smoky fire in a blackened grate, he sat on an upturned crate, a mug of tea in one hand, a fork in the other. An open can of cold baked beans, a saucer full of cigarette ends, and the *Sun* newspaper were before him on another upturned crate. He turned in surprise as we entered. Danny was seventy if he was a day.

'Ah, Danny!' My mother clasped her hands joyfully. 'So sorry to disturb your tea break. How are you getting on?'

Danny looked around critically, not in the least abashed at being caught on the hop. He sucked his teeth. 'I'm not gonna lie, Mrs Hartley, it's a long job. A very long job.'

'Right. But you'll have it done in a jiffy? This is my daughter Lucy, by the way. She's going to be living here. Lucy, Danny.' Anyone would think we were at a cocktail party.

'Well,' he shook his head soberly, not entering into my mother's festive spirit, 'there's a lot more than I thought. A lot more. I'd say you can forget about staying here for a bit.' He looked at me accusingly, as if I'd really got ahead of myself.

'Well – clearly!' I spluttered.

'No, not for a bit, I agree,' Mum said, patting my arm. 'It'll be a while before it's ready. But not too long. Danny's got it all under control, haven't you, Danny?' But Danny declined to answer. He stared around gloomily. 'And that's why I've got your old room ready,' she prattled on. 'Just for the time being. But I just wanted to show you how it was going.'

Slowly, I thought, as we bid farewell to Danny. He went back to his newspaper. It seemed to me he might be bedded in for the night.

Back in the house, I sensed a huge amount of tension coming to the surface as both my parents braced themselves for a horrific row. My father had a face like thunder, not thrilled at being caught on the back foot courtesy of something that had clearly been out of his control, and my mother was making her famous face, chin in the air, tight-lipped, defiant. There were quite a few things I would have liked to say myself, but given the amount of alcohol that had been consumed and the tired and emotional state of all parties, I heroically held my tongue. Instead I went to put the kettle on, seething inwardly.

It was about eight o'clock by now, and my mother declared she was having an early night, which was a huge relief all round. Dad quietly watched the television whilst I went out to the car for a case of clothes which I took up to my old room. I gazed around dispiritedly. I felt like a time traveller in this familiar room with its faded rose print wallpaper and candlewick bedspread, and not in a good way. If I was the depressive type, now would be the time for it to kick in. To think about how much I'd left behind, at least in terms of a normal London life, and wonder what a woman of my age was doing, moving back with her parents. I let out a long, shaky breath and steadied myself. Then I wandered down the passage, looking in all the old familiar rooms. I pushed open the door to my father's dressing room, where he now slept. On top of his chest of drawers were some pottery animals Helena and I had made at school. Inside his sock drawer I'd once looked for his military medals, to show the children. Instead I'd found letters from Michael. Thanking Dad for a Christmas present. But weirdly, referring to a loose tile on our roof, which he needed to get fixed in case it fell on someone in the garden. The next letter declined an invitation, on my behalf, to go to Ascot with them while Michael was away. It mentioned my car, which he said had a problem with the brakes. No one, except those who knew Michael well, and I include my father in this, would think it strange. But I'd gone cold. I knew exactly why my father had kept the letters. It made me catch my breath even now, but also feel extremely relieved to be here, and to be alone.

I went back to my room. I hung up my clothes and

put a few things in the bathroom. The rest, I decided, like so much else, could wait until tomorrow.

The following morning, over breakfast, I tackled my parents on more prosaic matters. Like where, in God's name, they'd found Danny?

'He's the Dugdales' chap,' said Mum in surprise, passing me the marmalade. 'Worked for them for years.'

'About a hundred,' remarked my father from behind his newspaper, clearly not the instigator of this farce.

'He seems a bit . . . glass half empty?'

'You're wrong, actually,' said Dad, clearing his throat. 'Danny's glass *is* empty.'

'And will the Dugdales mind if we return him to them and start afresh?'

'Not in the least,' said Mum. 'Cynth's been muttering at bridge about how she misses him in her herbaceous border.'

'He's a gardener?'

'Well, he's a jack of all trades. You know. Used to work on the home farm. Can turn his hand to anything.'

'Except one of them is a dead loss, because he lost three fingers in the combine,' came dryly from behind the *Telegraph*. Dad appeared briefly to roll his eyes meaningfully at me. Then he disappeared again. 'I've unpacked your car, by the way. Put all your bedding and cushions and books and whatever in the blue spare room, for the moment.'

'Oh Dad, you shouldn't have done that!' My father, as

ever, would have been up at six this morning. 'Some of those cases were heavy. I'd have done it!'

I sensed, however, that whilst it had probably taken him ages and been a Herculean task, this was something he'd wanted to do to make up for yesterday's disappointment.

'Nonsense, your father can manage; he's as strong as an ox! We're not entirely decrepit, you know.'

This, or words to that effect, was to become something of a mantra from my mother, repeated at regular intervals: and it was one which increasingly reinforced to me that they were precisely that.

After I'd rung the Aga man and organized a service, then got to grips with the Checkatrade website on my laptop and made some calls, sorting out two teams of local builders to come and quote, I had a quick bath, then went downstairs. I realized the house was silent. No sign of anyone. Finally, I pushed open the study door. Dad sat in his leather chair by the window, and Mum was on her knees before him, doing something to his leg. As I appeared, she stopped. They both stared guiltily, like naughty children. Dad hurriedly dropped his tracksuit trouser.

'What are you doing?'

'Just changing your father's ulcer dressing.'

I went forward and lifted his trouser leg. A ghastly sight met my eyes. A gaping wound was oozing with yellow pus. And not only that, something was moving. I made myself breathe. My father's eyes were averted when I looked at him. I steadied myself.

'Why isn't the practice nurse doing this?'

'I missed my appointment. It was on Tuesday. Something came up. But your mother's very able. She'd have been a nurse if she hadn't married me, you know. Didn't you always say that, darling?'

'Oh, I'd have loved it,' Mum said, sitting back on her heels, eyes shining. 'With a pert little cap and those dear little puffed sleeves. Skirt nipped in at the waist and—'

'Yes, but she's not a nurse,' I said curtly, cutting into her fantasy world, so horribly like my own. 'What's the surgery number?'

'Oh no, you won't get an appointment now, not if you've missed one. They're dragons!' my mother breathed fearfully. Meanwhile my father got up foghorning: 'Perfectly all right! Nothing whatever the matter!' and shuffled off to water his tomatoes in the greenhouse.

I got one though, an appointment. And later that day, drove him down.

'Dad,' I asked casually on the way into town, knowing from experience, with Ned and Imo, that these things were better broached in the car, side by side, and not face-to-face. 'Is it too painful to drive? Is that why you missed your appointment?'

He paused. 'Only at the moment. Be right as rain soon. Pressure on the pedals.'

'Right. And is that why Mum's driving?'

'Well, she's entitled to, darling, she's still got a licence!' But he wouldn't look at me. Gazed out of the window at the scenery, like Imo used to. Right. So nothing to do with him leaving the keys lying around – this was their modus vivendi. She drove, half blind and very fearful, because he couldn't. I licked my lips. And their house was too remote for them to walk, obviously. The bus? Yes, maybe later, the stop was only down the lane. But I knew they wouldn't countenance it now. Two old people on a bus with their pac-a-macs and plastic bags? No. Not yet. They were in denial as much as Helena and I were. Because why hadn't my sister and I thought this through earlier? Why hadn't we considered how two people in their eighties might get about in the country? But Dad had always been so capable, so strong, so indestructible. I realized the difference between a man in his seventies and a man in his eighties was huge. I swallowed, gripping the wheel tightly as I drove into the surgery car park.

As I waited for Dad in reception, I felt ashamed that we'd been so cross with Mum, whereas in fact she'd been protecting Dad. And of course, they weren't stupid. They both knew that if neither of them was driving, it would have been something of a crisis point as far as continuing to live at Pope's Farm, their beloved home for fifty-odd years, was concerned. The house my father had always said he'd leave feet first.

After a bit, Dad reappeared, looking uncharacteristically sheepish. I got to my feet. He glanced around warily, but the reception area, despite my mother's dire warnings of hordes of people, was empty.

'Maggots,' he said shortly. My jaw dropped. I stared at him, aghast. 'Which actually, she said, is not unusual.

Nature's way of getting rid of diseased flesh. I remember once one of my lance sergeants had them in North Africa. But not ideal.'

'No, *not* ideal,' I breathed, horrified. 'And we're not in fucking North Africa now, Dad.'

'No need to swear,' he said mildly, another expression I was to hear a lot, as my language got increasingly colourful. In direct correlation, in fact, to the increasingly apparent state of affairs.

At that moment the door directly opposite us, with 'Dr Gupta' engraved on a plate, opened. A young woman stuck her head round. 'Mr Hartley?'

'The nurse thought I should see a doctor,' he muttered to me. 'And Mike Bond's away.'

'Yes, of course! Can I come in too?'

'Absolutely not.'

'Yes, please,' said Dr Gupta. 'If you wouldn't mind.'

Try stopping me. I'd sprinted past my father, who, for once, was outnumbered, and sat down firmly by her desk. Dad shuffled in and sat beside me.

'I've written you a prescription for antibiotics for your ulcers and we'd like you to see the nurse again in three days' time. The penicillin should start to kick in soon and you'll be in less pain. Which must have been excruciating.' She eyed him carefully. 'Please don't drink on the antibiotics, and please come and have your dressings changed regularly. I see from your notes you haven't been for two weeks. I also see that you missed the carpal tunnel operation Dr Bond arranged. Was there any particular reason?' she asked gently.

'I was busy,' Dad said petulantly. He hid his gloved hands.

'Right, well, I've booked another one at the same hospital for three weeks on Thursday. I see, too, that Mrs Hartley missed her cataract operation. Any idea why that was?' She looked at me.

I opened my mouth, astonished. Cataracts? Carpal tunnel? I closed my mouth. 'No. But rest assured I'll get to the bottom of it.'

'Are you the carer?'

'Yes,' I said firmly as my father simultaneously roared 'No!'

'I mean, I'm their daughter. But I certainly will be—' Dad glared at me but I held my nerve, 'caring for them.' He went a bit purple.

'Right,' said the frightfully efficient Dr Gupta who was fast becoming my new best friend. 'Well, we have a cataract cancellation on Wednesday next week, at the same hospital. Shall I book your mother in for that?'

'Yes, please.'

After we'd collected his medication at the dispensary, my father and I walked to the car in stony silence.

'Interfering busybody,' he said as we got in.

'Actually, Dad, she's just trying to keep you independent for as long as possible. Entirely up to you.'

'She wanted to stick her finger up my arse last time I saw her.'

'That'll be your prostate. Did you let her?'

'Certainly not!' This was to be another mantra to add to my list, but I let this one go, thinking that, actually, his prostate was the least of my worries. Or at any rate one to be tackled another day.

I went back into town to shop after I'd dropped Dad at home. Then I returned to fill the fridge and the larder, which were horribly bare. Particularly when I'd thrown out everything beyond its sell by date.

'Nothing wrong with that!' they kept shrieking, hovering behind me as I filled a black sack.

'Cream from last month,' I told them, chucking in a blue-rimmed pot. 'Eggs from March.'

'Eggs keep forever,' my mother insisted.

'Sardines from 2001.' I was in the larder now.

'Ah, now they really will be fine,' said my father, lunging for them. 'Tinned stuff lasts years.' I wrestled them back, glaring at him. He looked taken aback. 'We've managed perfectly well on our own, you know. And a little bit of mould never hurt anyone.'

'Does one the world of good, actually,' agreed my mother. 'It's full of penicillin.' It occurred to me that apart from last night's little hiccup over the cottage, they'd definitely closed ranks and were presenting a united front. There'd been very little sniping, which was a good thing. Even if their barbs were aimed at me now.

My mother sulked for a bit in the scullery as I cleaned the fridge completely, but then she couldn't help creeping back as I refilled it.

'Ooh, what's that?' she said, fingering some greenery.

'Kale.'

'And what's that?'

'Flaxseeds. You sprinkle them on muesli.'

'Oh, we don't do muesli.'

'Mum, there's absolutely no nutrition in those stale Frosties I threw away. Just give it a go, eh? Or an egg? A fresh one, preferably.'

'And we like white bread,' she complained, as I filled the bread bin.

'Which is why I've bought both, and put a few loaves in the freezer so you can toast it. And I've got the jams you like, too.'

'You threw ours away.'

'They were thick with mould. And trust me, if Helena was here, it'd be quinoa, apple cider vinegar and Himalayan pink sea salt crystals all the way, so count yourself lucky. Now. Lunch.'

'A burger,' said my father stubbornly, going to the freezer. 'That's what I always have, unless you've thrown those away too. You get ten for a pound in the village shop. Ah, there they are, and your mother likes a chocolate cupcake with marmalade on top.'

'Did you get some?' she asked suspiciously, peering in my bag.

'I did.'

'But we don't eat yet,' Dad said, shocked, as I put some veg on the chopping board.

'No, I was just getting it ready. What time do you eat?'

'Ooh, about two?' he said, passing Mum a drink clinking with ice and lemon.

I glanced at the clock. 'So . . . that's a two-hour cocktail hour.'

'Got to have a little fun,' said my mother petulantly and I saw Dad's eyes gleam dangerously as he poured himself a particularly large vodka and tonic.

'I get that,' I said evenly, trying not to think of Dr Gupta, 'but maybe we'll eat at one thirty, otherwise I'll be starving. Anyway, I thought you said the De Courcys were coming? You surely weren't giving them marmalade cupcakes, were you?'

'No, no, they like the frozen burgers. But Nancy rang to say Archie's had an unfortunate fall. After lunch in St James's he went off to buy himself a hat in Lock's. Missed his footing on the way out. Just needed a couple of stitches.'

'Right,' I said faintly. 'And the Pattersons?'

'Reggie's brother-in-law died last night. He couldn't bear him. In fact, he advised him to fuck off over the parsnips last Easter, but he feels he should go and see Kitty, his sister. The one who farts as she walks, you remember. Outside church.'

'I do.'

'And then we have a little zizz,' said my mother firmly.

'Sorry?'

'After lunch. We like a little zizz.'

'But we don't like to sleep past five o'clock. We set our alarms.'

I nodded. No indeed. Because precisely one hour after that it would be cocktail hour again, and one wouldn't want to miss a minute.

After we'd all had home-made burgers and salad, which they pretended not to enjoy but I could tell they did, and whilst they were napping, I set about making a chicken pie for supper. Mum was worryingly thin: in fact I'd been shocked to see her arms when she'd taken her cardigan off, but if she subsisted on a diet of chocolate cake and gin, it wasn't hard to see why. I made three pies, small ones, and froze two, along with the burgers, all individually wrapped. When I'd finished, feeling soothed – cooking does that for me – I had a good look round the house.

Irene, I knew, still came once a week, but Irene, or Mrs Tully, as I still called her, had been coming since Helena and I were children, and was only marginally younger than my parents. Mum had tried to retire her once, but her eyes had filled up and so had Mum's, and so still she came. She hoovered a bit in the middle of the rooms, washed the kitchen floor, again, in the middle, flicked a duster around, but mostly she and Mum sat at the kitchen table and gossiped. Mum loved to hear about what was going on in the village and Irene didn't hold back. Dad, meanwhile, had a very comfortable morning reading all the newspapers in the study where Irene was never allowed on account of her moving things around – about twenty years ago, when she could. It was win-win all round, except, of course, the house was filthy.

As I poked around now, flinching at yet another dead mouse and trail of droppings behind a sofa, so rank even Hector wasn't interested, I realized that a mammoth task lay ahead of me. And this was merely what was visible. What lurked beneath was unimaginable. For now, however, I confined myself to the kitchen, which had almost made me gag as I'd cooked in it earlier, opening drawers stiff with grease, having to wash every utensil before I used it. I had to deal with that right now if I was even going to make another cup of tea in there. I found an apron in a drawer, and a duster, which I tied over my hair, knowing from last night that I might not wash my hair until I'd thoroughly cleaned the bathroom, and set to work. I was up a step ladder, deep in a revolting corner of the ceiling, flicking spiders and cobwebs down, when there was a rap on the back door.

'Come in!' I yelled, above Hector barking, knowing Danny was due to collect a final cheque for the time he'd spent stewing tea and beans in the cottage. It was sitting on the side. Nothing happened, so I yelled 'Come *in*' again, irritated. With a sigh I started to dismount my ladder, shouting for Hector to shut *up*, when the back door opened.

A tall, slim man, with blondish greying hair, an outdoors complexion and pale blue eyes appeared in the doorway. I stopped, mid-descent.

'Oh. Sorry to yell. I thought you were Danny.'

'Dan.'

'Sorry?'

'I'm Dan De Courcy.'

'Oh, right.' A bell rang somewhere: something to do with Helena.

'Don't tell me they've finally replaced Irene?'

'What? Oh – no.' I whipped the yellow duster from my head and glanced down at my pinny. 'No, I'm Lucy. Their daughter.'

'Oh yes. Of course.' He blinked. 'Gosh, I didn't recognize you. But it's probably been about a hundred years since I last saw you.'

'Dan! How splendid!' A voice boomed from behind me. My father appeared in the kitchen, refreshed from his sleep, looking ruddy-faced and bright-eyed. He was beaming delightedly as he rubbed his hands together. 'To what do we owe this pleasure?'

Dan looked rather abashed. 'I'm afraid it's not a pleasure, Henry. Mum asked me to come round. I'm afraid the hospital rang. I'm sorry to have to tell you, but Archie died this morning.'

12

'Oh Lord. I am sorry.' My father's hand went to his brow. 'Lord. That fall . . . ?'

'Proved to be fatal.'

'Archie?' I asked tentatively. So many names.

'Nancy's husband. And Dan, here's, step, step-father?'

'One more step, actually. Mum's fourth husband.'

'Ah.' Yes, I remembered now. Mum's best friend, Nance, had always been a bit of a goer. A serial husband bagger. But it explained the slightly awkward, but less than grief-stricken face of the man before me. I surreptitiously took my pinny off.

'God, I'm sorry,' said Dad.

'Well . . .' admitted Dan, uncomfortably. He stopped.

'Never liked the fellow?' offered Dad, helpfully.

'Oh, heavens no, I wouldn't say that. Just that, well, they only married last year, so . . .'

'Quite. Couldn't stick him myself. But luckily he didn't play bridge, so we didn't see much of him. Nance usually came on her tod. Ah, darling, Dan's here.' My mother materialized in a fresh floral dress; she always changed for the evening, but she'd forgotten to do some buttons up. I darted across to help her. 'Got some rather bad news. Archie's little fall knocked him out for good, I'm afraid.'

'Oh.' Her hand went to her mouth. 'Oh, poor Nance. How is she?'

'Well, she's not great, obviously,' Dan said soberly. 'And I wondered . . .'

'Oh! Oh yes, of course. I'll come. Wait a tick, I'll get my bag. Just pop up and do my hair. Wait there, Dan.'

'Drink, dear boy?' asked my father, as we went through to the sitting room and I surreptitiously ruffled my flat hair.

'It's a bit early actually, Henry, and I've got to drive back.'

'Oh yes, of course. Don't mind if I do? It's the shock, you know.' He made for the whisky decanter on the sideboard.

'Not at all.'

'Luce?'

'Not yet, Dad. Um, Dad, d'you think Mum will be all right? Won't she be very upset? Should I go with her?'

He looked surprised. 'Heavens, no, your mother thrives on drama, wouldn't miss it for the world. And Nancy,' he glanced at Dan, 'won't be exactly . . . devastated . . . ?' he ventured cautiously.

'Indeed not,' agreed Dan. 'I was stretching the truth when I said she wasn't great, she's just a bit shaken. But even she'd come to realize he was getting through her savings at an alarming rate. But hey, what can you do? It's her money, and I think they had a few laughs.'

I looked at him, liking him for that. In my opinion, it was entirely up to elderly people what they did with their money and I could sometimes get cross with Helena

149

when she wanted to talk to Mum and Dad about power of attorney and what they should do with their savings. It only made Dad tight-lipped and Mum anxious, and I knew she sort of meant 'so there's more when you go', and I knew Dad sort of knew too. So this was refreshing.

'He was wearing a sombrero when they found him,' Dan told us.

'Good God. Why?'

'That's what he'd bought from Lock's.'

'Christ. Bit odd. Not quite like other budgerigars, was he?'

'Not entirely. He thought he and Mum were going to Mexico for Christmas, and let's face it, Archie could barely get to Waitrose. Ah. Cecily.' He smiled kindly as my mother appeared with a great deal of make-up on, clutching her handbag and looking rather over-excited. 'You look splendid.'

'Do you want me to come with you?' I asked her, as we walked them to the door.

'Not a bit of it. Nance will want to tell all, which she can't do with you there. And, of course, she really *can* tell all, now that ... well. Also, we'll need to plan the funeral.'

'Tell me about it.' Dan rolled his eyes. 'She's already chosen the hymns.'

'And flowers, of course.' My mother was bustling outside excitedly now. 'Quite large displays, I should think, in that church. It's so dreary.'

'Easy, Mum. He's barely cold.' Although I couldn't

help feeling a frisson of guilt as I reprimanded her, for obvious, personal reasons.

'I hear you lost your own husband. I'm sorry,' Dan spookily echoed my thoughts, albeit along different lines, and I went bright red and couldn't look at anyone. But then neither could my parents, and since Mum told Nance everything, Dan no doubt knew the subtext, but because we were English, the motions still had to be gone through.

'Thank you,' I muttered in response. 'I'll come and get her,' I told him firmly, as my mother hurried around to the passenger side of his car.

He turned. 'Oh, there's no need—'

'No, I'd like to. In about an hour, so she doesn't get too tired, and comes back to eat,' I said quietly, out of Mum's earshot. My father was opening the door and helping her in.

'Actually, yes, good plan,' he said, equally sotto voce, his face clearing. Nance drank more than Mum, if it was possible. We met each other's eyes and communed silently, both knowing exactly what we were talking about.

As Dad and I went back inside and shut the front door, it reminded me of shuttling young children backwards and forwards: not wanting them back too late, too over-tired, too teary. It also occurred to me, as I went thoughtfully back to the sitting room with my father, that annoyingly, for once, Helena had not been wrong. Dan was rather attractive.

When I went to collect my mother later, mysteriously

I'd deemed it appropriate to switch my attentions to the bathroom rather than the kitchen. I'd scrubbed it to within an inch of its life, then myself. I'd also put on a clean pair of jeans, a rather attractive smocked top I'd bought in the Whistles sale, and washed my hair. Their house was only ten minutes away and I remembered the way from years ago: down this windy lane, then that one . . . right at the next, across the junction, and then right at the next sharp bend.

As I crunched up the manicured gravel drive so unlike our own, to the imposing Georgian façade, I wondered why Dan and I hadn't overlapped much during our childhoods. Probably because he'd been away at school when I was little and was the eldest of three brothers, the youngest of whom was my age. Also, Helena and I tended to only deign to show up with friends of our parents when there were girls of our age present, like the Dugdales or the Frobishers, and by the time we all realized how short-sighted this was, we were away at university. But I did vaguely remember his youngest brother, Milo, who liked to play French skipping with me. We used to fix the elastic round a tree at one end, then round one of our legs, as the other hopped about. I reckoned Dan would be about four years older than me. I tried to remember what Helena had said about him. Single, I knew, but why? Widowed? Divorced? And did he live here on his own? Commute to London? Was he reattached? So many questions.

It was Nancy who came to the door, looking rather pale, but bright-eyed. I gave her a hug and murmured my sympathies. She smelled amazing, as I recalled she always did. Mum and Nance had modelled together, back in the days when they twirled elegantly in-house for couturiers, rather than stalking down some foreign catwalk – she was a voluble, excitable woman who Dad said was both verbally and emotionally incontinent, which made her a natural ally of my mother's. Still tall and statuesque, always exotically dressed and with a penchant for silk turbans – peacock blue today – she was a very handsome woman. I followed her embroidered kaftan as she hurried through the hall with slightly too much alacrity, but then, as if remembering, her gait slowed and she bowed her head tragically. I suppressed a smile as I followed her in.

In her pale yellow sitting room, Nance resumed her spot on the heavily indented sofa cushions beside my mother. A box of chocolates sat between them, they had a drink apiece, and a box of tissues which didn't look terribly used. I deliberately didn't sit.

'Okey doke, Mum, let's go.' I turned sympathetically to her friend. 'Nancy's had a very difficult day. I think she needs some supper and an early night,' I said gently.

'Oh no, have a little drink, Luce,' insisted my mother. 'Just a small one.'

'No, I really think we should be away.'

'Oh, *do* stay, Lucy,' urged Nancy. 'Dan will be back in a mo, he's only gone to run the vicar home. And he was so pleased to see you today.'

I found myself sitting smartly in a yellow armchair opposite. 'The vicar's called already? That's nice of him.'

'Her,' said Nance. She glanced guiltily at my mother. 'Which of course is lovely, but I will rather miss our dear Reverend Hunter, who retired last year. For the funeral, I mean. He was so tall and good-looking, and with that shock of pure white hair – I honestly thought he *was* God.' She put a hand to her heart and went a bit misty eyed.

'Me too,' agreed Mum vehemently. 'Whereas Curate Leanne—'

'I'm sure will do brilliantly,' I said firmly, before they could get going on some massively uncomfortable character assassination based on gender and age and which I was already familiar with. And anyway, luckily Dan had appeared.

'Oh, hello again,' he beamed, breezing in smelling of fresh air and giving me, I noticed, an appreciative second glance, hopefully on account of the clean hair and spot of lippy. 'I hoped I'd catch you before you whisked Cecily away. She's been telling me what a trooper you've been since you've arrived.'

I glanced at my mother in surprise, aware that, thus far, I'd had mostly complaints.

'We do appreciate it, darling. Even if we appear to grumble,' she said sheepishly.

'And actually, your parents were the only ones who *didn't* have some help,' Nancy said, slightly accusingly. 'The Frobishers have got Camilla, and the Dugdales are now in Natasha's barn, and of course, I'm *so* lucky to have Dan.' She beamed at her son who raised his eyebrows and grimaced at me as he took a seat.

'Short straw, I'm afraid. Toby and Jilly are in North-umberland, and Milo's buggered off to the States with his hotshot lawyer husband. And now that Claire's bug-gered off too . . .'

Oh yes, I remembered now. His wife left. With her personal trainer. No – her *daughter*'s personal trainer.

'I'm sorry,' I said politely, echoing his own words earlier, about Michael.

'Dan's not, are you, darling?' piped up Nancy. 'She was frightfully selfish, and if she wasn't thinking about what she put into her body, she was thinking about what shapes to twist it into. Yoga and what have you. Poor old Dan barely got a look in. Now she and her toy boy instructor can self-obsess to their hearts' content.'

'Well, there are always two sides, Mum,' Dan said uncomfortably.

'And the children?' I asked, moving quickly on and ignoring Nancy's opening mouth. 'They're well?'

'Yes, very. Both in London. Tabby's just got married and Clem's probably about to. And I can work from home, so I've let the London house.'

'So have I,' I said in surprise. 'For similar reasons, actually. Well, sort of.' I suddenly realized Mum and Nancy were trying not to smile like pussycats and were being very quiet, for them. Almost purring. I sat up straight, realizing I'd fallen right into a trap.

'Right, come on, Mum, we're off.' I got to my feet, and so, reluctantly, did my mother. I crossed to the sofa; gave her a hand. Then I bent and gave Nancy a hug and told her not to move. I shepherded my mother out of the pretty yellow sitting room, followed by Dan. I couldn't really look at him as we walked to the door, but then, I couldn't really avoid it as I wrestled with the high brass knob: it was stiff. He came to my rescue.

'Here, let me.' He reached up and I removed my hand quickly, lest his should touch mine. I couldn't avoid his eyes, though, which were smiley and kind, and something else: weary, perhaps, with the knowledge that our mothers were collectively being more unhelpful than they could imagine. He shrugged despairingly, clearly not one to dissemble, and I grinned back in recognition. Then I bid him goodbye.

'You're very quiet,' said my mother when we were almost home. 'What are you thinking? He's very nice, isn't he?'

'He is, but I wasn't thinking that.' I turned into the drive and pulled up in front of the house. I turned to her. 'I was wondering how on earth I'd managed to revert to my adolescent self quite so seamlessly, with you and your friends organizing my social life and you taking centre stage as Mrs Bennett.'

My mother grinned, and it must have been a relief: she'd been sitting on it for ages. 'Well, you barely had an adolescence, if you remember. Wouldn't *let* me organize it, as Helena did hers, if you recall. You were determined to go it alone, and got it disastrously wrong, if you don't mind my saying so. So you can hardly object if I have a little go now.'

She cast me a triumphant glance and then got out of the car all on her own, without me having to go round and help. She shut her door with a flourish and started up the drive to the porch well ahead of me, but then I had banned high heels and found her some very acceptable low pumps, which at least allowed her to walk. Nonetheless, she had a new buoyancy about her, I decided, as I got out myself and closed my door. As if she was very much looking forward to her home-made chicken pie and a spot of cheese, and might even stay up to watch the news in front of the fire I'd laid, before going to bed in the fresh sheets I'd changed for her today. Well, bully for her, I thought, as I followed her up the gravel drive, realizing that it was me, for a change, who was exhausted, and in need of an early night.

13

A few days passed. My parents and I settled into a comfortable routine of shopping in the morning – my mother liked to come with me – and ticking off any long-avoided jobs in the afternoon. Bills that could no longer be settled by cheque and that, due to their ignorance of online banking, had been quietly ignored, were paid. The boiler was serviced. Wood for the fire was ordered so we didn't have to chop our own, and the gutters were cleared by a local tradesman: two things which I was horrified to learn my father had still been doing until relatively recently. They both took trips to specialists at the local hospital to confirm their minor operations and, as a result, I think, became less anxious (my mother) and less defensive (my father).

I'd organized some computer lessons for both of them, and had driven them into town for the first of many sessions, somehow knowing such instruction, like driving lessons in my youth, would be better not coming from a family member. Dad was reasonably adept in that he could at least email; my mother was a complete beginner, although I knew that once she got the hang of it – especially once she could flaming well see – she'd enjoy emailing friends and texting her grandchildren. Online shopping had been a complete revelation to both of them, and the morning we all sat down to place an Ocado order and then, hey presto, it arrived, was like the annunciation at Pope's Farm. I knew this would indeed be their saviour one day – one day being some unspecified date when I would no longer be with them and they'd be going it alone, which we all spoke of as if it would definitely happen, but all quietly knew it might not. My only slight qualm came when my mother asked me if I thought ordering an entire twelve-piece dinner service in a terribly attractive lotus leaf pattern, which she'd seen half-price on some dodgy American site, was an extravagance at her age. I assured her it most definitely was, wondering what monster I'd unleashed.

Mrs Cummings paid a visit, on the pretext of collecting for the parish magazine. She asked if the noises she'd heard last night had been ones of distress? Mum and I had been upstairs in her bedroom trying on her many dresses in the hope that some might fit me and they'd have another life – we're talking Dior and Chloé here. Not a chance with the dresses. I couldn't get them past my hips and we decided even Helena, who was whippet thin, might struggle. But Mum had insisted I force myself into one of the coats, which was beautiful quality. It was so skin-tight my arms stuck out at ninety degrees like a windmill, or a teenager whose mother insists the blazer worn in reception still fits, and I'd then been unable to extract myself. Dad had had to come up to pull me free as my mother collapsed in a heap on the bed. Hilarity, I'd told Mrs Cummings, as her eyes darted past me, taking in everything from the recently hoovered stairs and the washed parquet floor, to the smell of polish still in the air from the dresser. She left, looking disappointed.

And then, one morning, I awoke to a text from Amanda.

'Have decided to have a memorial service for Michael. Ned has sweetly agreed to take it.'

I stared at my phone. It was as if I'd been turned to stone. I'd been awake for ten minutes before I'd reached for my mobile and had been enjoying wallowing in the best spare room, a bedroom I'd known well as a girl but never slept in. My own bedroom was small, with a single bed, and since it was clearly going to be a while before I could move to the cottage, it had been unilaterally decided that I'd sleep in this much larger room, where there was a double bed and an en suite bathroom. In my youth I'd occasionally popped in to help Mum change the sheets, put flowers in a vase for a visitor, or borrow a book from the rather interesting guest bookcase, but had never had the pleasure of staying in here myself. I wondered, as I admired the spriggy Colefax wallpaper and the thick creamy curtains, not nearly as tired as the rest of the house on account of being used less, if this sort of look would work in the cottage? Or whether to go all pale wood, white walls and clean lines? I reached for my mobile to have a look at room set ideas on Pinterest, and suddenly all frivolous decorative notions turned to dust.

My mouth went dry. I read it again and shut my eyes. All at once I was back in my old life, transported to the horror of so many long and frightened years. Why? Why couldn't I just escape? Why did I have to be dragged back to All That when yes, all right, returning to the womb had not been exactly brave, but had at least proved to be busy, amusing and hopefully useful, and had totally taken my mind off my past. I hated Amanda. I just hated her. I also wondered if she'd ever go away. I sat up on my pillows and rang Ned.

'Mum.'

'Hi, darling. I've just had a message from Amanda. Apparently you said you'd take a memorial service for Dad.'

'Eh? No, she sent me a text saying she was thinking of planning one and that she was talking to you. I assumed the two of you had spoken. I was surprised you were agreeing to it, actually. I was going to ring you, but I only got the text late last night.'

I shut my eyes, feeling the familiar fury about being lied to and manipulated, which almost made me tremble. The audacity of these people: of this brother and sister act. The sheer mendacity and outrageousness. I would not have it, I wouldn't. Then the fear.

'Can I say no? Is it up to me?'

'Well, you can certainly say you don't want it.'

'I'll ring her,' I said, trying to keep the emotion from my voice.

'No, don't, Mum,' he said gently. 'I'll do it. I'll pop round and see her. Don't you get involved.'

'Really?' I felt a great wave of relief flood through me. 'Would you, Ned? It's just . . .' I fought back something: tears even, perhaps; certainly a large lump in my throat.

'Of course.'

I busied myself even more than usual that day, cleaning rooms as yet untackled. Helena's old bedroom, the boot room where Hector slept, the utility room. I concentrated on one at a time, doing each one methodically and thoroughly. I made a few puddings for the freezer because that was what my mother really loved, but made sure they were full of fruit, or eggs, or a bit of stodge, like bread and butter pudding. Having dropped my mother off at the chiropodist in the afternoon, since both she and my father were unable to cut her toenails – and I have to say, I'd felt a bit queasy when I'd looked – I came back and met a cheerful team of builders who gave me a reasonable quote and timescale for the bungalow. I'd just been to collect Mum when my phone rang. Without thinking, I popped it on hands-free speaker phone. It was Ned. He sounded grim.

'She's already arranged it.'

I gasped. 'I don't believe it.'

'Promise you. Invites have gone out already. Church is booked. Flowers ordered. She must have done it ages ago.'

I shut my eyes. Luckily I was at some red lights. I opened them as they went green. Took a deep breath.

'Is there anything we can do?'

'Well, she won't listen to me. Imo's hopping mad – as you know, she flew back yesterday. I won't be able to stop her storming round. Amanda says she'll have it with or without us, though.'

'I'll go and see her,' I said, seething. 'I'm the only one who can put a stop to this.'

'Or maybe just go along with it?' he said despairingly. 'Ned . . .'

'I know. I don't want to either. It's just . . . Amanda is almost, like, possessed.'

'I know.' And it was how Michael could get, too. Possessed was a good word, particularly coming from a vicar.

We said goodbye and my mother looked at me. Her face was a bit crumpled: scared. 'What is it?' she asked.

'Amanda wants a memorial service.'

She didn't speak. But her face, like my son's voice, made me realize how much he had woefully affected everyone's life: how even though I'd tried to limit the damage as much as I could, he had spread, insidiously, into everyone I loved and infected them with fear too. She leaned across and patted my hand. I gulped and we drove silently on, both quietly depressed.

My daughter, however, was made of sterner stuff. That evening, she rang. She was incandescent on the phone.

'She slammed the fucking door in my face!' she fumed, as I was dishing out the bread and butter pudding. 'I went round to tell her what I thought of her glorifying a man who'd bullied his wife and children for years and she screamed in my face that it was none of my business. She hustled me – literally, hustled me, as in shoved – down the hall, called me a heartless bitch and slammed the door on my foot!'

'I'll go,' I told her. 'I'm the only one she'll listen to. Who she'll have to listen to.'

'And I'll come with you.'

'No. Thank you, darling, but I think I'll be better alone.'

She was quiet. 'Don't go to her house,' she said softly, and I could tell she'd had a really horrible experience. 'Meet her somewhere public. And tell me and Ned where you're going.'

I paused. Went cold. 'OK.'

My parents, as a rule, went to bed early. Really early, at about nine thirty – making it to the news was a big night out – which Camilla Frobisher, who'd sweetly telephoned to see how I was getting on, and to arrange a coffee, had caustically told me was the only silver lining. When they'd gone up, comparatively sober these days, just the one bottle of wine between the three of us at supper and with a great deal more food inside them, I sat in front of *Newsnight*: not listening, not seeing anything. Just thinking. Remembering. The time he took Imo's phone from her bag and erased all the contacts he didn't know. When he rang her boss and told him she was thinking of leaving. The times he'd wondered aloud if I'd meant to drive so fast across that crossroads? Send that motorbike flying? If actually, there was no such thing as accidents, that everything was premeditated. The time he'd found a photo of Ned and a friend, Sam, their arms linked, and—

My mobile made me jump. It was a number I didn't recognize. For one ridiculous moment, because of where

I'd been, I wondered if it was Michael. Then I came to. Picked it up. My voice, when I said hello, was almost a whisper.

'Hello, Lucy?' said a much clearer, male voice on the other end.

I cleared my throat, rattled. 'Yes?'

'You sound miles away. It's Dan.'

'Oh. Hi, Dan.' I rallied. Well, a bit. Not really. He was from my new, pleasant life, that I couldn't really live any more.

'Sorry, I've just realized how late it is. I've been away and only just got back.'

'It's fine.'

'I was just wondering, seeing as we both seem to be in the same boat on the geriatric parent front, whether you'd like a night off?'

'Sorry?' I wasn't firing on all cylinders.

'Pub supper? Give them the slip? Leave them in front of beans on toast and *Holby City* one night?'

'Oh. I see. Um . . . yes, that would be lovely.'

'OK.' He sounded surprised at my lukewarm enthusiasm. 'Tomorrow any good?'

'Tomorrow I think I'm going to London.'

He was quiet. I hadn't suggested another day.

'Friday?' he said tentatively.

'Yes, Friday,' I managed. There was a pause.

'You all right?'

It was the kindness in his voice that almost made me choke. Something I was so very unused to in a man, unless it was my son, or my father. I couldn't speak for a moment: felt my eyes fill with tears which spilled silently down my cheeks. 'Yes,' I managed to gasp. 'I'm fine. See you Friday.' And then I put the phone down and wept.

The following day I drove to London, hands clenched on the wheel, teeth gritted. I knew I had to get this over with and that, if I left it even a day, it would hang over me like the cloak of doom. Ridiculous, I told myself, that it had had such an effect on me. A night's sleep – well, four hours, I'd tossed and turned for much of it – and a fresh dawn had assured me that I was being faintly foolish, here. Amanda couldn't go ahead without our consent, surely, and even if she did, so what? So what if she had her stupid, pompous service and we weren't there? Oddly, though, the ramifications of that, for me in particular, had me gripping the wheel even tighter as my eyes grew huge with a different fear. A glance in the rear-view mirror told me that my face was very pasty and slightly sweaty, too. I breathed from the diaphragm, like Helena told me she did before she went into the boardroom to present to a client, and turned on Radio 2, hoping for some cheerful, sing-along music. 'Amarillo' came on, but even the thought of Peter Kay's face failed to lift me.

I'd left my parents clearly rather excited at the prospect of a day without me. Mum had even clasped her hands with glee.

'We'll have the Millers round,' she said to Dad. 'Hetty rang me yesterday, to see if we were free.'

'Why can't you have them when I'm here?' I asked.

166

'Oh, we can, of course, darling, but – you know.'

Without me they could raid the drinks cupboard and have a lot more fun. I felt like a jailer. And rather sad, actually. I certainly didn't want to spoil their fun.

'She just means we have to be a bit careful who we have with the Millers. Hetty's incontinent and doesn't always make it, and Bertie gets a bit muddled and inappropriate with the young. He can be inclined to be saucy.'

'Right. Do I count as young?'

'Oh Lord, yes. Even your mother does, and she doesn't mind at all.'

Hence her skippy excitement. A saucy afternoon with flirty Bertie and without her flinty-eyed daughter watching her flutter her eyelids and chuck it down her neck.

'But we'll ask the Ashleys with them,' Dad said decisively and I saw Mum's face drop. 'Joan missed her vocation as a Lieutenant Colonel and keeps us all in check, but we suffer her for Roger.'

'*Love* Roger,' agreed Mum, brightening again and bustling to get a fish pie I'd made out of the fridge, whilst my father hastened as much as he could on his much improved, but still healing legs, to open the cellar door in the hall. But I strode past him.

'One case or two?' I asked meaningfully, eyeing him beadily at the top of the horrifically steep stone steps he was planning to descend. Mum had quietly admitted that he'd fallen down the last few once, and it was on that basis that I'd banned it, planning to move a selection of cases up to the scullery. In fact I'd planned to do that today.

'Oh no, darling, just a couple of bottles of the Merlot, if you wouldn't mind,' he said, chastened. And then when I was down there: 'Actually, make it three? And a bottle of the Yquem, perhaps?'

I brought them up and put them on the side in the kitchen. 'Just make sure she *eats*,' I said, eyeing my mother, in full earshot.

'Who's she, the cat's mother?' she trilled happily, fluttering to open the napkin drawer.

'No, the impossible teenager,' I said grimly, getting a trifle out of the freezer to defrost, and then leaving them to it, off to embark on my own, far less enviable day.

As I beetled up the M4, I checked my face again. My mouth seemed to have all but disappeared, and I wished with all my heart I was with my irresponsible, kind parents, doling out fish pie to my mother, keeping an eye on Dad as he tottered to the fridge – now that his legs were healing he refused to use his stick – and staying in that warm, nest-like excuse of a life, forever.

I'd arranged to meet Amanda in Brinkley's in Hollywood Road, round the corner from her flat in Tregunter Road. It was a bustling, upmarket bistro, full of thrusting young executives. I'd deliberately suggested somewhere on her doorstep in the hope that she'd like to be allowed back in, which would prevent her from breaking a plate of spaghetti on my head. We weren't due to meet until one o'clock, though. I glanced at my watch. Ten forty-five. Before then, I was popping home, because Josh had emailed me a few days ago to say that, try as he might, he couldn't get the heating to work without some weird ticking noise accompanying it. It was driving him mad, and did I have any suggestions? I did, a plumber, but I knew that would be expensive and I'd have to pay, so I told him to take it off the timer. He emailed back to say he'd tried that and the ticking prevailed. Did I have any other ideas? Before he installed a brand-new radiator in the sitting room and sent me the bill? I'd told him I'd pop by when I was next up, and thus, seething slightly, but knowing my eccentric plumbing needed the experienced touch, I drove round to my house. It felt mighty peculiar as I turned into my old road, but luckily, the momentum of having an annoying tenant was enough to keep me from dwelling on worse.

He came to the door – which naturally was weird, as I'd only ever put a key in before and opened it myself – barefoot in jeans. He wore a crumpled white shirt which hung loose, and a rather surprised expression on his face.

'Oh. Right. Yes, of course. Sorry, I was working. I completely forgot the time.'

'No lectures today?' I asked, as he stood aside to let me in.

'Reading week, as it's euphemistically called. It's actually a bit of downtime for the freshers to recover from their mid-term hangovers.'

I smiled. 'Oh yes, I remember. No sooner have they gone, than suddenly they reappear again in a heap. Oh, golly. You've changed it around.'

I'd stopped. He'd been leading me down to the

kitchen, but I'd obviously glanced into the sitting room en route. He'd moved the dining table into the bay window, and the sofas to the back. Switched the whole thing around.

'Problem?'

'No, not at all. I like it, actually. Don't know why I didn't think of that before.'

'Well, it works for me because I work in the window where it gets the most light.'

'Oh, right. Not in the study?'

He made a face. 'Bit gloomy.'

He was right, it was. The back of the house faced north. And the more I looked around, the more I liked what I saw. He'd hung his own pictures, which were modern and huge and cheerful, most unlike the gloomy Victorian oils in heavy gilt frames Michael favoured, and he'd flung colourful throws over the sofas and even the table. His papers and files were spread chaotically over a lovely deep red, fringed paisley shawl. The whole house, even the kitchen – the sofa had a cream linen throw – looked completely different and I was pleased. I told him so.

'Oh really? I rather imagined you liked it the way it was since you'd clearly had it that way for years.'

'My husband didn't like change. He came from the sort of family who only decorate once in a generation.'

'Ah, OK. Some grand, baronial pile in Scotland?'

'No, a mock Tudor in Esher, I think. He just had delusions of grandeur.' Josh glanced at me in surprise. There it was again, that unfiltered thought. 'Sorry. I must stop speaking ill of the dead. It's a habit I've rather got into and it's very unattractive. Lead me to the ticking radiator.'

He opened the cupboard door to the boiler above the sink and turned on the heating. We listened. In a few moments, things began to get a bit ticky, as I knew from experience they would as it revved up, but also, if I turned it off, then quickly turned it on again, at length it would all calm down.

'See?' he told me triumphantly.

'Yes, but give it a moment. Or even a few minutes. It usually stops.'

'Not in my experience, but coffee? While we wait?' He was going towards an attractive blue fifties-style kettle. Brown feet, I noticed. Tanned.

'Please.' And that did feel weird. Someone making me a coffee in my own kitchen. I perched on a stool.

'I do that too,' he said, suddenly. 'Speak ill of the departed.'

I looked at him. 'Oh – you mean . . . ?'

'Agathe. I try not to, but it's so close to the surface, I sometimes can't help it. And weirdly, it feels dishonest not to, even though it's disloyal and people think badly of you, if you know what I mean.'

'I do.'

'I'd like to say we went our own amicable ways, but we didn't. She buggered off with my best friend and I can't forgive her for that.'

'No. Nor him, I imagine.'

'Nor him.'

'So you lost both of them.'

He shrugged. 'I suppose. But I hate them both any-way, so it's fine.'

'I'm sure you don't really,' I said gently.

'Oh, I do. When you realize it's been going on for years and that every single memory you have has been compromised, it is possible to hate, which is a blessing. I wouldn't want to be moping around feeling sad.'

'True,' I agreed. 'I'd hate to feel sad, and I don't. I feel . . .'

'Liberated?'

I blinked. He was smiling, eyes crinkling. Hair dark and rumpled. Specs on the counter as he made coffee. Quite handsome.

'Yes. Definitely. Until I'm reminded of him again, then I sink. He was a bully,' I told him helpfully.

'Ah.' He passed me a mug. 'And why should you be reminded of him?'

I told him about Amanda and the memorial service. I don't know why I did, but on the other hand, why not? It was the only thing on my mind and I'd always worn my heart on my sleeve. I wasn't about to stop now, just because I didn't know him. In fact it was eas-ier, not knowing him. Like talking to a hairdresser. Which was perhaps why he'd talked candidly to me. He listened.

'Oh no, you don't have to do that. You're the wife.'

'Really? I mean – legally, or something?' I said hopefully.

'Well, I don't know about legally, but if neither you

nor the children want it, I don't see how she can force your hand.'

'Watch her,' I said grimly, sinking into my coffee.

He was observing me. 'Another bully?'

'Runs in the family,' I muttered.

He nodded. 'Well, just — hold your nerve. Tell her your memories are unhappy and you don't want to glorify him.'

I almost reached for a pen in my bag to jot it down, but managed not to. 'Yes. Yes, I will. Anything else?' I asked anxiously.

He smiled. 'Well, I didn't know him. But was he very religious?'

'God, no. Not in the least.'

'Well then, say he'd have hated it. Went against all his principles, or something. Good heavens, you're right, it has gone off.' He cocked his head and listened. Silence.

'It does. But if I'm honest, it's more like fifteen minutes than five, and if I'm totally honest, one in about a dozen times it doesn't. The trick is to turn it on and off quickly, then put the radio on loud, or have a bath. By the time you realize it's irritating and go to switch it off — the ticking has stopped. Usually. Otherwise keep the radio on.'

'Right. I'll remember that. I haven't needed it up to now since it's been so warm but this cold snap—' His mobile rang on the counter. He glanced at it. 'Oh, sorry. I need to take this.' He picked it up and disappeared into the sitting room telling, presumably, a student on the other end that he'd just grab their essay and have a look.

However, he didn't reappear and I heard him chatting in the next room. I drank my coffee. It occurred to me that he was far more pleasant than when I'd first met him. And he'd been so open. I wondered if he'd mellowed because he was away from the hurt of his family. Whatever he said about hate, that must have caused terrible pain. His glasses were sitting on the counter where he'd left them and, on an impulse, I put them on. Definitely very squiffy making. Definitely not clear glass. I only just got away with taking them off when he reappeared. He'd seen me replace them on the counter though, and looked surprised.

'Oh, my son, Ned, has the same ones,' I explained. 'Only he's lost them. I was just – just looking to see what make they are.'

'Oh. Right.' He looked unconvinced.

'Anyway,' I drained my mug, 'I must be away. And thanks for the – you know. Words of wisdom. I'm off to put them into practice.'

He nodded and walked me to the door. But as I left and was driving off down the road I found, rather to my relief, that I wasn't thinking about what I was going to say to my sister-in-law. I was wondering instead what Josh's best friend had been like and how on earth Agathe had imagined he was a better option. He must have been quite something.

14

In the event, obviously, I didn't tell Amanda where she could get off. Or where she could stick her memorial service. Or in any way hold my nerve or defend my corner. She won hands down. She was ready for me, naturally. Armed and dangerous, with a half-drunk bottle of Chablis and a whole heap of bitterness. I'd parked in Tregunter Road, where I knew there to be meters, and walked, too casually in retrospect, still fresh from my not unpleasant morning, down the expensive street where she lived. The pavements were squeaky with money and I marvelled, quietly, at being back here. Tall, white stucco mansions, one of which housed the top-floor flat in which she lived, were fronted by immaculate gardens encased with black iron railings. Filipino house-keepers were watering pots full of hyacinths and spring bedding, and one emerged with a baby in a pram. I turned the corner and walked down Hollywood Road towards the smart, bustling restaurant, joining a few people arriving at the door, wrapped up in coats and scarves against this sudden dip in temperature, rubbing their hands cheerfully and commenting on it. I joined in the discussion, lulled by a sweet French woman's smile and her expression of horror at the unpredictability of the British weather.

I saw her first. She was poised at a corner table in the window, her back to the wall. I made my way across with a nervous smile. She looked incredibly glamorous as she always did: stick-thin, her hair very blonde and smooth, freshly blown dry by someone else's hand, and tucked under her chin, like a helmet. She was wearing a beautiful dusky pink tailored jacket, a silky cream shirt, and lots of expensive jewellery. Her lips were thin but thick with lipstick. She extended them in a smile and gave a dinky little wave of her fingers in a faux friendly gesture, but I knew better. It was all in the eyes. They were over-bright and glittering. She meant business. This was her moment. Amanda didn't have a job because she didn't have to work, and aside from lunches with other rich women, she had plenty of leisure time. The moment I saw her face I realized she'd been thinking this through for weeks and that I was woefully under-prepared.

As soon as I'd sat down and we'd exchanged a few pleasantries, before I'd even taken a sip of water or looked at the menu, she started. Her back straightened, she clasped her hands in front of her and spoke crisply and fluently as if I was at an interview. She even thanked me for coming. Then she told me, in no uncertain terms, exactly where the service was going to be: St Luke's, Chelsea; what the order of service was – she produced, not a draft, but a creamy stiff original from her bag; who was doing the readings; and who was doing the flowers (Lady up-your-bottom-someone she'd been at school with).

'Ned won't read,' I said quickly, when I saw his name

by one of the planned readings, which I knew immediately was a big mistake, because I'd fallen into her trap.

'Oh well, never mind. I'll ask a friend to do it,' she said sweetly, whipping the order of service card back from my hands. I realized I'd spoken as if it were already happening.

'I'm afraid none of us will come,' I said firmly. 'We don't want it, Amanda.'

Her over-stretched brow furrowed as much as it was capable. 'Well, how strange. Don't you think that will look rather odd? As if you're pleased he's dead or something?'

My breathing became a bit shallow. 'Well no, of course we're not pleased he's dead—'

'No, I didn't say that, I said it might *look* that way. But since you mention it, Lucy, *are* you pleased he's dead?'

'No, of course not!' I said, flustered, reaching for my wine glass. She'd already poured us both a glass, and although as a rule I don't drink at lunchtime, for once I was grateful. I took a swig.

She made a thoughtful face. 'It's just I haven't quite glimpsed you as the grieving widow yet. No tears at the funeral, from any of you, and I couldn't control myself. Sobbed all the way through. Now shock I understand, but that sort of numbness usually passes and gives way to terrible, searing agony, a realization of a huge void that can never be filled. A great aching chasm, anger even, as you realize the only man you've ever loved is never coming back, hm?' She put her head on one side, quizzically. 'Oh, scallops, please. With a small green salad.' This to the waitress, who was poised beside us.

'Um, the same, please,' I muttered, without looking at the menu.

'But you don't seem to be in that place at all. At first, I thought you couldn't bear to be in the house in London because there were too many fond memories. But now I realize you left because you couldn't wait to start a new life. Couldn't wait to rid yourself of all traces of my poor darling brother who, let's face it, was barely cold.'

'Amanda . . .'

Her voice was not raised but it had a horrible shrillness to it. The couple at the next table had already glanced across and taken in her clenched face and grim, set mouth. Her hand was shaking as she reached for her glass and knocked back half of it. It was then I registered that the bottle was half empty. Imo was right, I shouldn't have come.

'In fact, I've never seen such a merry widow. You couldn't wait to get a nice fat wodge of rent from my brother's house – a house that, by rights, incidentally, should probably belong to me, because it was bought with my parents' money. And which you'll no doubt sell for a fortune the moment the market moves, or when you snare a new man, which is doubtless what you fully intend to do under the guise of,' she made quotation marks in the air, 'Looking After Your Parents. In such a delightful, dutiful, caring way.'

I felt my blood rise. 'I *am* looking after my parents. And actually, Amanda, Michael bought the house but contributed nothing to the running of it. You know as well as I do, a weekly column in a small literary magazine brought in barely any money at all, whereas—'

'Oh, whereas *you*, you had your sparkling literary career, which you lauded over him, knowing he was the *real* writer in the family. The *real* wordsmith. But, oh no, *you*, with your tawdry, tuppenny-ha'penny career, churning out the same old rubbish. The same tired old detective inspector Suzie Woozie—'

I got to my feet. 'I don't have to listen to this.' I realized I was trembling. Her hand flew out and she seized my wrist.

'Sit,' she hissed. 'I haven't got to the best part yet.'

She had me in a vice-like grip; to shake her off would have been difficult. It would have caused a scene. Already the young couple beside us had paused in their meal. The girl, facing me, looked concerned. I sat, slowly. Amanda kept her grip on my wrist, though. Our scallops arrived. She had to release me. To run would have been cowardly; plus, I wasn't at all sure she wouldn't lunge after me. Another waitress appeared with the salads, removed the olives, and replaced them with a bread basket. She topped up the water glasses. It gave us both a moment to compose ourselves. To breathe. My heart was beating fast, though. Amanda still looked unhinged and wild-eyed. She poured herself more wine with a shaking hand. I sipped my water instead.

'The thing is,' she began, and her face suddenly buckled. I realized she was on the verge of tears. 'The thing is, Michael was all I had. Literally all I had in the world.

After our parents . . .' She fought for composure and I screamed inside.

Here we go again. I wasn't sure which was worse, the naked aggression or the self-pity. How many years had I sat and listened, first with horror and sadness, then compassion, then, increasingly, with frustration, to what was about to pour forth? About the two lonely, lost orphans who only had each other. And of course it was dreadful, but it was also hundreds of years ago, and many people had experienced similar tragedies and somehow overcome them, and gone on to live decent, fulfilled lives. And whilst it would always be with them, they hadn't let it define them. Amanda had. And always would, until she died. She would always be Orphan Annie.

I listened and nodded and looked sympathetic and picked at my scallops which were slippery and slimy. Like her, I thought, as I passed her a napkin. Tears were coursing down her face. Manipulative. Always. And of course she needed professional help, but trust me, she had it in spades. It was all she did with her life. Grief counsellor on Monday. CBT on Tuesday. Group therapy at the Priory on alternate Fridays. She needed to get *on*. I gripped my fork as I picked at my salad, wondering when I could leave.

'And now Michael's gone too, so I'm totally alone.'

'But you have friends, surely,' I said. I couldn't even force my voice to be kind. Michael and Amanda had barely been in touch; this version of their relationship was simply *not true*, and I would not collude with it. *I* went round, *I* saw her, because my husband wouldn't.

He couldn't bear her. *I* insisted she come for Christmas, made sure, if we were at my parents', which we nearly always were, that she came too, even though Michael would complain. *I* always insisted the children saw their Aunt Amanda. I was the one who invited her to school plays, carol concerts, even on holiday once – a complete disaster, but I'd done it. Michael had barely allowed us to leave the villa – oh, Amanda knew about her brother and to pretend otherwise was disingenuous – and Amanda got drunk every night, and told us tales of men who'd let her down. Or betrayed her. Lured by her glamour and her money and, to be fair, her brain. Amanda wasn't stupid. She could have done so much with her life. But these men soon realized what they had on their hands. A narcissist with a screw loose. And then they'd run a mile, lest they wake up in bed, as one poor chap did, being attacked with the heel of her stiletto shoe.

Likewise friends, even similarly rich, idle, self-obsessed ones, had not stayed the course. Amanda was incapable of talking about anyone but herself; her self-ishness knew no bounds. So any conversation would automatically be dragged back to her. My suggestion, therefore, that she could rely on a chummy network, was about the most cruel I'd ever been. I regretted it immediately. I should have let her rant on as usual. But I was so angry with myself for being here, for becoming ensnared in this mesh again . . . She stopped. Went pale.

'Friends,' she hissed. 'Oh, it's all right for you. Surrounded by family and mothers of your children's friends and Melissa across the road, plus your sister, a ready-made confidante. Have you any idea how impossible it is for someone like me to have a network like that?' Her voice rose and the girl on the next table looked alarmed again. 'Have you? And now that you've taken Michael from me, now that you've taken my only family member—'

'Hang on,' I interrupted sharply. 'What d'you mean, I've taken him?'

'Oh, don't think I don't know. Don't think I don't know that you somehow got rid of him, Lucy.'

I gasped. Pushed my chair back.

'Don't you dare,' she breathed.

I realized she was watching me intently, like a fox stalking its prey. I had to think fast. And not run. I pulled my chair back in.

'You wanted a divorce, and he wouldn't give you one, would he? But that didn't stop you, oh no.' She lowered her voice. 'A neighbour saw something. I know because I rang the police the other day. I wanted to know how the investigation was going – after all, we've heard nothing. They couldn't tell me, of course, but they said the next-door neighbour was helping with their enquiries. Someone else told me that, too.'

'Mrs Daley? She was away.'

I saw the surprise on her face. Realized, in that moment, she was bluffing. Mrs Daley had moved in a few years ago, replacing the young couple who'd once knocked on my door in concern, late at night, but she'd been in Canada at the time of Michael's death, visiting her daughter. She'd popped round the following week with some tulips, in sympathy. I watched Amanda regroup.

'The other one,' she said quickly.

'I don't have another neighbour. They've got builders in.'

She thought wildly. 'Round the back, then.'

She'd already given herself away, but this childish 'then', this afterthought, almost a playground taunt, when she'd run out of neighbours, drove in the final nail. Nevertheless, I couldn't help my mind flying to the house behind, and Amanda saw it happen: she watched as I visualized the tall, brick back exterior, three stories high, so much taller than ours. I used to see the top-floor lights go on and the curtains close at night, as no doubt they saw . . . what could they see? I forced a smile, my heart beating.

'You're mad.'

She didn't answer me. But she started to smile. A satisfied 'got you' kind of smile. I knew she'd made it up, but her wild stab in the dark had been more accurate than she could have hoped. I'd never considered the possibility I might have been watched.

'Why so guilty, Lucy? You've gone awfully pale.' The waitress appeared and asked if we'd finished. We nodded and she cleared our plates. I waited until she'd gone, thinking fast. When I spoke, I made my voice level.

'I'm surprised you don't know about that, Amanda. About the guilt. About it being another stage of grief. After the anger. So many bereaved people feel this way, and I must admit, I'm no exception. I feel terribly guilty. Why didn't I get downstairs quicker? Interrupt the burglar sooner? Michael might still be alive if I had. And I've read about it, about how people blame themselves. It's well documented. You might even have felt it after your parents died? Wondered, perhaps, if you and Michael had been there, if it might not have happened? Maybe you'd have been in a different hotel, or at least different rooms, had the trip been in the school holidays, say?'

I watched her eyes flash back to her childhood. To her own terror of that carbon monoxide filtering through the air conditioning and she and her brother not running into their parents' room saying they felt unwell. I knew I'd hit home. Knew she'd have covered guilt with her grief counsellor many times. I licked my lips and prepared to act like I'd never acted before. I adopted a tone of kind, caring concern.

'Amanda, I'm worried about you. I'm worried that some of your therapy sessions, particularly the group ones, encourage an over-active imagination. You've been exhibiting it a lot recently. Remember when you thought Colin and Trevor, in the flat below, were plotting against you? Taking your mail? And when you thought the Amazon man was spying through your letter box? I'm wondering if you should go back to your GP. Change your medication, even?'

Oh, if she could be manipulative, I could too. And I knew that her favourite topic, herself and her complicated medical programme, was the surest way to her egotistical heart.

'There's nothing wrong with my medication,' she snapped. 'I went to Austria in January, to the Holen, and was entirely irrigated of toxins, so that everything I take now has a better chance. And don't try to—'

'The Holen Clinic?' I interrupted sharply. 'Isn't that the one that's just been discredited? By some neuroscientist from Columbia University?'

It was the detail that got her. Not entirely invented, either, I'd skimmed an article a while back.

'Columbia . . . ?'

'Yes, it was in *The Times*. Apparently, the Holen's irrigation methods are highly suspect and there's a lot of controversy about it. I knew you were a patient so I followed it up online, in the *Medical Journal*.'

'I don't read – I didn't see—'

'No, you wouldn't, because it's encrypted. You can only get access if you're registered, which a friend of mine is. Hilary, a psychologist. I asked her about it. And obviously I didn't want to worry you. But since you've mentioned it . . .'

'Could she get me the report?'

Gotcha. 'I'll ask her. I'm seeing her soon.' I know of no one called Hilary. No psychologist.

The bill arrived and I quickly got my card out, indicating to the waitress I'd like to settle it now. She disappeared for her machine.

'Yes, because the Belgravia Clinic, where I go for my irrigation in London, are also setting up in Austria and are keen for me to go there, and when I said I'd been going to the Holen for years, they did actually raise their eyebrows . . . I thought they were just touting for business. It's just so hard to believe. The Holen is *so* well established . . .'

'Believe it,' I said grimly, giving an Oscar winning performance. It helped that I'd seen the article, but let's not forget, I'm good at this. I've had plenty of practice, with Michael's women. 'Go back to the Belgravia, Amanda, and ask them exactly what their reservations are. Ask to see the chap in charge, the one you really rate—'

'Dr Kaluigui,' she said, eagerly.

'That's it, Dr Kaluigui. Ask to see him. Have a proper meeting, and say you've heard worrying reports. Presumably his new Austrian clinic will have state-of-the-art equipment?'

'Yes, and it's on the lake, too. Fabulous views. Very luxurious, apparently.'

The waitress was back. I slipped the card into her machine and punched out the number. She tore off the receipt and handed it to me.

'Well, there you are. Now I've got to fly, Amanda. I promised I'd pop in on Helena while I was up, she's got the day off. But I want you to promise me you'll go, yes? To Dr Kaluigui?' I got to my feet, simultaneously plucking my jacket from the back of my chair and slipping into it. I furrowed my brow. 'Otherwise I shall worry . . .'

'Oh, I will,' she said eagerly. 'I'll ring as soon as I get home.' She knocked back her wine and made to get up.

'No, don't rush,' I told her, putting my hand on her arm and making myself lean in and kiss her cheek, which stalled her. I sure as hell didn't want to walk with her. For her to revisit anything. 'You stay and finish that.' I nodded at the small amount left in the bottle. 'Otherwise it's a waste. But please, let me know how you get on, hm?'

I gave her a steady smile: a really worried smile. And I touched her arm again, a gesture typical of Amanda, who was very tactile. My heart was beating fast. I turned and wound my way through the tables towards the door, praying she wasn't following me. She wasn't. As I went out, down the street, I saw her, still at the table. She was pouring the remains of the wine and getting her phone out of her clutch bag.

I turned and walked quickly away, heading around the corner to where my car was parked two streets back. Before I got to it, however, I had to take a moment. Had to stop. Lean against the garden wall of a convenient mansion. I shut my eyes. My handbag was clasped to my chest and my heart was pounding. I bent my head. I felt sick. I made myself breathe. It was a while before I could raise my head, and when I did, a young chap in a suit, a Barbour over his jacket, was striding by. He did a double take when he saw my face. I believe it might have been very pale.

15

I sat for a moment in my car, my heart still racing. Then I realized I was still on her territory and she could come past at any moment. I started the car in a panic, hands fluttering, and pulled out in a blare of horns as a taxi swerved round me. As the cabbie shook his fist and swore violently out of the window, I made myself breathe, calm down: I'd narrowly missed a collision. My face, when I glanced in the rear-view mirror, was ashen. I drove on carefully, then pulled in, far beyond Amanda's house, to recover. In the glove compartment I found a toffee and sucked it, needing the sugar. There was an old bottle of water too, which I sipped. I went over the horrible, horrible lunch in my head. I was reasonably sure I'd convinced her my guilty demeanour was about wishing I could have done more to save her brother's life. I was also sure I'd diverted her with her own imaginary health issues. But had she rung the police? Quite possibly, on a daily basis even, irritating the hell out of them, but I knew from my book research they'd tell her nothing. No details from an ongoing inquiry could be disclosed in case it got in the press. So the neighbour business was bollocks. One thing she had said, though, had startled me and then made me think. About knowing I wanted a divorce. There had been times when I'd wondered what she'd heard.

About a year ago, in a moment of madness, when Michael was away in Edinburgh reviewing a play, I'd contacted a divorce lawyer. Foolish, in retrospect, because ultimately I knew I'd be unable to go through with it, but I'd been desperate at the time. Melissa had found her for me, and I'd asked if we could just speak on the phone, or face-to-face, never write anything down. No emails. She hadn't batted an eyelid, perhaps used to such a request. I'd called her from my bedroom. Imo was across from New York and, since Michael was away, was staying the night. She was working in the study. She knew nothing; I didn't want her involved. Amanda had popped by that morning, unexpectedly, as was her wont. Imo let her in, had come up to tell me, then went back and told Amanda I was on the phone and I'd be down in five minutes. She made her aunt a cup of coffee and went back to work. When I came off the phone, having arranged to go and see the lawyer, I opened the bedroom door to find Amanda coming out of the bathroom opposite. Her eyes were glittery and bright, as they had been just now in the restaurant. She said Imo had said to use the loo up here, that it was nicer. She was all smiles. I'd said yes, of course. My voice had been low on the phone, and I'd been sitting on the opposite side of the bed, facing the street. I was sure she couldn't have heard. But she'd been unusually sweet as we'd drunk our coffee in the kitchen, admiring the garden.

When Michael got back, things had seemed fine. Well, you know. Normal. Then one day, I was upstairs in my walk-in wardrobe, sorting out clothes for a friend who was having a charity sale at her house, and he came up and found me. He'd discovered my secret phone, in the cellar, in an old trunk, right at the bottom. He'd found the lawyer's details. He'd hissed and snarled obscenities at me, circling me, spitting at me as I'd shrunk behind my clothes on hangers, right in the corner, until I was curled up and crouched down, my arms over my head. Then he'd gone, closed the door, and locked it. Yes, quite dark. The light switch was outside, you see, and he'd turned it off. Obviously he'd let me out later, and had even cooked supper that night. It was ready when I came down. Chicken in a creamy mushroom sauce. He'd turned the heating off upstairs so it was freezing, but downstairs, it was warm. We'd sat at the kitchen table which he'd laid with a cloth, flowers from the garden in my favourite jug, and he'd made conversation, to which I'd tried to respond. My phone, and the lawyer, weren't mentioned. Towards the end of the meal, Michael started to talk about the children, in general terms, about their lives, but in a scary way. He said he might go and visit Imo, in America. Alone. Did she still live on the twelfth floor? I never rang the solicitor again and he never went to New York.

But that was then. And horrible though it was to realize now that Amanda had, in all probability, had her ear pressed to the door, and then been plotting to tip Michael off at the same time as laughing with Imo and me in the kitchen – this was now. Michael was dead. And something else she'd said, inadvertently, was far more pressing. Far more pertinent. I realized I needed to see something for myself, as an insurance policy. It hadn't occurred to me, you see. Just hadn't occurred. And it should have done. I needed to check. I turned the ignition, making sure I looked all around before I pulled out.

When Josh came to the door he looked, understandably, surprised. I made a hopeless gesture, throwing up my hands in the air and adopting an I'm-a-moron expression.

'I'm so sorry. I've put my purse down somewhere. No idea where. I'm really sorry, but I'm having to retrace my steps. I've been back to the restaurant, and into a couple of shops; would you mind . . . ?'

'Oh no, not at all. Come in.' He stood aside, feet still bare. 'But I'm pretty sure it's not here. I'd have spotted it.'

'Well, that's what I thought, but maybe when I went in the study . . .'

'I don't think you went in the study?'

I made a guilty face. 'I did, actually. When you were on the phone. I was intrigued by you saying it was a bit gloomy and I didn't know why I'd never thought of working in the front room. I popped in to – you know – check out the light.'

'Right. With your purse?'

I shrugged in a menopausal middle-aged woman sort of way and said, 'God, these days, who knows?' Hopefully that was self-explanatory without loading him with too much information.

'Oh, right,' he said shortly. 'Well, let's see.'

He led the way down the hall, through the kitchen

and into the study. I glanced around keenly. There was the sofa on which Michael had slept that night. There, in front of it, the coffee table, on which he'd hit his head in the scuffle. The new rug, covering the nasty mark, despite the cleaning company's efforts. And the French windows, through which the burglar had burst. A blind was above them, which we rarely bothered to pull, since we were never in here at night, but no curtains. And there, down the garden, beyond the high wall, was the house. I stared. Plain grey London brick at the back, with a much prettier white façade at the front. Those top bedrooms, those windows, which I could just see, no doubt looked straight down here, into the study. With quite possibly a birds' eye view of the entire room. No lights had been on, of course, but there'd been that torch, earlier. And it had been a full moon.

'Not sure you'll find it out there,' said Josh, following my gaze.

I came to. 'No. No, you're probably right. I didn't go in the garden, did I? I would love to, though, now I'm here?' He looked amazed, as well he might. 'I mean, obviously my purse isn't here,' I gabbled. 'I must have left it somewhere else, but now that I'm here, well, it's ages since I've seen my roses, and I have to say, you've kept them in superb condition, I'm surprised.' I shored up what I hoped was a dazzling smile, simultaneously reaching for the French door, which happily was unlocked.

Josh scratched his head as he followed me out in bare feet. 'Well, you seemed pretty insistent. Didn't want to hand the place back with everything dead, so I have indeed watered and deadheaded, as instructed.' He gazed around, rather pleased. 'I actually found it remarkably pleasurable. Quite therapeutic.'

'Good, good,' I purred, but I wasn't really listening. My gaze was trained on the house at the back again. Yes. As I thought, the windows were extremely visible now, but the study was different. More restricted. I went back in. I longed to crouch. See if an inert body on the floor, or even a fully functioning one, sitting on the sofa, hands clenched, could be seen. If from that position, I could see more of the windows. He followed me back, bemused. Not much rose admiring seemed to have taken place. I sat down suddenly on the sofa. Picked up a Chinese vase on the coffee table that wasn't particularly pretty and peered at it intently. 'Gosh, this is lovely!'

'Thanks,' he said, bewildered.

I bent a bit lower, as if I simply couldn't study the Ming Dynasty, or even the Conran shop, unless I was low. Very low. My eyes shot up to the bedroom windows opposite. Yes, they were indeed even more visible, but it was so hard to tell if there was a proper line of sight, or if the top of the French windows precluded it. Susie Sharpe would know, but then again, she made a lot of it up. What I'd really like to do was go up to Ned's old bedroom and have a look down. See how much I could see of *their* interior, but then we were only two stories: it was different. And there was no way I could pretend I'd left my purse in that room. The only way of telling would be to go round there, to that house, and somehow have a look.

'I've taken up far too much of your time,' I said,

getting to my feet. 'You must be getting back to your work. Remind me what it is you lecture in?'

'Criminology.'

The vase, still in my hands, slipped through my fingers and smashed on the coffee table. I gasped, horrified.

'Oh God – I'm so sorry!'

'No, don't worry,' he said, as I hastened to pick up the pieces. 'It wasn't anything special. Only an old Habitat thing and actually Agathe bought it so – oh Christ, now you've *cut* yourself.' He sounded irritated, as well he might. This wretched, menopausal woman barging into his house, inspecting the roses for greenfly, peering round his study, picking up and breaking his possessions then bleeding on the glass coffee table. But *criminology* . . .

He was leading me, rather firmly, by the elbow, to the kitchen, and had run the tap, under which I obligingly held my finger while he rummaged around in a drawer for a plaster.

'Isn't that the study of . . . criminals?'

'Ten out of ten. At its most simplistic level. Although, to be more precise, it's the scientific study of the nature, extent, management, causes, control and consequences of criminal behaviour.'

'Consequences. You mean . . . prison?'

He was rather awkwardly handing me a piece of kitchen towel, a slightly alarmed look in his eye. 'Oh. Thanks.' I duly wrapped it.

'Well, on a very prosaic level, yes. Some sort of penal

institution, or rehabilitation. But it's not just about it being on an individual basis, but on a social one, too,' he said irritably, understandably baulking at condensing his huge, learned field of study into one sentence.

'Yes, I see. More than I appear to, actually, because I myself write detective novels. But although I do a lot of research, I'm never a hundred per cent sure I get my facts right. To be honest, Frankie – she's my editor – isn't always sure either. But we usually decide – if there's some really obscure point of law we're not sure about – that if *we* don't know, and we've been doing it for yonks, the chances are our readership won't either. I'm pretty lowbrow, by the way. So we just sort of fudge it. But you would know implicitly, I imagine?'

He was handing me a plaster now. No way was he fixing it round crazy lady's finger.

'One would hope,' he said rather pompously.

'So how long, would you say, a case of unpremeditated manslaughter would get?'

'Sorry?'

'How long would someone get for that?'

'Manslaughter, by definition, *is* unpremeditated.'

'Yes. Of course it is.'

'And it entirely depends on the circumstances.'

I licked my very dry lips. 'Suppose they were . . . very favourable. To the woman. I mean, the criminal. Or victim. No, criminal, obviously. Manslaughter person. Who by mistake . . . well, no, not mistake,' I struggled. Regrouped. 'Who by dint of her appalling circumstances failed to – you know – alert the police, to a dying body.

Until it was dead. It's for my book, obviously,' I added quickly, but I was sweating. Could feel the dampness everywhere. Running down my back. 'The one I'm doing at the moment. It's about a woman married to a horrid man.'

He smiled. 'That really is a how-long-is-a-piece-of-string sort of question,' he said, as I smoothed the plaster firmly round my finger, avoiding his eye. 'It would totally depend on the circumstances. The extent of the duress, the physical or mental cruelty; but as you probably know, at least two women recently, who very definitely murdered their husbands, one with a hammer and one with a knife, were allowed to walk free. So for the purposes of your plot line, I'd say someone who committed manslaughter by failing to provide another person with access to medical assistance, as long as his wounds had not been inflicted by her, could credibly be acquitted.' He must have seen the relief flood my face, some beatific light fill my eyes. 'For the purposes of fiction,' he added, nervously. He was looking at me carefully.

'Oh, yes. Yes,' I agreed quickly. 'For the purposes of fiction. And, when you say acquitted, it would definitely go to court?'

'Definitely. You can't just run around killing people. Even if there are mitigating circumstances.'

'No. No, of course not.' I realized my mouth was very dry. 'Could I possibly trouble you for a glass of water?'

'Of course.'

He ran the tap until it was cold, got a glass from the cupboard, filled it and passed it to me. As I drank, I was aware of his dark eyes upon me. Curious but kind eyes. I put the glass down carefully, keen not to break anything else. The first time he'd met me I'd broken a milk jug, but luckily he seemed to have forgotten. I don't suppose I made much impression either way.

'Thank you,' I told him, making myself meet his steady gaze. 'You've been very helpful.'

He followed me to the door. 'Are you going to be all right to drive? You look a bit . . .'

'Oh yes, I'll be fine. Thank you.' I forced a bright smile.

'And I hope you find your purse.'

He saw me look startled. He'd said it gently, however, not with any low cunning. I swallowed. 'Yes. Thank you.'

I turned and went down the steps to my car. It was around the corner, on a meter, now that I no longer had a permit. I didn't look back, but I was aware of the door not having closed, because I knew the sharp click it made, however softly you tried to shut it. And trust me, I'd tried many times. So I knew he was still on the top step, watching me as I walked away.

16

I resisted the temptation to go round to the house at the back, knock on the door, and under the spurious guise of a neighbour with a carpet moth invasion ask to see her top-floor bedrooms, since strangely, those were the only ones affected in mine and my immediate neighbour's house, and we wondered if it was endemic and the work of some well-drilled moth army who started at the top and worked down? I resisted, because although I hadn't believed Amanda, I realized the last thing I needed to do was draw attention to myself. I was calming down a bit. Gaining a sense of perspective. It wasn't that the view from the study had been in any way definitive or had eased my mind; more that speaking to a rational human being had made me realize I was overreacting here. Fear was often born of wild imaginings, I knew that. The mind was capable of terrible tricks, but the great thing was, to resist them. I felt a lot more like my old self having talked to Josh. I did feel very cold, though; shivery now that the rivers of sweat had dried, and I turned the car heating on full. As I wound my way through the London traffic I reached into the glove compartment and found the last remaining toffee. I sucked it, realizing I'd barely touched my lunch.

It had occurred to me, though, that moth notion; and I wondered, as I crawled in heavy traffic up the Fulham Palace Road, if that was what got me into so much trouble. My vivid imagination. Because even as Michael lay dying at my feet, one of those very cases Josh had mentioned, the wife with the hammer, had occurred to me too and I'd already visualized myself turning up in court, flanked by my white faced, supportive children, in a plain, navy blue suit and cream shirt, although not entirely plain, perhaps with some sort of detail on the collar. A scalloped edge, maybe. That's how far ahead of myself I can get. How far into another world. Interesting, though, that as I'd sat there, picturing the court case, I'd still considered it to be worth it. Letting him go. Even as I imagined the consequences. Would I do it again? Fail to call for medical assistance? I honestly don't think I can answer that. Yes, probably. It was just such a relief to be without him, you see. Waking up every morning and not feeling afraid.

There was a toot behind me. The lights had gone green. It was only to sit in stationary traffic again, however, in a long queue for the Hammersmith roundabout, so I reached for my bag, retrieved my phone and surreptitiously checked my texts. Imo. Wondering how it had gone with Amanda and hoping I hadn't caved in over the memorial service. I glanced around to check for police, then texted back:

'It was as ghastly as you predicted. She's going ahead with it with or without us.'

A message came back immediately:

'Without us.'

I felt a ridiculous wave of relief, as if somehow we might escape, but texted back:

'Won't that look really odd?'

'What – like we did away with him or something?'

Flustered, I tossed the phone on to the passenger seat. The traffic was still at a standstill, though. After a bit I retrieved it. I texted:

'Am driving. Can't talk.'

I put it back in my bag, knowing it was on silent if she rang.

In an ideal world, I'd have seen both of my children while in London and that had indeed been my intention: to text and see if they were free for supper later. Imo worked very late in her new job, worryingly so, into the early hours sometimes, but she might have snuck out, and then the three of us could have gone to the Italian we liked. Except, this wasn't an ideal world, far from it, and the last thing I wanted right now was to see their dear faces. I couldn't relay the lunch to them in full, tell them what Amanda had accused me of, so I would have to lie, and I didn't want to do that. I could have just stuck to the memorial service, lied by omission, and tomorrow I would, when I rang them. But it was all too recent; too immediate now. And supper was so intimate;

they'd see my face, guess at something else, maybe. The phone was better, and tomorrow I'd lie my socks off as I had done for years.

I was quite used to that. Protecting them. As much as I could. And I'd listen to Imo's outrage at Amanda's preposterous behaviour, and Ned's calmer take on things, with more of an understanding of his aunt's state of mind, having seen a lot of it in his line of work. My son's job in a huge, diverse and sometimes troubled inner city parish, with a congregation of over 400, was often more therapist/social worker/psychiatric nurse than vicar, it seemed to me. They'd both know I'd had a grim time, though: that I'd been taken back to that familiar ghastly place, and they'd be concerned.

I drove on. Josh's awkward concern had been equally touching, and I wondered what on earth he must think of me. Not that it mattered, of course. He was far more intelligent than me, quite the professor when he got going about his subject, despite the shabby chic exterior. Or perhaps that accounted for it. Nevertheless, I hoped I hadn't come across as too barking. I decided I probably had.

When I reached my parents' house, I passed a sleek black car parked outside in the lane, with the Millers' chauffeur, Ron, fast asleep at the wheel. I recognized him from years ago: it had always been a source of amusement, the fact that we knew people with a chauffeur. Bugger, were they still here? I turned in at the gates. A couple of white vans were parked just inside, and scaffolding scrambled up one side of the cottage. Good. That was something, at least. The builders had made a start. Presumably they were beginning at the top and working down, patching the roof, which they'd told me was in dire need of attention. Jerry, who I'd liked enormously when I'd met him, and who had a quiet efficiency about him, was climbing down from a ladder, while his mate, Tod, was packing away their tools in steel boxes. As I got out of the car, they saw me and grinned.

'Good luck!' called Jerry, jerking his head towards Mum and Dad's house.

'Sorry?' I shut my car door.

'They've had a bit of a do,' he called cheerily.

I went rigid. 'A bit of a . . .'

I hastened towards the house. The front door was on the latch and I hurried through. Music was playing loudly, some old Nina Simone jazz. As I went through to the sitting room, my father was on the other side of the room by the stereo, crooning along to it at full volume, whilst Nancy danced. Nancy. What the hell was she doing here? Well, I say danced; she was swaying, actually – eyes half shut, turban askew, cigarette holder in hand, although there didn't seem to be a cigarette in it. Horizontal on a sofa, fast asleep, was Bertie. He had a napkin over his eyes, his mouth was open and he was snoring gustily. All around was the detritus of a lunch party: empty glasses, cheese plates and overflowing ashtrays.

Dad hailed me from over by the stereo system where he was clearly DJ. 'Darling! Come and join us!'

'Where's Mum?' I shouted.

'Upstairs, getting something for Hetty.'

He went back to his crooning, but unable to resist showing off now he had an audience, he sashayed across – as much as he was able – to sweep Nance into his arms. They waltzed, extremely unsteadily, around the room, giving me cheeky grins as they passed.

I forced a grin back. Dumping my bag, I went out to the hall and popped my head into the dining room before I went upstairs. The white linen tablecloth, soaked with red wine, had been propped up like a tent with two glasses underneath to stop it wetting the table. It was always my father's Heath Robinson solution to a spillage, although in practice it solved nothing. In the old days my mother would summon the French polisher the following day, but these days, they lived with the stains. A bowl of trifle seemed to have fallen off the table and Hector was busy licking it. I took it from him before he took the pattern off the bowl, simultaneously spotting – oh God, Mum's *teeth*. He'd licked those pristine clean too. I thought better of putting them on the table, realizing my mother could easily pick them up and pop them in her mouth, as had been witnessed one Christmas, and instead, put them in my pocket. Back in the hall I took the stairs two at a time and flew down the corridor to my parents' room.

My mother was flat on her back on the bed, fast asleep, snoring quietly. Her lipstick was smudged, hair in disarray, and she had eye make-up all down one cheek. Other than that, she looked fine, however. She even had a slight smile on her face as she slumbered. She also appeared to be clutching a blue silk skirt. No Hetty. I popped into all the other bedrooms, came back and gently shook Mum awake.

'Mum. Mum?'

She came round, blearily. 'Darling,' she murmured. 'Such fun.'

'Mum, where's Hetty?'

'Downstairs. Had a bit of an accident. Came up to get her a skirt.' She passed it to me, together with some clean knickers. Then her eyes shut and she went back to sleep again.

Oh right. That sort of accident. I took the skirt and knickers and raced downstairs. No doubt my mother, on her helpful mission, and on the point of going back down, had been unable to resist the lure of the bed. There was no sign of Hetty in the drawing room which my parents never used these days, or in the kitchen, and I was beginning to get a bit panicky. But as I pushed open the door to the laundry room, there she was, naked from the waist down.

'Hetty!' I gasped. She turned: smiled. I grabbed a towel from the laundry basket and thrust it at her, but she only looked down at it in her hands in surprise. I instantly wrapped it around her waist, tucking it in firmly.

'Are you all right?' I breathed. She was tiny, and still very pretty, her face like a small crumpled violet. But I sensed she was confused. Many machines appeared to be whirring in here. The washing machine, the tumble drier, Mum's old Kenwood mixer and – oh dear God, the ancient deep fat fryer, bubbling away furiously, full of boiling oil. I lunged and turned it off.

'Helena! How lovely!' Hetty exclaimed.

'It's Lucy, actually, and I've got you a skirt. I'll wake Bertie and get Ron to take you home, shall I?'

'I tried to wash my things,' she told me, 'but it's all so different. And Lorraine usually does it.' She looked upset and I realized she was shivering. My mother's silk skirt was going to be totally inadequate.

'I can imagine; so confusing, other people's machines. Tell you what, I'll wash it all later and pop it round tomorrow. Meanwhile,' I plucked some tracksuit bottoms of mine from the clean laundry basket, 'we're going to put these on, OK?' I took the towel away, drying her first, and sat her down on the stool by the ironing board. As I helped her into the warm, fleece-lined trousers I seethed quietly. My parents. *So* irresponsible.

'That's better,' she said politely, but she was still shaking.

'Good, good,' I purred. 'And now here's a lovely cardigan of Mum's . . .' It was mine, actually, but thick and warm; my mother only seeming to possess the flimsiest of clothes. I gently guided Hetty's arms into it, hoping I wouldn't break them; they were like twigs. Then I found one of Mum's pashminas, which I added for good luck. I shouldn't have gone to London. On so many levels. What an error that had been.

'I don't suppose you've seen my spectacles?' Hetty peered about myopically.

'No, but we'll find them. Come on, let's go and get Bertie.'

'Oh yes!' The mention of his name seemed to galvanize her, and I guided her back into the sitting room, relieved that the shivering seemed to have calmed down.

My father, by now, had collapsed in an armchair, eyes shut, arms hanging limply, but still singing gustily. Nancy was nowhere to be seen. I snapped Nina Simone off, irritated.

Dad's eyes sprang open. 'Hey! I was listening to that!'

'Dad, where's Nance?'

'Gone to find your mother and Hetty, upstairs. She thought you looked a bit shirty.'

'I am shirty. Help me get Bertie up, would you? I'll go and get Ron.'

Dad looked surprised. He sat up a bit and raised his eyebrows. 'Party's over?' he enquired.

'I think so, don't you?' I said sweetly.

As I shook Bertie awake my father roared helpfully: 'Bertie! Party's over!'

'Wha-a?' Bertie peered blearily into my face. He smacked his red-veined old chops and smiled. Tried to focus. 'Always fancied your wife, Henry.'

'Daughter,' Dad told him. 'But compliment accepted. Ron's outside, apparently.'

'Ah, Ron. Mustn't keep him.' Bertie struggled obediently to his feet, yawning and beaming at me as if he couldn't quite place me. Nancy reappeared.

'Your mother's asleep,' she told me. 'And I can't find Hetty but – oh there you are, dear.' She beamed at her friend, who I'd deposited temporarily in an armchair by the fire. 'You look cosy. Where are your specs?'

'I think I might have them,' Dad said abruptly. He

took a smallish, winged pair off his face. 'Where are mine?' He gazed around, peeved. 'Hope bloody Joan hasn't got them.'

'Christ – Joan and Roger, where are they?' I glanced around. Dear God, not more bodies unaccounted for.

'Went early,' Nancy told me. 'Joan still drives, but she likes to go in the light.' She smirked. 'She doesn't drink, of course. Frightfully dull.'

I liked the sound of Joan. I eyed Nancy beadily. She'd found a cigarette to light and was puffing away. 'Does Dan know you're here?' I asked. She froze, mid-exhale.

'No!' she breathed in a stream of smoke. 'Don't tell him.'

'We decided Nance needed cheering up,' my father told me. 'She's had a terrible time.'

'Terrible,' Bertie echoed.

'So we sprang her,' my father told me, trying to look important, but only succeeding in looking naughty.

'We tried to get her a You-ber,' Bertie informed me, 'but they said it was too far, so we got her a taxi from the station. Joan didn't approve, of course. Dismal old bag. Oh, there are your glasses, Henry.'

He bent slowly and picked up a pair of broken spectacles from the carpet: gave them to my father.

As the two of them examined the mangled spectacles, I beetled outside and through the gates to wake Ron. He struggled to attention immediately, ramming his cap on and starting the car, as keen as I was for him to get on the road. Under my instruction he drove right to the front door. Then we went inside and, between us, escorted Hetty and Bertie out of the house, and into the back of the car. Bertie protested loudly that he was quite capable of walking to the car on his own and shook us off, then headed straight into a rose bush. Once we'd sorted him out and picked the thorns and leaves off him, we poured him into the back seat with his wife. I saw the car safely round the corner, feeling slightly guilty about Ron coping on his own at the other end, but then I remembered the Millers were loaded, and had a live-in housekeeper. I hastened back inside. My phone stopped me, just short of the sitting room. It was Dan.

'Lucy? Did you call?'

'Hi, Dan. Listen, all's well, no need to worry, but the parents have had a bit of a party.' I swung around and headed outside into the drive again, out of earshot.

'Oh Christ. Where?'

'Here, I'm afraid. I went to London and they got a taxi for your mother. Sprang her. Their words.'

'Oh God. I'm in London too, had to come up unexpectedly for a meeting. She swore blind she wouldn't move and I left her food . . . Lucy, I can't really get back till tomorrow. Can you cope?'

'Course,' I told him firmly. 'But I might put her to bed here and take her back in the morning. She's a bit – you know.'

'God knows where that generation put it. I tried her gin the other night and it was practically neat.'

'Well, they don't, that's the problem. Put it anywhere, I mean. Because there's no flesh on them any more. Although your mum copes better than most. Anyway, I'll hang on to her, don't worry.'

'Thanks, Lucy. I'm super grateful. Oh, and see you on Friday.'

Somewhere dim and distant, in what I would like to think was a normal life, I realized I had a date. I agreed that I would indeed see him then.

I darted into the sitting room. There was no sign of Nancy again. For an old girl of nearly ninety, she was remarkably nimble on her feet. My father was on his, now, clearing up.

'I put Nancy to bed, together with your mother,' he said casually, as if butter wouldn't melt. 'They were both a bit tired.'

Up the stairs I went, leaving my father half smiling, and with an annoying hint of a halo over his head. Sure enough, there were the two old birds, fully dressed. I removed Mum's shoes and her glasses and Nance's great ropes of amethyst beads lest she strangle herself, and took off her shoes, too. I was about to remove her tur-ban, but hesitated, wondering what on earth I'd find underneath. Pulling the eiderdown over them both, I put another blanket on top, and drew the curtains. Then I turned off the light and went out.

When I got downstairs, my father had found the stereo button again. Nina was purring softly once more. He was efficiently clearing the dining room, clearly enjoying himself now. I helped him in silence, knowing now was not the moment. As he wound his way towards the kitchen, however, he made the mistake of putting his foot in Hector's water bowl.

I sprang to steady him. I took the tray of glasses from

him and helped him out, before his strange orthopaedic shoe got wedged.

'Easy, Dad,' I couldn't resist saying, as I eyed him carefully. His eyes accepted a tiny defeat. Making the most of it, I turned him around and headed him towards the stairs.

'Why not have a bit of a zizz yourself and come down and help me later?' I suggested.

He hesitated at the bottom. 'Might just have forty winks,' he conceded eventually. 'But I'll be back,' he warned. 'I won't be long.'

I watched him go, muttering about bossy bloody females and how hag-ridden he was, but he went, none-theless, and I knew I wouldn't see him again until morning.

I threw off my jacket, rolled up my sleeves and sur-veyed the chaos, then set about it. As I went back and forth to the dining room and sitting room, I realized I felt a hundred times better than I had done a couple of hours ago. I also realized I was humming along to Nina Simone.

17

Dan was waiting for me at the pub when I pushed through the door of the Rose and Crown on Friday. It was warm, softly lit, busy but not crowded, and he was perched at the bar with a beer, engrossed in a newspaper. It made a welcome change from seeing someone staring at their phone – not that I met many men in pubs, it occurred to me; indeed, I hadn't, for about a hundred years. I had the advantage of seeing him first and he was wearing a soft blue jumper which I could tell even at this distance was cashmere. It went rather well with his still boyishly pink complexion and his swept back fair hair. He turned and smiled broadly as I approached, folding away his paper and getting to his feet. I apologized for being late which I wasn't really, and he assured me he'd just got there, although when I looked at his half-empty glass it appeared he'd been there a while. When he'd ordered me a gin and tonic he asked after my parents, and I told him they'd finally recovered from the morning after the night before and explained about my day administering to the severely hung-over. On the down side, I told him, it had been exhausting, but on the plus side, it had had the advantage of rendering them horizontal and immobile on their respective beds as I'd popped in and out with soup and Alka-Seltzer, my father mumbling about the possibility of a dodgy prawn in the fish pie.

Dan chuckled as he paid the barmaid for my drink and passed it to me. 'They're incorrigible. After you'd dropped her off with Betty, Mum apparently spent the whole day lying on a sofa with a mask over her eyes, complaining that climate change had made the days much brighter than they used to be.'

'At least you've got Betty,' I told him, sipping my drink. 'She looked eminently more capable and sensible than our sweet but decrepit Irene.'

He made a face. 'Except she doesn't drive, which is annoying. But yes, I can at least leave Mum for a couple of days and be in London. As long as she's not snuck out by any reprobates, of course.' He grinned.

I grimaced. 'Sorry about that. We've had words about not leading the neighbours astray.'

We had, actually. When they'd recovered sufficiently, I'd sat my parents down like a couple of children and explained that I had to be able to go away, or even go on holiday, and not return to find the place trashed and the pair of them insensible. Not to mention all the damage limitation I had to perform with their friends' carers and children.

'It's our house to trash,' Mum had pouted.

'Of course it is, but aside from a chip pan fit to explode—'

'Hetty,' Mum interjected quickly.

'—you'd left an electric ring on high, with a bone-dry pan on top of it. Not for the first time, either. The Aga man's coming tomorrow, but until then, I think we avoid using a cooker you have no idea how to work. Plus, Bertie's got blood poisoning.'

'Bertie's always got blood poisoning,' interjected my father stubbornly. 'He never managed to clear it up since Egypt. It's a recurring condition.'

'Which, according to Lorraine, their housekeeper, reoccurs every time he sets foot in your house.'

'Or the McPhersons', to be fair,' he pointed out.

'They're much worse,' my mother agreed with a shudder.

I didn't remember the McPhersons, and asked Dan now if he knew them.

'Oh, they're a dreadful influence,' he told me as we were handed the bar menu. 'You don't want to let them go round there. He's got a horse down at Ronnie Taylor's yard. I once drove Mum and Archie there to go racing – didn't see them for three days.' He raised his glass and smiled, his eyes blue and twinkling. 'Welcome to my world.'

'Thanks,' I muttered, rolling mine back.

'Although I have to admit,' he looked a bit sheepish and lowered his voice, 'it's a darn site easier without Archie. He became my main charge.'

'Oh *really*? God, not even yours. An adoptee.'

'Exactly. When he married Mum, he was reasonably hale and hearty. He didn't half go off the boil quickly, though. I think he'd gone into training before, to snare her. Apparently he put in quite a few hours on the golf course, and then of course he gave the whole thing up when he moved into our house and never played a round again. He just sank into a sybaritic routine of lunching at his club in London once a week – which he could naturally afford to rejoin – and hobnobbing with all her friends down here.'

'Did you mind?' I asked him, as, having both ordered steak and chips, we moved to a table in the corner, which he'd reserved.

'What, that he'd clearly married Mum for her money?' Dan shrugged. 'Not really. As I said before, it's hers to do what she likes with. And she was clearly lonely after Piers had buggered off with her hairdresser. At least Archie was unlikely to do that.'

I hadn't met Nancy's third husband, but he'd been rather dashing, according to Mum. Quite a bit younger than her, in the mould of a Roddy Llewellyn, she'd told me. My mother's knowledge of the Royal Family is encyclopaedic, but she'd had to remind me who he was.

'You know, Princess Margaret's young beau.'

'Oh. No, not really.'

According to Mum, after flirting outrageously with Nancy's beautician, Piers had finally disappeared with her mobile – and nubile – hairdresser. That in itself was a mystery, since Nance was never without a turban. It had at least relieved her of the effort of looking twenty years younger, though, which, as she'd confided to Mum, was a blessed relief. All that plucking and bleaching and lifting cans of baked beans in the air . . .

'None of us siblings was too displeased to see the back of him,' Dan told me now. 'And since he'd only been married to Mum for three years, we did fight – successfully – to keep *his* hands out of the coffers. But there was no malice about Archie, so no, I didn't object to two old people getting together for companionship.' He shrugged. 'And I suppose, from his point of view, a more comfortable life.'

Our steaks arrived. 'Well, quite. Otherwise she's just rattling around in an empty house.'

'Until the next one appears.' He rolled his eyes. 'Husband number *five*!' he declared, miming a quiz show host opening a magic box.

I giggled. 'D'you really think?'

He sighed rather despairingly. 'Trust me, it's only a matter of time.' He poured me a glass of red wine and we tucked into our steaks. 'But beware, Lucy,' he waved his knife, 'you get sucked into this existence remarkably quickly. It's like quicksand. If you've got any aspirations to lead a normal life and continue with something even approaching a job, think again.'

'But you've been in London these last few days?'

'Well, I'm lucky in that I've reached the consultancy stage of life, the departure lounge, as I call it. I basically just sit on a few non-exec committees and advise – which sounds grander than it is. The real work starts when I come back to assess whether my mother's been as good as gold and pottering in the garden, or out on the razz with Claire McPherson.'

I blinked. 'Golly. I must make a note of these troublemakers. I don't remember them. Where do they live?'

He paused. Looked a bit awkward. 'Pains End.'

'Pains End.' I stopped. Put my fork down. 'But that's where the Carringtons live?' I went a bit cold, suddenly.

'Used to,' he said shortly. 'The McPhersons bought it from them about ten years ago.' He didn't look at me when he said it.

I swallowed. 'I didn't know that,' I said slowly.

'I'm sorry I brought them up, Lucy. I'd forgotten that was the house you were heading for.'

I met his eyes which were kind and truly apologetic. He meant on the night of the accident. The Carringtons had been hosting the party to which Helena and I had been invited. We never made it. And neither did someone else, in a tragic, more terminal sense.

'No, don't be silly. It's been years.'

He shrugged. 'Still painful though, I can tell.'

'Yes,' I admitted. 'Not a day goes by, actually.'

'Really? Actually, sorry, I don't know why I said that. I can imagine. It would never go away.' He shifted uncomfortably in his seat. 'I was there, as a matter of fact.'

I looked up sharply. 'At the party?' How odd. I'd never considered real life continuing in the wings whilst so much drama was happening somewhere else. In a quiet country lane. At a crossroads.

'It wasn't strictly my age group, but I knew Helena was going. In fact, if I'm brutally honest, I was only there because I knew she was bringing you.'

I glanced up at him in surprise. 'Oh! I don't remember—' I'd been about to say, 'I don't remember you,' but realized how rude it sounded.

He laughed. 'No reason why you should. I was Helena's friend, and even she was a couple of years younger than me. I just sort of – knew you from afar. When you came to the pub, sometimes.'

I remembered coming here, to the Rose and Crown, with Helena when I was home from university. Despite living in London, she still drifted back at weekends and met all her mates here: a fun, rowdy gang. Ant had been one of them. But when I moved to London, I no longer came down. I'd met Michael by then.

Dan grinned. 'I knew you were way out of my league, anyway. And then I heard you were seeing some incredibly smooth older man with a pad in South Ken. Knew I was beaten.'

'Michael,' I said quietly. 'I married him.'

'Ah.' He nodded. 'Yes, I knew that too.'

How different life could have been, I realized, if I hadn't. If I hadn't felt so emotionally scarred. So traumatized. Acted so impulsively after I'd killed Liam. If that terrible night had never happened. I knew I'd never have married Michael. I might have met someone at university. Or I might have come home every weekend from London. Gone to the pub with Helena's gang. Been chatted up by Dan, who already had his eye on me. The son of friends of my parents. A boy with the same upbringing, same values. I might have gone out with him. I might even have married this kind, intelligent man sitting opposite me. Lived a pleasant, peaceful life in the country. Been friends with other pony club mothers and organized church fêtes. Instead of which, I'd married Michael. I'd fallen for Michael because I felt

217

he'd understood me, and somehow absolved me, for Liam. In later life, I'd come to see that Michael had not been my absolver at all. In fact, he'd been my penance.

I shook my head. A regrouping gesture. 'What happened to the party?' I asked, my interest sparked suddenly.

'Actually, I'm ashamed to say, it carried on. No one knew the boy in question, of course—'

'Liam,' I put in quickly.

'Liam. And, obviously, everyone was devastated for you. Word spread pretty quickly. But you know what kids are like. Didn't stop the dancing and snogging.' He shrugged. 'Life went on.'

I gave a wry smile. 'At least you got to dance and snog.'

'Actually, I went home.'

I glanced up in surprise. He was looking a bit sheepish again. God, *why* hadn't I noticed him?

'Anyway,' he went on breezily, in the manner of one brushing aside an embarrassment, 'let's not dwell on that night. Tell me about the rest of your life. Tell me about your kids.'

I did, keen to move on too, and this was pretty much my specialist subject. I glowed with pride as I told him how lucky I'd been. Not always, of course. Imo had been a handful in her teens, and Ned had had his moments later, in a different, but perhaps more complicated way, but how lucky I'd been, given their father – although of course I didn't say that. So incredibly fortunate to have been blessed with two clever, well-balanced, functioning children who'd grown into the nicest possible adults.

'No spouses on the horizon?' He was digging into a

treacle tart now whilst I spooned up some sorbet, my children having taken some time. 'No wedding bells?'

'No!' I wailed. 'And why not? They're both completely gorgeous, inside and out, even if I do say so myself. So why am I not in Harvey Nicholls looking at hats?'

He laughed. 'They all do it much later, these days. Plus, I think they're more afraid of getting it wrong.'

'That's true,' I agreed. 'Especially after my shining example. Although they both claim it's not about that. That my mistake hasn't influenced their seeming inability to choose.'

'So . . . it was a mistake?'

'Oh God, yes, didn't I say? Total disaster.' I should have met you, Dan De Courcy. Kept my eyes on the road, slowed right down at that junction. Spotted the motorbike, and driven on to the Carringtons'. Then had a dance and a snog with you, before settling down with you, some six or seven years later. First in London, in a nice little flat, Clapham perhaps, then later in the country. Instead of having a shotgun wedding with two white-faced, anxious-looking parents. No, of course I didn't say that. He stopped a passing waitress with a smile and asked her politely for a couple more glasses of wine.

'Actually, I'd better have a coffee,' I told him. 'I'm driving.'

'Oh yes, of course you are. I'm ashamed to say I thought ahead and walked.'

'I must remember that. What is it, ten minutes?'

'If that, from both of us, yes.'

We were both silent a moment. It felt a bit awkward,

as if a plan had been hatched to walk to the pub on a regular basis. I think we both realized things had moved on a bit quickly and spoke at the same time.

'How did you—'

'What will—'

We laughed.

'Sorry.'

'No, go on,' he said.

'I was just going to ask what you'll do now Archie's gone. I mean, if he was your main charge.'

'Oh God, Mum's not far behind. She may be fairly nimble on her pins, but she's got galloping arthritis in her hands and wrists. Can't open a jar. Plus, left to her own devices she'd pretty much live on Walnut Whips and choc ices.'

'Tell me about it. Mum's diet consisted of marmalade infused cupcakes before I arrived. But you're in separate houses?'

'Lord, yes. I'm in the coach house, which I share with Archie's fleet.'

'His fleet?' I stirred my coffee which had arrived.

'Wheelchairs. Indoor, outdoor and all terrain. Shame he wasn't in one of them that day he tripped. But of course, he liked to show off when he was out with his mates. Gambol about like a gazelle. Mum's the same; she's frightfully competitive with her age group. Scans the deaths in *The Times* avidly, crowing with delight if someone younger than her has died. Only seventy-six! No age at all!' he mimicked.

I laughed. He was sweet. And amusing. Although we

did, inevitably, talk about old people a lot. Or children. I asked about his and he beamed. One daughter was married to an accountant, the other about to wed a sex therapist, which he tried, but failed to roll his eyes about.

I grinned. 'But she's happy?'

'Oh God, she seems to be on a permanent high,' he muttered. Then he grimaced. 'I really wish I hadn't said that.'

I laughed and drank a glass of water for the road as he paid the bill. I'd sort of offered but knew there was no way, and he'd batted away my attempt good-naturedly.

We stood up to go and he helped me on with my coat. As we walked to the door, Dan said goodnight to the bar staff who seemed to know him well. They watched as they polished glasses distractedly, but with a fair degree of interest, as we left together. It seemed to me we'd just arrived. Time had flown. A good thing, of course.

The night air was crisp and clear and the sky velvety black and studded with stars as he walked me to my car. Suddenly I wished I was walking down the lanes with a torch, as he was. I'd do that next time, I thought, as he got his out of his coat pocket. Next time, eh, Lucy? Helena would be crowing. I smiled inwardly at the thought of her face. We kissed lightly on both cheeks and said goodnight, and he promised to be in touch again. And why not? We weren't ancient, but we were old enough for things to move on, if they were going to – why hang about? I waved as he set off with his bright light, raising his hand as he went. No, I thought as I drove off down the lanes in the opposite direction, still smiling. Why not indeed move on?

18

The days went by. Two weeks, in fact, during which period I shepherded my parents to their respective minor operations, both one-day procedures, and both gratifyingly successful. Mum's eyesight was a revelation, talk about the scales falling, and Dad's hands, after they'd recovered from the post-operative effects, were warmer and much more mobile. His legs were healing nicely too, now that the antibiotics had kicked in, and since I'd insisted on the wearing of compression stockings daily. I'd had an email from Dr Gupta to that effect. When I wasn't ministering to the aged Ps, I'd watch in awe as the builders made lightning work of renovating the cottage. The work on the roof was completed now, and they were getting to grips internally. As I popped in and out with cups of tea, I'd linger to chat with Jerry and admire their handiwork.

Together we'd attended Archie's funeral, which, despite Nancy's original grandiose plans, had passed off in the local church in a quiet, dignified fashion, with Curate Leanne at the helm. In retrospect, I wondered if Nancy had been in shock that day with Mum. She certainly looked more upset than I'd ever seen her at the funeral, walking behind the coffin, head bowed, face pale. Dan was obviously there, supporting his mother with his brothers. We'd had another pleasant pub supper too, plus a trip to the local cinema, a sticky carpet joint we remembered of old. And then, all of a sudden, that cosy, comfortable way of life came to an abrupt halt. Because it was suddenly upon us. Something far less pleasant. Michael's memorial service. In St Luke's Church, Chelsea. And obviously we went, the children and I. Obviously. How could we not? It would have looked extremely odd not to, the three of us finally decided after some discussion on Zoom. We'd grit our teeth. Pretend there was nothing wrong with commemorating the life of a man like Michael. But I didn't put my parents through it.

Mum had had a fall a few days earlier: nothing major, but she'd missed her footing on the York stone terrace outside. Now she had a nasty bump on her head and a huge sticking plaster on her elbow. Plus, she was gabbling a bit: stumbling over her words, which she always did when she was anxious. So Dad and I decided they should stay here.

'Never liked the chap anyway,' my father remarked as we washed up the breakfast things together, Mum, safely down and breakfasted, but on the sofa with a milky coffee. She was watching Holly Willoughby, whom she adored.

My head whipped round to him. I knew, of course, but it was the first time he'd said it. 'Oh, it's lovely to hear you say that, Dad,' I breathed. 'Why didn't you say so, years ago?'

'I wrote to you, if you recall. Felt that was as far as I could go.'

He folded his tea towel over the Aga rail and shuffled back to Mum with his own coffee. Enough said. And throughout my marriage he'd never said more; never stepped in despite serious provocation: the ghastly letters, the veiled threats about my safety. Neither of them had ever said a word. For fear, no doubt. Just as I, through fear, had said nothing myself. Which of course perpetuates the circle. Vicious, isn't it?

I went up to change and came down wearing a dark green dress and holding a smart jacket and handbag. Dad had joined Mum on the sofa. Her feet were in his lap. They looked cosy. It wasn't so long ago that Helena and I had beetled down here to separate them as they'd lunged, screeching and flailing at one another, out of control. I liked to think I had something to do with this new dawn.

I smiled. 'Bye, you two. Dad, put the lasagne in the bottom oven for half an hour when you're ready to eat, OK? Just to warm, it's already cooked.'

'Will do, love. Thank you.' Then he gave me a steady look. 'And good luck today.'

'Yes, good luck, darling,' whispered my mother, her eyes anxious for me.

It was all they needed to say, and for me to hear. They knew. And I suspect Dad felt guilty about not coming with me, not being by my side. But he knew, too, that he had to stay with Mum, and that actually, if he was honest, the pair of them were more of a hindrance than a help on these sorts of occasions. When did that happen? I wondered, as I took an umbrella from the stand in the hall and went to the car. When would Imo and Ned go from not just looking out for me, caring in a quiet, distant way – which they already did, discussing me over their sweet sibling suppers, which they'd always had, perhaps more than other siblings might, courtesy of their circumstances – but to finding me a bit of a responsibility? To be passed from one to the other. Who's having Mum today? Who's checked in with her? Eighty? Ninety, I hoped. As I strode to my car with a straight back and purposefully in my heels, I decided I'd be ninety if I was a day before anyone had to look out for *me*.

Helena was waiting for me outside the church, Ant and the girls beside her. My sister's eyes searched mine as I approached, worried for me.

'Helena didn't want us to take another day off school, being a tiger mother,' Tess told me. 'But we'd already told Mrs Turner so there wasn't much she could do about it. It was a fait accomplished.'

'Accompli,' Helena corrected absently. She was looking a bit thin and clenched, albeit elegant in a smart navy coat and taupe silk scarf. She glanced about nervously. 'Come on, we've left it as late as we possibly can. Amanda's been in there for ages, we have to go in.'

'What about Imo and Ned?' My eyes darted about for them.

'They had to escort Amanda. She was getting . . . you know. I said to go on ahead and I'd wait for you.'

Oh. Right. Typical Amanda. She'd already nicked my

children. Helena waited for Ant and the girls to go ahead. She held my arm a moment, then rummaged in her bag and passed me a mint imperial.

I glanced at her nervously. 'Can you smell it?'

'A bit.'

I'd stopped to be sick in the churchyard. Right around the back; no one was looking. It was why I was late. I took the mint gratefully and she squeezed my hand.

'Come on. Soon be over.'

The organ was playing Elgar's 'Nimrod' as Helena escorted me through the nave of the huge galleried church. I'd previously only been in here to attend a charity carol concert a few years ago. It had been a joyous, celebratory occasion with an orchestra, trumpets, choir and packed pews. A cast of thousands. Today, it was a different story. Most pews were empty. At the front, admittedly, there was a fair sprinkling of congregation; Amanda had done quite well drumming up some support, but heaven only knew who these people were. Her own friends and neighbours, I imagined. She did have some, even if they went fitfully in and out of favour. But I also recognized the Bakers, the Franklins and the Taylors, all couples Michael and I historically had supper with, but with whom I'd lost touch. Nice enough people but social friends, rather than proper ones like Melissa, to whom I told everything, and who I wished was here today. She'd rung me last night from San Francisco, and we'd spoken for about an hour. She'd wished me all the luck in the world – and courage, too, she'd added. *You'll need it.* She'd repeated it again in a text this morning, which she must have set her alarm in the middle of the night to send. 'Courage, mon amie.'

My other friends had no idea about this event, and if I'm honest, knew nothing of the real Michael. I'd kept up the façade of a decent marriage, although some, like Maggie, my author friend, I'm pretty sure saw through it. Simon and Millie Taylor I'd met through Michael, and they turned as I approached. The Bakers, too, nodded and smiled consolingly. They'd all written to me when he'd died, but I'd contacted none of them since. How the hell had Amanda got hold of them? Then I remembered she'd asked to read my condolence letters: told me people's kind words helped. I hadn't asked for them back, I hadn't wanted them, so of course she had the letter-heads. I took a shaky breath. All my senses seemed to be in overload. There were flowers everywhere: on the ends of the pews, two huge pedestals by the altar, on all the stone ledges. Creamy white, overblown displays frothed extravagantly. The lilies, which I hated anyway, with their huge, confrontational heads and yellow staining stamens, were heady and strong. I breathed through my mouth to resist their scent, hoping they wouldn't make me feel sick again. This must have cost a fortune.

With my heart beating right at the base of my throat, we paused at the front pew. Helena's hand was still under my elbow. I didn't want to catch anyone else's eye so I kept my head bowed as together we slipped along to where Ned and Imo were sitting either side of Amanda. She was dressed entirely in black with a huge hat and veil, at odds with the rest of the women in the congregation who were more colourful, regarding a memorial service as a celebration of life, rather than a mourning of one. As I tucked my skirt under to sit down, I inadvertently spotted a few of Michael's Soho friends in the row behind. Pete who ran the pub. Tony, from the neighbouring Italian restaurant. The Greene brothers, Bob and Gerard: the former a reformed gambler, the latter a living and – just about – breathing one. Florid of complexion and with red-veined eyes, wearing a camel hair coat, he looked frail and shaky, as did the rest of his pals. In the very old days they'd come to the house, to drink and play cards in the kitchen, staying up late. A few awkward smiles were exchanged. I sat down next to Imo who kissed me and tightly squeezed my arm.

Amanda leaned across, her eyes full of tears. She took my hand. 'Are you all right?' she quavered.

'Yes, fine, thank you.'

Luckily I was fairly sure I looked pretty pale after the puke, and as her eyes scanned my face, I realized she was disappointed. She'd wished me more perky, so she could reprimand me. She wasn't well, I must remember that, I told myself as we both sat back, and as the vicar cleared his throat and came forward. I mustn't think of her as a manipulative bitch; she was damaged. She couldn't help herself. I saw Ned murmur a few words of support to her and I caught his eye gratefully.

The vicar reminded us that we were here to celebrate the life of a very dear man. I scanned the order of service sheet in my hand. It wasn't the one Amanda had shown me in the restaurant. Even though I'd only had a brief look before she'd whipped it away, I could see it had changed. And no, of course she hadn't sent it to me. Hadn't asked for my advice, or approval. But then again, I'd said I wanted nothing to do with it. I caught my breath in alarm as I read, but the vicar was enjoining us to stand for the first hymn, 'Praise My Soul the King of Heaven'. After that – and thank heaven for a splendid choir – we had a few prayers. And then Ned made his way to the front to give a reading.

Having said that he wouldn't, he'd rung me to say he deemed it better to toe the line, but had insisted on a Bible passage, and not the mawkish poem his aunt had wanted. Amanda had grudgingly suggested the well-known, uncontroversial letter of St Paul to the Corinthians, which he delivered beautifully. The mawkish poem came next, read by a friend of hers, a similarly skinny and expensively dressed woman, with the face of a twenty-year-old and the neck of a fifty-five-year-old. She tried to put as much emotion as she could into the sentimental twaddle Amanda had no doubt spent hours sourcing on the internet, but happily, her taut facial arrangement precluded it. She sat down, no one particularly moved, perhaps too fascinated by the overblown lips delivering it.

I'd already spotted from the racecard, as Dad always called it, what was next, but nothing could prepare me for the horror of what was about to unfold. Amanda slid past us, and didn't just stand at the front like Ned, but made her way to the pulpit, ascending the spiral stone staircase to the top. It took her ages, her head bowed in a sombre manner. As she turned to face us, though, and as her eyes roved around the congregation, it was in a much less misty fashion. There were no damp eyes, no swallowing either. And when those bright eyes finally came to rest, they were firmly on me. It was a look I knew. It was challenging. Triumphant, even. I took a deep breath and held it. It seemed to me the rest of my family did the same. This was her moment.

It started predictably enough. In a high but reasonably calm voice, she detailed her and Michael's happy childhood. The loving parents they'd shared, the delightful house in the country – Esher wasn't mentioned. She told us about the rambling garden, and the games they'd played. The rural idyll they'd enjoyed. And then, tragedy befell the family. Everyone looked and felt, I'm sure, very sad. It was a dreadful story. Amanda told us, however, that one good thing did come out of the tragedy: she and Michael bonded over their loss, became inseparable. To give their grandparents a rest, every summer they stayed with the Taylors in Norfolk, sailing every day and living a Swallows and Amazons existence. I saw Millie and Simon glance at each other. It was the first I'd heard of Michael's enthusiasm for sailing; he'd told me he hated it and stayed behind to read books, but who's to say. Anyway, so far so bland. I almost began to relax.

But then she got going. She told us how, after Michael married, everything changed. How, bit by bit, that bond had weakened. Disintegrated. I felt Imo stiffen beside me. How, despite the best efforts of both siblings, something was lost forever. Something was keeping them apart. Some force, beyond the control of these two lost children, these babes in the wood, was stronger than even their most desperate efforts, and was determined to drive them apart. A glance told me Ned's face was white, Imo's purple. I put a hand on her arm. She was trembling.

'We tried so hard,' Amanda told us, in a voice choked with emotion. 'We tried desperately to hold on to our love.' The vicar was frowning, looking perplexed. 'But it seemed the darker side of love, the jealous, possessive side that Jesus warns us about, and which Ned, my darling nephew, has just reminded us is always there, would not let me in. Love is patient, love is kind. It is not self-seeking, and – most importantly – it does not dishonour others.' Her gaze rested on me. 'Isn't that what Jesus taught us?'

My breathing became laboured. She'd tricked Ned into that reading, of course she had. It was the one Amanda had wanted him to read all along. The one that served her purpose. I couldn't look at him. I knew he'd be looking stricken.

'Love does not delight in evil,' she told us softly, quoting entirely out of context, for her own convenience. 'Evil,' she repeated quietly, to a horror-struck, silent congregation. 'For that is what it is, to keep a brother and sister apart.'

'Bollocks!' Imo was on her feet, shaking with rage. 'You're the evil one, you mad cow! How dare you even suggest such a thing? How dare you stand there, protected by some pious institution, when my mum did everything to include you? Your brother wrecked my mother's life, he nearly wrecked all our lives, and now you're trying to extend his legacy beyond the grave – how fucking dare you!'

'Imo – darling—' I was on my feet. She shook me off.

'No, I *will* not let her get away with that! Just because we're in a church, I *will* not!'

Ned had his arm around her shoulders. He tried to lead her away. The vicar was looking horrified. But she shook Ned off, too.

'Haven't we suffered enough at the hands of your family?' Imo screamed to Amanda up in the pulpit. Amanda's face was white. Livid. 'Isn't it enough that a bullying, frightening, *terrifying* man was able to control us for so long?'

Ned had her elbow in a vice-like grip now and was leading her away. And actually, she was done. Spent. She broke suddenly into noisy sobs. As one, we vacated the front pew, and with Ant, Helena and the girls hot on our heels, legged it down the aisle. Helena dashed to catch up with her niece.

'Quite right, darling,' she hissed. 'Quite *fucking* right.'

We all sped down the nave, through the ante-room, out of the door. Down the steps we went, the spring sunshine glaring at us. Tess and Maudie were silent for once, their eyes huge and frightened. Imo was still shaking with noisy sobs. So many tears. So many years. Only we knew. Ned knew too, and I realized he was pale and struggling to compose himself. The sight of his face was too much for me. I burst into tears. We all held on to each other and Helena did too, her arms around us, holding on. She knew enough. Even Ant didn't try to calm us. Although he did nip back to shut the church door. It was only when Tess and Maudie joined in the group hug and Maudie rubbed her heroine's back and, echoing her mother's words, murmured, 'quite *fucking* right,' as if permission had been given for all sorts of misdemeanours, that hysteria turned to hysterics. That fine line between the two worlds that gives the word its meaning was crossed. A lot of hiccupping and repeating of Maudie's phrase occurred, and then, with much laughter and tears, we all mopped ourselves up. We came to our senses and calmed down. Ant, who always had a clean hanky, passed it around as Maudie, delighted to have broken the spell, tried not to beam triumphantly.

Suddenly our heads turned as we heard singing. The choir was soaring above the rest.

'We have to go,' Ant said at once, taking the lead, which was so unlike him. 'That'll be the final hymn.'

We all agreed, nodding and murmuring our accord.

'We *can* go, can't we?' I said, mopping my eyes. 'Don't have to go to the wretched drinks thing she's organized?'

'Of course we bloody can,' declared Ned, in a most unecumenical manner. At that, we moved off collect-ively, out of the front gate.

'No – she's having it at the Bluebird,' I remembered suddenly, sniffing hard and jerking my head towards the Fulham Road. 'We need to go left.'

Hurrying to get away as quickly as possible, we has-tened, heads down, around the side of the church and Helena and I fumbled in our bags for tissues. Helena

233

passed one to Imo, who was very quiet now. As she took it wordlessly, I hoped, I prayed, for my darling daughter. Prayed that there wasn't something darker, something incredibly frightening and sinister that had provoked that outburst. Something that I didn't know about. I had asked her once, twice, even, and she'd always said no. But would she say that? To protect me? She was that nice.

'No,' she said in a low voice, her hand on my arm. She stopped me in the street a moment. 'No, I promise. I know what you're thinking.'

I exhaled shakily. Regarded her with huge relief. Helena had stopped too, and I think she'd heard the exchange and understood. A shadow cleared from her face, in recognition. Being my sister, it's possible she'd asked the same question of her niece in the past. I blew my nose and we made to move on, to follow Ant, Ned and the twins, not to the Sydney Arms, the obvious watering hole which Michael's Soho mates might fall into, but to the Builders Arms in Britten Street.

We still hadn't got past the vast church. It was enormous. We quickened our step. Ahead of us, a side door opened. I stiffened in alarm. The hymn hadn't finished; it was still in its final throes. Yet someone appeared to be leaving early. A blonde woman emerged on her own. She was wearing a short, pale grey suit with a fox fur collar. As she turned to go in the other direction, taking the path through the churchyard to Andrews Street, I saw her profile. I realized it was Ingrid Schroeder.

19

The pub was disappointingly full. Everyone was eating and looking pretty permanent, but luckily, at a large table in the far corner, a party of youngsters were looking set to leave. My sister's no slouch at this sort of manoeuvre: she's got very sharp elbows. She hovered and pretended she hadn't seen the group at the bar also set to stage an ambush, and had her bottom on a chair the moment someone moved theirs. Ant, well used to such an operation, deftly cleared away the glasses and popped them on the bar, ignoring the glares of the usurped party. He then ordered gin and tonics all round and brought them to our table. The twins, thinking for one mad moment they'd got one too, sipped, and realized it was lemonade.

'You could have made an exception today, Ant,' Maudie reproved him hotly. 'We've had a very traumatic day. In fact, I think I've got PTSD.'

'Bollocks, you've enjoyed yourselves enormously. You love a bit of drama. And anyway, I have made an exception. It's lemonade, not water.'

'You're only saying bollocks because Imo did,' Tess told him. 'It's not something you usually say.' She turned, starry-eyed, to her cousin. 'I thought you were magnificent, by the way.'

'Magnificent,' her sister echoed.

Imo grinned sheepishly and sank into her gin. 'Can't believe I actually *did* that,' she said in amazement. 'I mean – where did that come from?'

'The heart,' Helena told her. 'And if you hadn't done it, I might well have done it myself. Why should we all sit there listening to her lies? Our silence giving credence to them? You were right, she thought she had us trapped.'

'It's my fault,' I told them. 'I should have been brave enough not to go. Not to put us all through it. And that poor vicar . . .'

'I'll go and see him,' Ned said. 'Leave him to me, he'll understand. And trust me, it won't be the first family fracas he's witnessed. I once had a punch-up at an actual funeral, by the grave. Two wives and a body – both current wives, incidentally.'

'No!' The twins were gripped. 'What – like, bigamy?'

Ned entertained the girls with his tale of marital deception which meant the rest of us could talk quietly without the twins overhearing.

'I don't think we ever have to see Amanda again after this, do you?' said Imo in a low voice.

'Certainly not,' her aunt said crisply as I hesitated.

'She literally has no one else—' I began, but my sister's face was right in mine.

'After what she's done? After what she said in there? Tell me you have more backbone than that.'

'No,' I agreed quickly. 'No. You're right. Never again.'

The relief that flooded through me, that somehow I'd been given permission to cut all ties with Michael's family, was almost as huge as when I realized he'd actually died. Or, should I say, when I'd killed him. I was trying that out occasionally in my head. Trying to get used to it. It had been far harder than I'd thought it might be. In the early days, I'd kidded myself I'd been so numb with shock I'd been unable to move. But the moment I admitted the truth to myself, it rang alarm bells. And not in a ding-dong sort of way, more of a high-pitched screech. And the thing was, I'd fantasized about it so often, Michael dying. It had been a constant preoccupation. Sometimes it was all that got me through the day. And then, blow me down, a friendly burglar handed me my dreams on a plate. What was I to do, your honour? That was where the fantasy took a dive, as your honour reached for his black cap, or perhaps that didn't happen any more. But anyway, as I was led away in handcuffs. Down to the cells. I took a deep breath. Fell into my gin.

'Lucy?' I realized Helena, Ant and Imo were all staring at me.

'Mum, are you all right?' Imo looked worried.

'Yes, why?'

'It's just you weren't answering us and you've gone absolutely white.'

'Have I? No, I'm fine.'

'We were wondering if we should order some lunch?'

'I'm so sorry, but I couldn't eat a thing. Also, I have this irrational fear . . .' I glanced at the door.

'That she might storm in in her widow's weeds and make a terrible scene?' said Helena. 'She won't.'

'But Mum, you go,' said Imo softly. 'I know that feeling. Of wanting to be a million miles away.'

I thought of her in New York. Looked at her gratefully.

'Yes, go,' Helena agreed, suddenly realizing too. The old terror surfacing. 'If she so much as sets a foot in here, Ant will sort her out.'

Ant, the mildest of men, and the least likely to sort anyone out, was looking at his phone, but glanced up at his name. 'Eh? What? D'you know, it says here that in the sixteenth century the cure for female hysteria was lower pelvic massage.'

Maudie's head whipped round. She seized his phone, and as her father tried to grab it back, tossed it to Tess.

'But that a cure for the now defunct medical condition,' Tess read quickly, 'was made possible by a new technological advance – the *vibrator*.' Her eyes widened.

'*Thank* you, girls.' Ant snatched it back.

I grinned and stood up. 'Well, on that note, I'm off.'

'God, imagine Ant trying to calm three women down with a vibrator outside church.' Maudie's eyes boggled.

'And the vicar walks out,' said Tess. 'Typical of some *man*, though, don't you think, to decide female hysterics are caused by sexual frustration.'

'Like all we need is *them*,' agreed her sister, 'and their – you know.'

'Dicks,' whispered Tess.

Imo came round the table to hug me. 'Will you be all right driving?'

'Perfectly all right. Will you?'

'I came with Ned, in an Uber.'

'OK.' We hugged hard. An awful lot was said in that hug.

'Text me when you get to G and G's.'

'Will do,' I promised.

My son was also on his feet to say goodbye. His quick nod assured me he'd look after his sister, and then I left. The thought of food actually made me gag, but I knew they'd share a hamburger, bolster each other, and that with Helena at the helm all would be well. I didn't always, but right now I blessed my sister for being the captain in the family, and allowing me, on this, and many other occasions, to be the crew. We'd always scrapped and argued, but we'd also always been there for each other, always had each other's backs. Particularly on the rare occasions when only your sister will do. Like when she needs to be injected in the bottom for IVF at a very specific time of day, on a number of very specific dates. We'd always risen to the occasion. I remembered her grief when the first round of treatment didn't work. How I'd knelt before her and held her as she'd sobbed and sobbed, Ant with his head in his hands, helpless on the sofa beside her. And then the sobs of joy when she came round to tell me the next round *had* worked. She'd literally fallen through the door with tears streaming down her face, shouting with laughter, as we'd held one another. We've always been a rather loud, emotional family. See my parents on this score.

As I drove through the pretty Chelsea streets, I wondered if that was the problem. Michael had once told me that I was emotionally incontinent, which had astonished me, because he had no idea how much I kept inside. But perhaps if he'd married someone as constipated as he was, as damaged and repressed, for fear of exposing himself and getting hurt again, of being abandoned, as he'd once been as a ten-year-old boy, perhaps his life would have been happier too. Oh yes, I often tried to remind myself that there had to be two sides to every marriage. And that however much I blamed him for everything, in some way – in many ways, perhaps – I surely had to be culpable too.

I drove on through more familiar streets now, on the outskirts of Fulham, pretending I didn't know where I was going. Pretending I was in a bit of a daze. And that in some strange, compulsive way, my hands on the steering wheel just seemed to be taking me home. To my house in Sands End. How odd. How really very peculiar that not only did I appear to be parked outside my old house, but that here I was, walking down to the meter to get a ticket, and sticking it under my windscreen. Extraordinary.

I locked the car door and stared up at the house. I knew he was in; the sitting room lamp was on in the bay window. And I knew that if I took a few steps to the left I'd be at the correct angle to see him at the round table he'd moved there. The one with the fringed paisley throw. Maybe wearing a crumpled white shirt and jeans. Bare feet. I took a deep breath. I badly needed to speak to him. It was going to be acutely embarrassing, particularly, I realized, as he was someone I didn't want to embarrass myself in front of. Which was why I'd pretended I wasn't driving here. But there was no one else to turn to about this. I'd decided that. Regrettably, it had to be him.

To stop myself from chickening out, I put one foot in front of the other and climbed the steps quickly. I rang the bell. I heard light footsteps coming down the passage, which should have alerted me, but because I was running purely on adrenalin, it didn't. The young woman who stood smiling in the open doorway was slim, blonde and stylish in a casual, leggings and ballet pumps sort of way. It was a look I'd tried myself once, but failed to pull off, my bottom looking enormous, my legs short and fat.

'Hello?' She smiled enquiringly as I failed to speak, transfixed as I was by her beauty. That mane of blonde hair.

'Oh! Hi. Um . . . is Josh in?'

'Yes, he is. Come in.'

She stood aside, still smiling, then shut the door. She overtook me to lead me down the hallway. 'Joshy!' she called out, as she went. *Joshy.*

I followed her down into my – or perhaps her – kitchen, where a pan was about to bubble over on the cooker.

'Oh no you don't!' She lunged for it, and just managed to catch it before it came to fruition. 'Thai green curry,' she told me as Josh appeared behind us from the sitting room. 'Or it will be, if I manage to find a lime and some coriander to shove in it. I'm Tilly, by the way.'

She flashed another relaxed smile, her whole demeanour

reeking of smart schools, skiing holidays, swimming pools in the country and basically the sort of life I'd have liked Imo to lead. I say Imo, because I'd say she was closer to her age than mine, or maybe somewhere in between. Mid-thirties, perhaps. Either way, she was a lot younger than me, and fabulous. I turned from this vision to behold Josh, whose hair was tousled. He looked as if he was still engrossed in his work, and more than a little surprised to see me.

'Oh hi!' I breezed, as if it were the most natural thing in the world to pop in on him yet again, disturbing him and his new girlfriend. 'I was literally just passing,' I kept the smile going. 'So I thought I'd check up on the heating.' This was going to be so hard with Tilly here. Might have to be abandoned.

'Oh. Right.' He still looked mighty surprised. 'Well, no, it's fine. Seems to be working well.'

'No ticking?' I made a stupid ticking noise and moved my finger like the noisy second hand on the *Countdown* clock.

'I've got used to it.'

He was gazing at me, bemused. Tilly was too, although when she realized I was embarrassed, she had the perfect manners to turn back to her curry sauce. She gave it a stir.

'Good, good,' I breathed as if that really was the most tremendous relief.

'Tell you what,' Tilly said suddenly, 'there isn't even dried coriander in the larder, so I'm going to pop to Waitrose.' She grabbed her purse on the island, her manners, her poise, her confidence in the security of her own position and her sympathy for the awkwardness of mine, not deserting her for one second. In the twinkling of an eye, with another radiant smile and then the shrugging on of a gorgeous little navy jacket, she was gone.

I felt a huge menopausal blush surge up my neck as I tottered, unasked, to a kitchen stool. I perched. Stared at the familiar slate tiles.

Josh frowned and moved around the island to perch on the other one. There was a lengthy pause. Then he spoke. 'Suppose you tell me what this is all about?'

I took a deep breath. Was about to tell the most gigantic lie, but then made it a slightly smaller one. I looked up.

'I have a friend,' I said carefully, 'who thinks she might have killed her husband.'

He stared at me. 'Right.'

'She doesn't know where to turn. Because obviously she can't go to the police, for fear of what the – you know – consequences might be. But on the other hand, she can't really live with herself. No, that's not quite true. She can, some of the time. Some of the time she's fine. But she's conscious, the rest of the time, of the sword of Damocles potentially about to fall. She's wondering, since she didn't actually lay a finger on her husband, but maybe wilfully manslaughtered him, whether in fact she'd get off anyway, and it would be better to 'fess up and not live with the fear. She doesn't know.'

'I see.' He was silent. Watching me.

'And since you're a professor in criminology, and not

the police, I thought you'd be a good place to start. Hypothetically. On behalf of my friend. She doesn't know any lawyers. And she also thought they might be a bit close to the . . . you know. Law.'

'I see. Well, hypothetically, and on behalf of your friend, there's no such thing as wilful manslaughter. I believe we covered this before, when we were talking about researching your book. Manslaughter is a mistake. Did your friend make a mistake? Would you like to tell me the circumstances?'

I briefly outlined how my friend's husband had surprised a burglar, who'd pushed him, and caused his frontal lobe to rupture on a coffee table. But how, because he was such a monster, my friend had left him to die.

'I see,' he said when I'd finished. 'Well no, that's murder. Because intent was there.'

I felt the blood drain from my face. 'Yes,' I whispered. 'Yes, I rather thought it might be. Told her it might be.'

'But of course, if there were mitigating circumstances, which again, I believe we've discussed before, in relation to the book you're writing . . .'

He knew. He definitely knew. 'Yes,' I said miserably. 'We have.' Murder. Not good. Not good at all. There was a silence.

'I do write books,' I said in a small voice. I realized I wanted him to know I didn't lie about everything.

'I know.'

'Oh,' I said, surprised. He'd checked me out. I didn't know if this was a good thing or a bad thing.

He folded his arms and leaned back on his stool. 'Can you tell me about the sword of Damocles?' he said at length. 'I'm wondering if it's held by someone. Someone whose windows you tried to see into last time you were here, when you were crouching down in the study, smashing vases. Do you believe they saw something? And, if so, have you asked them what they're going to do with this information? If they even have any?'

I stared at him. 'No. I haven't.'

'Well, I think that's the first thing you need to do. Establish if your fears are even grounded. On behalf of your friend. And whether whatever evidence they have is even admissible. It may not be. How long would you say your friend sat on her sofa, watching her husband bleed to death?'

I gazed at him in horror but his eyes were not accusatory. I licked my lips. 'I'm not sure. About fifteen minutes?'

'OK. Well, that could have been shock.'

'Yes.'

We were silent.

'But it wasn't,' I whispered.

'I would advise your friend against that sort of confession. Who's to know, let alone the woman herself, what she actually felt at that moment? In the eye of the storm, as it were.'

I nodded.

'Prison is a very lonely place,' he went on. 'A very scary place.' I felt my forehead erupt in beads of sweat. My breathing became very shallow. I looked at him.

What must he think of me? A murderer. A key went in the front door.

'How would she do what you suggest, my friend?' I asked quickly, coming to. 'Establish who saw what?'

He jerked his head to the house behind. 'Well, I suggest she pops round and talks to them. Don't forget, she's the grieving widow, and so far the police have come up with nothing. She's outraged. She could say she's conducting her own inquiry, and was there anyone up there that night who was awake and might have seen something? They'll probably say – well no, it was the middle of the night, and anyway, the police have already asked, or something.'

I inhaled sharply at the simplicity of this. No moths. 'Yes,' I breathed gratefully.

Tilly came sailing down the passageway. 'The corner shop, would you believe!' She brandished a bunch of fresh coriander. 'Catering to the metropolitan elite. You shall have your Asian-inspired chicken swimming in aromatic coconut, monsieur.'

He turned: smiled. 'Well done, Tills.'

She glanced at me and, clearly registering my pale and sweaty face, did a double take. 'Would you like a cup of tea or anything?' she asked kindly.

I was being drowned in kindness here. By this lovely, caring, perfect couple. 'No, thank you,' I managed. 'I really must be going. I've taken up far too much of your time.'

I eased myself off my stool, and realized it was a bit sweaty. I walked towards the door. I had to pause a moment, however, en route, to shoot out a hand and steady myself on the kitchen door frame. Most of the time I'm fine, you see. In my cocooned, unreal little world. My bubble. But here in London, and after a morning like today's, realizing Amanda was still after me, still had an agenda, it was all so real. Was always going to be real. Was never going to go away. However much I hid in the country and pretended it would. It was like that play, *An Inspector Calls*. One day, he would. That, I imagined, was what had brought me round here today. To seek some sort of closure myself. Before someone else sought it for me. To be author of my own destiny. I raised my head and removed my hand from the wall. I didn't glance behind, because I knew Josh and Tilly would be watching me with concern. Instead I moved on down the hallway, opened the front door, which was easy, because it was mine, and went outside. I was about to shut the door behind me when I realized Josh had followed me down. He held the door in his hand.

'Let me know how she gets on,' he said quickly.

I looked at him with some surprise. His dark brown eyes were kind. I nodded mutely. Then I turned and moved on, down the steps.

20

I made my way down the street, around the corner, and then down the road parallel to mine. It was a long street, like mine, so it took a few minutes, but when I gauged I was roughly in position, I looked up. The next-door neighbours in my own road, the Crosbys, were having a lot of work done, their scaffolding sticking up into the sky, a blue tarpaulin flapping in the wind. It wasn't hard to work out the house I wanted. I paused before the black and white chequered pathway with its wrought-iron gate, and looked up at the white front door at the top of the steps. Number forty-two. Through the neat front garden full of late spring bulbs and up the stone steps I went, subconsciously noticing the tasteful urns of white lobelia by the door. There didn't appear to be a doorbell, so I lifted the heavy brass lion's head knocker . . . and then put it down again, softly.

What exactly was I going to say? What, if anything, did you see on that particular night, the night of the twenty-fourth of March, at about one in the morning? Naturally I'd say that. But if I was to be the grieving widow, overcome with frustration at police ineptitude and conducting her own enquiries, I had to take a moment to get into the part. I also had to be a wee bit careful here. Because if, in the fullness of time, I had literally no other option than to tell the truth and then use mental cruelty and coercion as a defence, I couldn't be too extravagantly grief-stricken. It might not go down well later in court. So it might be best to be merely interested for now. Pragmatic. Wondering why on earth I hadn't called and asked before.

I gazed up. The house was taller than mine: more imposing. I made myself knock and waited. Oh, thank the Lord, no one at home. I was off the hook. I turned, relieved. But then, just as I was going back down the steps, the door opened. I turned back. A young girl of about eighteen, wearing tiny denim shorts and an even tinier black top, peered at me through a flop of white-blonde hair. Fulham seemed to be littered with platinum blondes.

'Oh hi,' I smiled up. 'Um, are your parents in?'

'No, 'fraid not,' she muttered. A more sulky blonde than the one I'd just met in my own house. She'd deigned to take the earpiece from her ear but was clearly annoyed at being dragged from a screen, although she clutched another, smaller one in her hand.

'Any idea when they'll be back?'

She shrugged. 'Dunno. Mum's out. Who are you?'

'Oh – I'm a neighbour. My house is behind yours.'

'Uh.' No further interest. I was too old. Too boring. Neither did she offer to take a message. Just go, old woman. But I wouldn't. I persisted.

'When you say out,' I went on doggedly, 'do you mean she's shopping, or away, or—' I stopped suddenly, mid-sentence: stared beyond her, transfixed. Because behind the sulky teenager, on the hall chair, ornately carved in bleached wood and positioned below an elaborate rococo mirror, was a pale grey suit jacket. It had a fox fur collar. It was beautiful. And familiar. I'd seen it not two hours ago. It was Ingrid's. My eyes came back to the girl, so very pale blonde, so clearly Nordic. Suddenly I couldn't speak. The girl looked incredulous at my dumbness. Eventually I found my voice and thanked her, stumbling over my words, mumbling about having to go. Then I turned on my heel and left. I heard the door shut behind me.

My heart was pounding as I made myself walk fast. Escape. Ingrid. Shit, *Ingrid* lived there. I couldn't think. Couldn't take it in. My mind whirred. Suddenly I remembered her saying, when I'd been pretending to be interested in kitchens, that she lived close by. Literally around the corner, she'd said. I hadn't given it much thought at the time. I'd just been so intent on meeting her, not on her territory, but on mine, at the club.

My brain scrambled on, falling over its thoughts, which were jumbled, racing. Ingrid lived there. Jesus Christ, Ingrid. I carried on walking down another street, to get some distance, and think. There was no reason why Ingrid should have known our houses backed on to each other when I rang her, or when we'd met for lunch, either. All we shared was a high garden wall. In London, that was no call for neighbourliness. But later . . . maybe she'd realized before me? I shook my head, trying to think. When I'd seen her at the church, earlier, I'd decided she'd have heard about Michael's death through

Millie Taylor. After all, that's where I'd first met Ingrid, at dinner there. That had been the simple reason for her presence today, which I'd already worked out, but what if – what if she really had seen something that night? And when, belatedly, she had realized it was Michael, had said something to Millie? Who maybe, in a weak moment, and over a couple of glasses of wine, had told Amanda?

As this hypothetical chain of events unfolded in a nightmarish fashion in my head, I turned and fled back to my car. I let myself in with fumbling fingers. Then I sat and stared out at the sky. The clouds were racing, propelled by the wind, too fast, disturbingly fast, like my thoughts. I tried to remember how Millie had greeted me at the memorial service. I'd slipped in head down, hadn't really acknowledged anyone. But had she glared? Millie was one of the very few people I knew who felt compelled to keep in touch with Amanda, by dint of old family ties.

I'd thought Amanda was lying when she'd implied someone had seen me murder her brother, someone who lived behind, but what if it were true? She'd told me the police had mentioned a neighbour, but she'd also said – someone else told me that too. I'd thought it just another glib lie in her web, adding weight to the police story, realizing perhaps I wouldn't believe they'd tell her anything; but what if that had been genuine? What if my instincts, usually so spot on with my sister-in-law, had been wrong? What if, for once, amongst all the manipulative lies, Amanda had been telling the truth when she said a neighbour saw something – but had simply got confused about where Ingrid lived? Not confused about what she'd seen, though. But surely if that was the case, the inspector would have called by now? The sword would have fallen? Or not yet. Not quite yet, perhaps. But imminently. Hence her blistering attack on me in church. Perhaps she was reeling me in, even now. Slowly. Letting everyone know what a bitch I was, so that when it came to pass, at the court case, they could all recall and say ... golly. Remember that eulogy in church? About the mean-spirited wife? Freezing the poor sister out? Perhaps Amanda was enjoying herself. Letting me know she knew. For the second, or possibly third time that day, I felt sick. Very nauseous. And full of dread. Trembling, I fumbled in my bag for my phone. I tapped out a message.

'My friend has been round. The neighbour wasn't in, but it turns out she's a friend of the dead husband. My friend is now in terrible trouble.'

I stared at my phone, hoping for an immediate response, but of course, nothing happened. Naturally it didn't. Josh was no doubt enjoying a late lunch of Thai green curry together with fragrant jasmine rice, with his delightful and beautiful girlfriend. He was probably even now uncorking a delicious Chablis to go with her fabulous cuisine. He might perhaps glance at his phone later, after they'd repaired to the bedroom for a spot of afternoon delight, but he might not even answer for a few days. Maybe a week would go by. He may not find the time, what with all the dissertations he was marking, the seminars he was planning, the lectures he was writing, and the energy he was expending on keeping up with his younger, physically demanding, playful girlfriend. I, meanwhile, would be driving my very old car, in my very old green dress, back to my parents, with whom I lived, as their carer. Which was sad, but not half as sad as things were about to get really quite quickly. Particularly given my family's performance at the memorial service today. Amanda was not going to forgive us for ruining her big day in a hurry. The elaborate reeling in might well be sped up. She might want her pound of flesh sooner, and she'd make damn sure that flesh was mine.

21

An hour or so later, I arrived at Pope's Farm. As I walked through the hall and into the sitting room, my parents were getting to their feet. They greeted me like small children who'd been terribly, terribly good and were eager for praise.

'We washed everything up,' my mother told me proudly. She immediately took my arm and led me through to the kitchen, which was spotless and gleaming. She'd clearly been waiting for this. 'We didn't think it was worth stacking the dishwasher for just the two of us, you see. And I even washed the floor.'

'Well done, Mum. You didn't have to do that.'

'Oh, I don't mind, these days. Now that you've removed all that terrible grime and grease, it's a pleasure to keep it clean.'

'Good.' I raised a smile.

'Exhausting day?' asked Dad sympathetically, as we went back to the sitting room. Unlike my mother, he was less likely to ambush one on arrival. He bustled to get me a drink from the table in the corner.

'Pretty,' I agreed, chucking my bag on a chair and leaving it at that. And neither of them asked me for more, for which I was grateful. As far as they were concerned, it was over. Done and dusted. All ties were severed and honour was perceived to have been done with Michael's family. As I sank into the white wine my father handed me and then down on to the sofa, I tried not to imagine their shock and horror when they realized it was just the beginning.

'We're so glad you're back in daylight, darling,' said my mother, hovering over me. She was actually focusing on me too, I realized, through clean and up-to-date spectacles. 'Because we're dying to show you the cottage. It's come on leaps and bounds.'

'Bring your drink,' said Dad excitedly. I noticed he was also still on his feet. He rubbed his hands together. 'If you're not too tired? Long day?'

'No, no, I'd love to.' It was the very last thing I wanted to do. I just wanted to lie down on my bed upstairs, shut my eyes and think. 'But just let me change my shoes.'

'Here.' Like a magician, Mum produced some wellies from behind the sofa. They were hers and therefore tiny, but I took off my heels and somehow squeezed my tired feet into them. As I heaved myself up and put my drink aside, I realized they were already waiting for me in the hall. I raised a smile, and my game, and together we traipsed across; or at least I did. My parents were practically skipping with excitement. They'd rhapsodized about daylight, but it had almost gone, so I fished out my phone and used my torch. I steadied Mum as she attempted to gambol ahead, gambolling not being her speciality.

'Easy,' I warned, as she nearly tripped over a tree root. 'Shut your eyes,' she commanded as we got to the front door. Dad was already opening it, and reaching for the light switch inside.

I did as I was told. She led me in and I could hear her excited breathing in my ear. I hadn't been in here for a few days. Aware the builders were extremely busy, I'd just left a tray of tea outside with a shout to Jerry. Clearly, those days had been pivotal. I knew all the cement mixers and building equipment had been removed because I'd seen them outside on the lawn. I also knew the joiner and the plasterer had arrived because I'd seen their vans.

'Da-dah!' sang my father. 'Open your eyes!'

All was very bright, and very sparkling. In fact, it took my eyes a moment to acclimatize. The ceiling positively sang with spotlights, and in their gleam, a glorious open-plan space was illuminated. The fact that there was no segmented hallway or pokey rooms was not a surprise, that much I'd already witnessed. Most of the internal walls had come down a while ago, but nothing could prepare me for the spaciousness, now that the more decorative tradesmen had worked their magic. The large, bright room with its pale wooden floor, its recently plastered walls still drying, albeit with a few electric wires hanging, was a revelation. The transformation from ugly fifties interior to elegant spacious living was extraordinary. I realized it was pretty much ready for painting. The windows were all new, and stylish sash, and at the far end, generous French windows with wide panes led on to the garden. My parents turned their delighted faces to mine, to gauge my reaction. I lit up accordingly.

'It's amazing!' I enthused, and so thrilled were they

that they didn't spot the effort it was costing me to be animated.

'Isn't it?' Dad squealed, and my father doesn't squeal. 'And look – look at the kitchen.'

But my mother had already raced ahead – yes, raced – and was disappearing through a wide archway. I followed into an elegant space, with arched, spotlit alcoves which mirrored the entrance. The pale wooden floor ran throughout, and a pantry, minus a door, was in the corner. At the other end was another French window.

'Obviously once the cupboards are in it will look a lot better,' Mum was saying, stroking the slate shelf in the pantry. 'But isn't it neat? Don't you love it?'

'I do,' I agreed, following them as they shuffled out and down the hall to the bedrooms, realizing they loved it. And it came to me, as I don't think it had come to them, that of course, it would be ideal for them. Not me. It was all on one level. It was clean. It was new. There were two double bedrooms.

'One for you,' Mum was telling me, 'and one for guests, or when Imo and Ned come.'

And without all the hazards of the seventeenth-century farmhouse they currently inhabited. Even though it was dark outside, I could tell that those large sash windows rendered fabulous light in the daytime, and faced south. And Mum's sight, much improved by removal of cataracts and new glasses, was nevertheless not what it used to be. Pope's Farm was dark, with mullioned windows, and lots of hazardous corners. It also faced north. It had two twisting staircases and two inglenook fireplaces, which they still used, it being too expensive to centrally heat the whole house. Even though we'd banned my father from chopping logs and I'd organized a delivery, he still insisted on bringing them in, in a large, soggy tarpaulin: breathing heavily as he carefully stacked them one by one in the log basket, because the idiot boy, as he called the odd-job man who swung round on his motorbike of a Thursday to mow lawns in the summer and occasionally chop logs in the winter, threw them in the basket any old how. But here, there'd be no logs. Because beneath these smooth boards, Jerry had installed underfloor heating. And even if one of them ended up in a wheelchair – my father, possibly, with his ulcerated legs and bloated feet – he'd whizz around these shiny wooden floors and glide through the wide archway to the kitchen, where the addition of a tiny ramp would see him outside to a small terrace and manicured garden. Instead of stumbling into the four acres of tangled rose gardens, herbaceous borders and moss-ridden lawns, not to mention a long-abandoned tennis court I knew he fretted about next door.

It struck me, suddenly, that Helena and I had been very remiss. We should have done this years ago. Not waited for a crisis to pre-empt it. We should never have fallen for Dad's lies about how they were managing tremendously well. Not that we did, really. In our hearts, we knew they were fibbing, but it suited us to go along with the lies, telling ourselves it was what they wanted, and who were we to be controlling and dogmatic? And meanwhile getting on with our own busy, and often very difficult, lives.

'And you can entertain in here,' my father was saying, as we all went back to the living room. 'If it was me, I'd have a table against this wall, which you could then pull out when people come. *Comme ça*.' He made an imaginary rectangle with his hands.

'And you could have your desk here,' Mum was saying. She pretended to sit, facing the French windows, demonstrating with a flourish of her imaginary pen how I'd write. Then she paused, pen in hand, to gaze out at the view. I imagined her there, writing her thank-you letters. Before going to her pantry, which she'd never had, and had always wanted. To prepare a little light lunch for her and Dad. 'Because you will write again, won't you?' She turned to me anxiously. 'Helena and I see you doing that again, here. Well away from – well. You know.'

My former life. My disaster of a life. Which was still chasing me. I'd clearly been discussed, at length, on the phone by the two of them. That didn't come as a surprise to me. Mum and Helena were very close. And I don't say that with any hint of jealousy at all; in fact, I'd often felt it let me off the hook. They spoke every day, sometimes twice a day, and I wasn't really like that. I'd never felt the need to clock in with anyone, and throughout my marriage, had deliberately not done so with Mum because I didn't want to worry her. I'd have had to lie constantly, which would have been so exhausting.

Instead, I suppose in a cowardly fashion, I'd let Helena do it for me. 'I'm sure she's fine, Mum, sure *they're* fine. You probably haven't heard from her because she's writing.' And then a quick text to me: 'Ring Mum.'

No, there was never any hint of favouritism. It was just that some children needed their parents more than others, and although one might assume I'd be the obvious candidate for a lifebelt, with my dysfunctional marriage, it was Helena, with her very happy family, who needed it. It was always Helena who made the calls. When she got home from work, in her beautiful white designer kitchen. Jacket flung on the sofa behind her as she got supper, phone clamped between ear and shoulder, simultaneously supervising the twins doing homework at one end of the long island. The one with the least time. The one who couldn't possibly be here. What would happen to them, I wondered, with a sudden jolt of panic, when I wasn't here either? When I wasn't *permitted* to be here? Detained, at Her Majesty's Pleasure? Helena couldn't possibly replace me. She had a full-on, full-time job and school-aged children. They'd have to have a carer. Because although I could definitely leave them for a couple of days, the more I was here, the more I realized what an absolute necessity I was. Yes, they'd come on leaps and bounds and the crumbling had been far less dramatic these last few weeks, but I knew, in my heart, it had only been temporarily arrested. In a year or so's time, without someone's watchful eye, something else would start to give.

I watched as they squabbled now in the corner, about some whizzy sound system they wanted to show me, which, despite the house having only bare bones, had been installed along with the electrics.

'You press *this*,' Mum was hissing.

'No, you don't, you press *this*.'

'Oh, you *stupid* man.'

This was how quickly things could degenerate into their usual bickering. I nipped across to officiate. Both their faces were pink as I took the remote they were fighting over.

'Here.' I showed them. 'All you do is literally touch this one, with the arrow, to start it. And this one to stop it. That's all you do.'

'Put it on,' Mum said eagerly.

'You do it. Like I showed you.'

She took the remote back. Looked flustered for a moment. But after some initial hesitation, she did. The Brahms violin concerto, full of loss and longing, miraculously floated through mysterious speakers. It was too clever by half and I saw Mum's eyes widen in wonder. My father's closed in rapture. He loved Brahms. Mum began to dance, in a floaty, ethereal way, arms outstretched like a ballerina, around the room. My father, eyes still shut, gently swayed, his hands conducting.

'Wonderful,' he breathed eventually. 'And so fiddly, all my gramophone records. I'd almost given up.'

'Dad, *stop* it. Ant changed you over to CDs years ago!'

'It broke,' he said simply. 'The machine.'

'So get it repaired.'

'We forgot,' he said shortly. Or didn't know how. Or where to go. So they had lived without music, Dad's greatest love, even beyond books. I realized now I'd hardly heard it since I'd been here, except for that old Nina Simone the other day – and now I thought about it, that had been a gramophone record. And historically, music had been on all the time. The soundtrack to my youth. I felt angry on their behalf. Angry at the world overtaking them. I *would* not get like this, not ever.

'But this whole house has been Spotified,' Mum said proudly. 'We told Jerry we all like Brahms and Chopin—'

'And Dire Straits, we knew you liked—' Dad put in quickly.

'So he put it all on a thingy.'

We were moving towards the front door now, preparing to go. Before we left, I made Mum turn off the music. Then I switched off the lights and took their arms before we embarked on the darkness. We had to return, however, as my mother had taken the remote with her. They gave the interior a last lingering look as I turned on the light to nip inside.

'It's gorgeous,' I told them, switching off the light and shutting the door. 'And you're right, I'm going to love it here.'

No need to say any more at this moment, I thought, as we linked arms and went back to the house. No need for any further discussion. Just take one day at a time and let things naturally, and, I feared, irrevocably, fall into place.

But what of this place, the farmhouse? I thought, as I lay alone in bed later that night. I tossed off the heavy bedcover and turned over to face the wall. Could we rent it out? It was so run-down. Sell it? Dad would never agree. And who would keep an eye on them? Could we have a carer in here? Eventually I fell fitfully asleep, it being only a small comfort that my parents were sleeping very comfortably down the hall, dreaming of dancing to Brahms.

22

The following morning, I lay in bed staring at the crack of cold light creeping through the gap in the curtains. In a succession of terrible nights, that last one had to be up there with the worst, but then the bar was quite low. The odd, fitful doze I'd managed in the small hours had featured pale yellow roses crawling over a brick wall, tasteful, like her grey fur jacket and the white lobelia on her step. I'd admired those roses for years. Wondered what variety they were, even looked them up in my gardening books. In my fitful dreams, however, the roses were full of greenfly and thorns. A flashing light had also featured, in Ingrid's top-floor window, which I couldn't decide if I'd seen or not from the study on that night. Had I imagined it? Roses. A light. Thorns. My eyes were full of fatigue. I shut them again. When my phone beeped, I jumped. I opened the message, full of dread. It was Dan.

'Pub supper some time this week?'

I sank back on the pillows, relieved. For some ridiculous reason, I'd thought it was her. I composed myself. And a response.

'Good idea. Why not.'

'Wednesday any good?'

'Perfect. I'll fit it into my frantic schedule.'

I could afford sarcasm about my socially barren life, because I knew he liked me. I didn't have to play hard to get. And let's face it, it was only going to be a fleeting romance, if my worst fears were founded.

My phone had been in my hand since about six o'clock in any event, as I'd tentatively researched murder and the sentencing thereof. I say tentatively, because I knew from my Susie Sharpe sleuthing that too much research could lead to trouble. Susie had once got involved with a terrorist trafficking ring, who had kidnapped a young girl, with intent to ship her out to Pakistan and into an arranged marriage. Naturally she'd infiltrated the gang and rescued the girl. A few weeks later there'd been a knock at the door. Two gentlemen from the security squad in Whitehall wanted to know why I was so terribly interested in Al-Qaeda's extremist rings and could they possibly look at my computer? Of course they could, and of course I gabbled away and explained and made copious cups of tea and showed them all my notes and books, and eventually their faces softened. They nodded silently, murmuring something about having to be very careful. Them, or me? I wasn't sure, but I was very glad to see the back of them, and from that day on, Susie and I mostly used library books when we needed sensitive information. I wondered if the local library would yield anything helpful now, but then, if I was in court, might some boot-faced librarian slide quietly into the witness box declaring I'd borrowed a mass of tomes on murder and produce the volumes? Or, if I cannily didn't borrow, might she remember me spending hours in the research section, unheard of in this digital age? My imagination, as ever, knew no bounds, which was perhaps why I normally kept it under control by writing. I had a vague instinct I should reach for a pen and scribble something now in an attempt at displacement therapy, but instead, I raised myself wearily out of bed and tottered to the bathroom. I felt utterly exhausted and the day hadn't even begun.

After I'd brushed my teeth I leaned my hands on the porcelain basin and stared at my reflection in the mirror. What I couldn't stand, I decided, was the not knowing. A neighbour of my parents, a farmer, had many years ago knocked someone over while driving away from a pub, late at night. A vagrant, who'd wandered out in front of his car. But the farmer had been drinking, so in panic, he'd driven on. The police had drawn a blank. Months later, he'd given himself up. And the publican confirmed he'd been drinking. He went to prison, but only served a year as he was such a model prisoner. He's still farming now, down the road. Should I do that? I wondered. Give myself up? Go to the police? I stared into the mirror for clues. After a while I splashed my alarmingly pale face with cold water and went downstairs to make breakfast.

I'm told that first thing in the morning and last thing at night are the very worst of times for nightmarish thoughts, but that during the day, if kept busy, it's possible to put all terror aside so that the whole affair actually becomes unreal: it becomes something so ridiculously awful, the mind has surely just invented it overnight. And so it was with me. As the days went by, and with no sharp knocks on the door, or threatening missives on my phone from Amanda, it started to seem like a surreal dream which receded into the distance with every passing day. Thus one slips easily into a false sense of security. Only occasionally, when I took Mum for her flu jab, for example, and had to park outside the police station because the surgery car park was full, or when Dad, en route to pick up his new ortho-paedic shoes, commented on the beauty of the Georgian courthouse in the market square, did I feel that sharp stab of reality: that loss of breath that takes one from feeling perfectly normal to sick with fear in seconds flat. The mind does have a remarkable coping mechanism, however, so that by the time I met Dan, I was, if not totally relaxed, at least relatively sanguine about the situation.

We'd both walked, and arrived at the pub door at pre-cisely the same moment. We laughed at our staggeringly predictable middle-aged promptness, cheeks glowing, wrapped in our coats against the unseasonable nip in the evening air. Neither of us, having grown up in the coun-try, were the least worried about walking down dark lanes on our own, or even cutting across a crisp ploughed field as I'd just done. Obviously one had to dress for the occa-sion, which involved reasonably sturdy boots, but my days of high fashion were long gone. Anyway, Imo told me they were frightfully edgy when she'd asked me to send her a photo of them, together with one of Dan – I'd directed her to Facebook – but only, she'd told me, if teamed with a floaty dress, which she'd picked out for me online last year, and which I dutifully wore. I'd wondered if the look wasn't too young for me, but Dan seemed to give the whole ensemble an appreciative glance after we'd kissed each other's cold cheeks and taken our coats off.

We were just being led by one of the waitresses to exactly the same corner table we'd had the last couple of times, which he assured me with a laugh he absolutely hadn't organized, when his phone went. He frowned, irritated, but when he saw who it was, he took the call.

'Right . . . OK . . . OK. Yes, stay there, if you can . . . I won't be long . . . No, no worries, I'll be back . . . Yes, quite sure.'

He pocketed the phone and looked worried. I raised my eyebrows enquiringly. 'That was Betty. She was just about to leave when Mum took a tumble. She says she's perfectly OK, and she's popped her on the sofa . . .'

'Oh, but you must go.'

He scratched his head and looked torn. 'I'm sure she's fine. It's just . . .'

'No, no, definitely. We'll do this another day.'

'Or we could both go,' he said, as it occurred to him. 'And I'll run you back later. There's loads of food in the freezer. I could shove an M&S pie in the oven? I'm not sure it'll just be the two of us, but . . .'

'Yes, why not? Good plan. Come on, let's both go. I love your mum, and it couldn't matter less if she joins us. Anyway, I know you'll worry if we don't go.'

We left the pub, crossed the lane, and set off across

the fields, following a footpath with our torches. And actually, it was lovely to be walking through the plough in the soft night air, our boots marching in unison.

When we arrived at the house, Betty was already putting her coat on in the hall. 'Sorry, Dan, I would have stayed, but our Lily needs me to babysit, and what with Pete and his bad leg . . .'

'Yes, yes, absolutely. You must go.'

'But she really is fine,' she reassured him. 'It's just, I knew you'd want me to ring you and—'

But Dan had gone. With a fleeting thank you to Betty, he'd disappeared into the sitting room. I followed him. Nancy was on the yellow sofa by the fire, propped up with tapestry cushions.

'I told her not to ring you,' she whisper-hissed, her eyes flashing with anger beneath her turban. '*Told* her I was completely fine. What was she thinking?'

'Where does it hurt, Mum?' Dan said, crouching down and ignoring her. We heard the front door shut as Betty left. 'What did you fall on?'

'My foot,' she told us. 'I just rolled off the side of it, down the step to the kitchen, and felt something go. And yes, I might well have done a ligament or something, but there is absolutely *nothing* to be done until the morning, apart from leg up with an ice pack, which Betty has already done!' A pack of frozen peas was indeed nestled against her foot, which did look a bit swollen.

'So sorry, darling,' she said, reaching out for my hand with her thin, bony one and rolling her eyes at me above

Dan's head. 'All this could have been conveyed on the phone, while you two had a lovely supper. But wretched Betty beat me to it!' She was clearly livid.

I grinned. 'Couldn't matter less, Nance. We'll eat with you here.'

'You will not,' she retorted. 'You'll eat in the kitchen, while I have mine in here, which I was going to do anyway in front of *Gardeners' World*. Which I like to watch alone,' she said very firmly. 'No, actually, have it in the dining room, at the small round table in the window. Not the big one. Light the fire, Dan, and draw the curtains. And the candles are in the sideboard drawer in there.'

He laughed. 'I don't think we'll do that. We'll eat in here with you.'

Oh, right. I wasn't sure about candles in the dining room either, but I could see that Nance very definitely wanted us to eat on our own and was not to be thwarted in her plans, so surely we could leave her and Monty Don to it and eat in the kitchen?

In the event, we all had trays on our laps in front of the TV. Dan nipped across to his mother occasionally to turn the bag of peas when he thought they were getting a bit warm, and to put a tea towel around her foot when it was overly cold. It was sweet, actually, if a little over attentive, but then I knew from friends that my own family was ridiculously laid back and under attentive. Imo teased me about it, recalling countless childhood occasions when I'd sent them to school with near pneumonia, or others such as a particularly hairy sea wall in Cornwall which I'd let them walk along. The raging sea was on one side, a forty-foot drop on to concrete on the other. Imo swears I'd called up, after Helena had vaguely voiced concern: 'Darlings, if you're going to fall, fall this way, on to the concrete.'

So no, I wasn't used to a family that rearranged cushions behind my head, as Dan was doing for Nance now, whilst, to her credit, she grumbled about his fussing, or, equally mindful of my needs, wondered if I'd like some more fish pie, since I seemed to have polished mine off in a nano second? As Dan widened his eyes in mock incredulity at my empty plate, Nance and I laughed.

'I've always been greedy,' I told him, none too seductively. 'In fact, when I was young, Mum used to make me wait until everyone else had started and was well under way so I didn't finish before them.'

'Which surely only made you bolt your food more!' observed Nance, triumphantly. 'Your mother certainly had some strange ideas.'

I grinned, well used to Mum and Nance sparring with each other, which was only part of their friendship, and surely oiled the wheels. Much as their shared love of the hard stuff did, I thought, watching Nance drain her small glass of wine and waggle it at Dan. He made a face and shook his head back.

'Spoilsport!' roared Nance, clearly absolutely fine. No fluttery, dizzy, after-effects there.

So yes, we were still at the minor tumbling stage, I thought, with Nancy and my parents. But what next?

Would they all take more of a tumble one day and drop down dead? Ghastly, obviously, but perhaps a blessing, and something they all hoped would happen. A quick exit. Or, would they tumble, but survive? End up in a ridiculously expensive care home, wired up to all manner of machines which kept them alive, if not kicking, for the next five years? Impossible to say. But guiltily, I knew that given the admirable level of vigilance Dan provided, the latter would most likely be true for his mother, one day. Which was commendable, obviously, but didn't half have financial implications for the next generation. That probably wasn't a problem here, because Nancy was loaded, but my own parents were not. And although we'd collaborated and borrowed to get the bungalow up to speed, there was no more in the pot. I had a feeling I'd have to go back to work if any more was to dribble through, which these days really was a dribble. Plenty of time in prison, to write, of course, I realized suddenly. And plenty of material, too. Who knew who'd be on my top bunk? A serial murderer, perhaps, with a grisly tale to tell. Or a child molest—

'You all right?' Dan's face seemed to be right in mine. He was leaning over and peering at me anxiously as he attempted to take my tray from me. I loosened the white-knuckle grip I appeared to have on it and nodded mutely. My palms were sweaty as I let go. I didn't trust my voice.

'You do look awfully pale, darling,' said Nance, with a frown.

'No, no, I'm – I'm fine,' I told them. I raised a smile.

'Bit ambitious with the second helping of fish pie.' Dan took my untouched plate on the tray for me. 'Let me help you in the kitchen.'

I followed him through, taking Nancy's tray, glad he hadn't said: 'No, you stay here with Mum,' as I thought he was about to. Although juggling three trays would be a feat, even for a capable man like Dan, I thought, as I watched him throw everything in the dishwasher, quickly wipe down surfaces and toss ready meal cartons in the bin. He turned to face me with a smile and I'd already straightened my back and rearranged my face to accommodate a much chirpier expression. It took a bit of summoning but was still achievable.

I could see he was slightly disarmed as he regarded me appreciatively. He scratched the back of his head sheepishly. 'Gosh, it's extraordinary . . . I mean, honestly Lucy, you really haven't changed that much since we were young.'

I laughed as he moved towards me. 'Oh, now that really is stretching it.'

'And luckily, you can't remember me when *I* was young,' he said softly. 'None taken, by the way.' I laughed quietly. He was resting his hands lightly on my shoulders now and I tilted my face up. If ever a girl needed to be kissed, it was me. Kiss away all my worries and troubles. Make the bogeyman disappear. And when he did, it was lovely: gentle and tender, and he held me very close, too. I could feel his heart thudding against mine before we drew back and I suspected my own was doing the same, unaccustomed as it was to such activity. But the lighting was harsh and overhead, and the door was still open, and his mother was in the next room. We made wry faces at each other and stifled a laugh apiece.

'Another time, I think,' he murmured.

'Quite.'

'And now I think I'll take you home.'

'I could walk?'

He made an appalled face. 'Don't be ridiculous.'

He went to the kitchen dresser for his car keys and I noticed his face was quite flushed and happy, as I suspected mine was too. Yes, this was nice. Felt right. He shouted to Nance that he was running me back and I popped my head in and said goodbye. She looked curious and excited, her eyes wide as I pecked her cheek. But I gave nothing away.

'*Do* come back, my dear,' she murmured, grasping my hand. 'Dan would *so* love it.'

I grinned and agreed that I would, and then Dan took me home. We did kiss again, before I got out, with more passion than before, and then laughed as we realized that here we were, in a steamy car, snogging outside my parents' house. It was too absurd. I got out and shut the door, agreeing to meet again soon, but with fewer interested parties. As I let myself into the darkened house, I discovered I was still smiling. I had an idea Dan might be too. I turned out the few lamps my parents had left on and poked the smouldering log into submission in the grate. The dishwasher was humming cheerfully in the kitchen. Hector was asleep in his basket. I made to go upstairs. Out of habit, I checked my phone. One message from Imo, hoping I was OK, another from Ned, and one from Josh which made me stop, halfway up the stairs, on the landing.

'Sorry, thought I'd sent this and wondered why you hadn't replied, then just found it unsent. Bit disorganized – I've been away:

OK, that doesn't sound good. Tell your friend I'm happy to advise her if she'd like to meet.'

23

I stared at the screen. Went a bit cold suddenly, shocked. I read the last text I'd sent him.

> 'My friend has been round. The neighbour wasn't in, but it turns out she's a friend of the dead husband. My friend is now in terrible trouble.'

My living hell, which had been slumbering quietly at low-level anxiety, came roaring back to life like Caliban from his cave. I felt sick: nothing placatory there. I messaged back:

> 'That is so kind of you would love to meet. Is tomorrow any good?'

I needed to do this now. Immediately. I stayed still on the landing, waiting. It seemed to me I wouldn't move from this spot until I knew. The text had been sent an hour ago and I hoped he hadn't gone to bed. It was only ten o'clock, though. Dots began to dance on my screen. He was back within seconds.

> 'Tomorrow is fine. I'm teaching but could meet you close by. There's a Pret in Melrose Street. One o'clock?'

I frantically messaged back.

> 'Perfect. Thank you.'

I stared out of the landing window at the almost full moon, obscured by a thin veil of cloud in the night sky. It wasn't perfect. Of course it wasn't. My wording was as obfuscated as the moon at which I gazed. Nothing could be perfect any more. I'd effectively killed my husband. I was under no illusion about that. But a kind man was going to advise and help me, which was something. Just as another kind man had cooked me supper tonight. Strange how life can turn, like that, on a sixpence. One moment you're perfectly fine, or you've allowed yourself to think you are because the alternative – walking around in a state of high alert and high anxiety at all times – is unsustainable; and the next, you're not. You're meeting a man in a sandwich bar in London who, given your predicament, will spell out the consequences of your actions to you. Your actions taken in an extremely short space of time but as a result of years of provocation.

In a remarkably cool manner for one for whom the bell was so imminently to toll, I went on up the stairs to bed.

I managed to maintain the cool, collected manner to my parents the following morning. They hardly batted an eyelid when I said I was going to London to look at some furniture for the cottage. OKA, in the Fulham Road, I told them, was my focus. In fact they looked rather pleased that I was so enthused. It was also convenient, they told me, because they were lunching with the Frobishers, and Camilla, their daughter, was picking them up.

'And she's dropping us back,' Dad told me. 'And worry not, Camilla is more scary than my old company commander. She'll have us back here at three o'clock on the dot, and no more than barley water will have passed our lips.'

'More's the pity,' grumbled Mum.

I knew this was stretching the truth, but also knew they were in good hands. I rang Camilla to thank her.

'Oh, it's no problem. I have to do something with mine or they go a bit stir crazy. But I limit it to one couple at a time. And frankly, I've banned Nance.'

I smiled. 'She's incapacitated anyway, I saw her last night. She's done something to her foot. Laid up.'

'Ah. Well, sadly that won't detain her for long; she's a spirited old bird. Unlike that wet fish Daniel who flaps around looking after her.'

I so wished she hadn't said that. I knew from Helena that Camilla had a sharp tongue: was a bit of a cow, in fact. But I still wished she hadn't said it.

I found the Pret a Manger in Melrose Street quite easily and pushed through the plate-glass door.

The café was busy with lunchtime regulars, and by the time Josh arrived, I'd already made headway in quite a burgeoning queue. He appeared beside me with a smile. A social peck, we mutually decided was appropriate, since we'd met a few times already, and it was performed in a perfunctory manner. Nonetheless, a ridiculous frisson spiralled through me.

'Coffee?' I asked, wanting to break the ice quickly as we approached the counter.

'Please. An espresso.' He reached into a fridge for a chicken salad wrap.

I ordered the same but with a cappuccino, and insisted on paying since he was doing me a huge favour by meeting me. I wanted to make this as businesslike as possible in order to pick his highly intelligent brain.

The place was packed now, but we found two bar stools at the counter in the window, which luckily were reasonably private.

'Thank you for meeting me,' I told him as we settled ourselves down, trying but failing to keep the anxiety from my voice.

'No problem. And I wanted to apologize. That text I sent you last night was unconsidered, and in retrospect, rather alarmist. I've given it some thought since, looked into it a bit more. I can't say for sure, but I honestly think you're overreacting here and that there really isn't anything to worry about.'

'Oh!' I wanted to kiss him. On the lips. I very nearly did.

'I know I said before that intent constitutes murder, but on reflection, this is more nuanced. The thing is, there's no legal compunction to actually save a life. If you're taking a walk in the park and someone is drowning in a lake, you don't have to jump in.'

'Really? You can just watch them drown?'

'Obviously it's not a natural reaction, but it's not criminal. However, this is slightly different. It wasn't a case of jumping into deep water. It was a case of picking up a phone.'

'Yes.'

'Which I think makes it voluntary manslaughter – rather than straightforward manslaughter, which, as I said before, is a mistake. But not murder.'

'So better?' I breathed.

'A bit. But still custodial.'

I swallowed. 'Right.'

'But I don't think you're nearly there yet. I mean at the court door. So I really think – calm down.'

I noticed we'd dropped the pretence of 'my friend'. I was so incredibly encouraged by his words there was no way I was going to protest.

'How long did you say you sat there for? When he was unconscious?'

I went very still. Forced myself to tell the truth. 'I think I lied a bit, when you asked me that the other day. I think it might have been more than fifteen minutes.'

He gazed at me. With dark, bottomless brown eyes. Didn't say anything.

'But you didn't look at the clock.'

'Well, I—'

'You didn't look at the clock,' he interrupted fiercely, holding my gaze. 'OK?'

'OK,' I breathed. 'But the woman at the back . . .' I told him about my fears. About Ingrid. About how I knew her. Had realized who she was on the doorstep. Then I told him about her links with my sister-in-law. About Amanda's insinuations in the restaurant. Her mental state.

'Your sister-in-law clearly has psychological problems

and is taking her deranged thoughts to their absolute limit. Encouraging you to come along for the ride. She's playing on the fact that guilt is an overriding emotion when anyone dies.'

'She is,' I said eagerly, 'deranged. And the guilt thing, I've read about that. In fact I even mentioned it to her.'

'It's a natural reaction. You think – oh God, was I responsible in some way? Was it my fault?'

Then I told him about a new fear. About a light being on, in a top-floor bedroom of Ingrid's house, which had kept me awake. A sudden flashback to that top room being briefly lit up. I didn't know if I'd imagined it, I told him. Didn't know if my mind was playing tricks in the small hours. I told him about her being at the memorial service. And about Amanda's threatening speech.

Josh listened. He shrugged when I'd finished. 'That eulogy was just some story your sister-in-law sold herself in her solitude and depression. Some victimhood balls she no doubt elaborated in her mind. Perhaps even came to believe. But I think her building up to something more, something accusatorial, is a figment of your own over-active imagination, if you don't mind me saying so. Because trust me, if Ingrid and Amanda were cooking something up together, you'd have heard about it by now. The police would have carried out door-to-door enquiries with all the neighbours ages ago. If anything came up, if she did have a light on, then turned it off and was awake, watching you, she would have acted by now. Told the police, even. The mind is capable of playing cruel tricks on us, Lucy. If this is a new, recent worry, I think you've imagined it now that you know where Ingrid lives. I think you can relax.'

I gazed at him, speechless. 'Oh, I will, I will,' I breathed happily, when I could find my voice. 'I mean – if you think I should—'

'Look, Lucy,' he interrupted, 'I realize you're taking my words very literally, here. But I'm not a detective. Not even a criminal barrister. I'm an academic. I'm absolutely no oracle on the subject. You should know that.'

I swallowed: looked down at my lap. 'You lecture on it,' I said quietly, wanting to believe.

'Yes, but more on the psychology of the criminal mind. It's your sister-in-law who fascinates me, actually. She's just the sort of woman to stab a lover in the chest.'

I told him he could well be right, and gave him a brief résumé of her life, hers and Michael's, but I kept it brief, because now that he'd assured me this was Amanda's mind spiralling out of control and doing its damnedest to take me with it, I was actually keen to talk about something else. Anything else. I found the matter and manner of Michael's death so horrific, that I either wanted to think about it ceaselessly on my own, or bury it in a box. It wasn't a subject up for cosy discussion and neither was Michael. He was a monster. But he was my monster. And if I wasn't going to jail for killing him or, as the more rational part of my mind told me, letting him die, I didn't want to talk about it.

'You've been away?' I asked conversationally. I was unable to touch my chicken wrap. Instead I sipped my coffee.

He looked surprised that the subject was closed so abruptly. 'Yes, back to France. All very last minute but I took the children skiing for a few days.'

'Ah. Lovely.'

'Lucy, I'm not a psychologist either. But facing things and not running away is sometimes the best course of action. I take it you've already been questioned by the police?'

'Yes,' I whispered. But I only remembered it as a blur. Perhaps because I didn't want to remember it. It had happened very soon after the event. After ... the body ... had gone. In the sitting room, wrapped in my dressing gown, which I'd been allowed to get from my bedroom. A few questions from a kindly policewoman. A younger one, beside her, taking notes. I remembered telling her I hadn't woken at the noise of the break-in, because I'd been wearing earplugs, which I often did. Especially when I knew my husband was coming in late. So no, I hadn't woken when he'd returned, or when the French windows had been forced. But then, later on, I'd stirred: and with some instinctive intuition that Michael wasn't beside me, put an arm out to his side of the bed. Empty. I'd been puzzled. Then I'd gone downstairs. Seen him on the floor unconscious. Realized we'd been broken into. I'd called the emergency services. The policewoman had nodded. It had suddenly occurred to me, you see, that there'd be a time lag. Between me finding him, and ringing 999. I knew the pathologists would spot it. Estimate the time of death. And if, by chance, a neighbour, or a passer-by, had heard the break-in and reported the time, I needed a reason not to have woken. Plus, I did use earplugs occasionally. I even had some handy. When I'd gone up for my dressing gown, I'd slipped some into the pocket, with a trembling hand. Not that she'd asked to see. The policewoman. As I say, I don't think about that interview much. In fact, this was the first time I'd let myself consider it, in detail, at all. Let alone speak of it. It had been airbrushed from my mind.

'Lucy?'

I swam to the surface. It was a long way, though. I'd been far away. As I focused, I realized Josh was staring at me. I regrouped.

'Sorry?'

'I said, was there was an autopsy? A coroner's report?'

'Oh. Yes, there was,' I said.

'Which both concluded that there was no mis-adventure?'

'Except for a shove in the chest and a fall, no.'

'And no inquest.'

'No.'

He nodded. Looked thoughtful. 'Well then, I suggest you forget all about this. And I would block your sister-in-law on your phone. That way you'll have no contact with her ever again.'

I stared at him in wonder. I loved this man. Where had he been all my life? He was making mine so simple, so straightforward. It was extraordinary how another perspective could do that. I realized that now he'd sorted my life out, I wanted to ask him so much about his. I wanted to ask if he was on better terms with his ex-wife,

283

if they were managing to be civil. Clearly they were, if he was allowed to take his children skiing. I wondered how old they were. If Tilly got on with them. I was sure she did – she was gorgeous. I pictured the four of them whizzing down the slopes together: blue skies, snowy mountains. That beautiful girl, erasing all the misery of Agathe – oh yes, I remembered her name.

'Lucy? You'll block her calls?'

'Oh yes – yes, I'll do that,' I agreed. Would I? Block her? Or would I be too scared? Not with someone like this beside me. But of course, he wouldn't be beside me. He belonged to someone else. 'Is Tilly a good skier?' I blurted out stupidly, involuntarily.

He looked confused. 'Sorry?'

'Well, I imagine she went with you? Skiing?' He frowned, then at length, a small smile began to play around his lips. He put his coffee cup down. 'Tilly cooks for me. I found her through a colleague of mine at work, another lone male. She's about half my age, Lucy.'

'Oh!' I stared, confused. 'But – but she called you Joshy. I thought—'

'She says I behave like a baby in the kitchen so she gives me a baby name. Accuses me of not being able to boil an egg. She was preparing a meal for the friends I stayed with when I first came over from Paris. I'm having them to lunch next Sunday, by way of a thank you. She's away – skiing, as a matter of fact – with her boyfriend right now. So she made it before she left. The chicken dish is sitting in the freezer as we speak.'

He was clearly amused. But I was still getting my head

round this. Today was turning out to be completely extraordinary in so many ways. Taking so many unexpected turns for the better, in a manner I was so totally unused to that it was hard to assimilate. Tilly was a cook. Of course she was; she had all the hallmarks of the well-bred girls I used to work with who did that sort of thing. She had a boyfriend. Naturally she did. Naturally.

'Would you like to come?' Still the amused smile.

'Where?'

'To lunch, on Sunday, with my colleagues. A French professor and his wife.'

All my Christmases appeared to have come at once. All of them. I put my coffee cup down and sat up straight. I gave him the most radiant of smiles.

'Oh, I'd *love* to come.'

He grinned. 'Great.'

That was it. Great. And I was sort of – speechless. My whole world had spun on a sixpence again. But this time, the right way.

'Unless, of course, coming back to the house . . . ?'

'What? Oh – no! Not a problem at all! Love my old house.' I beamed widely. He looked disconcerted, as well he might. 'I mean,' I gabbled quickly, 'I might not go in the study—'

'No, quite—' he agreed, equally quickly.

'But anywhere else—' God. Did that sound a bit – you know. Forward? 'I mean – the sitting room, the kitchen,' I said rapidly.

'Exactly.' He grinned. Clearly diverted now. And then he glanced at his watch. 'Actually, I have to go. I have a

285

tutorial in ten minutes and I need to collect my papers. See you on Sunday, then. Oh – and thanks for lunch.'

'No, thank *you*,' I breathed, hopefully not too gustily. I seemed to be puffing and blowing like a force ten gale. I was very pink too, I was sure, as I stood up. He pecked my cheeks – hot cheeks, I was convinced – and then, whipping his navy scarf around his neck in that very stylish French way, he gave me another huge grin. *God*, he was good-looking. And then he was gone. I gazed down at my chicken wrap, enraptured. Suddenly I was starving. I sat and guzzled it down in minutes flat and drained my coffee. I *wasn't* going to jail. Amanda *was* a lunatic. An attractive man *had* invited me to lunch and clearly found me attractive and enjoyed my company. I wanted to sing, I wanted to dance. Instead, I left the café, and pushing through the door to the street, raised my face to the heavens and sang '*Hoorah!*' to anyone who was listening. A passing wino gave me a wink, but everyone else ignored me. A fool, on a high, in London.

Still glowing, I made my way back to my car and down the Edgware Road, towards the M4 and home. The traffic was light for once, and I whizzed along making good time. Ed Sheeran came on the radio and I turned him up loud and sang along. As I belted out the chorus to 'Photograph' it seemed to me that the only fly in the ointment, the only slight fly, if you could even call it a fly, half a fly, perhaps, was that I now appeared to have two men in my life. Only one that made my heart soar, admittedly, but I also knew that he might not even be in my life. Might simply have asked me to lunch to make up numbers. Far more likely. But still, it was a lovely conundrum to have. To possibly have. And a lovely *friend* to have, I decided, forcing myself to be sensible, if that's all he became.

Ridiculously, though – and I feel you know me well enough for me to tell you this – I imagined myself introducing him to Ned and Imo. Except – Ned had already met him. Had *liked* him. My heart gave a foolish leap. Josh. Joshy. I smiled. Dear Tilly. *Lovely* Tilly. So young. Of course she was. How could I even have *thought* such a thing? It was verging on the perv – no, no it wasn't. But she was so refined. Not that he wasn't. But he was more right-on than she was. More woke, as it's now called. Tilly's boyfriend was probably in the City. Whereas Josh . . . well golly, I'd find out, wouldn't I? Cosmopolitan, classless, liberal intelligentsia, was where I'd put him. And age? Hmm . . . difficult, I thought, as I came off the motorway. I gave it some thought as I wound through the lanes. A tiny bit older than me, I'd like to think, but I'd hazard that was wishful thinking. The same would be ideal. Younger . . . more tricky. And stressful, as Nancy had discovered. What was it Mum had said? All that maintenance. All that grooming. All that plucking, dieting, waxing and exercising. Baked bean tins had come into it too somewhere, although I couldn't quite remember where. Exhausting. And expensive.

Well, I'd write a book, I decided as I pulled into the drive. To pay for it all. Of course I would. Hadn't I already sort of decided? That needs must, to pay for the cottage? Well, now they *absolutely* must. And he'd like that, I thought, as I got out of the car. Men did. And don't forget, he'd looked me up. In a good way, we now assumed. And I could hardly say – d'you know what, Joshy, I don't really do that any more. The writing thing. I just sort of, care for my parents. That wasn't terribly attractive. Kind, but not sexy. Yes, men liked the books, even if they weren't Booker Prize winners. *Especially* since they weren't Booker Prize winners. One had to consider their fragile egos. Nothing too threatening. Although I was sure Josh wasn't like that. Those were the old Michael days. He was too enlightened for that.

Lamps were on in the sitting room window and smoke was spiralling from the chimney, signalling the parents' safe return from the Frobishers. On the way in I caught sight of my reflection in the hall mirror. I paused for a moment. My hair was badly in need of highlights. And it was growing, actually, like a bush. It needed trimming. The thickening waist could do with some trimming too. I'd see about those Zumba classes in the village hall. How *could* I have gone to London looking like this?

As I went to poke my head around the sitting room door, my parents beat me to it. Mum was on her feet, opening the door from the other side so that I nearly flew through. Dad got up quickly from his armchair by the fire, putting his newspaper aside. Both their faces were pale.

'Oh darling, we've been so worried,' blurted out my mother.

'Worried? Why?'

'No, not worried,' said Dad quickly. 'We're sure it's nothing. It's just – the police have been round, love.'

'The police? Why?' I stared at them.

'They've caught the burglar.'

'What?' Even as I said it, though, I knew.

'The one who broke into your house. You know. The one who had a scuffle with Michael.'

'Except now, of course,' my mother informed me, her pale blue eyes wide behind her spectacles, 'he's not just a burglar. He's also a murderer.'

24

I gazed at my parents, who looked terribly old suddenly. I felt that awful sinking feeling one does at times
like this: when the lift rising smoothly and inexorably
to the top floor, suddenly fails, stalls – and then crashes
to the ground.

'Right,' I said, forcing myself not to betray any emotion. Forcing myself to stay calm. 'Right, well, that's
good, surely?' I said, coming in and sitting by the fire.

'Of course it is,' said Dad buoyantly, sitting down
again, opposite me. 'I told your mother it was nothing to
worry about. I don't know why she's got so upset.'

'But why would the police want to talk to you, darling?' she said, clearly very worried.

'Well, to let me know, I'm sure.'

'But they said they had some questions they wanted
to ask you. It didn't seem like a formality to me.'

'To tie up loose ends, no doubt,' said my father. 'Go
down tomorrow, love.'

'Down?'

'To the station. They asked if you'd drop by.'

'Oh.' I stared at him. 'Oh, well no, actually, I'll go
now,' I said slowly. I got to my feet. 'I'd rather.'

'Yes, I should,' said Mum quickly. 'Get it over with.'

Dad shot her a look. 'There's nothing to *get* over,' he said irritably.

'No, no I know, but—'

'Cecily, for once—' They were talking over one another.

'It's fine,' I cut in. 'Dad, Mum is rightly anxious. It brings back . . . memories. And I'd rather go. Have you had some tea? How were the Frobishers?' I made myself function.

'I'll put the kettle on and make your mother one,' Dad was saying. He shuffled towards the kitchen, knowing I was asking him to take the helm. 'And the Frobishers were on good form. Sent their love. We'll see you in a bit then, love.' His eyes were anxious too, though, as he filled the kettle at the sink, and I wondered what the police had said.

I drove down to the local town in a very different condition to that of the girl who'd vacated this seat at the wheel not ten minutes ago. That almost teenager, full of skippy excitement, trading one man in her head for another, was no more. This was no girl; this was a woman. A very tired one at that, hunched over the wheel. I tried to think. It occurred to me I'd thought very little about the intruder. At the time, the police had told me these sorts of break-ins were very common, about six a week in Fulham, they'd said wearily, and I'd sensed they thought they had little chance of catching him. Even though a run-of-the-mill burglary had stepped up to a murder inquiry, it was still the run-of-the-mill burglar at the helm: slippery as an eel, clever enough not to have been caught before, and not to be caught again. They'd gone through the motions of fingerprints – there were none, so gloved, I suppose – and I imagine there was no DNA either. I told myself to calm down, or as Imo would say, 'Calm yourself, Mother,' joshing me. I found myself wishing she was here, with me. Ned, too. But Imo was so good in a crisis.

I parked in front of the police station in the market square and realized it couldn't look less intimidating if it tried, this little brick and flint cottage, in a small market town. It even still had its Victorian blue lamp above the door. It occurred to me that many years ago I'd taken my cycling proficiency test here. In the back yard, with a dozen or so other ten-year-olds from my local primary school, watched over by a kindly copper. There was no cause for alarm. I locked the car, went inside and gave the policewoman on the front desk my name.

A few minutes later a man in a suit appeared and asked me to follow him. That was when my heart began to thump. A plain-clothed policeman. And I was being taken to a room, not just details taken at the front desk. As he gestured for me to sit down opposite him at a small table, the same policewoman slipped into the room and stood in the corner. I breathed deeply, forcing myself to stay calm, telling myself there was nothing to worry about.

The policeman waited for me to settle. 'Thank you for coming in, Mrs Palmer. I'm Detective Sergeant Turner, and this,' he gestured at his colleague, 'is PC Williams.'

I nodded and managed to look him in the eye. 'I hear you've caught the burglar,' I said conversationally, receiving it as the good news it surely was. 'That's good.'

'Yes, the Met took him into custody yesterday. He was breaking and entering a few streets away from your house and the tiny bit of DNA they have on your French windows matches his. Also, he's now confessed. The Met have asked us to continue the investigation.'

'Oh, right. That's unusual, isn't it? For a burglar to confess?'

'Not if we're accusing him of a more serious crime, namely manslaughter or murder.'

'So he's only confessed to the burglary?'

'Correct.'

'And did he—'

'Mrs Palmer, would you mind if I asked the questions? This is our inquiry.'

'Oh. No. Of course not.'

'Would you like anyone to be present?'

I took a deep breath. 'You mean a solicitor? No – I mean . . . I don't need one, do I?'

He shrugged. 'You're not under caution. And therefore you can stop the interview at any time, if you feel you'd like to.'

I nodded, mute. Dug my nails into my hand beneath the table.

'Mrs Palmer, our suspect maintains that when he ran from your house in Gresham Road, the deceased, your husband, gave chase down the garden. That he was perfectly unhurt when he left.'

I stared, horrified. 'But – but that's just not true! That's a lie! When I came down, Michael was lying in a pool of blood by the coffee table!'

'Quite so.' He stared at an iPad before him and I wondered if this was being recorded.

'What – so you mean—' I was thrown; thinking aloud now. 'You think Michael came back inside and then fell? But surely there'd be mud on his shoes – from the garden. Or – or you think – someone pushed him *then*? But who, that's so unlikely!' The detective stayed silent and I realized I was talking far too much. But then the silence grew and was appalling. Endless. 'I mean – you're surely not suggesting . . . you're surely not just going to take the word of a common thief!'

The word 'common' hung in the air like something Leslie Phillips would say in a *Carry On* movie. In a posh accent. A larky comedy from the sixties, except this wasn't a comedy. Not at all.

'Your sister-in-law, Amanda Palmer, told my colleagues in London that relations between you and your husband were very strained.'

I inhaled sharply. 'Yes. Yes, they were,' I agreed in a whisper. What was he implying? This was worse. This wasn't me being slow to call for help as Michael lay dying; this was me giving him a mighty shove. And they'd already spoken to Amanda. When? Recently or a long time ago? 'But I would never have . . .' I stopped. Licked my lips. 'Relations are strained in many marriages.'

'Indeed. And you said at the time, and just now, that

294

when you came downstairs, you found him unconscious on the rug.'

'Yes.'

'Not puffing back up the garden, staggering a bit in the dark, drunk, disorientated, making no sense. Whereupon you had a flaming row and you gave him a push?'

'No!' I was horrified. 'And God – if anyone says I did, if the woman at the back – I would never have done that!'

He considered me, evaluating me. The room was very quiet and still. I sensed the policewoman behind me, but she made no sound.

'Tell me, if you would, please, about the woman at the back.'

I licked my lips. They were dry as dust. 'I've changed my mind,' I said huskily. 'I'd like a solicitor. And I'd like to speak to my daughter first.'

'Of course.' He nodded efficiently and closed his laptop. I imagine he supposed that the look he gave me was inscrutable. But there was an element of satisfaction in it. An element of a job well done. His job. I watched him tuck a pen away inside his jacket. I wanted to ask him if he had any idea what it felt like to be owned by someone. I wanted to tell him that, had I given Michael a push, that too would have been understandable. But I never laid a finger on him. Just as he never laid a finger on me. He was far too clever. Never a bruise, not one. Just dark enclosed spaces where I could contemplate potential accidents as he called them. There was a lot I could say.

'And I'd like to go home.'

'Naturally. PC Williams will see you out. We'll be in touch, Mrs Palmer.' And with that he got up and left the room.

After a moment, the policewoman came round and waited for me to get up and follow her. She was totally expressionless. A very different young woman to the one who'd smiled at me in reception and asked me to wait, please. And he, my interviewer, was definitely not an older version of the nice young copper who'd over-seen my cycling proficiency test. The one who'd smiled as I'd completed winding through some cones. With trembling hands I pushed my chair back and followed her out.

Outside in the car, I rang Imo. No answer. But her phone was always off at work. I sent her a message.

'Please ring me when you can.'

I was about to start the car but she rang back immediately. Because I would never normally write that.

'What is it? What's wrong? Is it Granny?'

'No, it's not, it's me.' I had to pause a moment. Fight for control. 'Darling, I'm outside the police station in Thame. I've been asked lots of questions. I have a feeling they're going to ask me some more. I need a solicitor.'

There was a silence. Then: 'Shit. OK. Don't do any-thing. And don't go for their duty solicitor, if they offer. I'll get you one. And I'll come down.'

'Thanks, darling,' I whispered.

We rang off and I stared out at the drizzle on the windscreen. I wouldn't ever, *ever* worry her. And I despised mothers who did. Who loaded their own problems on to their children. Melissa had talked to her children far too much. Lauren, her eldest, had been very weighed down: very affected. I'd kept Michael's treatment of me from them as much as was humanly possible, always. Except of course it wasn't always. Possible. Both had witnessed enough and Imo had once found me . . . anyway. I'd done my best. Because I didn't want them to be damaged. But this was different. This required prompt, clever action and I needed Imo fast. I sat there. My mind was racing. Most of this was palpably not true. Michael giving chase was ludicrous. He'd have been catatonic. I was amazed he'd even got up from the sofa. The slightest shove would have had him over like a ninepin. But the intruder told it differently. Well he would, wouldn't he, in the words of Mandy Rice-Davies. Lying through his teeth to stop them pinning a murder charge on him. Inventing a story about being pursued. And now I'd stupidly mentioned Ingrid. Who might not even have been in the equation. I shut my eyes. Imagined the detective now on the phone to the Met. Telling them to conduct another house to house, particularly concentrating on the houses at the back.

It seemed to me I stayed like that for a very long time. But at length, I reached for my keys and started the engine. I drove slowly home. Was I in serious trouble? I wasn't sure. Surely they wouldn't let me go home if I was? Surely they would have cautioned me, which he'd mentioned? From my work, I knew that was the step before being arrested, which I definitely hadn't been. So that meant they had no evidence. Although he had asked me if I'd like anyone with me. Why? To frighten me? Was that even allowed? And the interview room – so intense. Surely if they just wanted some clarification of events that night, they'd have popped round? But of course, they had. And I'd been out. This should have just been a cosy chat in the sitting room with a cup of tea. Biscuits, even. I began to relax. I'd only been in that ghastly room because I'd gone to them, and it was the only place they had to talk. And surely if the Met really thought I'd done it they'd have come down themselves? Had they just asked the local branch to go through the motions for form's sake? I made myself loosen my grip on the wheel. I was overreacting as usual. They were obviously going to re-question everyone concerned. No, not re-question, just ask for confirmation of what had actually happened that night.

As I parked in the drive, I got a text from Imo.

'Helena and I will be down first thing tomorrow.'

I messaged her back:

'Darling I have an awful feeling I've overreacted. I'm sure we could talk on the phone.'

'We're coming,' came the immediate response.

Slipping my phone into my bag, I couldn't help feeling relieved. Imo *and* Helena. The cavalry.

25

Helena and Imo did indeed arrive the following morning. I'd had to tell whoppers to my parents along the lines of them both having the day off and wanting to hotfoot it down to see the cottage, but neither of them believed me.

'But they're both so busy . . .' said Mum anxiously as she passed me the marmalade over the kitchen table. 'Helena never even has a day off if she's ill.'

Dad was silent but he didn't look at me. And last night, he'd diplomatically said they were very tired after all the excitement of the Frobishers and were going to have an early night. At eight thirty. I'd thanked him with my eyes. Up until then I'd done rather well: had said on my return that there was nothing at all to worry about, and that the police were just making routine enquiries, now that they'd caught the intruder, which was absolutely standard procedure. I'd cooked us all scrambled eggs on toast and watched *Gogglebox* with them, which we all loved. But at one particularly hilarious moment, I hadn't laughed, and Dad had looked my way and caught me staring into the middle distance, no doubt looking rather tragic. That's when he'd suggested an early night.

Luckily Helena had sent me an inspired text saying – 'Please tell Mum how excited I am! How lucky that Imo and I are both off together!' – which I was able to show her over breakfast. She took the phone as I passed it to her, then got her reading glasses out of their case and peered. She read it aloud slowly, word by word, as old people do, and then her face cleared with joy.

'Oh! How marvellous! And what a lucky coincidence!'

I took the phone back. 'But she says she's booked a table for lunch at the Rose and Crown just for the three of us, because apparently we have to go through all the power of attorney and inheritance tax stuff.' I rolled my eyes.

'Power of . . .'

'Remember the girls are going to do that for us,' said Dad helpfully, but his voice was gruff. 'Take all the business side of things out of our hands.'

'Oh, that's good.' Mum's face cleared again. 'Yes, you were finding it all a bit much, weren't you, darling?'

That wasn't happening yet. The power of attorney. It might, one day, and Helena had discussed it with Dad, but at the moment he was still quite capable. That's what I mean by whoppers. For the second time in twenty-four hours, Dad and I communed with our eyes, and I thanked him. I also tried to convey that I'd talk to him later, but it was quite hard, all that, in just one glance.

My mother's no fool, but she was clearly convinced because my father was, often the narrative of their marriage. Added to which, she was already so full of skippy excitement about the cottage that when Helena and Imo did arrive, she could barely pause to kiss them on the cheeks, hurrying off immediately to find them some wellies. When we all got to the cottage door, she then informed them it was shoes off.

'I thought you always said that was naff,' commented Helena, nevertheless doing as she was told on the threshold. She then boggled at the little white slippers in a cellophane wrapper we were handed.

'What's this, Granny?' exclaimed Imo in wonder.

'They're from the local spa,' Mum explained. 'They let me have a few, because I go there regularly now for my toenails. Lucy takes me, and my frightfully nice girl gave them to me. And your father.'

'Dad! Pedicures at a spa?' Helena blinked at him.

'It's more pruning of the rhino tusks, actually,' Dad drawled. 'With hedge clippers. But yes, they do mine too. So much cheaper than a chiropodist.'

'Neither of us can reach, you see,' Mum explained. 'And your father's were growing out of his socks.'

'Oh please.' Helena was horrified.

'Come on, let's go in.' Dad was equally excited and impatient, I realized, and in we shuffled, in our spa slippers.

More had happened since last I was here, and Imo and Helena rightly oohed and aahed over the shiny granite worktops and wooden cupboards now in situ, all the drawers sliding noiselessly in and out. Mum demonstrated and Imo, rising to the occasion, joined in, hamming it up like a schmoozing saleswoman. 'The drawers don't so much slide as *glide*,' she purred in a low voice, demonstrating, and we all laughed. Yes, I made myself. And actually, it was so lovely having my family around me, particularly these two highly intelligent women, I felt better already. How could anything ghastly happen? I was sure it would all be fine.

When everyone had gushed sufficiently, we headed back for a quick coffee in the kitchen, exchanging snippets of news. As Helena showed our parents photos of the twins on a recent school trip to France, I put a chicken pie for two in the oven and told Dad it would be ready in half an hour. Then, with huge hugs all round, and promises to come down again soon, the three of us set off in Helena's car.

The car was silent. For some time. At length, Helena spoke. She tried to keep her voice light.

'Well, that little house has got Mum and Dad written all over it.'

'It's a no-brainer,' I told her. 'And actually, had this just been a normal day, we could well be doing just that. Going to the pub to talk about what to do with Pope's Farm, when they both move into the cottage.'

'It is a normal day,' put in Imo from the back. 'The more I think about it from the little you've told me, the more the whole thing is absurd.'

'I agree,' said Helena staunchly. 'But let's do this over lunch and a glass of wine. I think I'm allowed to sip a small one for the road.'

The pub was full, so it was good that Helena had booked. I could see her looking around with interest at her old haunt, as I had done when I first moved here. When we'd got our table and ordered our food, she leaned in and folded her arms on the table. She fixed me with her blue, Hartley eyes.

'OK. Suppose you tell us exactly what happened at the police station.'

I took a deep breath and filled them in, trying to tell it as verbatim as I possibly could. It took a while, and they both took a moment to absorb, once I'd finished. I could see the cogs whirring.

'R-ight,' said Helena slowly. 'So they asked if you wanted someone present . . .'

'But they didn't charge you,' finished Imo.

'No.'

'Which is odd, isn't it?' asked Imo, turning to her aunt. 'Scaremongering, d'you think?'

Helena shrugged. 'Possibly. And the whole story about Michael legging it after the burglar is total bollocks, as is the suggestion that you came down and had a furious row with him, presumably about him being pissed and incapable of giving chase, and gave him a shove.'

'Exactly.'

'Exactly, as in, you didn't?'

'No, of course I bloody didn't!'

She nodded. 'Luce, I had to ask. But surely then,' she frowned, 'if that's the case, you have nothing to worry about?'

I felt my mouth drying again. 'I . . . didn't call the ambulance immediately.'

They stared at me. I saw Helena's eyes widen slightly. Not Imo's, though. In hers I saw a flash of recognition.

'How long?' She leaned forward intently. 'How long did you wait?'

I took a deep breath. This old chestnut. 'I think about half an hour.'

Neither my sister nor my daughter recoiled in horror at this news, though Helena's mouth pursed a bit. Then they both sat back and digested it for a moment.

'So it could have been longer?' asked Helena.

'Conceivably. But I've since learned,' I leaned in, lowering my voice, 'from someone I know, someone who's an expert in these things, that there is no actual legal compunction to save a life. For example, if someone was drowning—'

'Hang on,' interrupted Imo. 'Jesus, Mum, who? Who have you talked to?'

I explained about Josh, the criminology professor, saying criminology professor about six times. Obviously not someone I'd met in the street. 'Ned's met him,' I said. 'He really liked him.'

'No one else?' asked Helena quietly.

'No.' I felt stupid. 'No one else.'

They looked at each other. 'I wouldn't see him again,' said Helena.

'OK. Except – he's asked me to lunch. With other people,' I added quickly. 'Won't it look a bit odd?'

Of course I'd cancel if necessary. Now that my world had changed for the catastrophic, Josh was low down my list of priorities. Who was that woman who'd considered having her eyebrows plucked professionally, maybe even having them tinted to remove the grey? Not the one sitting here.

'Yes, it might,' agreed Helena slowly. 'Important to

carry on as normal. All right, go, but don't *talk* about it, OK?' She struggled but failed to keep the bafflement from her voice. I could see her and Imo thinking, God, we always knew Luce/Mum wasn't brain of Britain, but this level of stupidity is unreal.

I lowered my head. Hard to explain. About always having been on my own. Always fighting my constant battles, alone. Always keeping Michael to myself. Hard to explain, when you've been locked in a dark cellar, sometimes for hours at a time, how it had felt to talk to someone who seemed incredibly kind and concerned and who knew about these sorts of people. By whom I meant Michael and Amanda. Understood the way their minds worked. But when I raised my eyes, both pairs of eyes regarding mine were kind.

'It's all right, Mum,' Imo said gently. 'I get why you told him.'

I nodded. Made my mouth move a bit, but couldn't smile.

Helena leaned across and squeezed my hand. I nodded mutely. They both gave me a moment.

'Do you think, if it came to it, you could possibly bring yourself to talk about Michael to anyone else?' asked Helena gently.

'Who?' I whispered, but I knew.

'The police,' she said quietly. 'These days, there are very many more women who are coming forward, with lives like yours. Who, because of what they suffered, are being dealt with leniently.'

'Would it have to be . . . public?'

'You mean a trial?'

'Yes.'

'I don't know.'

'And newspapers?'

'Possibly. But as,' she hesitated, 'your – friend – told you, and just going by the zeitgeist, I have every confidence that even if it did go to trial, and to the press, you'd be dealt with fairly.'

Dealt with. I felt very cold, I realized. And the pub was warm as toast, a fire in the grate beside us. 'It's not really that,' I said, forcing myself to raise my voice above a whisper. 'It's just, if it was public . . . if it all came out. All of it . . .' I trailed off.

'Ned and I would know the extent of it,' Imo said gently.

I looked down at my hands. Tears began to stream down my cheeks. I couldn't stop them. More and more they poured, like a valve that's been bursting and suddenly opened. Imo darted to sit beside me and held me tight but I couldn't stop. I was gasping, eyes shut, shaking. Luckily my back was to the rest of the pub but I was oblivious to everyone else anyway.

'Mum, we know,' Imo said.

'No,' I managed, 'you don't.' She didn't. Ned didn't. It had been my life's work. The only thing that kept me going. And writing stupid, frivolous books as a decoy. To keep it from them. I blew my nose into the tissue she'd handed me which was wet already from mopping tears.

'OK, we don't know everything,' she said softly, still

holding me tight. 'But we know enough. And can take it now. We're adults.'

I nodded, but I wasn't sure they could. Not all of it.

'And if we don't know, we can imagine. Which might even be worse.'

'He never hurt me physically, you know that, don't you?' I glanced at her. It was very important she did. She nodded quickly.

'Of course, you've always told us that, and we believe you. And Mum,' she paused to make me look at her. 'You have to believe he never laid a finger on Ned or me, either.' I did know that, but it was always a huge relief to hear it. 'But there are other, subtler ways. Particularly for an intelligent man like Dad. And you have to know, hard as it might be, that yes, Ned and I suffered, and we kept some of it from you, too, but not from each other. We always had each other.'

Relief swept through me. 'You talked about it?'

'Always. We made each other. We had a pact. Told each other everything. The threats he made. And that definitively kept us sane.'

I remembered their regular lunches, dinners, whenever Imo was across. Ned often going to see her in New York. I felt my breathing come down a bit. Helena looked fit to burst a blood vessel, but she was silent. I knew there was a lot she could say about all of us remaining silent, how we should all have spoken out – including her, to some extent – but couldn't. For fear of reprisals. That's what you did, for love. And we were the lucky ones, we three. We had that. Love. Michael didn't.

'I'd have left him for an hour,' said Helena.

'I'd have left him there all night,' replied Imo.

For some reason this struck us as unbearably funny. We exchanged looks and then snorted, all quietly horrified at our hysteria. Eventually we got ourselves under control amid strange looks from the rest of the pub, who can't have been totally unaware of my sobs earlier. I might avoid this place for a while.

'Can we get back to the police?' asked Helena kindly, and I agreed we could, although Imo stayed beside me. She moved her knife and fork round so that when our food arrived seconds later, we tucked in, ravenous, to fish and chips, side by side. Helena, who barely ate, and certainly not this sort of food, toyed with a very English-looking ham salad.

'I'm not suggesting you go straight to the police and say you left him to die because he was a cunt. I'm just saying, don't forget *why* you did it. If and when the time comes.'

I nodded, throwing in chip after chip. Cunt. I liked that.

'Also, Luce, there's no way the police *can* find out how long you left him, don't forget.'

'Oh.' I put my fork down. Told them about Ingrid. How it had slipped out at the police station. Imo asked why I'd even thought someone might have seen something? I told her about Amanda: my lunch with her.

'OK,' she said slowly. 'But that's just Amanda's little threat? One of many? Scattergun approach? A shot in the dark that hit a target?'

'Yes, more than likely. Scared the living daylights out of me, though. To the extent that I even started to imagine things, that this woman had turned a light off, the better to watch me.'

'But you didn't go round?'

'I did, actually.' I told them about seeing the daughter. Watched, as they valiantly resisted the temptation to put their heads in their hands.

'OK,' said Helena, as calmly as possible, 'but obviously no more contact, all right?'

'All Mum's doing is being honest,' Imo said reasonably. 'Acting like a normal person would, who's not under suspicion. Maybe frustrated by the slowness of the police inquiry?'

'That's true. Also, since you're not under caution,' Helena swept on, 'and if you can bear it, I think you're better off answering the police's questions on your own. If you can bear it,' she repeated.

'I can. You mean, it looks suspicious if I have a solicitor? I've already asked for one.'

She hesitated. 'It does look more honest, I suppose. But they may not even be back. But if they are, if it gets to the point of being cautioned, we'll get you one then. OK? Personally, I think they put the frighteners on you by asking if you wanted one, and with the burglar's version of events, just to gauge your reaction. To see if by any remote chance you looked guilty. Perhaps prompted by the Met. But they don't believe it any more than a jury would.'

A jury. Helena signalled for the bill. She'd abandoned her ham salad. Imo was efficiently scanning through her phone contacts, murmuring to Helena about lawyers. People she knew. Helena was responding with her own suggestions. They'd moved on. And actually, in a way, I had too. After they dropped me back at the house, at the end of the drive out of sight of the parents, and we'd all got out and hugged hard, I stood for a moment in the lane as they drove away. I felt better. I was even beginning to feel an element of 'bring it on'. I find that can happen when one takes a scary situation to its worst possible conclusion. And aside from the court case, there was a potentially even worse situation around the corner: prison. But I felt I could almost contemplate it now, purely because it was surely more questionable. More – not necessarily remote, but debatable. The world had moved on, hadn't it? Away from the patriarchy. Men were no longer allowed to abuse women, in any sense of the word. Of course, I couldn't be sure. But as I went inside, I found myself thinking about what Helena had said: about what I knew from news-papers was called coercive control. She hadn't said it, but that's what she'd meant: there was a lot of it about.

I went to the kitchen for a glass of water and spotted my parents through the window over the sink. They were sitting outside in the sunshine, on a bench sur-rounded by budding cow parsley. Mum was wiping her nose and tucking a hanky up her sleeve. As we exchanged a wave, I thought about how I'd tell the court every-thing, if I had to. Spill the Michael beans. With my head held high. Keeping my voice steady. In my navy suit, with my cream shirt. The one with the scalloped edge. I knew I could do it.

26

The following morning, Helena rang. 'All right?' she demanded briskly.

'Yes, fine, thanks. You?'

'No, this isn't a social call. I'm just ringing to check we didn't leave you in a hole yesterday, but I've literally got two minutes.'

I smiled. I could feel her looking at her watch. Sensed she was in the office already, at ten to eight. I'd showered and dressed but that was as far as I'd got.

'Yes, I'm really fine. But much better for seeing you two.'

'Good.' A pause. Unlike my sister in a hurry. 'I forgot to ask if you'd seen Dan.'

I smiled again. Two smiles before eight, not bad. I saw what she was doing here. The world continues to turn. 'I have, actually. Once or twice. He's nice.'

I sensed her beaming on the other end. 'Isn't he?' she purred.

'But slightly over-attentive to his mother, apparently.'

'Nance? Who told you that?'

'Camilla Frobisher.'

'She would,' Helena snapped. 'He dumped her.'

'No. Really? Dan did?'

'When the ghastly Torquil left her she thought she

was a shoe-in with Dan, but she underestimated him. After a few dates, he made his excuses. Nance might have been one of them, I don't know. Anyway, don't make the same mistake, Luce.'

'What?'

'Of underestimating him. There are hidden depths.'

'Good ones?'

'D'you think I'd be mentioning them if they weren't? Anyway, I've got to go.'

We hung up and I marvelled yet again at how my sister fitted so much into one day. Management buyouts, equity partner meetings, criminal procedure advice plus relationship counselling – all in a day's work. I wasn't quite sure what I'd been doing with my life.

A second later, she was back. 'My point is, Luce, you need to carry on as normal. For you, your sanity, for Mum and Dad, for the kids, but also from the police's point of view. This could go on a while. Hold your nerve. And don't get all jumpy and confessional. Keep calm and carry on.'

'Got it.' About five minutes ago actually, oh sister of mine.

Nevertheless, less recently, perhaps not. Perhaps I'd been hiding. I'd certainly been avoiding a few messages I'd received. One from Frankie, wondering about lunch some time. I tapped away now and agreed I'd look at dates if she sent me some. One from Josh, letting me know it was one o'clock on Sunday, to which I said great, look forward to it. Then I replied to a text of Dan's, agreeing to meet him for supper the following Wednesday. I put my phone down beside me. Life going on as normal, but how normal was that? To be seeing two men? Except . . . I was doing nothing of the sort, was I? I was spending time with two nice people. Friends, that was all. I conveniently forgot about the kiss in the car. Which, in the scheme of things, was immaterial anyway, I decided, as I got to my feet. Because anything I did right now was basically irrelevant. All I was doing was rearranging deck chairs on the *Titanic*. Oh, I knew what was coming. I was facing up to the blindingly obvious by the minute. I took a deep breath to steady myself. Then I made my bed, tidied my room, tucked my phone in my pocket and went downstairs.

Fortunately, perhaps, my parents were now in a parallel universe: immersed in their own little world of soft furnishings, glass candlesticks, side tables, place mats, and faux flower arrangements, they were somewhat oblivious to anything else. Or at least Mum was. Consumed by catalogues, online shopping and trips to Dunelm – which apparently was far cheaper than Peter Jones, historically her spiritual home – she'd even picked out a recliner chair she'd seen, before my father quietly reminded her I might not need a chair that gently eased me to my feet. He caught my eye.

I'd managed to have a quiet word with him in the greenhouse. My mother was a bit under the weather, nursing a cold she'd had for days, and was under a rug on the sofa in front of *Cash in the Attic*. The timelessness of the greenhouse was a comfort: I remembered coming in here as a child to help him plant tomatoes.

I took the other ancient Lloyd Loom chair opposite my father's at the far end and watched as he sprinkled sweet pea seeds into a tray. He'd made a furrow in the warm earth with a lollipop stick and was carefully picking a few seeds out of the palm of his hand. Hector was lying at his feet and his old Roberts Radio was on low, tuned to Classic FM. As I sat there, he waited. He picked up another packet of seeds. Tobacco plants, this time. Mum's favourite. Eventually I cleared my throat.

'Dad, Helena says I'm not allowed to get confessional, but—'

'Then don't,' he interrupted sharply. His gaze was steady for one with eyes so rheumy. 'I don't need to know, Luce.'

'No,' I said uncertainly, wrong-footed. 'It's just – I know you're not stupid. And I know you know they both came down here to give me advice—'

'But that the fewer people who know about that advice, the better. Helena's right, love. We're here if you need us, but you don't need to tell us anything. Keep shtum.'

My heart began to beat fast. What could he know? He put his seed packet aside. Regarded me over his reading glasses. 'The thing is, Lucy, under immense pressure, it's possible to feel immense guilt. You felt it all your married life. Michael persuaded you you were permanently in the wrong. Permanently culpable. As far as I'm concerned, there's little you could do that would be wrong. But don't let his influence cloud your judgement. Even from the grave.'

'Right. No.' God, I had no idea my family knew so much about my crap life. How naïve of me, in retrospect, to believe I'd kept it to myself. All I'd kept were the dark spaces. And not even all of those. And people talk, whatever you might think. Imo to Ned. Helena to Imo. My parents to Helena. I watched Dad tip a few more tiny black seeds into the palm of his hand and sprinkle them again, in a line. Beside him were a row of bulbs already planted in pots for later in the year: dahlias. My father was eighty-six. How did he know he'd even see them come up in the autumn? How did he imagine he'd see any proper growth in the chestnut sapling he'd found broken off by the wind, and was carefully dipping into root hormone powder to stimulate it, before planting in a terracotta pot? He didn't. He was doing it because that was what he'd always done, and what was expected of him. He was doing it for future generations, and he was doing it for love. That was why we all kept buggering on. I'd also imagined I might tackle the subject of the cottage with him, but then I realized I wouldn't. Some things were best left unsaid. Instead, I got up from my chair, and went to refill the heavy galvanized watering can from the tap in the yard, which I knew he found a struggle to carry back when it was full. I delivered it to him, then disappeared inside to make some egg mayonnaise sandwiches for lunch.

A few days went by. And still no sign of the police. I began to wonder if Helena was right, and they'd just been trying to frighten me. The weekend approached, and within a twinkling, I found myself arriving at Josh's house for lunch. Well, my house. I'd actually been sitting round the corner for fifteen minutes until I'd deemed myself fashionably late, but not overdoing it. It occurred to me, as I waited, that Melissa, back from Silicon Valley, would be horrified if she knew I was here and hadn't popped in. But although I was making myself carry on, I also knew I wasn't up to that. Melissa knew a lot about me, but not everything. The advantage of seeing Josh was that, despite having met me so recently, he knew what was consuming me. There was an odd sort of relaxation in that. Of course, it wouldn't be mentioned. But it was there, unspoken, in the room. I didn't have to pretend it wasn't.

Naturally I'd thought long and hard about what to wear: it had been a pleasurable diversion. In the end, I'd settled for a long, slightly boho skirt Imo had given me for my last birthday, a pair of lace-up ankle boots, and a thin cream cashmere jumper tucked into a wide belt. I'd added a short, faux-suede jacket from Zara. The vibe I was hoping for was arty chic. As I rang the bell clutching my bunch of tulips, it occurred to me that my heart didn't beat like this as I was waiting for Dan.

Josh flung wide the door, bestowing on me a beaming smile. I basked in its glow for a moment. God, he was – oh, get a grip, Lucy. To be fair, though, he hadn't smiled at me much before. Most of our exchanges had been of a serious bent. This new social dynamic caused his eyes to crinkle, which I loved: it was something Ned had, smiling eyes. He was wearing a blue shirt and a perfectly ordinary pair of chinos, but he somehow made it look

Parisian and chic. I beamed just as broadly back and we kissed lightly on each cheek. As he shut the door behind me, he said quietly:

'OK?'

'Yes, thanks,' I replied, knowing that this was more than just a social enquiry.

I followed him through into the sitting room where his friends were already sitting. They both rose to greet me, smiling, as Josh brought me through and introduced us. Francis was middle-aged, small and balding, but his bright, twinkly hazel eyes didn't miss a trick, and Trisha was soft and fair, with slightly windswept curls. But no frowsty clothes, as some academics are known for, perhaps because, as I was quickly to discover, she wasn't one. I'd got that wrong. She had a garden design business, which was much more manageable for me, conversationally, than the French literature her husband specialized in. After some initial chat, we went through to the kitchen together to arrange my flowers, and fell happily to Dutch or English tulips. These were Dutch. We discussed which lasted the longest, and whether to trim the stems or put anything in the water, all of which I was very au fait with. When we'd set the vase on the table, I even offered to show her my garden, which of course wasn't mine at all, but sort of was. We had a laugh about that and I opened the French doors and showed her anyway.

As we walked around my old patch she bent with interest over some white narcissi, which, if you were lucky, kept going with their pale nodding heads right into May. Prolifically, too, bridging the gap between the forget-me-nots and tulips. They happily needed little tending, although I couldn't resist pulling a few weeds from around them. Trisha instinctively crouched and did the same, so that when Josh and Francis appeared in the open French windows, nursing a glass of red wine apiece, we were talking so much we hadn't heard them. We both straightened up, rather guiltily, our hands full of weeds and dirt. Josh widened his eyes theatrically.

'Is this what's known as garden shaming?' he enquired dryly, and we laughed.

'You'll probably get a bill, Josh,' Francis told him. 'Knowing my wife. Can't tell you the number of women who've asked for garden advice and then been charged.'

'Ooh, what a terrible fib!' Trisha declared, her eyes dancing. 'Once,' she turned to me, 'an acquaintance – not even a friend – asked me to stop by and have a look at her garden. I was there for two hours. She picked my brains for the entire time as we walked around – she even took notes! Drew a plan! I'm afraid my daughter was so incensed when she heard, she insisted I bill her.'

'My daughter would be the same,' I told her. 'She used to be astonished when I wrote copious notes to would-be novelists whose manuscripts I read – but they were mostly young and I didn't mind. One elderly chap did treat it as a weekly seminar, though, and I had to keep it from Imogen.'

'Oh, you write books?'

It had slipped out, perhaps because so much else really mustn't slip out. But it wasn't something I brought up, as a rule. People were too interested, and I always felt I'd stolen the spotlight, somehow, in some sort of power grab. On the other hand, if I didn't mention it, hostesses were often put out, saying – I put you next to Gerald because he's writing a novel!

'What sort of things do you write?' asked Trisha, which was always the first question. I could see Josh looking at me with interest, perhaps wondering how I'd describe it.

'Oh, just silly detective stories,' I said quickly. 'Very much beach reads.'

'That's amazing,' said Trisha, nonetheless impressed, and followed up with the question that was always next, where I got my ideas. That one I always fudged. Michael. Always Michael, and his cruelty, which gave me, not my ideas, but the imaginary world he propelled me into. With a gutsy heroine so different to yours truly; indeed, the woman I wished I was. My fingers would fly over the keys as she got to the bottom of every unsolved police investigation, every injustice, reopening inquiry after inquiry – cold cases being her forte – perhaps on the tearful insistence of some poor family whose child had gone missing years ago; some gap year student who'd never been found. And eventually, of course, Susie does find her, alive and well, and married, incidentally, in Papua New Guinea. Happy, too. Because, it transpires, she'd been desperate to escape the clutches of her controlling mother. The one who'd asked Susie to find her. No, Michael never appeared in my books – or read them, thank the Lord, having given up after erroneously

319

failing to recognize anything of our life together. But the influence was there.

I smiled. 'Honestly, I have no idea. I think it's just a process of osmosis, everyday things I pick up subliminally and use in my stories. Things I'm told, maybe – who knows?' I spread my hands expansively. 'I expect people ask the same thing about your garden designs, don't they?'

'Well, it's not quite in the same ballpark as yours, creatively, but you're right, it does all spring from the imagination,' she admitted with surprise, liking the seriousness with which I'd treated her subject. And I knew I was safe. I'd neatly turned the tables, as I always did, so that whoever had asked the question had forgotten what they'd asked, and taken the baton. But as we drifted into the house, and Trisha explained about one garden she'd done recently for a nightmare client, who basically wanted a mini Highgrove, a series of little rooms, I could feel Josh's gaze still on me, not so easily diverted.

If it was strange to be sitting at my own kitchen table, albeit with a different cloth on it, and being served food from my own oven I hadn't cooked myself, that feeling passed quite quickly. Plus, the food and wine helped enormously. Tilly's Thai green curry was a triumph – and the roulade she'd made to follow, which Josh had just about remembered to defrost, was delicious too. And Francis and Trisha were a delight. They clearly knew Josh extremely well – after all, he'd lived with them when he first came over – but they went back much further than that: Francis and Josh to Cambridge days, which intrigued me, because Francis looked a lot older. They mentioned crowding into a union bar to watch Nelson Mandela being released and I remembered doing exactly the same in my student days, as did Trisha.

'So we're all the same vintage,' she observed, glancing around. Her amused eyes rested on her husband.

'Yes, all right!' Francis spluttered, his mouth full of roulade. 'Ask Josh what he puts in his cornflakes – it's not my fault the man dyes his hair!'

'What rubbish!' Josh roared, eyes popping, face flushed. I was enjoying seeing him like this. We were near the end of the meal and he was a bit pissed, and flustered from doing the cooking. He was also often the butt of his friends' jokes, and a bit exposed, particularly when Trisha insisted on recalling how she'd first met him. It was bad enough, she told me, leaning across the table, going out with someone from the university when she was only at the secretarial college down the road, but meeting Francis's friends, especially Josh, had been terrifying. Particularly when he'd asked her whether she thought existential literature was de trop.

'I didn't even know what de trop meant, let alone existentialism!' she shrieked. 'Was still devouring Jilly Cooper!'

'Ooh, I didn't,' groaned Josh, putting his head in his hands. 'What an out and out twat. I was probably trying to impress you. Probably jealous of Francis.'

'What rot, you were escorting that Priscilla number at the time! With the waist-length hair and legs up to the penthouse.'

I reached for my drink. Ah, interesting. He might be my age, but I was seriously punching. Trisha might just as well be describing a supermodel.

'Priscilla Rivers was a travesty, as well you know,' Josh retorted. 'Sorry, Lucy, this is incredibly boring for you. What Trisha is trying to do here is lampoon me with my terrible track record with the female sex. Rather inappropriately, I might add,' he wagged a jovial finger at her as he raised his glass to his lips.

'Point taken,' she demurred, with a grin. 'Quite fun, though, and somewhat irresistible.'

'Lucy, you'll have to excuse us.' Francis put a hand on my arm. 'We seize any opportunity to discredit our oldest friend, I'm afraid. We're very badly behaved.'

I smiled, loving this sort of banter, and knowing that the opposite was true: that by showing him more than capable of taking any joke that was poked at him, they were revealing him not as the serious-minded academic, but someone who was full of fun and didn't take himself too seriously. I wondered if Trisha in particular was doing it more deliberately than her husband, showing me his lighter side? If so, I was flattered.

Later, as they were preparing to leave, and I decided I would too – it would surely be odd to linger – Trisha and I found ourselves alone in the kitchen, putting on our jackets. Josh had taken Francis into the sitting room, suddenly remembering a publication by a fellow professor which he'd brought and wanted to show him.

'It's been lovely meeting you,' she told me with real

warmth, her eyes sparkling as she retrieved her suede bag from the island.

'And you too,' I told her, really meaning it. Trisha was a honey. She lowered her voice.

'And I can't tell you what a relief after Agathe.'

'Oh – no. We're not – you know . . .' I flushed.

'Oh no, I know.' She put a hand on my arm. 'I know you're not. It's just, it's such a blessed relief to meet some-one like you, even as – you know—' She blushed too. 'A friend.'

I couldn't help myself. I also lowered my tone. 'But I mean, surely she can't have been that bad? They were married for years . . .'

'Fourteen. He got married much later than us, and she's beautiful. But chilly. And he's not, he's warm. Trouble is, he's so easy-going – when you get past his reserve – he gets sidetracked by beautiful women who snare him. He doesn't see it coming. And of course, they were all no doubt lovely to begin with, everyone is. When they're trying. Who was it said – "What one loves about love, is the time before they find out what one is like . . ." Or something like that.'

'Cedric,' I told her, rather pleased with myself. 'In *Love in a Cold Climate*. My favourite book.'

'That's it! I love it too. Well, by the time Josh found out what Agathe was like, it was too late. Mimi, his eld-est, was on the way.'

I was loving this. Absolutely gripped. I glanced at the door but we could still hear them chatting. 'And they're totally over?' I whispered, knowing I could: knowing she was absolutely straight, and not the type to say later, with a twinkle: 'Your new friend was asking all about your marriage . . .'

'Yes, for good. He finished it, eventually. Even though she started it, leaving him for his best friend. She decided she wanted him back – quite recently when he went back to see his kids – but he said no. There was no love there. No warmth. And to be fair, I don't think she was capable of loving him any more than she did. That's just the way she was, and he realized it. He also realized it wasn't enough. Not for the rest of his life.'

'Right. Is she devastated?'

'Not at all. She's not like that. She gave a Gallic shrug, apparently, as Josh nonetheless wept, and went off to the market on the Left Bank, which she always does on a Saturday.'

'And his girls?'

'Well, obviously, that kills him. But Agathe's not a bitch. She said he can have them as much as he likes, which is why they then went skiing. It will probably suit her, actually, this arrangement, in a way. She's quite selfish. I can easily imagine her saying – oh, have them for six weeks over the summer.' We heard footsteps. Trisha straightened up. 'So if your parents *do* decide to take the plunge and want some help with their new garden, I'd be more than happy to take a look.'

'I think they might,' I agreed, snapping to. 'They've done all they can inside, it's only a matter of time before they're planning the outside.'

'Touting for business *again*?' Francis mock-staggered

into the room. He put an arm around his wife's shoulders and squeezed her tight.

'Shameless,' muttered Josh, shaking his head.

'Absolutely not!' Trisha said indignantly. 'I was merely telling Lucy that if she sent me a photo of her parents' patch—'

'Yeah, yeah, we believe you.'

And thus, in a convivial fashion, we all made our way down the hall, to the front door. We said the most cheery of farewells, all telling our host we'd had the best time – oh, and to be sure to tell Tilly the food had been delicious. His eyes lingered enquiringly on mine as we kissed goodbye, though, and I saw Trisha look away quickly with a smile. She hurried down the steps, taking her husband's arm to propel him with her.

'It was lovely to see you,' he told me softly.

'And you too,' I agreed quietly. Our eyes met for a moment longer, and then I followed the aptly named Goodfellows down the steps to the street. We set off in opposite directions. I didn't look back, but I was sure Josh waited until I was around the corner before he shut the door. In fact, I know he did, because once again, I heard that familiar loud click as it shut.

27

I drove home with a broad smile on my face, obviously. How could I not? And yes, music blaring too, of the soppy uplifting variety. I needed to preserve these moods whenever possible, knowing at the back of my mind they would be rare. And transient. But today had been good. When I got home and pulled into our drive an hour or so later, the fine rain which had been threatening was falling steadily. In the lamp-lit, warm sitting room, my father was watching the rugby in his favourite armchair, a fire burning in the grate. When I'd first arrived, the fire had only been lit in the evenings, on the dot of five to six, in time for the news. The house had been permanently cold during the day, as Dad maintained it was too expensive to heat the whole place, but now that logging was under control and I'd had the chimney swept – I'd been sternly told by the sweep it was a chimney fire waiting to happen – the fire was lit at midday when necessary. It was chilly today. Dad hailed me cheerily as I came in.

'Hello, love!'

'Hi, Dad.' I glanced around. 'Where's Mum?'

'Hm?' He glanced away from the rugby. 'Oh, her cold was a bit worse, so she took to her bed.'

'Oh, right. Is she OK?' But I'd already dumped my handbag on a chair and was on my way to her.

'Perfectly!' he called after me. 'Heavens, how my daughters fuss.'

And he didn't. Never had. And neither did Mum. They could be at death's door and still claim they were perfectly all right. Just as our children complained of being sent to school with a stinking cold, so Helena and I could claim the same. The apple doesn't fall far. I softly pushed open the bedroom door, which was ajar. The room was dark and chilly. The heating hadn't come on yet and the curtains were open. Darkness filled the latticed window.

'Mum?' I whispered, approaching the bed. 'Are you asleep?'

'Oh, hello, darling,' she said groggily. 'No, not really. Just dozing.'

'Oh, OK.' I perched on the side. 'How d'you feel?' I peered. She looked pale in the half-light.

'Absolutely fine. Tip-top. It's just a rotten cold.'

'Have you taken anything? Nurofen? Paracetamol?'

'No, darling, I told you. It's just a cold.'

'OK, hang on.'

I nipped downstairs to make her a Lemsip, and found some Nurofen. I took them up.

'Can you sip this? It's not too hot.'

She didn't move, so I gently raised her back up with my hand and propped her up on the pillows. She drank some of it, sipping slowly, but then shook her head.

'OK.' I lowered her back down. 'In a mo, d'you think you can drink the rest?'

'Yes, darling.' Sleepily.

'And could you swallow the ibuprofen?'

'Oh no, I don't think so. I'll try the drink, though.'

'OK. Let's have another go.'

I raised her up and she almost managed the rest of it, then seemed about to gag so I lowered her back down. She shut her eyes. I felt her hand on the covers. It was cold. I tucked her in properly. Then I shut the curtains and felt the radiator beneath them. It was coming on, good. For the moment, though, I found an old storage heater in the spare room. She seemed to have fallen asleep again, and knowing that was the best thing, I crept out and left her. I was a bit cross with Dad, though, toasty warm in front of the fire when I came down.

'Could you not have given her some Nurofen, Dad? And the room was freezing.'

'Hm?' He just about looked up from a missed try. 'Hopeless pass from that wretched number eight, he should be shot for that.'

'Dad?'

'What, darling?'

'Mum, upstairs. Too cold.'

'Oh, nonsense, Luce, she gets colds all year round, she'll be fine. We both do, despite the so-called flu jab. If the back row were stronger they'd get it to the forwards quicker, that's the problem.'

Later on, I got us some supper, which we ate on trays in front of an old Inspector Poirot movie which he loved. And I have to say, when I checked on Mum later, she seemed better: warmer, certainly. I turned the storage heater off. And she was sleeping soundly, her breathing soft and regular.

The following morning, however, it was a different story. When I went in quite early, she was still asleep, but her breathing was shallow and rapid. When I felt her forehead it was hot. Damp, too.

'Mum? Mum!' Alarmed, I shook her awake.

She stared at me with blank, confused eyes. 'Hels?'

'No, it's Luce. How d'you feel?'

'De Courcys will be here soon, must cook—' She tried to get out of bed but she was shaking and feeble.

'No, no, Mum, the De Courcys aren't coming. You don't have to cook.'

'Bloody dog – eaten all the bird food again! Look!' She pointed to the corner of the room.

'No, Mum, Hector's downstairs.'

'What's going on?' My father had appeared from his dressing room. He was in the doorway in his pyjamas and dressing gown, tying the cord.

'It's Mum. She's got a fever. Ring Dr Bond, would you, Dad? Ask him to pop round.'

'Oh no, he doesn't do home visits any more. That went out with the ark. And he's probably still away, anyway. She'll be all right, love. I'll make her a cuppa.'

'Pass me the phone.'

Dr Bond was a friend and had been their doctor for years. Helena had pasted his mobile number to their bedroom phone a couple of years ago, when he'd said they could always call him. Of course, they'd never done so. Not even when Dad's ulcers had leaked all over the bed. Wouldn't want to be any trouble. My father hobbled in with a sigh and passed me the old-fashioned receiver. Mike Bond answered almost immediately. He listened, and said he'd be over in half an hour. Amazing. You wouldn't get that in London. But then I wasn't on first-name terms with my doctor in London. I tried to make Mum drink something but she wouldn't, kept muttering about having to feed the birds, and how the squirrels took all their seed unless she put it in a special place.

Mike Bond arrived sooner than he'd said. He took one look, felt her pulse, didn't even bother taking her temperature, and told me to call an ambulance. He quietly told me that the delirium was possibly due to a urinary tract infection, in which case she would likely need a drip. But he also wanted to rule out pneumonia. Actually, no, hang on, he'd do it. It would be quicker. He pulled out his mobile.

'Pneumonia? No, surely not,' my father was bleating feebly. 'Surely just a dose of flu?'

My mother was coughing uncontrollably now, sitting up in bed supported by Mike and me. As she retched, her thin, frail body racked and heaved with the effort. Green spittle was trickling down her chin and nightie.

'That's it, Cecily, now breathe. Breathe gently now. In . . . out . . . in . . . out – excellent. OK, well done.' He laid her back down again as the coughing fit subsided, then quickly asked me for warm clothes. I flew to the wardrobe and found a coat. We gently sat her up again and eased her out of bed; together we wrapped her in her dressing gown, then her coat, and found her slippers. I popped some socks on first. My father, all the while, was looking on helplessly. Alarm was in his eyes now and he made way for us, as Mike and I shuffled her past. She wasn't really walking; she was being half carried. I'd wondered about waiting for the paramedics and the stretcher, but Mike told me when elderly patients were delirious like this, it was a struggle to keep them on it: they often scrambled off and were deceptively strong. The stairs would be a hazard.

'Will she be all right?' I whispered in the hall, out of earshot of my father. I couldn't help it, I was scared.

'If we've caught it, there's no reason why she shouldn't be,' was all he said, and I was so glad Helena had had the foresight to tape his number to the receiver. He was young – well, my age – the son of some friends, and completely brilliant.

Helena. Should I ring her? No, not yet. She'd only flown down a few days ago. I'd leave it until . . . well. I'd leave it for a bit.

Two kind and caring ambulance women were very soon outside, opening the back doors. They came forward making soothing noises, asking her name, and we all helped my mother inside. She didn't resist, thank God. Indeed, she looked around, wide-eyed with wonder, as we got her into the brightly lit ambulance, like a child going into Santa's grotto, I thought. The women sat her down gently in a seat and she complied as she was efficiently strapped in. I asked if I could travel with her, and they said I could. Everything happened so fast, before she had time to question it. And then, as they were about to shut the doors, I turned and saw Dad in the driveway, in his dressing gown. He looked so lost.

'Hang on a sec.' I hastened back. As I did so, I saw Mrs Cummings, also in her dressing gown, pop her head over the garden fence. 'Dad, are you going to be OK?'

'Anything I can do?' she called, in a falsetto voice. I hesitated, wondering if actually, yes, maybe a pot of tea, a boiled egg. But my father roared in before I could utter.

'Absolutely not!' he boomed. Then he hissed to me: 'I do *not* want that bloody woman coming round here.'

'No, quite right,' I muttered. 'No, thank you, though!' I called back over the fence. I lowered my voice to him. 'And I'll ring you from the hospital as soon as I can. But I wouldn't ring Helena.' I refrained from adding, 'yet.'

'Certainly not. Busy girl. And no need.'

He drew himself up to his full height, and suddenly he was the tall tank commander of yesteryear, going into the desert at the front of his men, standing up in his gun turret, like in the black and white photo in the downstairs loo. He shot Mrs Cummings a glance and I found myself feeling grateful to her for precipitating this change in him. I gave him a quick peck on the cheek and ran back to the ambulance.

Off we went at quite some speed, with blue flashing lights, siren blaring, even jumping traffic lights – the full bollocks, as Imo would say. The journey seemed to daze my mother and she sat there quietly without a word. In fact, I wondered for a moment if Dad were right, if we were overreacting. The minute, however, the ambulance stopped outside the hospital, that terrible rasping cough, together with the green slime, began again. She started to shake violently. After that, I was a mere spectator. The ambulance crew jumped out and ran round to open the doors. We were met by a team of two, one a capable male nurse with a wheelchair. When they'd lifted her into it, off he shot.

'Should I come in?' I asked his colleague as we trotted alongside her, down the corridor.

'Just wait in the waiting room when we get there, please. We need to assess her and do some tests. You'll know as soon as we have any results.'

I was jogging to keep up with her. She was still shaking and hacking away and looked terrible, what I could see of her, bent double as she almost was now, in the chair. Her tiny frame was heaving with the effort. I felt panicky. Why so small? Surely I'd been feeding her? But she ate so little. Some grey swing doors were approaching and I bent down in front of her, without interrupting the flow of the chair.

'Mum? Mum – I'm going to be right outside, OK?' I said loudly. 'You're in good hands and I'm right here, all right?' She looked alarmed and it occurred to me she didn't recognize me for a moment. 'Mum, it's Lucy, OK?'

'Lucy,' she repeated and her face cleared a bit with recognition.

The male nurse shot me a sympathetic look. 'All right, love, we'll take her now.'

'Yes, of course.'

And they were gone. I stayed still for a moment as the doors swung shut in my face. Then my shoulders slumped and I turned in defeat. She'd be OK. She'd be absolutely fine. Of course she would. And heavens, she was in the best place. The finest hands. We'd got her here in double quick time.

I got myself a black coffee from the machine and took a seat at the back. It was still early, but already it was noisy with children. Worried parents were trying to calm them. A television above the nurses' station was showing CBeebies. An old wino was stretched out on the three chairs beside me, fast asleep and snoring. Understanding, suddenly, why that seat had been free, I moved to one at the front. Now I was squashed between an enormous man with breathing difficulties and a small boy who couldn't stop crying. Actually, I'd stand.

I leaned against the wall in the corner, registering now that I looked a fright. I'd thrown a jumper and coat on, but I was basically in pyjamas and Ugg boots. Although these days it could easily be taken for leisure wear, I realized, looking around at the track-suited crew. Happily my phone was in my coat pocket. I took it out and checked it. No messages – good. No family members I had to reply to and lie to by omission. I wouldn't reply, I decided, if anything came through from Helena or the children. Could easily just be out of signal. I also held off from ringing Dad. I'd wait until I had something concrete to report, and if it was bad, I'd go home and tell him myself. I shut my eyes. Please God, don't let it be bad. Please God, don't let me have to break terrible news to my father.

334

Finally, some people left and I nipped to a chair. They'd left a copy of *The Times* behind, so I made myself read it from cover to cover. That was no quick feat, so when I glanced at the clock, an hour had passed and it was mid-morning. The waiting room was thinning out so, confident I'd keep my chair, I approached the desk, behind which sat a team of nurses. They didn't look up. I cleared my throat, and asked about Mum in an apologetic, British way.

A ginger-haired nurse looked away from her screen and regarded me wearily. 'Name?'

'Cecily Hartley.'

She scanned her computer. 'We'll let you know.' She resumed her tapping.

'Right. Thanks.'

I crept back to my seat. No news is good news, I told myself. If there was anything badly wrong, they'd come and find me. Time ticked by.

'Lucy?' I'd been in the far corner of the room, scrabbling around for another newspaper on the plastic coffee table. I glanced up. Dan was standing over me in an old Barbour jacket. He looked kind and concerned.

'Oh – Dan! Gosh, what a coincidence. What are you doing here?'

'Mum rang your mother for a chat this morning and got your father. He told her what had happened. I've just dropped her off. To sit with him and have some lunch.'

'Oh, that's so kind, thank you.' Dad had been on my mind. 'He'll cheer up immeasurably with Nance there.'

'Exactly. And Mum's delighted to be in a strong cap-able role for once. She was heating up soup we brought and telling him it'll all be fine when I left them. Will it be fine?'

I swallowed hard. 'Who knows. I mean, she's eighty-four. It's an occupational hazard at that age, isn't it? Death?' I made myself say it.

He looked at his shoes. Nodded. 'It is.' We went to a couple of free seats at the front of the room and sat. 'Your father said it might be pneumonia.'

'Possibly, yes. And she's so frail. I'm not sure I see her recovering easily.'

We sat looking glumly at the floor. I was pleased to see him, though. It was horrid being here alone. Worrying alone. So kind of him to come, and I told him so.

'Oh no, no trouble. These places are the pits on your own. And Lucy, good that you're – you know. Facing it.'

I shrugged. 'Being realistic.'

'Exactly. When Dad died, my brothers were so taken aback and I thought – surely it must have crossed your minds?'

'Helena will be like that.' It occurred to me that Helena would be devastated. She relied on Mum more than she would ever admit, whilst I'd weaned myself off her a bit, with difficulty, for fear of worrying her, at a younger age. 'Were you close to your father?'

He hesitated. 'Ish. No, if I'm honest. Not really. But we got on OK. It's just, I was the eldest, so expecta-tions . . . you know.'

I managed a smile. 'Except you've done fine?'

'Sure, but always hoping he approved. And he didn't always. Milo and Toby had it easier, I think.'

'He'd approve of you now,' I told him. 'Looking after Nance.'

He gave a wry smile. 'Perhaps that's why I do it. Wondering if he's watching. Influencing me from beyond the grave.' My father had said something similar recently to me, about Michael: don't let it happen. Dan shifted in his seat, a regrouping gesture. 'But I certainly don't want to do it forever. I'd like my life back.'

'Well, you won't have to,' I consoled him soberly. 'As discussed earlier.'

'Quite.' He grinned. 'Sorry, Lucy, shouldn't really be discussing it. Can't think why we are.'

'I can. Much worse to pretend it's not happening. I find it helps to go to the – you know. Worst outcome.' I swallowed. Found my mind fleeing from it, nonetheless. 'My main worry is Dad . . .'

'Your dad's as tough as old boots. Like my mum.'

'He was . . . and still is, sometimes. But he's a softy at heart. He adores her. Plus, I don't know if I see him in that cottage on his own. With maybe me at Pope's Farm. God, you're right, why am I even talking like this!'

His hand closed over mine. 'It's shock. And one thing is for sure, if you were at Pope's Farm, you wouldn't have to be on your own.'

I wasn't certain what he meant by that, but then I understood. I felt my eyes widen. Oh. Right. Well . . . maybe. Or perhaps he was just being complimentary? Saying I was too much of a catch, in a general way, to be

337

on my own? I mean, not right now, obviously, in my pyjamas and coat. But trying to buoy me up? Yes, that was it. So kind. Which he was, I realized, as he went off and came back with a couple of coffees. And if Mum died, I could really do with someone like him. Strong, caring, dependable. So I didn't have to deal with my grief-stricken, elderly father alone. I'd always known Mum would go first. She was so much frailer. And I also knew that this lengthy wait I was having was because she was struggling in there. Poor darling Mummy. I hoped at least it would be quick. If it was as bad as that. I felt a bit faint.

'Shouldn't you ring Helena?' I was startled. Then I realized he really did fear the worst, and I also remembered this was how Martin, his father, had gone. He obviously knew more than me. Knew it probably would be quick.

'How long did your father . . . ?'

'Six hours. From the time they took him in.'

'Shit.' I regarded him in horror. 'I thought we were talking days.' I scrambled for my phone. He stayed my hand.

'Listen, every case is different, obviously. Let's find out more, first. Have you asked at the nurses' station?'

I nodded, suddenly feeling really quite faint. I put my coffee on the floor, about to spill it. That wasn't helping either. The caffeine. 'But they were hopeless. And snappy, too, which is unnecessary.'

He looked at the redhead, who was eating a Curly Wurly. So not that stretched. Dan got up and strode to the counter. I saw him override her excuses and ask to see a doctor. Explained that we'd been here hours; some information, surely? The sulky nurse sighed. Then she picked up the phone.

'Someone will be with you shortly,' she told him.

'Well, if they're not, I'll go and find my mother myself,' Dan told her.

'Your mother,' I whispered, as he sat down.

'Think I got away with it.'

As he crossed his legs I realized that this was what had been missing from my life. Someone who looked after me. Looked out for me. I felt really light-headed now. Dan told me to put my head between my knees, which I did. I fervently hoped I wasn't going to pass out. Once, when Michael had . . . anyway. I'd obviously been standing in one position for too long. In the broom cupboard. He'd had to bring me round. He'd looked scared. Perhaps he'd wondered if he'd killed me? Dan had his hand on my back as I leaned forward, which was nice. Comforting. He stroked between my shoulder blades and told me to breathe deeply. I did. Felt better. Was able, at length, to sit up. I gave him a weak smile. He put his arm around my shoulders and gave them a squeeze. I didn't feel nearly so alone. He left it there as I recovered.

Suddenly the swing doors flew open. A young male doctor, in jeans and a checked shirt, white coat flapping, strode through. He had a stethoscope around his neck. He scanned the waiting room.

'Mrs Palmer?'

I stood up immediately. 'Yes?'

He came across and smiled. 'Well, it's not often I'm the bearer of good news, but your mother is stabilizing. Looking a bit better already, in fact. She's suffering from a urinary tract infection, but a drip and antibiotics will sort that out. And the suspected pneumonia was just that, suspected. She has a chest infection, which presents similarly, and will likewise respond to the penicillin. You brought her in just in time. She should make a full recovery.'

I stared at him. Couldn't speak for a moment. Then: 'Oh! Oh wow.' Dazzled, I turned to Dan. 'Oh, Dan – isn't that marvellous?'

Dan gave a thin smile but something passed over his eyes. A shadow perhaps. 'It is. It really is. Wonderful news,' he said flatly.

Later on, and with the benefit of hindsight, I came to wonder if this moment was pivotal, even if, at the time, I didn't realize it. Dan had hoped I'd need him, and in that moment, I didn't. And he knew it.

28

'What a relief,' I beamed at the doctor. 'I cannot thank you enough.'

'Well, as I say, prompt action on your part, so we caught it. Would you both like to . . . ?'

'Oh no, she's Lucy's mother,' said Dan, and actually, I was already on my way. Giving Dan a radiant smile and mouthing 'thank you!', I fairly skipped off down the corridor beside the doctor. I did turn back briefly and the swing doors had been propped open by a nurse, so I was able to see him still standing at the end there. He cut a slightly forlorn-looking figure, a long way away. He raised his hand in farewell.

My mother was now in a large ward full of elderly women. Every bed was occupied and they all looked terribly old and frail. Most were asleep. Luckily, her bed was by the window, which made it relatively private. She blinked and smiled weakly in recognition as I approached.

'Dehydration,' she told me, and I realized she knew exactly who I was. 'So they've had me on this thing,' she nodded at the saline drip running into her arm, 'for ages now.'

'I always say you don't drink enough.' I sat down, kissing her papery cheek.

'Actually, you always say I drink too much.'

I grinned. 'Fair enough.' Jokes too. That lapse in mental control earlier had frightened me. 'Oh Mum, I'm so pleased you're OK. How do you feel?'

'A bit feeble, and a bit chesty too. But apparently I've had some extremely strong antibiotics which should do the trick. They're good, here.' I thought of the sulky nurse outside. But good where it mattered, at the sharp end, thank the Lord. Thank the blessed NHS. Her eyes were shutting a bit and although we were holding hands, her grip was weak.

'Mum, I'm going to leave you to sleep now, but I'll be back later, OK? I'll bring Dad.'

Her eyes fluttered open. 'Oh no. No need to fuss.'

'He'll want to see you. And I'll bring anything you need. Your pashmina, maybe? And a clean nightie and sponge bag.'

'Oh, I won't need all that. I'll be going home later today.'

'I doubt it,' I told her firmly. 'No saline drips at home, but I'll check with the doctor. I should think a couple of days.' She looked alarmed, but I'd spotted the young doctor again, about to leave another patient. He was giving an elderly lady a kind smile and patting her hand before he went on his way. I beetled up.

'I'm so sorry,' I breathed, as a nurse looked on reprovingly. 'But my mother, in the bed by the window. How long d'you think she'll be here?'

He glanced across. 'She can go home tomorrow,' he told me. 'As long as she doesn't overdo it.'

'She won't,' I told him.

'But I'd like her on that drip for another eight hours.' And with that he was gone, followed by the watchful nurse. I hastened back to my mother.

'Just one night,' I told her, and saw her face clear with relief. I'd deliberately pitched it high so that this came as good news. She relaxed into the pillows.

'Well, I still think it's a silly fuss. I'm as right as rain now, but I expect I can manage that.' She slurred the last few words, her eyelids flickering. I squeezed her hand gently and told her I'd be back, early evening, with Dad. And then I left.

Outside, in reception, I rang my father. Told him the good news.

'Oh darling!' he bleated. He had to take a moment to steady himself. Then he shouted to Nance: 'She's fine!' His voice cracked with emotion when he said it, which brought tears to my eyes. I swallowed. I was so pleased I'd beaten Dan to it; he was doubtless en route to pick his mother up. Not that he'd want to overtake me, but it was lovely to give my father the good news myself, and hear his voice.

It was lovely to see his face, too, when I got home half an hour later; Nance, indeed, had already departed. My father, bathed, shaved and dressed rather nattily in red cords and a pale yellow shirt, damp hair combed back, was coming out of the front door. He'd clearly heard the car and was eager for more news.

'No drama. Apparently we caught the UTI and the chest infection before they became a problem, and apart from that she was just very dehydrated.'

'*You* caught the chest infection and the whatchama-callit,' he told me, giving my shoulders a squeeze as we walked back into the house together. 'I was absolutely hopeless. In denial. Wouldn't have done a thing. Would have told myself she was fine and brought her a cup of tea. For days, probably.'

'Well, that's natural, Dad,' I told him gently. 'We none of us want to face reality, and there was a good chance it could have been a bad cold.' There wasn't, but I wanted to give him this.

'Well, thank God you were here, love. Can I see her?'

'This evening,' I told him. 'In visiting hours. She's just in a normal ward now, out of A&E. And home, as I say, tomorrow.'

He nodded, eyes bright, not quite trusting himself to speak. In a moment I saw him straighten his shoulders as he set about tidying the newspapers from yesterday, putting them in the recycling pile in the kitchen. Then he came back and insisted on taking the ash out of the grate himself, laying the kindling, and generally getting the house bright and cheerful for her, even though she wouldn't be back until tomorrow. I realized he'd thought the worst, as I had. At least I didn't have that, I thought: the terrible grief my father would of course have one day – but not right now – of losing his life partner. The love of his life. I'd been spared that, with my life partner. But an empty, lonely feeling prevailed instead.

'Nance must have been pleased,' I said. 'When you told her?'

He chuckled, bending down with almost superhuman ease to put a match to the fire. 'Nancy's a tough old bird. I think she'd almost moved in. Was practically rearranging the furniture.'

'No!' I was shocked. But then, not really. This was how Dad's generation spoke – and acted. And Dad was an attractive man. It was no secret that Nance had always fancied him, and let's face it, who wants to be lonely for the last decade of their life? And Nance might be Mum's best friend, but she'd always had very sharp elbows. I tried not to be horrified. Husband number five.

'Much too bossy for me,' he grinned. 'And she practically bathes in gin; we'd be permanently pickled. It would never do. No, your mother's a much kinder, softer person.'

I saw his eyes fill as he gazed into the flames which leaped up from the crumpled newspaper. I gave his shoulder a squeeze as I passed. 'She is,' I murmured.

'Like you, love,' he said abstractedly. But I didn't answer. 'Anyway, enough of me, what about you?' He straightened up, rubbing his hands together. 'I reckon that Dan's after you.' I smiled and went into the kitchen to put the kettle on. 'And he's not a bad prospect, either,' he called after me. 'Got loads of dosh, courtesy of his consulting work. On all sort of boards. You wouldn't starve.'

I grinned and reached up to the shelf for the teabags. 'You're as bad as Helena,' I called out. 'And no doubt Nancy's been stirring the pot while she was here? Putting him forward as a candidate?'

There was no answer. I poked my head round the door as the kettle boiled. 'Dad? I said—'

'Yes, I heard. I was thinking about it. She didn't, actually. But Nancy's a selfish old girl. I think she was keen in the beginning, but not so much now. I think she's realized she likes that boy single, and at her beck and call. Not sure the reality of sharing him with someone else is that attractive.'

'Oh, right.' I went back to the fridge for milk. 'God, Nancy's shown herself in her true colours today, hasn't she? And I bet she thought she was covering herself in glory, playing Florence Nightingale and offering tea and sympathy.'

I heard my father chuckle from the next room. 'Funny how that often happens in a crisis. Brings out the best in some people, and in others, brings out the worst.'

I thought about that later as I was driving my father to the hospital, armed with *Vogue*, grapes, and some clothes for the morning. About how good Dan had been at the hospital, and how unlike his mother he was. I wondered where that softness had come from: his father had sounded a bit dictatorial.

'How well d'you know Dan?' I asked, as casually as I could, but not getting away with it.

Dad sat up, pleased. 'Not terribly well, actually. He was in London until his marriage broke up. But he always seems like a nice boy. Kind.'

'Yes, he is kind. He was brilliant at the hospital.' We were at some red lights and I quickly checked my phone.

'Helena's fond of him?' he offered.

'Yes, I know.'

'Darling, you shouldn't text and drive.'

'Sorry.' I dropped my phone on my lap as the lights went green. 'I wasn't actually using it, just looking. And I'd really like to know why that's so different to reading a map.'

'Not different at all, but plenty of people drive up the backside of a lorry reading maps.'

My mother was positively perky when we arrived in her ward. She'd been eyeing the door, waiting for us, and was sitting up in bed. The hospital gown was grim and I immediately handed her a pale grey pashmina which she took gratefully. Together we arranged it artfully around her shoulders, this sort of thing being important to Hartley women.

'Thank you, darling,' she said as Dad gave her a kiss. I watched as they gazed tenderly at one another for a moment.

'All right, old girl?'

'Never better.'

'Gave us a bit of a shock.'

'I like to keep you on your toes.'

'As long as you're not turning them up.'

We giggled, never a family for public displays of affection. Better at silly jokes and pashminas, which she was readjusting round her shoulders.

'They took my earrings,' she told me indignantly. 'Said I might hurt myself on them. I said I'd been wearing earrings in bed for sixty years and I hadn't suffered an injury yet.'

''Elf and safety,' I told her. 'I'll take them home for you. Are they in here?' I bent and looked in her little cabinet. Dad, sitting on the other side of the bed, just blinked a lot and took her hand. For once he seemed rather lost for words. The little old lady, last seen being carried into the ambulance, was a very different kettle of fish from the one sitting up swathed in cashmere, demanding her Chanel clips.

'No, Becky's got them,' she told me. 'Becky!' she tried to call out, but her voice was thin. It nonetheless carried enough, and I turned to see the sulky redhead, from the waiting room, turn her head as she tucked in a patient. She came across, smiling.

'More lippy, Cecily?' She grinned.

'No, but thank you, darling,' my mother purred. 'I just wondered if I could retrieve my earrings. This is my daughter Lucy, and my husband, Henry,' she said, extending her hand as if we were at a drinks party. 'Becky's been wonderful,' she told us. 'She's been looking after me. Marvellous girl.' I was surprised. I realized Becky didn't even recognize me. It occurred to me then, that when I'd imagined she'd been staring at a screen, online shopping, perhaps, she'd doubtless been madly organizing beds remotely. Or some other urgent medical task. And no lunch break, so just shove in a Curly Wurly. I gave her a grateful smile.

'Thank you. So much.'

'I'll get your sparklers,' she told Mum with a wink.

'They're in the safe,' Mum told us as the nurse moved on. 'And Becky told me they're the nicest things in there.

Everything else . . .' She shuddered, looking around at her inmates in horror. 'Well, you can imagine.' Her voice was a bit louder now. She was clearly feeling a lot better. 'And this one,' she hissed, jerking her head at a catatonic woman next door, deathly pale, mouth open, eyes shut. 'I mean, she might as well be dead. Look at her, poor thing.'

'Mum . . .' I warned nervously.

'In fact, *half* of these poor creatures, if they were animals, honestly, no sane vet—'

'Yes, yes, OK,' I interrupted hurriedly, wondering if she hadn't had quite enough saline and should come home now. Quite punchy. Dad was still gulping and staring adoringly, and it occurred to me that this moment might not come again: when he might tell her something rather tender and lovely. Three seemed a crowd, suddenly.

'Tell you what, to save Becky coming back, I'll go and get your jewellery from her. Dad, I'll see you out there. I've got a quick phone call to make. I'll see you tomorrow, Mum. Pick you up early.'

Before either of them could argue, I was on my way. Becky was straightening up behind the counter in the waiting area, having clearly locked a safe beneath it. As she handed me the earrings, a diamond ring and a Cartier watch, I thanked her for all she'd done. I also agreed I'd be back any time after seven, because, she told me, the ward badly needed the bed. I took a seat at the front where I did indeed get out my phone, for about the tenth time that day. But no. No message. And no reason

349

why there should be one, of course, I thought, pocketing it slowly. I mean, yes, I'd left a long, chatty one after the lunch. But it was a thank you. He was hardly going to text back saying – thank you for your thank you – was he? No man would do that. A girl might. Might say – lovely to see you! But not a man. The television above the nurses' station was on again: the news. I tried to distract myself with the political situation in Scotland. More cries for sovereignty. Then I got my phone out again and read the message I'd sent.

'Can't tell you how much I enjoyed lunch and what good fellows the Goodfellows are! The curry was delicious and I think you should take all the credit. Tilly would insist! Many thanks again. Xx'

Obviously I'd laboured long and hard over it. The kisses had been a difficult decision, but surely it would be odd not to? I practically left kisses for the window cleaner. And surely we'd almost had a moment at the door? But . . . perhaps I was deluding myself. Perhaps I'd been a bit pissed? Although I hadn't thought I was over the limit. I felt slightly foolish, all of a sudden. A bit out of my depth, which made me feel panicky. It was an old, familiar feeling that I'd sworn to myself I'd never feel again. I had vowed I'd never again put my emotional health in someone else's hands, that *I'*d be the one in control, *I'*d be the one calling the shots, wearing the trousers. Which was why Dan was a much more . . . suddenly I froze. Stared at the television. Listened to what George Alagiah was saying.

'A man has been arrested in connection with the murder of the theatre critic, Michael Palmer. Mr Palmer was found dead at his home in West London earlier this year, following a break-in. Andrew Parker, seventeen, has been charged with his murder.'

A photograph of a young blond boy flashed up on the screen. 'In Herefordshire, the River Wye has once again burst its banks . . .'

I turned away, shocked. Stared blankly into the middle distance. George Alagiah's mellifluous tones drifted on.

29

When my father came and found me a few minutes later, I was still sitting there, staring blankly at the wall. He bounded up, looking jaunty and happy.

'All right, darling? Let's go.' He rubbed his hands together. I turned my head and looked at him blankly. 'Luce?' he said as I got to my feet. 'What's wrong? You're as white as a sheet.'

'Someone's been charged with Michael's murder,' I told him. But my voice sounded odd. Distant. 'It's just been on the news.'

'Oh!' He looked astonished. Then his face cleared. 'But that's marvellous, darling. I mean – clears it all up.'

'He's seventeen,' I told him. There appeared to be no saliva in my mouth.

'Right.'

'There was a picture. He looked . . . like a child. Like Ned did, at that age.'

'OK, well—'

'He's probably – you know – a petty thief. A local lad. Chancing his arm. Nicking laptops, that kind of thing. Not a murderer.'

My father shrugged. 'Well, unintended consequences and all that.' He looked at me carefully, as if searching behind my eyes. 'Come on, love,' he said gently. 'Let's go to the car.'

We began to walk out. I kept my head bowed. I could sense he was recovering his buoyancy beside me, fairly bounding along by the time we got to the front doors. Not particularly fussed that a young lad had been arrested for Michael's death, still very much with his dear wife in the ward down the corridor. And d'you know, he didn't really feel they were doing enough in their declining years. He felt that the moment had to be seized. That now that his ulcers were under control, and her eyes and everything else – waterworks and what have you – they might go on a cruise. But I wasn't really listening, I was wondering how Andrew Parker had grown up. Fatherless? Possibly. Unemployed, almost certainly. Did he even have a home? Was he on the streets? Seventeen . . . I felt a bit sick. I let us into the car and let Dad ramble on as we drove away.

He was telling me about a trip the Frobishers had taken. Just around the Balearic Islands, so not far, but hot and sunny and—'Don't you think it's odd that they didn't come and tell me?' I said suddenly, cutting into his chatter.

'Who?'

'The police.'

He looked surprised. 'Well no, love. They're just concluding their inquiry.'

'But Michael was my husband. And I was questioned.'

'Well yes, of course you were, you were there, in the

house. But they will have questioned lots of people. They don't have to come and tell you how they're getting on.'

'Don't they?'

'Not to my knowledge, although actually, Nance did think she heard the door, but when we looked, no one was there, so who knows?' He smiled: patted my knee. 'Look, I know it's a shock, and particularly to hear it on the news like that, but once you've got your head round it you'll be so relieved. I wasn't the biggest fan of Michael, as you know, but to have found the man who ended his life is surely a good thing. It gives a sense of closure.'

Boy. He was a boy. And he hadn't ended Michael's life. I had. My heart was beating very fast. My mouth was dry. I held on tightly to the wheel. I mustn't look at Dad. Mustn't say anything. Worry him. I licked my sticky teeth.

'Yes, of course,' I whispered. 'Just the shock. That'll be it. Tell me about the Frobishers' cruise.' And he did. About how they'd sat at the Captain's table most nights, and how Jeannie, because of her dodgy knees, had had a wheelchair when they reached Formentera; a lovely cabin girl had scooted her around. Not that they went far, just into the main square for lunch. And not that he'd need a wheelchair, his legs were so much better, but nice to know it was there. A team of medics on board too, no doubt a defibrillator in every cabin! He told me Dickie had had the dressing on his septic toe changed by a very saucy blonde and I managed a feeble laugh. They'd asked Mum and Dad to go with them next year and they'd said no. But maybe they should change their minds?

'You should,' I managed, as we pulled into the drive. 'You'd enjoy it.'

Dad fairly skipped from the car. As soon as we were inside, he bustled to his study, muttering about being convinced he'd put the brochure Dickie had given him somewhere. Maybe in his desk . . . ?

Luckily his study was the one room he'd forbidden me or anyone else to clean, on the basis that yes, it was messy, but it was *his* mess and he knew where everything was. Happily, this was untrue, because he spent ages looking for things, so I knew it gave me a few moments. A few moments to hold on to the back of the sofa, bend my head, shut my eyes and think.

OK. OK, they'd said murder. But surely that should have been manslaughter? Surely, if the boy had been a petty thief, there's no way he'd intended to kill? It had just been a mistake. So manslaughter. But why had they said it? This was the BBC, not some local radio station. Why had it been on the national news in the first place? Because Michael had written for a national newspaper once? Probably. And Helena told me there'd been a bit on the news when he'd died, not that I'd seen it. Had in fact deliberately avoided it. And so therefore – I whipped out my phone. Yes. Two missed calls. One from Imo, one from Helena. They'd both left voicemails. Plus a text from Ned. All were along the same lines. I listened to Imo's voicemail.

'Soo delighted, Mum! They've got him. All that worrying for nothing! Now you can relax – oh, thank God. Ring me!'

355

Thank goodness my phone had been on silent. I sat down and quickly messaged back on our family WhatsApp.

'Such good news! I saw it too! Can't talk now cos Mum and Dad need supper.'

No. I deleted the last bit. No lies –

'cos am getting supper, but will ring you all tomorrow!'

I added a row of smiley faced emojis to keep them happy.

'Da-dah!' My father appeared in the doorway, brandishing an Abercrombie & Kent brochure. 'Found it. Darling, you've still got your coat on. And don't let the fire go out.' He hastened to put a log on. It had become something of a leitmotif for my father: not letting life go out. I straightened up. I removed my coat and went to hang it up.

'Shall we have fishcakes tonight, Dad? There are a couple in the freezer. And we could watch an episode of *The Crown*.'

'Good idea. And let's have a G&T while you rustle it up.' He hurried to the drinks cupboard and poured a couple of large ones. Amazing how fast he could move with a bit of adrenalin. I took my drink to the kitchen with me. I'd drunk half of it before I realized the pan was burning on the hob, with nothing inside it.

The following morning, it seemed to me I'd never really been asleep at all. I'd spent a fitful and frightening night in the gloaming, that terrifying place where the sweet release of sleep is always on the horizon, but never quite achieved. And where hallucinations are common. I got up wearily and prepared to collect my mother. Before I left, I arranged my face into a bright smile and popped into Dad's bedroom to let him know I was going. He was already shaving at his basin in his paisley dressing gown.

'I'm going to start driving again, now that my legs are better,' he told me, covered in Trumpers shaving soap. His eyes were defiant. 'No reason why I shouldn't?' His chin jutted.

'No reason at all. Although I might come with you for a bit. It's been a while since you've done it.'

He hesitated, about to protest, but then realizing he'd done well to get the general concept through, went back to listening to the *Today* Programme, which ordinarily made him roar with rage, but this morning saw him soaping himself merrily.

My mother was up and ready to go, already sitting bolt upright in the chair by her bed in the ward. She was dressed in the clothes I'd brought her yesterday, clutching her handbag. Her overnight bag was packed and ready at her feet. She was also beautifully made up. Now that she could see, her make-up was much less erratic.

'Hello, darling.' She stood up as eagerly as an eighty-four-year-old woman can and came towards me. We kissed and I took the overnight bag. Mum then made her way to the nurses' station to say farewell. Anyone would think she was checking out of the George Cinq, as she insisted on shaking hands with all the nurses, some of whom had no idea who she was, thanking them all profusely, and scolding me publicly for not bringing chocolates or flowers. Business as usual.

In the car which, despite her bravado, had taken us a while to totter to, she chatted away excitedly, along much the same lines as my father. They'd obviously discussed it yesterday, and her only worry seemed to be whether House of Fraser in High Wycombe would be up to cruise wear, or whether she'd have to go into Marlow?

'I don't want to end up looking like Jeannie's sister-in-law who went with them last year,' she told me. 'I saw the photographs. She looked like an extra in *Hawaii Five-O*. So I think we need some specialized boutiques.' She eyed me nearly as defiantly as my father had done, daring me to disagree, or worry that they were both too old for such a trip.

'Marlow it is,' I told her calmly. Luckily, like Dad, she was too distracted with her own life to notice anything unusual about me. I also knew that my children's and Helena's lives would be carrying on apace, and that having exchanged texts, and felt a great wave of collective relief, they'd forget, for the moment, about speaking to me. But I did wonder if Josh had seen it. The news. Not necessarily. It was only a quick news flash. It could have been on other programmes, but I'd looked online and bought all the papers – yes, all of them – and it was only a tiny column inch on a couple of inside pages. Easily missed.

I dropped Mum off at home, helping her from the car, and made sure they had some breakfast organized.

'Too much fussing!' my father complained when I added honey to the table he'd already laid in the kitchen. Bread was poised to pop down in the toaster, I noticed, and some bacon about to sizzle on the Aga. 'We're not invalids, you know.'

'Perfectly capable!' my mother agreed, bustling to put the kettle on, although Dad intercepted and filled it himself. He guided her to a chair. 'After all, we've been managing quite nicely for sixty-odd years!' she said as she sat.

Well, the last one was debatable. But in the small part of my brain that wasn't preoccupied with my own drama, I made a mental note to back off and see how they coped. I told them I was going shopping for myself, and that I needed a few things from Boots. I also told them I might be quite a while and that Mum wasn't to overdo it. Doctor's orders. Mum barely heard me, but Dad gave me a nod. When I left – my mother tucked under a rug on the sofa, I was pleased to see – they were muttering about whether the Frobishers would be up yet, or to leave it a while longer? They glanced at me furtively, Dad perched beside Mum on a chair as I came downstairs with my handbag, clearly wishing I'd go so they could discuss it properly, in private.

I drove down the familiar country lanes. The hedgerows were a vivid green and bursting with creamy May blossom. It was a bright, cold morning with a beautiful pale blue sky, but on closer inspection, a late ground frost singed and mocked the hedgerows for their show of colour. Why did I feel that was prophetic? Relieved to be alone, I rehearsed in my head what I was going to say.

I had no radio on, no CD in; only the quiet purr of the engine as a soundtrack to my thoughts. It was still early when I reached town, which was just waking up. There were precious few office workers here – they mostly went into Oxford – so it was mainly shopkeepers who greeted one another cheerily, fishing out great bunches of keys, opening up their doors.

The blue glass in the lamp above the police station door was glowing slightly in the sunshine as I parked outside. I got out and locked the car. Then I took a deep breath and went inside. A young uniformed officer was on reception. He looked up in slight surprise to see me at this hour. 'Can I help?'

'Yes, I'd like to . . .' barely a whisper. I cleared my throat and tried again. 'I'd like to speak to the officer I was interviewed by the last time I was here.'

He looked even more surprised. 'And you are?'

'Mrs Palmer. I believe his name was Turner? Detective Sergeant Turner?'

'Someone taking my name in vain?'

I turned around to see the man himself, coming up behind me, smiling. He was still in his coat, having clearly just followed me in. He'd been really rather intimidating previously, and I was surprised by his cheery demeanour. He didn't recognize me immediately, but when he did, his face cleared.

'Ah, Mrs Palmer. Good news from London. No doubt you heard?'

'Yes. Yes, I have. And that's what I'd like to talk to you about.' I wasn't calm. Not calm at all, and possibly this showed. I'd meant to be very composed, but I knew my voice, my agitated mannerisms – my twisting hands, the licking lips – were somewhat giving me away.

He looked taken aback for a moment. Then his face softened. 'I'm sorry, it must have been a shock. I can see that. To hear it on the radio. And actually we did send a police liaison officer round to break the news yesterday, but no one was in?'

'Oh. My father wondered. He got to the door too late.'

He spread his hands apologetically.

'Well, thank you for that. But I wonder if I might have a word anyway?'

'Yes, of course.' This was a different man now. He was polite, kind, mannerly. No doubt the man he was in real life, when he wasn't questioning murder suspects. He led the way down the corridor to the same interview room, probably the only one they had. Before he went in, though, he popped his head into the coffee room where his staff were still waking up. He asked Holly to come in, please, and bring the file, if she would. The same girl as before put her cap on and came in behind us, giving me a smile. Perhaps she'd heard the news too. May even have been the one who'd popped round.

I waited until we were all seated at the table. They were relaxed and easy in their chairs. I opened my mouth. For a moment I had neither wind nor words to draw on. But then it came out.

'I'd like to confess.'

There was a silence. Turner frowned. 'Confess?' He looked confused.

'To my husband's murder.'

Slowly they both sat forwards. They didn't speak, they just waited. Then I saw Holly reach for a button on a machine: Turner stayed her hand.

'You see, I killed him. Yes, Andrew Parker, the burglar, knocked him down, knocked him out, but I found him still alive when I came down. I didn't ring the ambulance until he was dead.'

Silence prevailed. Turner looked at me intently. If this was a tactic to make me talk, it worked. I gabbled on. 'My husband was a monster. A bully. A tyrant. I was terrified of him. We all were. I spent my life running scared. He didn't beat me, but he did other, more terrible things, more scary things. Nothing visible, he was too clever for that. But the things he made me do. The threats he made about my children . . .' I shook my head. 'All sorts. Horrific. When I saw him lying there, I knew I wanted him dead. Had often thought about it. I left him there until . . . you know.'

I looked at my hands, clenched before me on the table. The nails of one were digging into the back of the other. There was a trace of blood. The girl, Holly, saw it too.

'How long did you wait for, Mrs Palmer?' asked Turner quietly.

'I don't know,' I whispered.

'You were in shock?'

'Yes, but – no. Not really. I felt very rational. Very calm.'

'Not panicky.'

'No. And you see, the boy, the young lad, he would

have just pushed Michael and run. He just wanted our phones, money, whatever. I, on the other hand, wanted him dead.'

Turner was still regarding me intently. 'But only you can corroborate this. There was no one else in the house.'

'No, but the study blinds weren't pulled, you see. And the woman at the back, behind us, was up. I saw her light on. Only briefly. Up to now I've persuaded myself I imagined it, but I know I saw it. When I came down.'

Without taking his eyes off me, he put his hand out. Holly passed him a file. He opened it. Read for a bit. 'Mrs Schroeder?'

'Yes.'

'We have spoken to her.'

'I thought you would have.'

'She said she didn't see the break-in, she must have been asleep, but she woke for some reason, perhaps she heard a shout, and did see you arrive in the room. She said the French door was open and there was a man on the floor. She saw you crouch down and reach for your phone a moment later. She saw the light from it. Saw you put it to your ear. That's why she didn't ring the police herself, report what she assumed was a break-in. She says the emergency services arrived soon after.'

I stared at him, astounded. Dumbfounded. At length I spoke. 'But . . . I – I didn't. That just didn't happen. That's not true. It was just in my hand, my phone. For ages. I sat there for ages, in the dark . . . it seemed like ages.'

'Not according to Mrs Schroeder. And not according to you, either. A statement was taken from you at the time. You told the police officer you wore earplugs and didn't hear your husband come in, but when you went down, he was already dead on the floor. You phoned the police immediately. What do you say about that?'

'I retract it. I made it up,' I whispered.

'I see.'

He paused. Read the notes again. Finally he looked up. He folded his hands in front of him. 'Of course, shock affects people in many different ways, Mrs Palmer.' His voice was kind. 'Many people, when something terrible happens, can be in an almost trance-like state, despite feeling completely lucid. And time, in those circumstances, is often not in line with our perception of it. What feels like hours can be moments. And the mind works in mysterious ways, after a trauma. Particularly given the condition of your marriage. It's possible, in your guilt since the incident, you persuaded yourself you were responsible.'

I stared at him, stunned. 'You don't believe me.' My voice was no more than a breath.

'I suggest, having spoken to Mrs Schroeder, who is an un-shocked, independent witness, that her timeline is more accurate. It also concurs with your account at the time. It's possible you've had too much time to think since, and become disoriented and confused. At the time, you gave the same account as Mrs Schroeder.'

'But I told you, I want to retract that. You see – there's an innocent young lad, a boy, his whole future – and – and you see, years ago,' I rushed on, 'there was another young boy. That's the thing. Another teenager. Only two years older than this one, nineteen. Liam Stephens, perhaps you remember? Perhaps you were here? Not you,' I glanced wildly at Holly, 'you're too young. But you might have been?' I implored Turner.

'I'm sorry,' he said slowly. He frowned. Shook his head, confused. 'I . . . don't understand.'

'I knocked him off his motorbike in 2001. It wasn't my fault, but he died. I killed him.' I was licking inside my cheeks for saliva. 'I thought you might remember?'

'I came from Tetbury, five years ago,' he said slowly. He was looking at me very carefully. My head was pulsing. It felt like a vein was leaping out of my temple. Like Michael's used to.

'No, no, then you wouldn't remember.' I nodded feverishly. I could feel myself sweating. 'You're right, it would have been before your time. But you see, my point is, I was responsible. Inadvertently, but still, I did it. I ended his life, and I don't want to end another. I can't be responsible again, I just can't.' My voice was rising, cracked even. This didn't sound as good as it had done in the small hours. Or in the car, when I'd rehearsed it. Not as clear, as rational. I tried to explain again, but I was falling over my words. 'Because now, you see, there's this other young boy. And I simply cannot have that on my conscience, don't you understand? Don't you see? It would be—'

'Mrs Palmer,' Turner interrupted me sharply. 'The young boy, Andrew Parker, or Parks, is a gang leader. A drug dealer. He has a host of previous convictions. His particular gang roams the West London streets where you live, in a calculated, ruthless manner. Last summer, an elderly lady was beaten up and killed for her jewellery by Parker. The Met know this, but there was not enough evidence to prosecute.'

I was taken aback. A gang leader. A drug dealer. But still, I felt dogged. Determined. I pressed on. 'So – so what you're saying is, you're going to prosecute him for this one, is that it?' My voice sounded a bit shrill. 'Pin this one on him, hm?'

'Mrs Palmer, we're talking about a violent, serial offender. A very nasty individual. It's lucky you didn't come down the stairs earlier, or he might well have killed you too. I very much doubt he gave your husband a little push.'

Turner's eyes were pale hazel, almost yellow, like a tiger's. Steady, intelligent eyes. Focused. They didn't leave my face. I was mesmerized by them. I didn't know what to say. The silence in the room was heavy, thick with portent. I swallowed. Eventually I spoke. 'So . . . what should I do? Now? I mean – I've told you what happened. Are you going to pass it on? To the Met?'

'Of course. I shall speak to them directly.'

'And I'll wait to hear?' It sounded as if I were at a job interview.

'Yes, you will be hearing from us. Because I think it would be in your interests for us to keep you informed. In the interests of your . . .' he hesitated. For a surreal moment I thought he was going to say sanity. 'Anyway. I can see this has come as a terrible shock. I regret not persisting in contacting you previously. It was remiss of me. We should have persevered. And I believe it would be wrong to keep you out of the loop now, particularly in light of what you've said today. But please think carefully about any statement you might wish to make.' He leaned forward again: folded his arms on the table. His eyes searched my face. 'I've seen people, usually women, confess to crimes they didn't commit, for all sorts of reasons. And unfortunately, if you insist enough, you reap what you sow. But too often, in circumstances like this, the mind plays tricks on us. It's well documented. Don't forget that, Mrs Palmer. Is there someone at home for you?'

'What d'you mean?'

'Someone to look after you.'

'I don't need looking after.'

'But is someone there?'

'My parents.'

'Good.'

He closed the file. Then he pushed his chair back and got to his feet. Holly stood too. They were waiting for me. At length, uncertainly, I followed suit. There was so much more to say. So much I needed to say. But there was nothing I could do about it. Turner went to the door, opened it and waited. I hesitated, but went through, under his arm. He peeled off into the staff room without another word, the file under his arm. Holly's eyes were kind as she ushered me down the corridor to reception. No, I realized as she opened the front door for me and held it, her eyes were not kind. They were concerned. Worried. And all I could think was – why isn't anyone listening to me? After all these years of keeping silent about Michael, when I finally decide to speak out, why won't anyone hear me?

30

I drove back down the lanes feeling dazed and disconnected. The late spring sun was low in the sky and dazzling in its intensity. The road shimmered, mirage-like, before me. I pulled the visor down, but it didn't help much and suddenly I was glad of the searching spotlight, focusing on me, finding me out: looking into every corner of my soul. I pushed the visor up and embraced it. Was he right, Turner? Was Ingrid right? Was I imagining things? Had my mind overcompensated for the numerous times I'd fantasized about Michael dying? And let's face it, it had been a constant preoccupation. One minute he was stepping off the pavement, half cut, into the path of an oncoming car when – thud. It was all over. The next he was driving too fast – a regular occurrence – and meeting a lamppost head on, as he misjudged a corner. No one else was hurt, obviously, but the car concertinaed and he was killed instantly. I shook my head, gathering myself together. Banishing all those old thoughts. That old life.

Instead, I concentrated on what Turner had said. Sometimes, in times of extreme stress and shock, and after trauma, the mind plays tricks. Distorts the past. The timeline can shift, or, more specifically, lengthen. A minute seems like an hour. Except I knew . . . I *knew* . . .

didn't I? I gripped the wheel feeling – what was that word Imo had taught me? Gaslighted. That was it. She'd used it with reference to her father. It was from a movie of the same name, with Ingrid Bergman and – Cary Grant? The husband who drives his wife insane: planting seeds of doubt, until she questions her own reality. Michael had done it, constantly manipulating me to imagine I was in the wrong, doubting my own memories, my perception of the truth. Jesus Christ, was it happening again? In which case, *was* it me? Was *I* the one who misremembered events? Had I deliberately coughed in Michael's ear every two hours, as he once said I had, intentionally waking him, so that I was afraid to go to sleep (and wasn't allowed to sleep in the room next door)? I had to pull over suddenly, off the road, on to a grass verge. Was this yet another situation I'd got wrong?

My hands were shaking as I removed them from the wheel which I'd been clutching. Had I been mad all along, and had Michael been right? Did I deliberately smash his mother's antique bowl? He even showed me the pieces on the floor: told me I'd stepped over them for two days. He said the same of Imo and Ned, that they'd taken things of his. A watch, belonging to Michael's father. The family Bible. Stolen them. He punished them for it, and then we'd found those things later, locked in drawers. It made me feel better, remembering the children's experiences. My parents, too, who he said never thanked us when they came to our house, although my mother always wrote – Michael had made it plain he didn't count a phone call. But Michael destroyed the letters. Before I got to them. So they stopped coming, my parents. To make it easier for me.

Turner couldn't have known, of course, what he was doing, by going down that misremembering route. But by God he'd hit some buttons. Found some raw nerves. I waited for my heart rate to come down a bit. Waited for it to stop racing. And I made myself relax my shoulders. Breathe, Lucy. Breathe.

I put the car into gear again and drove on. But I kept my speed very slow. Because I wasn't entirely sure I was all right. Wasn't entirely sure how to deal with what had happened back there at the station. Of course, I should have been leaping for joy. Not only had I confessed, but it had been rebuffed. Ruled out. The police weren't having it. They had their man, thank you very much, and they'd been after him for a while. No wonder they'd left questioning me to the provincial branch – no neurotic housewife with a fit of conscience was going to get in the way of the Met. Retract him from their clutches. A nasty piece of work, I told myself. Parks, not Andrew. A drug dealer. A violent criminal. Who assaulted old ladies. *Killed* old ladies.

I didn't drive home; I drove on into Oxford. I knew where to park, behind the Old Bank Hotel, which had become a brasserie. I found a seat inside, on the banquette bench against the wall, and ordered a coffee. I sipped it slowly. The place was busy, bustling. A fair amount of students, some prospective, I thought, looking at their nervous, eager faces, together with their parents. Some professors, too, I decided. A pair beside me, middle-aged women, were talking earnestly, their noses almost touching over the small table. Good. Good. Thank heavens for clever, preoccupied people. I sank back on the leather seat, watching, watching. Huge murals hung on the walls. Why so big? Oil paintings, with too much colour. I averted my eyes. The place ebbed and flowed. More young people came in. My coffee was cold, but I sipped it still. Eventually a young waitress came across and asked me if I was all right. Yes, why? It was just that I'd been there a long time. Three hours, and they wondered ... I gazed at her, shocked. Then at my watch. Three hours! The women beside me had been replaced by a young couple. I stumbled an apology, paid for my coffee and left. I was horrified. It was as if Turner had deliberately sent me there, to vindicate him. As if he'd been watching. Three hours. I knew too, that on the day Michael's bowl had been broken, I'd dusted the bedroom. Which was unusual, because normally I left it to our cleaner. Was it me? Was I actually insane? Had *I* locked Michael's possessions in a drawer in my desk, the ones he accused Ned and Imo of taking, and then wiped it from my brain? Had I thrown my mother's letters in the outside dustbin, before Michael had a chance to look at them? I saw myself lifting the lid, glancing furtively about, dropping them in. Was I, in fact, out of my mind?

I walked around the clothes shops in the High Street. Old familiars: Jigsaw, Whistles. Then across the road to the covered market. It was cold, and I didn't have a coat.

I picked things up, bracelets, jumpers, scarves, but I didn't try anything on, or wrap anything around my neck. I wanted to be an anonymous person amongst many other anonymous people. And I hoped the exercise would do me good. With that in mind, I started to walk to the Ashmolean. But when I got there, it was enormous. Huge, honey-coloured columns, vast looming steps, with great flags advertising some exhibition, towered over me. Had everything here always been so big? And the antiquities were so old, on the ground floor, in the Roman section. How old? AD 26? How was that possible? The very idea made me tremble. How many millions of people had lived since then, since this tiny scrap of copper I was looking at? How small and insignificant was I? I felt very cold. I left the museum in a hurry. And when I eventually got back to the car, it was getting dark.

There was a car I didn't recognize in my parents' drive. I drew up alongside and switched the engine off. The lights were on behind the drawn curtains in the sitting room, and smoke was coming from the chimney. I got out and went inside. When I went into the hall, it was beautifully warm. Good smells were coming from the kitchen.

'Ah! Darling! You made it.' My father greeted me warmly, coming out from the sitting room. He rested his hands on my shoulders. 'Good heavens, you look all in. Dan popped round to see you. He dropped Nance off at the Pattersons for supper and called in for a drink. We thought we'd all have supper!'

Dan appeared behind my father in the sitting room doorway, tall and smiling in that blue cashmere jumper that matched his eyes. Dan again. I felt a wave of irritation. He was always popping up unexpectedly, wasn't he? He came across and kissed my cheeks warmly.

'Blame your parents,' he told me apologetically. 'Apparently chicken pie is imminent, and I was press-ganged into it. I tried to ring you, but your phone is off.'

'Yes. I turned it off.'

I followed them both and took in the cosy scene. Mum had popped out from the kitchen to tell me that before I fussed, she'd been in bed all day, and could now be heard back in there singing along to the radio. My father and Dan repositioned themselves by the fire. They were nursing drinks and resumed their chat, happy and relaxed, and suddenly – suddenly I was so incredibly pleased to be here. I felt something drop from me, like a dead skin. This, surely, was real life? Cosy and safe. Not that horror story I'd been reliving out there, frozen to some dark past that refused to leave: that insisted on dragging me back, haunting me. Here, I knew I'd got nothing wrong. Knew I'd broken and hidden nothing. Had angered no one. Had only pleased people, which was all I ever wished to do. I looked into Dan's hopeful, smiling eyes. I knew I'd be so safe with him. As I joined the pair of them by the fire, warming my hands but declining a drink, not sure how my head would cope with it, I watched him joking with Dad. Teasing him, about how he and Mum were clearly fitting up the cottage for themselves, on the pretext of giving it to me. He'd obviously been shown around.

'It's practically got your slippers under the bed, Henry! I'm surprised you're not in there already!'

Dad threw back his head and roared with laughter. 'We've been rumbled!' he told me, turning to me, his eyes damp with mirth. 'Dan's seen straight through our little ruse, I'm afraid – he's said the unsayable.' He peered closer at me. 'You all right, love? You look awfully pale.'

'Yes, fine. Well, I must say, Dad, the thought hadn't escaped me either. Or Helena or Imo, for that matter. We were waiting for you to break cover.' I was still in a state of upheaval, but my head began to feel a little less chaotic.

'Really, darling?' My mother appeared from the kitchen where she'd clearly been listening keenly. 'And you wouldn't mind?' She looked anxious, but also excited as she came in.

'Not a bit. It's far more suitable for you than me. But what would you do with Pope's Farm?'

'We thought sell it,' Dad said firmly. He made his fabled face, the one with the jutting chin, which meant he was serious. It occurred to me dimly that we were having a very personal chat in front of Dan, but somehow, that felt fine too. It occurred to me, also, that Dan knew about Liam. Which was a huge tick. And that I could tell him about Andrew Parker. About what I'd done, and that he wouldn't judge me. Wouldn't be appalled. At how I'd ended the lives of two young men.

374

That his sort of love would be unconditional. That he'd actually do anything for me. Which was what I needed.

'There's a nice young couple in the village, with small children,' my father was saying. 'They love the house and have asked us a couple of times. You know, to give them first option. If we ever decide to go.' It was the first I'd heard of it, but then, it wouldn't have been in my parents' interests to tell me. Not when they were determined, with every fibre of their beings, to hang on to it. Now, of course, they were determined to go. So it was a different matter. 'Unless you or Helena wanted it?'

'But we don't want you to feel obligated to live next door to us,' Mum said quickly. 'If you see what I mean. We'd love it, obviously. But we don't need it. We'd be totally independent in that bungalow.'

I wasn't really up to speed with this conversation. I tried to assimilate what they were saying but I realized I'd lost the thread, momentarily, so I had to ask Mum to repeat what she'd said.

'I said, we could be completely independent, over there.'

'For the minute,' I replied, coming to. 'For the minute, you'd be fine. But since we're saying the unsayable, no one's invincible.' I forced a smile, but actually, it didn't seem the effort it would have been an hour ago. Not half as bad as I'd thought. The fire behind my legs was lovely. 'And maybe I would want to live here? Maybe you'd be hard pushed to get rid of me?' I gazed around. Took in the faded chintz covers on the sofa and armchairs: the old velvet curtains, the worn Persian rugs. It was warm and familiar. And – yes, OK, that word again. Safe. Womb-like. It occurred to me, I really would like to be here, forever.

'It's a jolly nice house,' Dan said appraisingly, glancing round. 'Mum's always been jealous.'

'*Has* she?' This pleased my mother no end. She came and perched on a sofa arm, avidly. She looked very fresh, for one who'd left hospital so recently, dressed in a pink frock and a pearl-grey cardigan. But then if she'd been in bed all day she'd probably have spent most of it asleep. And no drink, I was pleased to see.

'Yes, she's always saying how hers is too big, and how manageable this is. Prettier, too.'

'Well, of course it is prettier. It's Queen Anne,' purred my mother delightedly. Nance would never have admitted this to her, they were fiercely competitive. And it wasn't Queen Anne, actually – it missed the period by a long way – but my mother never let the truth stand in the way of a good story.

'Needs work, of course,' said Dad, turning to Dan in a man-to-man sort of way. 'The roof is sound, but the lean-to on the study side leaks like buggery.'

'Probably take that down?' suggested Dan.

'Oh yes, I've always wanted to do that. And have a lovely conservatory there instead,' said Mum eagerly.

'Orangerie, you told me,' Dad reminded her, raising his eyebrows. 'I've run scared ever since.'

They all laughed, and actually I joined in. And then, on my mother's instruction, we drifted through to the kitchen, where the curtains were drawn, and the Aga was warm. The room looked inviting. I was surprised to see Mum had laid the table beautifully, with a cloth, flowers and candles. She saw me look.

'I *can* do it,' she told me quietly. 'Just wasn't really trying before.'

She'd had a shock. They both had. A nasty one. Neither of them was ready to go yet. To be gathered, as my father would say. But they knew they had to make a fist of staying on. As if to illustrate, my mother then produced a pie from the oven, which was not one of mine.

'Stop it,' I told her, as I sat down. I was feeling better by the minute.

'Yes, but it's a cheat, actually. It's leftover chicken in a chicken soup sauce with frozen pastry on top. But heavens, it works. Look!' She cut into it and we all marvelled. Even when we tasted it. Hardly Cordon Bleu, but extremely edible nonetheless. And Dad had made a fruit salad for pudding.

The evening wore on in a convivial manner, with much joking and banter. Not from me, but nobody seemed to notice, and I felt more restored. I was still in disarray but I began to feel a little less wild. I'd get there. I knew early mornings and last thing at night would be bad. That all sorts of doubts and worries, not least about my own sanity, which I was now convinced Turner had been about to mention, would come flooding back. But this was miles better than that awful police station. That freezing stop in the lane. That concerned look on the waitress's face in the bistro. That terrifying museum. This was home.

Eventually, Dan stood up and said he had to go. Had

to get his mother before the Pattersons rang him and demanded her immediate withdrawal, informing him they'd locked the drinks cupboard. Forbidding my parents to get up – although Dad wasn't having that and rose slowly from his chair – he thanked my mother for supper. Said he'd had a lovely evening. I walked him to the door.

'It was lovely to see you,' he told me, slightly shyly. 'I felt a bit bereft when I left you in the hospital, yesterday.'

I remembered him standing at the end of the corridor. 'You did look a bit forlorn.'

He looked surprised and I realized I shouldn't have said it. That good manners precluded me from saying ego-denting things like that. I wasn't quite functioning properly. Wasn't quite picking up the social nuances. 'It was lovely to see you too,' I added quickly, and realized I meant it. This capable, kindly man soothed me, I decided. But I did need to be on my own, right now.

He recovered his equilibrium. 'Is the pub too predictable, or shall we venture into Oxford? London even? Live a little?'

'Not Oxford,' I said quickly. 'Or London. And actually, I love the pub.'

He smiled. 'Let's do that, then. Tuesday?'

'Tuesday it is.'

We could hear my parents clattering about in the kitchen, and to my relief, Dan didn't move towards me. I certainly wasn't up for that. Instead, he turned and made his way, which showed a level of sensitivity. As I shut the front door, though, I realized he'd looked very pleased as he went to his car. There was a spring in his step: renewed vigour. A sense of second chance about him. And I was pleased too, I decided. I went back into the sitting room, arms folded consideringly across my chest. Let's face it, he was a lovely man.

My father was stacking the dishwasher, forbidding Mum to help, as I went through into the kitchen. They turned as I came in. Their faces were open and expectant.

'Jolly decent, isn't he?' said Dad, faux innocently.

'Jolly.' I smiled, and bent to blow out the candles.

'And such a *kind* man,' my mother told me. 'D'you know, he'll pick Nance up from the Pattersons' now, take her home, pop her in the bath, and then put her to bed. He supervises the whole thing. Every night.'

I turned to her slowly, in surprise. 'He baths her?'

'She got stuck once,' she told me. 'It's frightened her ever since. She couldn't get out.'

'Oh.'

'And she can't bear showers. Says it's like being rained on.' She made a face. 'But that's a fib, obviously. It's her hair.'

I put the candlesticks back in the cupboard, but then I paused a moment, still digesting this. I pictured the nightly ritual. Somehow, I wished she hadn't told me that.

31

It's well documented, of course, but it is nonetheless extraordinary how restorative a good night's sleep can be. And I'm not a good sleeper. I often require medical assistance. But when I do sleep, unaided, for nine hours on the trot, which I'd just done, I feel empowered. I was surprised I'd managed it, frankly. How odd. Usually when my mind's in turmoil, I get about an hour and a half. It must be this house, I decided, looking around at the faded floral wallpaper. I definitely slept much better here. I got up, showered and dressed, and then, hearing my parents already about, went to my shopping in the corner of my room. Yes, I had made one purchase yesterday on my way back from the Ashmolean, in the Cornmarket. I picked up the plastic bag and took it downstairs. Popping my head around the kitchen door where my parents were having a quiet breakfast, I asked my mother how she was.

'Radiant!' she declared. 'Never better. Must have another dodgy turn.' I shot her a reproving look. Then I asked my father if I could use his study.

'Of course, darling.' He looked surprised. 'What are you going to do in there?'

'Oh, you know. This and that.'

He looked confused, and then his face cleared in recognition. He nodded; looked pleased. I grabbed a black coffee and departed.

In the study I carefully cleared a space, transporting his messy piles to the floor, replicating their exact positions. Then I sat down at his desk in the window. It overlooked the paddock where Helena and I used to keep our ponies, and where the local farmer now grazed a few sheep. It was a lovely, familiar view and swept up to the hill beyond, where we used to ride. I drank it in for a moment, realizing I hadn't seen it up to now, this being the only window in the house that afforded it. Maybe I'd see it every day, now. I reached into my Ryman's bag and drew out six spiral bound, A4 notebooks. Three were pink, and three were green. Then I took out two packets of black, thin-tipped pens and, removing one, wrote number one on a pink notebook and circled it. I turned over the first page and at the top of the right-hand page wrote – Chapter One – and underlined it. I already felt a lot better than I had done twenty-four hours ago, but just that simple act was deeply calming. I stared out at the sheep in the meadow. They were last year's lambs, so ewes only now, all the boys having gone to market. The girls didn't look too fussed about that. After about twenty minutes – I know, not long, although no doubt subliminally it had been months, with all sorts of ideas kaleidoscoping around my head like so many bees – I set off.

Susie was at home, a scenario I liked a lot these days, her domestic life becoming as important as her professional one: gradually the balance had shifted. She was sorting through the post, which was all for her since she lived alone, her husband having left her, when a particular envelope caught her eye. It was brown and handwritten in a shaky, familiar hand. She stared at it for a long moment and then quickly opened it. It was from her adoptive mother who she hadn't seen for years, her biological mother having taken her place after revealing secrets about the adoptive one which were too hard for Susie to take.

> *Dear Susie,*
>
> *I know it's been six years since you asked me not to contact you, but something has come to light which I hope will convince you to change your mind.*

And thus, I was off. No idea where. But into another person's world, someone else's drama, well away from anything that was happening in my own. Shielded, protected, soothed. Perhaps like a class of aerobics, followed by one of stretches, followed by a run in the park, who knows? Each to their own form of escape or therapy. All I know is that when I looked up – hungry and in need of a pee – I also felt calm and whole. I went to the loo, grabbed a piece of cake from the kitchen, and came back. I set off once more and then, after a while, exhausted, knew I'd finished for the day. I closed the book. Sat back and stared out at the sheep, head cleared. Full, but cleared. And in that clarity, it came to me. As things often did, in that moment. Of course. It was obvious. Indeed it was as clear as the bright blue sky I was gazing at. I glanced at my watch. Only one o'clock. Which was fine. I'd missed the rush hour, and if I went now, I'd be back before the evening one started. Perfect.

There didn't seem to be many signs of my parents in the kitchen or garden, and then I realized they were in the sitting room, the remains of a ham salad on their laps, watching the news.

'We didn't know whether to disturb you,' said Mum, rather guiltily. 'You seemed busy, but there's plenty in the fridge.'

'Yes, don't worry, I'll get my own. Drinking lots of fluids, Mum?'

'Yes, loads. Your father gives me a glass of lemon barley every time he sees me, you know I can't abide water.' She made a face. 'And I'm about to have a nap. I slept for hours yesterday.'

'Good. Um, I'm popping out. Be back probably about supper time, but if I'm not, start without me, OK?'

'OK!' Their faces brightened and it occurred to me that in their present contentment they were quite pleased to have the house to themselves. After all, they'd been used to that sort of modus vivendi for many years, and much as I loved Imo and Ned, there'd been times when they'd gone back to school or university when I'd been relieved too, although sometimes for different reasons, to do with their father.

As I drove along the A40 in a light drizzle and happily only light traffic, I rehearsed a few pithy sentences in my head. But then, knowing that actually I was better on the hoof in these sorts of circumstances – see my performance yesterday – I turned on the radio and caught the end of the Jeremy Vine show. He played the sort of easy listening conducive to maintaining equilibrium and morale.

The London traffic wasn't too terrible either, plus I knew the best route, so I arrived at forty-two Arlain Road in good time. I slotted the car right outside. As I climbed the steps to the tall, white, stucco-fronted town house, I realized it had only a fifty-fifty chance of occupancy, but this sort of place usually had a housekeeper, so some clue to whereabouts might be ascertained. I could return. Steps came down the passage after I'd rung the doorbell, but then, no housekeeper, or even sulky daughter appeared. This time it was Ingrid herself.

She'd opened the door with a smile, but then, as she recognized me, looked surprised. She blinked. 'Oh, it's you.'

'I'm sorry. I know I should have phoned or emailed you, but I was terribly afraid you wouldn't see me and I badly need to speak to you.' This came out in a bit of a rush.

She digested this silently: looked thoughtful. Then her face softened. She gave a small smile, nodded, and opened the door for me. Her blonde hair was up in a ponytail and she was wearing black leggings and an assortment of grey and black vests. She had trainers on her feet.

'I haven't got that long,' she told me apologetically, 'I'm on my way to the gym.'

'I promise I won't keep you long,' I told her, surprised at her tone. This was very different to the unfriendly, uptight woman I'd previously encountered at lunch in my club.

She led me through a beautiful pale grey hall lined with mirrors, framed photographs and architectural prints. A delicately carved bust sat on a console table flanked by two huge vases of white lilies. I followed her into the kitchen which was so different to mine on the other side of the wall it took my breath away. Pale limed wood and Swedish in design, obviously, it was ultra-modern and achingly chic. There were two white leather and chrome bar stools either side of the island which she pulled out. We sat down opposite each other. The island was smooth white marble and completely bare. No mess, no clutter. Ingrid clasped her hands loosely before her. They were not heavily jewelled today: in fact she had no rings on at all. She waited. I took a deep breath.

'I came to see you, because I now know that you witnessed my husband's death. The police told me.' She remained expressionless. Her pale blue eyes held mine. 'The thing is, Ingrid, it doesn't tally with my own recollection of events. Timewise, that is.'

'I saw on the news they got the man who did it. Isn't it all over now? Should we be comparing notes?'

'Possibly not, but I'm going to plough on anyway. I need to know. And the police didn't tell me not to talk to you. Did they say anything to you?' She didn't reply. I blundered on. 'You see, I know I sat there for a long time while Michael was on the floor. And yet, you say I called the police immediately. The moment I came down.' She remained silent but a muscle went in her cheek. 'Can I ask where you were?' I asked.

'In the top bedroom. In the attic. It's the spare room. I sleep there sometimes. Usually when my husband's at home.'

'Oh . . . right. And he sleeps?'

'In ours.'

'I thought you were separated?'

'We are, but he stays here sometimes. When he's in London.'

'That's civilized.'

'No, he insists. It's his house. And if I want to stay here, it's part of his deal. And I do. Want to stay. My house is my life's work. I put my heart into it. And I wouldn't get it in any divorce settlement.'

'Oh. Right.' A rare glimpse into someone else's world. I reorientated myself. 'So . . . he was in the main bedroom.'

'Fast asleep. And I was reading upstairs.'

'With the light on.'

'Yes.'

'But you didn't see him break in? The burglar?'

'No.'

'So . . . when did you look out? Why?'

'For some reason I went to the window when you appeared. Maybe I heard something. I turned off my lamp to see better. I saw someone on the floor. Then I saw the smashed door, realized there'd been a break-in. I thought about getting my phone, but then I saw you check him, Michael, and dash to get yours. So I didn't.

I've told the police all this. I watched you make the call and then, very quickly, it was all sirens and blue flashing lights – I gather you had them out again the other night. I told the police all of this when they came round. Told them that it all happened very quickly.'

I stared at her. 'You see, it's so strange. Because my own feeling is that it happened very slowly. That I sat down. On the sofa. In my nightie. For quite some time. And watched the blood seep out of his head. My recollection is that I did nothing. Some may say through shock, some might say through deliberate design. I know what I think. But I probably need to keep that to myself. Anyway. I remember sitting there, in the dark, until I was really quite cold. Apparently shock does that to you, it does chill you. The police said that was no surprise. It's why they wrap trauma victims in blankets. But it may also be that it's cold to sit still for so long in a thin nightgown. Again, I know what I think. I remember checking him occasionally, using the light on my phone. I didn't time it, but I reckon I sat there for at least half an hour. Waiting for him to—'

'Don't say it,' Ingrid interrupted grimly. She leaned forward, her hand on mine. She gripped it. 'Don't say the word,' she breathed. Her expression was urgent. I blanched in astonishment. Saw something in her eye. Something like gritty determination.

Eventually she spoke. 'You sat there for two hours and ten minutes,' she said softly. I inhaled sharply. Couldn't speak for a moment. I stared at her.

'You watched me.'

'Yes. I sat with you.'

'For that long?' I whispered.

'Yes. Me upstairs, and you, in your white nightie, next to him. I'd seen you in that nightie before. In the garden. At night. Locked out.' My breathing became very shallow. I felt that horrible, panicky feeling return. 'When your husband locked you out, sometimes in the winter. I saw him open the door, once. I didn't know then it was Michael. Didn't know you were the couple I'd met at Millie's dinner until much later. He was just the odd man who lived at the back. And you were that poor strange wife. I assumed you were the wife. He left you there for ages, in the garden, and you sat in dark corners, where he pointed, in the flower beds, crushing your plants. I saw you from my top-floor room, whenever Lars was here. Once, I nearly rang the police. Or social services. But I didn't. I don't know why. I wish I had. I think . . . because he didn't push you out. You seemed to go willingly. He sort of . . .' she hesitated. 'Let you out. Like a dog. I should have done, should have said something, I realize that now. But I told myself it was domestic. Private. And I was having my own domestic turmoil here. I had a husband having sex with a friend of my daughter's down the road. Same age. Seventeen. That's where he'd returned from, that night, when I was in the spare room. I wasn't reading, obviously. Just . . . awake. Thinking. Thinking. Then I saw you.'

I stared at her, dumbfounded. Eventually I found my voice. 'But . . . we had lunch. And you and Michael had already had lunch—'

'I told you,' she interrupted, 'I didn't know it was you. Or him. That you were that couple. How could I? I didn't know you were the woman at the back, as I called you. Did you know where I lived, when we met at Millie's?'

'No. I had no idea.'

'And the police didn't talk to me for ages. The first time they came, early on, I was out. They spoke to Sophia, my daughter, who said we were all asleep. By the time they returned, I'd just been to the memorial service, with Millie and Simon. Millie had casually mentioned, when you came in with your family, that you and Michael lived right behind me. When your daughter got up in the church and told us what he'd done, what a bully he was – suddenly I went cold. I knew. I realized who you were. I was so shocked, I left early. I couldn't stay there any longer. I felt sick. Really sick. The police came round that afternoon. I was still very angry.' She gave me a flinty look and raised her chin defiantly. 'I told them what I'd seen.'

I stared at her in astonishment. 'You did that for me?' I whispered.

'I did it for us.' She closed an elegant fist and placed it firmly on her heart. 'For other women like us. Women who suffer. On account of … And don't forget, you didn't do *something,* you just did nothing. That is very different, in my book. I wish I could do nothing and Lars would die.'

She picked up a packet of Vogue cigarettes and lit one with a gold Ronson lighter. She snapped the lighter shut and exhaled a thin stream of smoke. She regarded me coolly. I couldn't speak. After a moment, she got up and made some mint tea. She put a white china cup in front of me.

'Thank you,' I said quietly.

'What for?'

'For protecting me.'

'I wasn't protecting you, it's what I saw.' She looked at me keenly. 'I spoke to the police on the record. They came again yesterday. I was far more scared. Wasn't full of rage and adrenalin. But I stuck to my story. Except, of course, it's not a story. It's what I saw. I'm scarcely going to lie twice, am I? Scarcely going to falsify evidence?'

'No,' I breathed quickly. 'No, of course not.' I gazed at her, amazed. She was much braver than I was. Much stronger. She was quietly sipping her tea. Smoking her cigarette. How scary that must have been yesterday: forced to back up her story. But she'd done it. Stuck to her guns. I found her remarkable. And admirable. Her composure. Everything about her. She was gazing beyond me now, deep in thought, and I moved my eyes from her face and looked beyond her too. I was facing her garden. It was beautiful, full of plants I liked, albeit more formal. Small box hedges, alliums, a grey slate terrace, white walls. At the end was the dividing wall. Above it, the sloping roof of my house, a storey lower than hers. The house next door to Ingrid's was a nursery school. It was empty at night. The other neighbour, I could see, had a tall line of conifers: Leylandii. They would afford complete privacy. She would be the only one with any sort of view. I wondered what else she'd seen, over the years. I wasn't sure I wanted to know. My eyes came back to her. She looked much younger than I remembered. Softer. No make-up, I realized.

'You're different to when I first met you,' I said uncertainly.

She came back to me and gave a wry smile, remembering. 'I was nervous. At your club. I got there horribly early, I remember.'

'Oh . . . I didn't realize . . .' Nervous.

'I'd met you at Millie's, and I'd already had lunch with your husband. It didn't sit well. I don't date married men. I shouldn't have met Michael, but my confidence had been at an all-time low. Luckily he wasn't my type. And I badly needed that lunch with you. Badly needed the things you were promising. My business was hanging on by a thread. You said you wanted a new kitchen. And that you might get me published, that you could talk to people. I knew what that would do for me. But still . . . I didn't like myself much at the time. For meeting you. But I felt I was being manipulated at every turn. By Lars . . .' she made an ironic face. 'By you, as it turned out.'

I looked down at my hands, ashamed. 'Yes. I was manipulating you. And I know that feeling. It's horrible.'

She shrugged. 'You were in your own little world of shitty despair, and I was in mine. We were both trying to muddle through. Find a way. But I'd decided, before I met you, that I needed a mask, a protective layer. I played it deliberately cool. Tough. You can see I had my reasons.'

'Yes. You did.'

A silence prevailed. I wanted to ask her how things were now, if her business was still precarious. If she'd made any decisions with regard to her marriage. If she was going to stay with Lars for the sake of the house. But I knew it was far too complicated. Life was. It was never black and white. It was grey, smudged and messy. As Tolstoy reminds us, every happy family is alike, but every unhappy one is unhappy in its own way. I wouldn't ask her about it. Wouldn't ask whether he was still with the young girl, or if it had played out. If that was what she was banking on. Sitting on her hands and waiting, as I had done that night. For something to give. I was sure she wouldn't want to talk about it. None of us did. We were veterans of different wars and we didn't choose to parade our scars.

I drank my tea in silence. She seemed to have forgotten about the gym. About me, even. She was looking past me again, deep in thought. I noticed the kitchen wasn't as pristine as I'd thought. There were pictures of her daughter on the fridge, fixed there with amusing magnets. And a pile of library books on the side, her card on the top, which surprised me. Very few people went to the library these days. I could tell I'd misjudged her. She was just battling on, like so many of us. She just did it in a different way. Under a different guise.

I finished my tea and we sat in silence, but it was a companionable one. It had a degree of comfort to it, for both of us, I hope. I gazed out. The drizzle I'd arrived in had abated and the sun was just about to make an appearance: to peep out around a bank of cloud above the roof of my house. Not quite, but the rays were there, gathering strength.

At length I sighed and got to my feet. I gathered up my keys and my bag. She got up too and walked me silently to the door. Before she opened it, though, we looked at each other, and then we hugged. I don't think either of us instigated it, neither of us opened our arms, it just seemed like a natural thing to do. We held on to each other for a few moments, in silence. We'd been so close, separated by only a slim brick wall. But we'd both been in our living hells.

'Good luck,' she whispered, as we stood back, blinking a bit.

'And you too, Ingrid. I can't begin to thank you for what you've done, what you've—'

'Shh.' She stopped me. 'Don't. I didn't, remember?'

I smiled. Nodded. 'No. You didn't.'

'Don't let me down.'

'Never. I'll never tell a living soul,' I told her fiercely, and I knew I wouldn't. Not to anyone. And she knew it, too.

She opened the door and I went down the steps. At the bottom I turned, remembering something. Something she'd said which tapped me on the shoulder now, but which I'd previously passed over. I'd been so absorbed by her version of events that night.

I looked up at her. 'By the way, what did you mean

about sirens and blue flashing lights? Having them out again the other night?' I asked.

'Oh.' Her face cleared. 'Didn't you know? I assumed you would. The guy in your house was rushed to hospital. Peritonitis, apparently.' She made a face. 'Which I gather is pretty serious.' She sighed bleakly. 'It's all happening in our neck of the woods, isn't it?'

I stared at her. My voice, when it came, sounded unfamiliar. 'I had no idea.'

She shrugged. 'Other people's lives. They pass us by, don't they? When we have only one perspective. When we're so caught up with our own.' She gave a wry smile and closed the door.

32

As I stood in that quiet, leafy street, the pavements damp with rain, I felt my world tilt. My head seemed strangely airy, but I made myself digest what she'd said. Blue flashing lights and sirens. My house. Where Josh now lived. And he lived alone. To call for an ambulance would have gone against all his natural instincts. He must have been in terrible pain. Peritonitis was excruciatingly painful. I imagined him reaching for the phone, having resisted for a long, long time. I found myself making haste past my car, and in another minute, I was arriving at the front of my old house and leaping the two steps to the front door. I rang the bell urgently. I'd recently found a key at the bottom of my bag so I could always use that, but after a few moments, the door opened. It was Tilly. She looked surprised, and then pleased to see me.

'Oh, it's you. Good, come in.' She stood aside.

'Is he all right?' I breathed. I realized my heart was pounding somewhere up near my throat.

She made a doubtful face and wobbled her hand horizontally. She shut the door behind me and spoke quietly. 'He's getting there. But he's been super rotten. Really ill. Burst appendix. I only heard because I thought it was odd he hadn't been in touch. He'd asked me to make him something and I needed to deliver it. I kept texting, but then I rang and he eventually answered. He could barely speak, so I knew something was up. I barged my way in here with a bucket full of chicken soup, although he's not very hungry.'

'Where is he?' I asked, as we went down the hallway.

'Well, believe it or not, he's in the garden. Wrapped up in hundreds of blankets, obviously. And I was a bit nervous about it, but he says he feels worse inside. I've literally just trundled him out, but he's only staying there for ten minutes, then I'm bringing him back in again. We don't want pneumonia on top of everything else.' She gave me a wry smile. 'I've designated myself head nurse, by the way.'

'Good for you,' I told her as we went into the kitchen.

She stopped short of the open French windows. 'I'll let you go out,' she said quietly. 'He won't thank me for letting you in.'

'Oh – because . . . ?'

'Doesn't want anyone to see him like this. I don't count, obviously.' She grinned and went back to the cooker where she was heating something pleasant-smelling on the hob. She gave it a stir.

I looked out. I could see him, seated at the end of the garden with his back to me. He was on the lawn, under the old pear tree. I went out on to the terrace and stood, watching him for a moment. Then I tiptoed down the garden. He was sitting in what looked like a hospital wheelchair, blankets dripping down from either side. I popped my head around, tentatively. His eyes were shut. His face was very pale and waxy: unshaven and gaunt.

He'd tilted it towards the dappled sun which was heroically staging a comeback through the leaves: it made mottled patches on his white face. He didn't hear me, and I crouched down beside him. Studied him. His cheeks were sunken and he looked dreadfully thin, the stubble of his beard quite grey. I gazed at him for a long moment. I realized it was a face that brought a lump to my throat. Tears to my eyes. I touched his arm gently. He was asleep. I was about to straighten up and tiptoe away when he slowly opened his eyes. I saw some faint shock in his eyes. He gave himself a moment.

'You.'

'Yes, me. Hello, you.'

'Hello back. Who asked you in?'

'Tilly. She tells me you're being a difficult patient.'

'She's the worst sort of nurse. Hectoring. Bullying. Tell her she's fired for opening the door.'

'Why shouldn't she open the door?'

'I look like shit.'

I smiled. 'You don't. You look pale and interesting. How are you feeling?'

'Better.'

'Don't lie. Peritonitis is serious. Why are you even home?'

'I escaped. The hospital was beyond dreadful. I couldn't stay there, not another minute. I thought I'd die.'

'Well, you probably will, now you're home. Were you on intravenous antibiotics? Getting fluid through a drip?'

'What makes you such an expert?'

'Ned had a burst appendix which briefly became peritonitis. He was in hospital for two weeks. Do you have medical insurance?'

'Don't be fucking stupid, I'm a teacher.'

'Oh well. We'll manage.'

'We?'

'Tilly and me.'

He met my gaze. My eyes were frank and honest and his were too. What was the point of being otherwise? I saw his well up slightly. Realized he couldn't speak. When his voice came, it was thick.

'I couldn't possibly reply to your thank-you text. Not mentioning it would have been lying through omission, and mentioning it . . . would have looked too much like a cry for help, however cheerily I composed it. "Oh, by the way, I've got galloping peritonitis." I tried a few times and deleted it.'

'How very British.'

'Didn't want you charging up if you didn't – you know . . .'

'What?' He didn't answer. 'Feel it?' I asked softly.

'Exactly.'

'I feel it.'

After a moment he spoke. His voice was blurry with emotion. 'I feel it too.'

I wanted to cry. I felt my eyes well up. I took his hand which was cold and dry: enclosed it in mine. We both squeezed but his grasp was weak.

'Thank God,' he muttered. 'I thought I'd got it wrong. I've got so much wrong, in this department, over the years.'

'Oh, me too.'

'Don't get competitive.'

'I'd win hands down.'

He gave me a sad smile. 'We each have our own narratives. Unhappy ones. But important to get it right eventually, I feel.'

'I think so too.'

We stayed like that for a moment. Then I felt his other hand. 'I'm taking you in, you're cold.'

'I feel like Mr Rochester.'

'And I feel far too much like Jane.'

'Meaning?'

I hesitated. Wondered whether to go ahead with it. But then I did. 'Well, in the spirit of full disclosure, which seems to be our theme, I was worried you were too much for me. That I was punching above my weight. And that now I'm only in with a chance because you're an invalid.'

He looked astonished. Then he tilted his head back and hooted a cracked laugh to the heavens. 'Rochester was blind, wasn't he?'

'My point entirely.'

He was still smiling as his face came back to me. 'Are you always so honest?'

'Fatally so,' I said ruefully. 'It's a problem. Emotional incontinence. But I've learned to hide it, over the years.'

'Please don't. I think it's your supreme attraction. I've been used to so many closed hearts. So much coldness. I long to say what's on my mind the moment it arrives. Have longed to, for years. Like you just did. Please kiss me, Lucy, I can't reach.'

I did. Gently. His lips were cold. Too cold. In another moment I'd turned the chair around and was whipping him inside.

'That didn't last long,' he grumbled.

'You're freezing.'

'I'm not, and I feel better than I have done for days.'

When I'd shut the French windows, I went around to crouch in front of him. My eyes scanned his face. I had to admit there was a slight colour in his cheeks and a light to his eyes. That may have been the fresh air, of course. I like to think not. We smiled at one another, communing silently.

Then I straightened up and darted to feel the radiator, which was on. Good girl, Tilly, she'd overridden the heating. On the stove, the soup was doing a little more than simmering, Tilly having tactfully removed herself. I took it off the hob and was about to get some bowls out when I heard a few coughs from down the hallway. Having announced herself, Tilly appeared.

'I was going to make sure he ate it,' she said hesitantly, 'but since you're here . . .'

'Oh yes, do go,' I beamed at her.

'OK, great.' She looked relieved. She came around to bend down in front of him. 'Right then, Mr Bolshy,' she grinned. 'I'll be off. Don't give Lucy as much trouble as you gave me, or I'll be telling Mrs Goodfellow.'

'Oh God, not her,' he said weakly.

'The Goodfellows don't know?' I asked.

'No one knows. Apparently recovery from this particular strain of peritonitis is extremely rapid and no one *needs* to know.' She eyed him beadily: gently prodded his chest. 'Behave yourself, Joshy. No more toys out of the pram.' She straightened up and then, flashing us both a winning smile, shrugged on her little jacket. She promised to be back tomorrow, with more soup. Oh, and she was charging him double. He'd been double trouble.

'Thanks, Tills,' he muttered gratefully as she left.

When she'd gone I poured the soup into two bowls and let it cool for a moment as I set the table. Then I wheeled him up and made him eat it. He did, actually, quite successfully. Although his hand shook and he got a fair bit down his dressing gown, which made him bark with rage as I wiped it off with a dishcloth.

'Like a fucking baby!' he roared, or tried to.

I shrugged. 'I suggested I do it for you, or put a napkin in your neck, but you wouldn't have it. What would you normally do now?'

'What's normal?' he growled. 'I only escaped yesterday. Gardening, probably. Or tennis. Yes, tennis.'

I ignored him. 'Sleeping. How do you get upstairs?'

'We're going to bed?'

My mouth twitched. I waited. He sighed. 'I walk. I'm quite capable of walking, it's just that wretched girl went to the hospital and got me a wheelchair. Came home on a bus on my own.'

'Idiot. God knows what you caught on that. Come on, let's give it a whirl.'

I pushed the chair down the hall to the bottom of the stairs and then helped him haul himself out of it. Together we made a very slow and shaky ascent, me with one arm around his waist, and him holding the banister tightly. In that way we made it to the bedroom. I knew he wouldn't want any help from there on in, so I diplomatically went to the loo while he got slowly into bed. When I came back, he was under the duvet, tucked in up to his chin.

'How d'you feel?'

'About six. Go away.'

I grinned. 'I'm going. But sadly for you, I'll be back. Have you got water?'

He didn't answer so I poured a glass from the bathroom and put it on the bedside table. 'OK. What's Tilly's number?'

He sighed. Then jerked his head in defeat to his phone on the side. I gave it to him and he scrolled down and handed it back to me. I tapped it into mine.

'And Trisha's?'

He groaned. 'Is that really necessary?'

I assured him it was, and actually, he was getting very drowsy now. I knew he wanted me to go. His eyes were shutting, so when I'd got the number I drew the curtains, shut the door and went downstairs. I sat on the bottom of the stairs and rang Trisha. She was in a meeting, but she came straight out. She was appalled and furious with him at the same time. And clearly worried. We decided I should go, and that she and Tilly would manage, and that she, Trisha, would not take no for an answer.

'He won't want you nursing him at this stage,' she warned me. 'It's too demeaning for him. He's proud.'

'I know, that's what I thought. It's why I rang.'

'So you disappear. And I'll keep you posted regularly. I'm coming round now, can you leave me a key?'

'I'll put one under the flowerpot.'

'Stupid fool. Imagine if Tilly hadn't persisted? If he were coping alone?' I shut my eyes. I didn't like to imagine, actually. Knew, from nursing Ned, how serious the condition could be, how easily it could turn into sepsis, be fatal. 'Some men think no fuss is honourable,' Trisha went on. 'Not mine, of course. Mine's in bed if he so much as gets a tickle in his throat. Go, Lucy, and I'll be in touch.'

I rang off, loving the way she took my presence here for granted. My need for regular updates. She'd already been leaps and bounds ahead of me at that Sunday lunch, I just hadn't dared to go there. And now it appeared Josh hadn't dared either. Hadn't dared to be vulnerable. Neither of us had, in case we got – you know. Hurt. More hurt. Which neither of us needed. So I'd gone briefly for the safe option. I shut my eyes. Dan. I knew I'd led him up the garden path, but in a way, I hadn't. I just hadn't been brave enough to say no. To go for the other path. Hadn't been bold enough to text Josh and say – 'You've gone a bit quiet, what's up?' Like the young would. Imo. Helena, back in the day. I hadn't wanted to be rebuffed. I knew I had to go and see Dan, explain, and I knew that would be hard, for both of us. Most of all, for him. But at least I was doing it now, and not in three or six months' time, when I was feeling stronger, less unstable, and when I knew I'd got it wrong. Or I might have been in too deep and unable to: might even have been living

with him at my parents' house. With them in the bungalow. A cosy little set-up.

It gave me a sudden jolt of horror, that vision. Because
I knew I'd be back on my feet soon, now that the bogeyman had gone. I knew that my nightmare of a life was
receding, like an ever-decreasing tide, away into the distance, and that I wouldn't need him. Thanks to Ingrid.
Thanks to that remarkable woman in the house behind.
And I'd never say a word about what she'd done. Not
even to Josh. I'd take it to my grave. I'd made her a sol-
emn promise, and I'd keep it. And I would forever
be astounded, humbled and grateful to her. Hope that
one day, I could do the same for someone else, another
woman like us. I adjusted my position on the stairs and
adjusted my mind back too, to Dan. Back to what could
have been. It would have been very wrong to be with a
man I liked very much but didn't love, and whose pro-
tection I didn't need any more.

And if I'm honest, in a corner of my mind, Dan's level
of protectiveness had worried me. It reminded me too
much of someone, in the early days. It was awful to even
suggest it, but a couple of things had brought to mind
the old Michael. The way Dan would appear, unexpectedly. At the hospital. At my parents' house. Like Michael,
in his blue MG, outside a girlfriend's supper party. The
way Dan – sweetly, no doubt – assumed I needed support. I was tarring him with a horrible brush, and no
doubt his motives were completely kind, but it felt too
similar. That level of care for his mother, too. Was it
control? Would it only be a matter of time before he was

calling me Little Luce? And I'd thought him the safe bet. I'd thought Josh was the risk. Too attractive. Too cool. Too amusing. Too clever. But he was more vulnerable than I could ever have imagined. And I don't mean the illness. And nor was I pleased about it, that vulnerability. I didn't chalk it up in a smug, same-as-me-mate sort of way. It was more that the glimpse I'd had of it, of his thirst for proper, spontaneous love, reminded me of my own. If I dared unleash it. If I loosened the reins on my emotions. That glimpse had been salutary. A lesson in using more than one's eyes, or one's brain.

And over the years, throughout my married life, I'd trained myself to use those two very forensic, scientific senses. It went against the grain, however, and I'd spoken the truth when I'd told Josh that, by nature, I was emotionally incontinent. But guilt over the things I'd done – Liam, and then giving my children Michael as a father – had persuaded me my gut instincts were poor. So I'd tried hard to use my head, to get things right. But not this time. This time I was using my heart. And although I wasn't naïve enough to think I'd definitely got it right, this ... thing with me and Josh, whatever it was – I didn't even know what to call it, we were so very much at the beginning – I knew I was choosing life. Hope. Daring to be me. And not, by dint of having been through so much, just plumping for a soft, safe landing. I blinked. Or not, as the case may be. I could have been heading for the rocks – who knows? No one can glimpse the future, however much they rack their brains, weigh up the pros and cons, write

405

comparative lists. But by listening to the heart – my instincts, which I'd once written off – by consulting those, I reckoned I at least stood a fighting chance.

I got up from sitting on the stairs. I was standing by the hall mirror. My hall mirror, the overmantle, with the gilt frame. It was one I was used to seeing my reflection in a lot. My cheeks were flushed and my eyes bright, reminding me of someone. I realized it was myself, years ago, when I was young. When I had my own light, my crushes, my possibilities. Could it be that light was back? I went to get my coat from the kitchen and put it on. Then I plucked my phone from my pocket and sent Josh a text, which he'd get when he woke up, saying I'd gone, but bad luck, I'd be back. Then I sent Dan one, saying I needed a chat, and could I pop round tonight. I pocketed it and headed for the door, shutting it behind me as softly as possible.

I tucked my key under the flowerpot for Trisha. As my feet tripped down the steps, it seemed to me they were lighter than they'd been for a very long time. Indeed, I wondered if I'd ever so much as tripped down these steps in my life. Like a dancer, almost. That made me smile, as dancing used to be a strong suit, and had come naturally once. Still smiling foolishly, I passed a young guy in the street. He grinned back, surprised. I was embarrassed and glanced down at my feet, but as I rounded the corner out of sight, I threw my head back and laughed softly to the heavens, much as Josh had done in the garden. Then I hastened away to my car.